Mr. UGLY

BENJAMIN ALLOCCO

Black Rose Writing | Texas

ISBN: 978-1-68433-965-5
PUBLISHED BY BLACK ROSE WRITING
www.blackrosewriting.com

Printed in the United States of America
Suggested Retail Price (SRP) $21.95

Mr. Ugly is printed in Baskerville

*As a planet-friendly publisher, Black Rose Writing does its best to eliminate
unnecessary waste to reduce paper usage and energy costs, while never
compromising the reading experience. As a result, the final word count vs. page
count may not meet common expectations.

Mr UGLY

PART 1
HIGHWAYS

1

They packed the jeep faster than Janelle would have liked. Vacation was over, but she wanted to linger. A childish sentiment, she knew, like asking for Christmas two days in a row.

She wedged her pillow against the window while Richard settled in beside her. She caught him looking at her legs and flashed him a flirty smile. He did that thing with his mouth where he twisted his lips to the side, embarrassed or trying not to laugh, which she found unbearably cute. She drank him in with relish, knowing it would make him uncomfortable. He was a bit of a prude in public.

Not so much in private.

Of course, the consequences of their relationship, if she could call it that, would need to be addressed once they got home. Yet another reason to stay. But their bags were loaded, stacked so high in the back they blocked the rear window, and Jeff had filled the tank last night, so there was no need to stop on their way out. Time was up.

Time is an asshole, Janelle thought.

She resisted the urge to lean against Richard. She planned to unbuckle her seatbelt at some point and use his thigh as a pillow. He had nice thighs.

Jeff backed them out of his cousin's driveway, his phone blurting directions.

Soon they were on the highway.

Jeff hogged the wheel just as he had on the drive down. Amy practically shoved him from the driver's seat at a rest stop around 8 a.m. He relented, bragging that he wasn't even tired, and proceeded to fall asleep in the passenger seat ten minutes later.

They drove with the windows up and the music low. Janelle listened to Spotify until her phone died. She didn't sleep on Richard's thigh. She dozed, woke at one point to Amy flopped over beside her, black hair pooled across the middle seat. Richard was driving, talking to Jeff. She caught the words *draft pick* and *make the playoffs* and went back to sleep. They tried to revive a few road games—the Alphabet Game and 20 Questions and a half-hearted attempt at I Spy—but they had exhausted these on their way down. The boredom became oppressive. Their legs cramped. They flexed their toes and stretched and yawned and parked every few hours at rest stops where they stood on picnic tables at overlook points that overlooked nothing.

Twenty-four hours passed this way.

The sky turned a second time to dusk.

A thunderhead snuck out from behind the moon.

Then it was Janelle's turn to drive.

The storm must have been traveling north, because they didn't hit it until after the Iowa-Minnesota border, with less than 200 miles left. Lightning cut jagged scars in the darkness like cracks around enormous doors. Nobody said *tornado*, but as they crossed through a curtain of rain into a downpour you could drown in standing up, Janelle searched the radio for weather stations and found an oldies channel calling for nothing more than intermittent thunderstorms.

They agreed to push through.

She slowed. Her passengers lost their initial excitement, and the storm's fury became little more than background noise. They slept, leaving Janelle to fight the wind and rain alone.

She let her thoughts drift back to California. The sun and the beaches. The overpriced restaurants with their delectable seafood. Visiting the Bay early in the morning and the fog that filled it, hiding Alcatraz and making the Golden Gate Bridge seem to float. Jeff kept reminding them how the bridge was a popular spot for suicides and wondered aloud if they would see one if they came back each morning, which got everybody yelling at him to shut up before they threw him over the side. That only made him grin, but it wasn't funny. Janelle kept picturing someone ducking under the railing and leaning back, taking a long breath before letting go. She couldn't help imagining what that would be like, falling backward, the underside of the bridge silhouetted against the blue sky while the water neared unseen behind her head—then the *wallop* of water and a hard cut to black.

Thanks, Jeff, for implanting such morbid thoughts.

There were better things to remember than the Bay. Like lying on the futon with Richard pressing against her.

He slept beside her now, in the passenger seat, his head on the window, making it steam.

In fact, much of the jeep had gone steamy since the storm came.

She reached her hand to feel lukewarm air blasting from the vents. Not hot enough to prevent condensation. She almost woke Jeff to ask if something had gone wrong with the heat, but when she swiped at the windshield to create a clear spot, she saw the first sign for Fairfield. They were minutes from their first destination—Richard's father's house.

And maybe she didn't want to admit that she couldn't handle her portion of the drive. Maybe she wanted to pull into Richard's driveway, park the car, and *then* wake everyone up with a shouted, "We're here!" She knew they saw her as the shy, timid member of their group. As much as she loved Amy, if one of them was a superhero and the other the trusty sidekick, she knew very well who would be sitting at a computer while the other was out there kicking bad-guy ass. This, she believed, was partly why Richard never thought of her *that way* until she practically threw herself at him.

Later, she would wish she slowed down or pulled over. These untaken courses of action would haunt her, and she'd curse the determination that fueled her now.

It happened the instant she crossed the overpass into the city limits. She had swiped a round porthole into the fog of the windshield and was leaning forward, squinting through it, when something dashed out of the median to her left. A flash of movement followed by a *whack-thud* that shuddered through the vehicle.

She slammed the brakes. The tires shrieked, and the force flung Janelle and her passengers into their seatbelts. The jeep skidded across the pavement at a 45-degree angle, teetering on the passenger tires before settling again. It all happened in a matter of seconds, and while time did not slow as people say it does in a crisis, it seemed to stutter, as if Janelle lost synchronicity with her body. The moments strobed by in a series of blinks, then came back as memories she pieced together. Now she felt her frozen lungs and forced them to take air. Her hands gripped the wheel so tight her knuckles hurt, and she heard rain beating the roof and hood. The jeep sat in the center of the two-lane highway, the headlights cutting across the median. The rain so dense she couldn't see beyond the first hints of grass. The engine idled, and the defroster blew uselessly. The clear patch she had swiped in the windshield filled in.

"What just happened?" Jeff gasped.

Richard placed a hand on Janelle's thigh. "You okay?"

She knew she should respond, but her jaw locked.

"Nelly," Amy said, poking her head out from behind the driver's seat, "you all right? Did we hit something?"

Jeff put an arm around Amy, like he could shield her from the accident that had already occurred. "We're in the middle of the road," he said.

Janelle heard him, but the words were gibberish.

"Janelle. We're in the middle of the road."

At last, she eased her foot from the brake and guided them to the left shoulder.

Were you supposed to pull over to the right? She couldn't remember.

Amy touched her arm, gently. "Did we hit something?"

Richard squeezed her thigh. "Nelly?"

Her mouth was ash-dry. She forced out the words. "I… I think so."

The wipers slashed. *Thud-squeak. Thud-squeak.* The dashboard radio showed that it was 2 a.m. Tuesday morning. They were behind schedule, and most of the world still slept. She hadn't seen many cars since the storm hit, which she was grateful for now.

She shifted the jeep into park and tucked her hands beneath her thighs where they couldn't shake.

"The four-ways," Jeff said.

"What?"

"The hazards."

She couldn't find the button.

Richard reached over and pushed it for her.

Amy and Jeff wiped their windows. "We're in Fairfield?" Amy said.

"Yeah."

"Should we, like, call someone?"

Jeff cracked his door.

"Hey," Amy said.

He paused with one leg outside. "It's my mom's jeep."

He went out to assess the damage, leaving the door open. Amy hesitated, groaned, then followed. They stood in the headlights, already soaked. Amy spoke what appeared to be charged words. Jeff ignored her and approached the bumper at a crouch, directly in front of Janelle, the flashers intermittently painting him yellow-orange.

"It's probably nothing," Richard said.

She tried to replay the moment of impact in her mind, but the details were lost in the quick-cuts. She'd seen movement, hadn't she?

Jeff tapped her window. She fumbled with the buttons, then eased it down. "Bumper's cracked. And there's sort of a dent in the grill." Water popped on his lips. "I think there's blood."

Richard's grip tightened on her leg. "Blood?"

"It's hard to tell with the rain." He held out an open palm, but there was nothing on it. If there had been blood, it washed away. "I thought I saw some in the grill."

Richard started to speak, stopped, removed his hand, unbuckled, and eased open his door.

He glanced back at Janelle, opened his mouth, closed it, and went out.

Janelle thought she should go, too, but her body wouldn't move except to roll the window up.

Shock, she thought. *This is what shock feels like.*

The rain slowed.

Across the highway, in the southbound lane, a pair of headlights flicked on and flashed the high beams once, twice. Her friends stood upright and faced them. She expected the lights to draw near, but they remained at the same distance, unmoving.

Jeff called out, "Okay! Thank you!" He turned to Janelle, grinned, and gave a thumbs up.

She had no idea what this meant.

Amy came to the window. "There's someone over there," she said. "He says we hit a deer. He's having car trouble or something. Jeff wants to see if we can help."

"A deer?" Janelle rasped.

"Yeah."

A deer. That's all it was.

"You okay?" Amy said.

Janelle had never been in an accident before, let alone the cause of one. Deer or not, she'd hit a living thing.

I think there's blood.

"Uh-huh," she said, unconvincingly.

"Jeff's parents are loaded. They can handle the repairs."

Jeff and Richard squinted at the girls, their faces shining.

A tear ran down Janelle's cheek, surprising and embarrassing her.

Amy reached through the window and pulled on the handle, easing the door open. "It's okay, boo. We're good. Let's stretch. We're basically home."

Janelle nodded, shut off the jeep, and stepped out.

The storm had reduced to little more than a fine mist, enough to disguise her wet cheeks.

Richard threw an arm around her shoulder and squeezed. It seemed a forced, chummy gesture, how you might reassure a buddy who'd lost a game. "You okay?" he said.

"I think so."

He took his arm back.

"Sorry I freaked," Jeff said. "I was just— Remember junior year, like two weeks after I got my license, I kinda sorta totaled my dad's car? I think I was having flashbacks. But it's fine. Really. Like, don't worry about it. I'm just glad everyone's okay. Plus, we're basically home."

Janelle didn't like them staring at her. "Let's see what this guy wants."

They crossed the median, the earth squishing beneath their feet.

It was a beige pickup truck parked on the far side of the southbound lane. A road jack raised the rear wheel off the pavement. The man standing beside it wore a pair of black denim overalls with a black t-shirt. He was soaked, hair matted so tight to his skull it resembled a swimming cap.

"Hell of a thing," he said. He rocked forward on the balls of his feet. His voice was deep, with a slight southern twang. "That deer sure took to your headlights. I watched him come outta the field like a shot. Spooked, I guess. Seems y'all came out all right. Could use your help here."

Jeff said, "We don't know much about cars, but we can take a look."

Janelle inspected the wheel and the jack propping it up. The tire seemed to be full, far as she could tell. She was more curious about the Jetta parked behind the truck. A silver car. Dark and empty. She wondered if the man had been towing it. She didn't see any ropes or chains.

"Damn wheel near to fell off. I ain't no mechanic myself. Could use a lift up the road a ways. If you'd be so kind as to provide one, that is."

Something about the way he carried himself unnerved her. She couldn't say exactly what.

She was still shaken up.

The guy just wanted a ride.

She knew better than to offer him one, as did her friends. Stranger danger and all that.

"Doesn't look blown," Jeff said.

"If you get in there and see the axel, it's all bent to hell. No idea what did it."

Janelle thought the guy winked at her. She turned to Amy for confirmation, but Amy was facing the way they'd come, holding herself with a seriousness that put Janelle on edge.

"What is it?"

Amy said, "Do you..." She shook her head.

"What?"

"I thought... I don't know."

Jeff approached the tire and got down on one knee, placed a steadying hand on the truck, and poked his head underneath. "It's too dark."

Richard trailed toward the truck's back end and nodded at the Jetta. "Whose car is this?"

The man reached into the bed of the truck. "Got a flashlight here."

Jeff lowered his shoulder to the pavement, craned his neck upward.

"There," Amy said, still watching the northbound lane. "What is that?"

"What's what?"

"Behind the jeep."

Janelle scanned the highway. She didn't see anything.

Then it moved. In the middle of the road, twenty feet behind the jeep. What could have been a bit of fabric lifted, then fell, caught in a sudden breeze.

She swung her attention back to the man. "You said the deer ran off?"

The man removed a flashlight, shaped like a car battery, from the truck bed.

"Whose car is this?" Richard repeated.

The man held the flashlight at eye level. To Richard, he said, "Look here a second." He flicked the light on, and Richard's face lit up, the light yellow in his pupils.

Richard raised a hand to shield himself. "Hey."

The man pointed the light at Janelle. Before she could look away, it blinded her. "Stop." The man lowered the light and a reddish-brown spot remained in the center of her vision. She blinked hard. "There's something in the road," she said.

She heard the man moving in front of her.

"I saw it too," Amy said.

"Miss?" the man said.

He must have shined the light on Amy next, because she hissed, "What the hell, man?"

Janelle's suspicion was rising into heart-hammering panic when Jeff said, "Hey, what are you—" He broke off and there came a series of wet smacks, like someone tenderizing meat.

Jeff grunted, then screamed.

2

Detective Ray "Al" Alverson leaned over the kitchen table, tipping himself toward the police scanner as if it might speak to him in confidence. A patrolman's voice reeled off the code for a routine traffic stop, and Ray leaned back and released his breath. He turned up the volume and hurried to his bedroom, came back a moment later, tucking a dress shirt into his slacks.

It was a slow night for the Fairfield Police Department, but it was going to pick up. The radio didn't know it yet, nor did the people on the other end.

But Ray knew.

He'd awoken at 2 a.m. as if someone had burst into his room banging pots and pans, jolting him from an unnerving dream about a haunted forest, the particulars of which he lost upon waking. He didn't think about what he did next. Though it was the middle of the night and his shift didn't start for five hours, he rushed to the kitchen to wait by the scanner.

It was just like the night his father died. He'd shot out of a sound sleep then, too, filled with dread and sorrow at the absolute certainty that something had happened to the old man. It had been winter, but he drove to his father's Eden Prairie townhouse in nothing but his pajama pants and a t-shirt. Ray found him face down in the hallway between the bedroom and bathroom, directly beneath framed photos of Ray as a boy, teenager, and finally the fresh-faced young man he'd been the day he graduated from the police academy. It was an aneurism. The old man had been on his way to the medicine cabinet, searching for something to ease his blinding headache and the weird feeling in his gut. Dead before Ray was out of the driveway.

He knew these things before any medical exam. He didn't question how.

Some stones were better left unturned.

The call came over the scanner, as he knew it would. Probable homicide on 169 South, between Belgrade and Riverfront. All available units respond.

He was five minutes out when Chief Obermeyer called, apologizing for waking him.

"You didn't," Ray said. He flipped his flashers on as he approached the entrance to 169. "Already on my way."

"Don't you sleep?"

"You call Bartie?"

"About to. Larsen and Vogel are en route."

Ray would likely beat them there.

"Take charge when you get there. I won't be far behind."

"You got it."

"And don't let patrol touch anything."

"Yes sir."

A patrolman was just setting up road flares at the entrance ramp. Ray slowed, rolled his window down, and flicked on the dome light. The patrolman recognized him and waved him forward. Ray raised a hand in gratitude and eased onto the highway. A state trooper blocked the southbound lane fifty yards back, at the nearest exit ramp.

More emergency lights ahead. Three patrol cars had parked diagonally across the lanes.

Ray parked on the shoulder behind them.

Even before he opened his door, he heard voices. An officer barking orders, someone shouting back, and the rise and fall of a woman wailing—a sound of despair.

Outside, the words were crisp and harsh:

"*I won't leave him!*"

"I said get back! Bevins, restrain her!"

"Miss, you need to come with me!"

"Don't hurt her!"

"He's not dead!"

"Get her away from those Goddamn bodies, Bevins!"

Ray pointed his mag light at the ground as he approached this drama. Two officers occupied the center of the road beside a couple of teenagers, a male and female. Fifteen feet beyond them, a third officer tussled with a second girl, who sank to her knees in the officer's grip and released another wail: *"He can't be dead! I won't leave him!"*

Ray flashed his badge to the patrolmen. He knew their faces, but couldn't place their names. "Arriving officer?"

"That's me," the shorter of the two said. "O'Henry."

"Officer Fowler," said Officer Fowler. "I just got here."

"We need to get these kids back."

The teenagers all appeared the same age—18 at the most. One Hispanic or Latina female, crying quietly. One African American male, restrained with flexicuffs, his gray shirt heavy with rain and flecked with diffuse brown circles Ray recognized as blood. He couldn't get a good look at the second female, who was now sobbing in the third officer's arms.

To the boy and the Hispanic, he said, "Are either of you injured?"

The girl shook her head. The boy did not react.

"What's your name, son?"

The boy stared.

"The detective asked you a question," Fowler growled.

"I had to do it," the boy said. "I couldn't get him off. I can't— I didn't— I couldn't get him off."

"What are those stains on your shirt?"

"I had to. I couldn't get him off. I couldn't—"

Officer Fowler said, "He's trying to say he smashed a guy's head in."

The Hispanic girl cried, "It was self-defense!"

"What's his name, miss?"

"Richard."

"Richard," Ray said. "Did you hurt someone?"

That fifty yard stare again.

"Okay, Richard," Ray said. "That's okay. Officer Fowler?"

"Yeah."

"Let's get this young man to the station."

The girl protested, "He didn't do anything!"

"It's all right. We just need to figure out what happened here, and the police station's warm and dry. It's gonna be a long night, but it doesn't have to be so wet and cold."

This seemed to calm the girl some.

Officer Fowler grabbed Richard by the elbow and dragged him off.

"Your name?" Ray asked the girl.

"Janelle Winters."

"And your other friend?" He indicated the wailing girl.

"Amy."

"Who called 911?"

"I did."

"Can you tell me what happened?"

"I— We— I was driving, and we hit something, because of the storm, and— And, there was a man. He said he had c— car trouble, and he— He started— He stabbed Jeff. I think he's—He stabbed Jeff, and Jeff's back there and I think he's—"

"Where's the man now? The one who hurt Jeff?"

"Richard got him. He took the— He used the, um, the, handle for the— The road thing."

O'Henry offered, "The jack."

"Yes," Janelle said. "The jack handle. He hit him in the head and I think he's—" She swallowed hard. "I'm gonna throw up." And she did, coughing gray vomit across O'Henry's boots.

"That's okay," Ray said. "Janelle? I want you to take it easy. Officer O'Henry here is gonna get you a blanket and ask you some questions, but you just take it easy, all right? I want you to tell him everything again. Try to calm down. Someone's gonna take you to the police station in a little while, and I'll be by to speak with you again. Does that sound okay?"

"Y— Yeah."

To O'Henry, Ray said. "Only detectives go beyond those cruisers. That's our entry point. Take anyone's name who crosses."

"Yes sir." O'Henry touched a front pocket, where the corner of a notepad stuck out. "Detective, there are two. I checked them." He shook his head.

He meant there were two bodies.

The third officer, Bevins, finally got the wailing girl to her feet. *Amy.* She walked like an old woman, with barely the strength to remain upright. She was too hysterical for a statement, so Ray told Bevins what he told the others, and she helped the girl to her patrol car.

A parade of emergency vehicles began to arrive.

Ray pointed his mag light at the car and truck on the shoulder. Two bodies lay prone beside them, draped in shadow. His pulse ticked up. He tried not to think of the way he awoke tonight, as if something other than professional duty had brought him here.

Called him here.

The boy lay on his back, fish-eyed, skin ashy, mouth slightly agape as if bemused, like he didn't quite know what to make of this predicament.

The second cadaver was also on its back. Also male. Probably older. Hard to tell, given the state of its head. Little remained thereof but pulp and bone. One eye had been forced from the socket to dangle by the optic nerve. The other eye might have popped. Ray couldn't find it. The mouth was a red gash, the jaw crooked and open so wide Ray saw that most of the teeth had been smashed out. In its right hand, it held what appeared to be a hunting knife. Closer inspection revealed a quarter-inch barb curving down the back of the blade, away from the tip. Ray didn't hunt, but he knew guys who did, and recognized this as a tool for field dressing prey. A gut hook, it was called.

Nearby lay a metal bar with a rubber grip for a handle. Strands of hair and brain like bubblegum clung to the end. The jack handle.

Richard got him.

He sure as hell did.

Ray glanced up at the sound of a vehicle crawling along the northbound lane. Headlights illuminated the jeep parked on that side of the highway. The headlights slowed, stopped, and emergency lights on the roof swept to life. A deputy jumped out, rushed forward, bent over something on the ground. A moment later, he straightened and waved both hands. "There's a body over here!"

. . .

It was a complicated operation for a department of their size. Fairfield didn't have the resources for a specialized CSI or forensics unit. Investigators worked major crimes on top of their specialized areas and kept forensic equipment in the back of their SUVs. There were eight investigators in total, all trained as crime scene techs, but Ray had the most experience, so he briefed the others as they arrived. While they waited for the coroner, he set up a tripod and took wide angle photos of the area, knowing they'd need more after dawn. At least they didn't have the rain to worry about. The clouds had blown off, unveiling stars and a sliver of moon.

They cordoned off both sides of the highway, set up battery-operated LED lighting, and maintained the southbound lane as the point of entry.

The coroner and Chief Obermeyer arrived at the same time. The coroner took her own photographs and notes, and Ray helped her flip the boy's corpse so she could inspect his back. She lifted his shirt with a gloved hand to reveal a series of stab wounds clustered in the lumbar region. She and Ray snapped photos, took measurements, and repeated the process with the corpse Ray thought of as Pulp-Head. After initial examinations, the coroner searched the bodies for identifying information and found wallets on both.

The boy was local. Jeffrey Patel. 18 years old.

Pulp-Head's real name was Ehblu Htoo, a 42-year-old resident of Charlotte Furnace, Kentucky.

"Kentucky?" Obermeyer said over Ray's shoulder. "That truck's got Minnesota plates."

They continued to the third and final body.

"Huh," the coroner said, standing above the corpse. Dr. Aire was a tall woman. Blonde and skeletal. A fellow detective once described her as *unflappable*, a term that stuck with Ray, as there was something birdlike about her frame and the jerky deliberateness with which she moved, reminding him of the robins that hopped around his front yard. Even her name had an avian quality. *Aire*. Now she tucked her gloved hands into her pockets but for her thumbs, so her bony elbows stuck out like featherless wings. "Looks like he fell from the sky."

Like the others, the man lay on his back. His head was turned to his left and his arms flung in that same direction, the right bent at the elbow above his head, right leg twisted at the knee, foot pointing away from his torso. The shoe had come off. The other leg pointed straight down. The skull above his right eyebrow had caved in. There was no swelling, but blood and cranial fluid had oozed down his forehead. He wore a t-shirt that should have been white, though the fabric around his midsection was stained a deep red.

Dr. Air took her photos and lifted the man's shirt to reveal a starburst pattern of wounds around his belly button. Obermeyer sucked his teeth, and Dr. Aire hummed through her nose. "Well," she said, craning her neck at Ray. "This man appears to have been stabbed."

Ray almost laughed.

She looked to the other side of the highway. The detectives over there were setting up scene markers, taking more photos, and collecting evidence.

Ray guessed her line of thinking. "He was running."

Aire nodded. "I'll bet that's his car behind the truck."

Ray had already figured that, and though he pieced together the timeline of events that led to these bodies lying in these locations with these wounds, he couldn't suss out the *why* of it. Here was a man from Kentucky driving a truck with Minnesota plates. He jacks up his truck on the side of the highway and waits for a good Samaritan to come by. And here comes a sandy-haired man in a silver Jetta, stopping to help. When he gets out of the car, the truck driver stabs him in the stomach. Somehow, the injured man escapes and runs into the southbound lane and either has terrible timing or intentionally jumps in front of a pair of fast-approaching headlights. The impact kills him, and when the kids get out to see what happened, the truck driver calls them over and attacks them, too. While he's stabbing his second victim, one of the teenagers splits his head open with the jack handle—and thank God for that.

Why, though? Why attack a group that outnumbered him so badly?

Was he trying to rob them? Or was he the kind of nutbag who got his rocks off by killing strangers?

Ray helped Dr. Aire bag and load the bodies into the waiting ambulances. He handed the scene off to Obermeyer so he could get to the station and speak with the witnesses. So far, everything the kids said lined up, but one of them was responsible for Pulp-Head's new look. As much as Ray hated to admit it, putting the boy in restraints had been the right move.

He returned his equipment to the back of his vehicle, opened the driver side door, climbed in, buckled, turned the engine over, flicked on the headlights, looked up—

And froze.

A teenaged boy stood in front of the vehicle. Curly black hair sagged down his forehead, slick with rain. He spoke animatedly, but no sound came out, as if he was in a soundproof room.

Ray reached for his door, taking his eyes from the boy for less than a second.

When he looked back, the boy was gone.

He sat for several long seconds, heart frozen, before he leaned over the steering wheel to better see the pavement, as if the kid had ducked down and out of sight. He couldn't have run off. Not in the literal blink of an eye between when he saw him and when he vanished.

Vanished.

It was an accurate description, and it unnerved him. People didn't *vanish*.

Sweat beaded on his forehead and moistened his palms.

Still scanning the area, he did what he would ask of any witness, replaying the events, focusing on the details. The curve of the boy's nose. The heavy texture of his hair. His clothes—tightly fitted blue jeans and a gray t-shirt with a design that might have been a band logo. The rapid movement of his lips and the sharp whiteness of his teeth. He'd been looking directly at Ray, his eyes wide and wild as he spoke with no voice. Whatever he'd been trying to say, it was important.

But there was something else about the boy. Something that kept Ray from running out of his vehicle and searching for this civilian who had trespassed onto a crime scene. Something that made Ray's hands tremble.

No matter. He had to check.

He reached again for the door handle.

Something thumped against the window and a big white face filled the glass.

Ray jumped so hard he bit his tongue.

Detective Ethan Bartov grinned at him. "Al?"

Ray cracked the door. Bartov stepped back and Ray pushed it wide.

"You all right?" Bartov said. "Did I startle ya?"

"I'm fine." Ray fought to keep his voice steady. A coppery taste filled his mouth. "You shouldn't sneak up on a guy with a gun."

"The chief wants me to assist with the interviews."

"I figured." Ray leaned out and spat a string of bloody saliva onto the road. It landed with a smack, swirling pink and white.

"Oofta. I guess I did startle ya."

"Not you. I think I—" Ray paused, not sure what he almost said, but glad he stopped. "Did you see anybody over here a minute ago? A civilian, maybe?"

"Civilian? I don't think so. Where?"

Ray gestured vaguely in front of the vehicle.

"Got a description?"

"Never mind," Ray said, even as he circled around the SUV, searching. Bartov followed him to the passenger side, then the rear, and back to the front to stand in the headlights scanning the empty field.

Could he have run into the field? There were no footprints. And the moon was bright enough now that he saw the treeline half a mile away. Nothing moved out there.

"What did they look like?" Bartov said.

Ray ignored him. "Let's get to the station. We've got a long day coming."

Ray got back in his SUV. Bartov shrugged and set off toward his own vehicle.

Ray turned on his flashers and did a U-turn and crept through the obstacle course of emergency vehicles. He tried to put the teenager out of his mind, but that face seemed to hover before him even now, framed beneath the mop of black hair. He'd seen that same face on the ground beside the pickup truck. He'd turned the boy over so Dr. Aire could get her photographs.

Jeffrey Patel. The murdered teen, trying to speak.

3

Gertie slumped sideways in her seat, head hanging out the driver's side of the van, bottle of Jim Beam half empty and open, pinned to her hip by a well-trained elbow. David stood in the road beside her, wringing his hands against a backdrop of dried vegetation and a rising sun.

"Someone's coming," he said.

Gertie righted herself with a groan. She checked for spills, found none, and searched around her crotch and under her ass for the cap of the liquor bottle. David gestured at the dashboard. She slapped at the bottlecap like it was an offending insect and spun it onto the bottle, slid the bottle under her seat.

"We almost wrecked last night," David said. "And you left the dome light on again."

She bit back a retort. Too tired to fight. It took enough out of her just listening to him.

She hopped onto the dirt road to stretch and get her bearings. Long periods of the previous night were missing from her mind, though she clearly recalled the dive bar outside of Charlotte Furnace where it started. She'd sat in the parking lot tapping the steering wheel and chewing her cheek while David told her not to be stupid, things would get better. But the despair had been building up for a long time and the dam could not hold forever.

Years of sobriety swirling down the shitter.

She had swiped the bottle of Jim Beam from behind the bar. Couldn't remember if that was before or after she fucked the cowboy who'd been eyeballing her since she walked in. It had been rushed, frantic sex, and she couldn't remember much of that, either. She took the cash from his wallet afterward and was not impressed. Then she was behind the wheel again speeding aimlessly down country roads, lost in the dark, screaming along to Bad Brains while David's shouts to slow down faded in and out.

Brown trees surrounded them now. She'd parked one tire directly on a pricker bush and there was a puddle of puke outside her door.

She had to piss, and would have squatted in the grass if not for David's waking words.

She squinted up the road behind the van, and sure enough, a big white pickup truck rumbled nearer, kicking up dust. A large house sat atop the hill beyond it. With any luck, she was on private land and the owner was coming down to shoot her.

She checked herself in the side mirror. Her short blonde hair frizzed out and greasy. She raked a hand through it to smooth it the best she could and hoped she didn't stink too bad.

The truck stopped beside her. She raised a hand. A middle-aged man rolled down the passenger window and leaned across the seat. He wore a red baseball cap. Face leathery from years of too much sun, but not unfriendly.

"You lost?"

"Actually, yeah. GPS stopped working."

"There's your problem. GPS won't get you far around here. Where ya headed?"

"Huntington." It was the first city she thought of.

"Boy. You're a ways off. You spent the night out here?"

"Some of it."

"Oughtta be careful, pretty girl like yourself."

David rolled his eyes.

"Well, you need to get back to 64 East. Keep going the way you're headed and take a left when the road ends. When that one ends, take another left, and another onto Route 7. Follow that to the interstate. There's not much between here and there." He thought a moment. "How are you on gas?"

She leaned into the cab to see. "About a quarter tank."

"Cutting it close. I got a can in the back. It's not full, but you might as well take what I got. Hate for you to get stranded." He popped open his door and lowered himself. He was older than she first thought. Probably early sixties. He took an ancient metal gas can from the bed of his truck. She unscrewed the van's gas cap and let him fill it. He smiled at her.

"Yeah, it ain't like it used to be," he said, picking up a conversation she didn't realize they were having. "Even around here. I never used to lock my doors, you know. Saw you parked out here, thought you might burgle me." He chuckled at this.

She shifted her stance. "Lot of crime out here?"

"Enough. Like I say, I lock my doors now. You know how it is." The sides of his mouth dropped along with his voice. "There's more and more Mexicans coming up this way. And you know who else. Let's just say it gets darker all the time, if you know what I mean."

"Lovely," David muttered.

The man went on, talking more to himself than her.

Gertie stuffed her hands in her pockets and contemplated the house on the hill.

The man returned the can to his truck and reiterated his directions, warning her like she was a child not to go down any roads without signs. She nodded and smiled and thanked him.

He clamored into the truck and leaned across the passenger seat again and noticed for the first time the lettering on the side of the van. "This is your van?"

"Yep."

"You're from New York, then?"

"That's right."

"City girl. That explains it."

"Upstate, actually. Central New York. It's mostly farmland."

"Sell furniture, do you?"

"Not me. I inherited the van."

"And you drove it all the way down here?"

"Couldn't afford a new one."

The man nodded. "They say the economy's stronger, but I don't know."

"And who knows what the queers are doing to the soil, right?"

The man didn't quite balk, but he regarded her more skeptically than before. "Well," he said, "you take care now." He sat upright and drove off.

When he was out of sight, she got into the van and turned around.

David fidgeted in the passenger seat. "What are we doing?"

"You see that house?"

"Gertie."

"I guarantee that racist prick has a wad of cash in a wall safe."

"Gertie."

"Right behind a big painting of a plantation."

"You got us cash last night. We're not robbing this guy."

She reached under her seat. She felt the bourbon bottle and pushed it aside for the plastic water bottle wedged beside it. She pulled the water out and drank. Warm, but it eased her throat.

"Not robbing. Burgling."

. . .

They stopped in Grayson for food and gas. She had plenty of cash to spare now. The man didn't have a wall safe, but a small freestanding safe he kept under a blanket beside his bed. A Colt revolver inside, a box of ammunition, some personal items wrapped in brown paper, and ten thousand dollars in cash. She counted out a grand and left everything else. David whined at her to leave, but it was this or days of petty thievery and panhandling. Such things were not difficult for her, but they were tedious and time consuming. David still didn't approve.

There were plenty of diners to choose from in Grayson. Chains, mostly. She settled on the most rundown she could find. A place called Sty Diner that was surprisingly clean on the inside. A couple construction workers ate at a far table. She sat at the counter across from a television above the cook's window. Onscreen, a local newscaster talked about the weather. The volume was too low to hear, but the numbers said it was going to be hot.

A woman with deep smoke lines around her mouth fiddled with a stack of receipts and took her order, calling her "honey" without looking up. Gertie ordered coffee and eggs over easy with rye toast, chugged a glass of water, and went to the bathroom to piss.

It was a single stall bathroom, so she undressed and washed with paper towels, wiping down her armpits and neck and lower half. She badly needed a shower. She figured she'd head to Huntington after all.

Why not? The latest lead had dried up, so they could do nothing but keep an eye on the news and crime websites and wait. The racist's money would buy a couple weeks at a cheap motel, and she could catch up on sleep.

And what then, she thought, after a shower and rest?

Best not to think too far ahead.

Her food waited at the counter.

David had elected to sit in a booth by himself. Sometimes, they needed space.

"You're from New York?" the waitress said when she sat down.

Gertie squinted at her nametag. *Martha.*

Martha clarified. "I saw your plates." She nodded at the big front window.

"Originally, yeah."

"Whereabouts?"

"I'm from upstate. Not the city."

"I didn't assume the city. I have family in New York."

"Sorry. It's just, most people hear New York, they think Manhattan."

"Mm-hm."

"I'm from Rockwall."

"My nephew goes to school in Rockwall. What brings you down here?"

She dipped her toast in the runny yolk and washed it down with a swig of coffee. "Looking for someone."

"Ooh, mysterious. You must be a bounty hunter."

Gertie wasn't sure if she was joking. "That a popular occupation around here?"

"You tell me." Martha nodded at the men in the corner. One of them, bearded, thick around the middle, raised his mug.

"Kidding," Martha said. "Derek and Dave couldn't catch a cold if it was hanging out their nose."

Gertie smiled. "Well, I'm no bounty hunter, either. Just trying to find an old friend."

"They in trouble, this friend of yours? Or are you?"

"A little of both, I guess."

"Well, I wish you luck."

The front door chimed, and another man entered. He sat at the counter a few chairs down. Martha had his coffee ready before his ass hit the seat. "The usual, Martie," he said.

"Gertie," David hissed from his booth. He pointed at the television above the cook's window.

The newscaster, an over-tanned man with 90's style frosted tips was saying something about a tragedy in Minnesota. Gertie strained to hear. The screen cut to plain white text over a blue background.

Ehblu Htoo, suspect in Estill County quadruple homicide, dead in Fairfield, Minnesota, after taking two more lives.

The latest victims were a recent high school graduate and a janitor. It happened yesterday morning. Almost exactly twenty-four hours before she sped drunkenly through the countryside, certain she'd never catch another break. And here it was.

She scarfed down the rest of her food. Through stuffed cheeks, she thanked Martha and slapped a twenty on the counter and bolted out the door.

.   .   .

She sat in the van flipping through her atlas. When they'd begun this road trip, she had a phone with GPS, but couldn't keep up with the monthly plan. According to the maps, Fairfield was near the southern end of Minnesota, a few hours from the Iowa border.

"I'm guessing thirteen hours," she said. "Without stops."

"You sure you're good for that?"

"I'll nap while I drive."

"Funny."

She gestured at the map taped across the glovebox. "Navigate."

David sighed and squinted at the paper. "Go back the way we came. We'll head through Cincinnati. After that, we'll need a new map."

She started the van and pulled onto the road. They said nothing for a while, passed through several towns you'd miss if you blinked. The day was sticky and hot and she could tell she had missed some soap under her right armpit, which was beginning to itch.

"Why Minnesota?" David said.

"Who knows? Why Kentucky?"

David had no answer.

"Don't overthink it. He doesn't plan."

"I guess. Just seems high profile. We used to have to dig to find him."

"He's getting bolder."

"Speeding up, too. I don't like it."

"That's not exactly surprising, is it?"

"I'm just saying. It's not good."

"Let's just get there."

Out on country roads again, she reached under the passenger seat between David's feet and found the handle of the plastic case hidden there. She pulled it out and set it on her lap and flipped it open to look at the tranquilizer gun and vials. She had filled the vials with a concoction she mixed herself. She'd labeled each according to the approximate weight of the target. Every time the trail picked up, she wondered if she'd get to use the damn things.

"You good?" David said.

She snapped the case shut and put it back, reached under her own seat and pulled out the liquor bottle. She held the amber liquid to the light, uncapped it, and poured it out the window. It flared from the bottle and splashed across the side of the van.

"Fine," she said.

They drove on.

4

Richard's cousin's place was a mid-sized apartment that probably cost an arm, leg, and firstborn child, considering its proximity to the bay. There was plenty of room for four guests. Amy and Jeff took the guest bedroom, Richard the couch in the living room, and Janelle the futon in the office.

It was their first vacation as a group, and for everyone but Richard, their first time seeing the ocean. The day of their arrival, they visited a handful of tourist sites and lounged on a nearby beach. Everything cost more than it should have, but nobody minded.

They went whale watching on the second day, and that night in bed Janelle felt the futon rolling like a boat and dreamed of riding on the back of a humpback that slid through the depths like a submarine. It took her down into the black and the cold, but she wasn't afraid.

She hadn't worked up the courage yet to make a move on Richard, but it was on her mind long before she packed her bags. She needed it to be part of this trip's memory. That was all she'd get long term with Richard—a memory. He'd been accepted into Columbia College, which was a huge deal for him, and a world away from Fairfield. He would never put it off to be with her, and she'd never ask.

Amy and Jeff had their paths, too. They'd both been accepted to UW Madison. That was how things went for them. Together since freshman year, a perfectly matched couple whose lives would sync up until they keeled over at the exact same time, ninety-something years old, nurses whimpering as their hands unclenched and they drifted into heaven with a collective sigh.

Janelle had no plans. She had procrastinated too long on college applications, then claimed she'd been planning to enroll in community college all along. She'd probably stay at Burger King until she selected a four-year school and a major, which meant she'd have to decide what to do with her life. What she wanted was for time to stop being so damn stubborn and let her and her friends stay together as long as they damn well pleased.

So she knew Richard had no part in her future, nor she in his. That was fantasy. But hooking up didn't have to be more than that, unless they wanted it to be, which was to say unless *he* wanted it to be. And if he did, then maybe they could find a way to push through whatever force had kept them apart for so long. Things would click. Not just for them as a couple, but for her, personally. Richard was always so put-together, so figured-out. He didn't have an insecure bone in his body. If they spent enough time together, maybe she'd absorb some of his better traits.

She'd been wedging herself closer to him since they were juniors, even though he'd been dating Christina B since sophomore year, and Christina B was the perfect female specimen. She could have been a model, and, worse, was a perfectly pleasant person. Janelle could never compete with that peppy personality and those boobs and perfectly round butt. Other than envy, she couldn't even find a reason to hate her.

The day after graduation, Christina B dumped Richard. He didn't talk about it, but she obviously wanted to date guys at college. No doubt she would dig her claws into the most handsome, charismatic one she found when she got there. The breakup hit Richard hard.

He was still mopey in California.

His cousin kept a stash of liquor she invited them to raid, and Amy brought flasks that looked like sunscreen bottles. By midafternoon most days, they were toasted inside and out. They'd make their way to a restaurant and giggle at the staff. On their third day, they successfully used their new fake IDs at a karaoke bar. Janelle made Richard sing "California Dreaming" with her while Amy and Jeff cheered them on. At the end of the song, Janelle pulled Richard close and pecked him on the cheek. Amy did her dog whistle and Jeff whoop-whooped.

By the time they returned to the apartment, Janelle was sloppy. Amy knew her intentions, so she slunk off to bed with Jeff, wishing Janelle good luck.

Richard poured water from the tap and made Janelle chug half the glass. She wrapped herself around him and let it all spill. The truth about her feelings. How patient she'd been. Richard muttered something about her being drunk. She nipped at his neck and pulled him in the direction of the office and the futon. He was stiff and awkward in response, telling her it wasn't right. Rejecting her.

Her plan was cracking open. She started crying. She was making a fool of herself, and confessed that she would never be a worthy follow-up to his previous relationship. He wiped her cheeks and kissed them and told her that wasn't it. She was just drunk, and that wasn't how this should go. They went to the office and left the door open. They made out on the futon.

She woke up fully clothed with his arms around her, spooning her.

She had a headache and her mouth tasted awful, but she was sober, and Richard was still there. She twisted around in his arms to face him. He was awake, dark eyes gazing into hers.

She kissed him under the chin. Found his lips. He kissed back. She pressed against him, grinding their hips. At last he stood and closed the door and returned to her.

The rest of the trip, they were a couple. They held hands. They made love each night, curling into each other's bodies. She could almost believe her fantasy was coming true. Good things waited for them, just beyond this curve in the road.

• • •

Wednesday morning.

Fairfield.

Her own bed.

She stared at the ceiling, clasping her phone over her chest like a corpse with a rosary. If she closed her eyes, she could almost imagine she was back in Richard's cousin's place. But the sheets weren't the same. Her bed was too comfortable. No pressure from the futon's metal ribs.

A full day had passed since the incident on the highway.

That was how people referred to it. The police. The news. Her parents.

The incident on the highway.

Jeff was dead.

Richard had killed a man. It was self-defense, but he'd still done it.

Those soft hands slamming metal against somebody's skull.

The trauma played on a constant loop in her mind. Blinking at the blind spot from the man's flashlight, seeing only the impression of movement as Jeff screamed. Her vision fading in slowly. She thought at first the man was punching Jeff in the lower back. Then she saw the knife. And the blood. The man knelt on Jeff's legs and held him down with a hand between his shoulder blades.

Richard made a noise in his throat like a gasp or a cough, dashed forward, pulled the handle out of the jack and swung it like a bat against the man's head. Sounded like a melon splitting. The man rolled off Jeff and onto his side, still holding the knife, face streaked with blood. Feebly, he swung the knife. He appeared to be laughing. Richard kept his legs clear and brought the jack handle down on the man's skull, crushing his forehead, though the man still grinned, still laughed. Richard brought the metal down again. And again. And again.

Jeff lay on his stomach, shuddering and pale.

Amy dove across him. She pulled the back of his shirt up. "Oh my God oh my God oh my God."

Janelle became unstuck. She demanded Amy's phone and dialed 911. She spoke rapidly in stuttering phrases so the operator told her to slow down and try again. She said they'd been attacked. Jeff was hurt. They didn't know what to do. Amy tried to staunch the bleeding with her sweatshirt. Jeff gurgled and coughed. Janelle stayed on the line even when Jeff went silent, went still, stopped shaking, and Amy shrieked, "What the fuck, oh God." She turned him over and started mouth to mouth while Janelle and Richard looked on, helpless.

The rain had stopped. No cars came.

Richard sat in the middle of the road, staring ahead, in the direction of home, the only one not crying. Janelle went to him, put her arm around him, tucked her face into his shoulder.

"I can't get him off," he said, his voice flat.

She thought she misheard him. Maybe he said, *I can't get him up.* Or, *I couldn't get him off.* It didn't matter. They were all in shock. Jeff was pale and still, and Amy kept shaking him and talking into his ear.

"Miss," the voice on the phone said, "are you still with me?"

Cops came. They put Richard in plastic handcuffs.

At some point, she sat in the back of a police cruiser and looked out the window as the town passed. She was taken to an old stone courthouse. Inside, she placed her fingertips on a piece of glass until a computer beeped, and a woman brought her to a small room with a cheap conference table and bad lighting where she sat for a long time with an itchy wool blanket on her shoulders, a hot chocolate going cold in front of her. A digital camera on a tripod in the corner.

After a long time, two men entered. Both wore button-up shirts and ties. The woman who brought her hot chocolate followed them. The men identified themselves as detectives. The skinnier, younger one was Bartov. The taller one, Alverson, had spoken with her briefly on the highway. He sat across from her with his sleeves half-rolled, revealing muscular forearms etched with veins. He asked the questions. She had already answered most. The skinny one took notes, though they told her the whole thing was being videotaped by the woman at the camera.

When they were satisfied, they told her how sorry they were and that her parents were waiting for her downstairs. The woman escorted her out past the front desk and into the lobby area, where her mom rushed to embrace her. She didn't see Amy or Richard.

At home, in the shower, she collapsed sobbing to her knees and let the water beat on her back until her mom knocked at the door and asked if she was okay.

She was toweling off when her phone buzzed. She had a message from Amy: *im out. u home?*

Janelle replied, *yes. u ok?*

Amy responded immediately, *no.*

so sorry. She added, *it's gonna be ok.*

how?

idk :(

There was nothing she could say. She wrote, *luv u*

Amy replied, </3

Janelle texted Richard again. There was no response.

Nightmares kept her from sleeping. As soon as she closed her eyes, she would see Jeff on his stomach and the man on top of him. She would jerk awake and find that she was crying.

Tuesday evening, the local news released details about the incident. Her parents took the house phone off the hook and, after a series of visitors rang the doorbell, hung a sign on the front door asking for privacy. Her social media accounts blew up. After a cursory glance through the comments, she decided to unplug indefinitely. Most comments were supportive or expressing their own grief. Others lashed out in frustration and outrage: how did the attacker, a wanted murderer from Kentucky, evade law enforcement for so long? Why hadn't the public been warned that there was a murderer in the area? When was America going to fix its health care system and get people the mental health support they needed?

A detective called and left a message, wanting to update her about the case.

She didn't call back.

She missed Richard. Couldn't help it. They had spent several blissful days together. Things had been perfect. She'd been prepared to talk to him about their future. She wanted him to hold her. She wanted to hold him.

How petty and selfish was that?

She didn't know what she was supposed to think or feel. She didn't want to feel anything.

There was a soft knock at her bedroom door, and her mother whispered, "Nelly?"

"Yeah."

The door opened a crack. "Will you come down for breakfast?"

She made no reply.

"You've gotta eat."

"Fine."

Her mother nodded, began to close the door, hesitated. "I scheduled a doctor's appointment for Friday."

"For what?"

"It's just someone to talk to. It might help."

"Fine."

Her mother went out, and Janelle lay there another fifteen minutes.

Her phone buzzed. Another text from Amy.

Jeff's calling hours tomorrow @ 4pm. Caldwell Funeral Home. funeral friday.

ok. ill be there.

<3 </3

Downstairs, a plate of scrambled eggs, bacon, and a buttered English muffin waited on the kitchen island. It had gone lukewarm, so her mother placed it on a pan and warmed it in the oven. She was using her vacation days this week. Her father would do the same next week. They didn't think Janelle should be alone, and the urge to chug the first thing she found in the liquor cabinet told her they were probably right.

Her mom rested her elbows on the island across from her. "How are you doing, sweetie?"

"I don't think I can go to school."

Her mom frowned. "It's summer, honey. You graduated two months ago."

"I mean college."

Her mom went stiff. "We can talk about that later."

"No. I can't go. I don't want to."

"Let's just wait before we make that decision, okay? You've got that appointment Friday."

"Fine."

Mom looked in the oven, brought out the pan and put the food back on Janelle's plate. Janelle had no appetite. She picked at the eggs and drank her orange juice.

Afterward, she tried texting Richard again. No response.

She retreated to her room and called his house phone.

His dad picked up. "Hello?"

"Hey, Mr. Becker. It's Janelle."

"How you doing, girl? You okay?"

"I guess."

"I know what you mean. You will be, though. You're a strong kid."

"Is Richard there?"

"He is. Just released, in fact." Was there an edge of bitterness in his voice?

"What do you mean?"

"They wanted to charge him."

"Charge him? For what?"

"They said he committed a homicide. I had to call a damn lawyer."

Janelle wanted to scream. Hadn't the cops listened to a word she said?

"But they let him go?"

"For now. I told them I'm prepared to sue."

"Wow."

"I guess you'd like to talk to him?"

"Yeah."

"Give me a sec."

Finally, she thought.

The voice that came on was not Richard's. "He's sleeping," Mr. Becker said. "He's been through a lot. I'll have him call you back, okay?"

Tears welled in her eyes. *Wake him up now, damn it.*

"Okay," she said.

"Take care now."

"Thanks. Mr. Becker?"

"Yeah?"

"Could you make sure he calls?"

"Course I will. Be good now."

Richard's dad was the high school gym teacher. Janelle liked him, but he forgot things easily. Students' names. Equipment. Days of the week. Messages she left for Richard.

She lay on her bed and considered texting him again. The police wanted to charge him? What were they thinking? He'd saved their lives. She wanted to let him know.

Eventually, she slept. She did not dream about the highway. Instead, she rode the back of a whale, but it did not swim through the ocean. It drifted through a vast, freezing void. She clung to its blowhole, slippery with blood. She felt something ahead. Something predatory in the dark, watching her—waiting.

She woke shivering and twisted in her sheets.

It was probably good her mom called a therapist.

5

At 0410 on Tuesday morning, while Janelle Winters sat numbly in an uncomfortable plastic chair in a dingy conference room and fought back another round of tears and Detective Ray "Al" Alverson leaned on the counter in the break room, sighed, and poured the morning's second cup of coffee and looked over his notes and steeled himself for the day ahead, Officer Rachel Bevins was pulling up to the Eagle Lake residence of Gerald Whitney, owner of the 2015 Toyota Tacoma the killer from Kentucky had been driving. Bevins had been second to arrive at the scene. She took it upon herself to comfort the girl whose boyfriend lay dead on the pavement. She had the EMTs check the girl, and she stood by while detectives tried to pry answers from her.

Bevins transported the girl to the police station and lobbed pleasantries at her, but the girl—Amy—never responded. Bevins struggled to leave her at the station. She thought about her own daughter. How one day her little Tonya would be Amy's age and just as helpless against the horrors of the world. She thought about this often.

Gerald Whitney lived in a mint-green ranch house next to a Lutheran church. The driveway was empty, and the lights were off. Bevins pulled into the driveway. Her headlights shined into the chasm of the garage, which had been left open. The contents cast spidery shadows: rusty lawnmower, snowblower, antique bicycle, snow shovel, pickaxe, rake, gardening tools hanging on the back wall, something in the far corner that glinted like a beetle's shell. A lot of people in these small towns didn't lock their doors, but even somewhere as quaint as Eagle Lake, it was unwise to display the contents of your garage like this. If Whitney's truck were in there, someone could have walked right up and drove off with it.

Bevins had called Whitney's home phone earlier and got his voicemail. In all likelihood, it meant he was asleep. Still, a chill ran up her spine when she saw that open garage.

She reported her arrival to dispatch and stepped out of the car, leaving her headlights on. She approached the front door, fishing the flashlight out of her belt and snapping it to life. She held it at shoulder height and illuminated the paver stones leading to the stoop.

She rang the doorbell three times before heading to the garage. The space was dusty and smelled of earth. The thing with the beetle shell in the corner turned out to be a motorcycle frame with no front wheel or motor. Bags of mulch stacked beside the backdoor. A screen door led to the house's interior. The inner door had been left open, so she could see straight through the foyer into what appeared to be the kitchen.

The smell hit her all at once.

She snapped open her holster and removed her service pistol and rapped the butt of her flashlight on the doorframe.

"Mr. Whitney?" she called. "This is Officer Bevins of the Fairfield Police Department. If you're able, please respond."

She angled her light into the foyer, peering as far into the corners as she could.

The smell made her queasy. She knew it well. Before the police academy, she worked for an animal control center. Part of her job was to remove carcasses from the roadway. All she had to complete this work was a filthy pickup truck with a low bed. She would go out and load (drag) the carcasses up into the bed before driving them to the dump where she unloaded their stiff bloated bodies, sometimes by shoving with both hands and feeling the rotten guts squishing under her fingers. The truck had no AC, so in the hottest months of summer her options were to bake in the cab or keep the windows down and breathe in the decay that wafted out of the bed. For years, she had nightmares about that smell—that it was in her apartment but she couldn't find the source, and she knew that one of those dead things had clamored out of its grave and followed her home.

It was an evil smell.

"I'm coming in!" she announced.

With her hand that held the flashlight, she pushed down the screen door's handle, hooked her pinky around it, and swung it open. The hinges shrieked.

She held her flashlight at neck-level and her pistol tucked against her torso as she entered the foyer. She found the light switch on the wall and flicked it, squinting at the sudden brightness before continuing into the hallway separating the foyer and the kitchen.

From the garage, all she had seen of the kitchen was a patch of tile floor and the front end of a stove. The source of the smell had been just out of sight. She saw it immediately upon entering the room, and though it went against all of her training, she shut her eyes for a full second before opening them again and finding the light switch beside her.

The dining table was pressed against the far wall. Above the table hung a chandelier of faux-diamonds. A line of clay pots of various sizes rested on the floor in front of the table. Bevins counted six in total. On the table lay a man's naked body. Most of it, anyway. It had been cut open from neck to groin. Some of the innards had been pulled out and wrapped around the chandelier so they seemed to be crawling up like creeper vines. With the light on, the viscera cast an orange-red glow around the room. The man's hands and feet had been removed and placed in the pots on the floor. Pale hands and calloused feet with yellow nails sticking out of the dark, fertile soil. She puzzled over the fleshy protrusion in the smallest pot before realizing it was the man's severed penis. His head was in the largest, but it did not sit directly in the soil like the others. It had been carefully balanced on a wire frame so it seemed to hover above the pot. The pink-white spinal column dangled out of it, just grazing the soil. Worse than the carnage was the expression of absolute calm on his face. In the far corner, the tools used to complete this vile display had been neatly stacked. Among them, a hacksaw, gardening sheers, and a spade.

Bevins could not hold back the bile. She bolted out of the house the way she'd come, knowing she would not admit to anyone but her department-appointed therapist that she left the scene without securing it, and while she vomited in the front yard and fought to control her shaking long enough to work the radio, she knew that no matter what she encountered in her subsequent years as an officer of the peace, this would be the night to haunt her when hope slipped away and she felt the forces of darkness gathering like a wave about to crash upon the innocent.

Ray's instincts about Pulp-Head were spot-on. The guy was a genuine psychopath.

36 years old, a second-generation American working IT for a security firm just across the West Virginia border in Huntington, he'd been living a normal, boring, average life until three weeks ago when he stopped at a sporting goods store on his way home from work, bought a hunting knife, and proceeded to murder his wife and two children. He mutilated the bodies before walking to his neighbor's house—a single mother of one—knocking on the door, and stabbing her 36 times in the abdomen. It was a small mercy her child was sleeping at a friend's house, but no mercy at all that the child discovered his mother's corpse when he was dropped off in the morning. The authorities recovered Htoo's car at a gas station in the nearby town of Olive Hill, where they discovered an elderly man strangled to death in the single-stall bathroom. Then there was the dismembered body of Gerald Whitney in Eagle Lake and the incident on the highway.

Other than his family and neighbors, Htoo's victims appeared to be chosen at random. A couple feds who came down from the Twin Cities field office called him a "disorganized offender," a term that lumped him in with serial killers like Richard Ramirez and David Berkowitz, though most of his profile did not fit this mold. He was of average or just above-average intelligence, grew up middle class with no history of violence or escalating behavior, and held a steady job for years while raising a family. None of his recent actions fit what came before. This aligned with the pattern set by other recent "spree" killers around the country. The feds didn't yet know what to make of it, and returned to the Twin Cities with their case files in hand, beaming like scientists on the brink of some great discovery.

Ray called the sheriff's office in Estill County, Kentucky, early Tuesday. The man was elated about Htoo's death. He walked Ray through the progression of their own investigation, what they had discovered in Htoo's home, the neighbor's house, and the gas station bathroom. He said it was without question the most gruesome case he or any of his deputies had worked in their combined history of law enforcement. The scene in Htoo's home was so bad one of the responding deputies—a 20-year veteran of the department—put in for early retirement the next day. When Ray told the sheriff how Htoo had come to his reward, and how the boy responsible was currently sitting in a conference room waiting for the county attorney to decide on charges, the sheriff replied, "Son, that boy deserves an honest-to-God medal, not a court date."

It wasn't up to Ray.

There was little question as to what happened that night, but self-defense laws were not as cut-and-dry as in the movies. In Minnesota, deadly force could only be used as a last resort. The books referred to this as a "duty to retreat." When force was applied, it should only be the amount any "reasonable person" might use in order to escape a threat. The state of Ehblu Htoo's body was the complicating factor. The pulpiness of his head, to be exact. It seemed quite clear that Richard Becker had not stopped swinging his weapon after knocking Htoo unconscious.

Never mind that the boy had just watched the man stab his best friend to death.

Legally, they could hold Becker for 36 hours without charges. They released him after 28. Two hours after that, the county attorney's office put out a statement praising the boy's actions. They said he had saved the lives of his two female companions and put an end to a deranged killer's trail of terror. By Wednesday afternoon, local news media had labeled Richard Becker a hero.

Ray hadn't slept or left the station since Tuesday morning. At Becker's release, he returned to his desk to prepare the final report. At least once an hour, one of the other investigators leaned over his cubicle wall and told him to go the hell home and get some rest. But Obermeyer had requested a full write-up, as though the investigation would result in Pulp-Head's post-mortem prosecution. In reality, the report was strictly for the public interest. A high profile case like this, Obermeyer had the whole city demanding answers.

Ray just wanted to be done with it.

He was reading over Dr. Aire's report about Henry Opal's wounds—the man who threw himself in front of the teenagers' jeep—when a notification popped up on his screen informing him he had an email from the agency that transcribed their interviews. It was a short message with a video attachment. The message claimed there were audio anomalies in one of the videos, making it difficult to transcribe. They had attached a clip of one such anomaly for his review. They didn't describe the nature of the problem, which seemed unusual. Typically, they'd just transcribe the thing and note any discrepancies in the write-up.

Ray hadn't reviewed the interviews since conducting them. A glance at the thumbnail attachment showed that the video in question was of his interview with Richard Becker. Ray hovered the cursor over the clip, but stopped from clicking.

This part of the station, referred to as the bullpen, was arranged much like any office space. Four cubicles on either side of the room with a walkway between them provided a semblance of privacy. The bullpen was almost always buzzing, so if you wanted true privacy, you had to go elsewhere. Ray's computer was an old desktop PC—not exactly portable.

The place was particularly crowded today. And noisy. Larsen and Vogel were laughing about something and Jensen and Fernandez were arguing about the Vikings' chances of making the playoffs.

Ray fished a pair of earbuds out of his desk and plugged them into his PC. He popped them in and leaned forward, squinting at the video thumbnail, still reluctant to play it. In that static square, the conference room appeared brighter than he remembered. Becker sat upright, his hands flat on the table. He'd made little eye contact during the interview, and his voice stayed low and steady when he answered questions. Ray thought there was something *off* about the way he held himself. He had interviewed people who were in shock before, but this was different. The boy seemed almost in a trance, and he kept twitching. A shoulder jerking upright, an eye fluttering, a finger tap-dancing on the table before abruptly cutting off.

But that wasn't what bothered him or kept him from playing the clip.

Even now, he struggled to comprehend what he'd experienced in that room.

Bartov had been there, but he didn't seem to notice anything unusual.

The email message mentioned only audio anomalies. Nothing about—

About what? What had happened in that room?

It had felt as though—

It seemed—

It was as if—

There was someone else in the room with them.

Ray, Bartov, Richard Becker, and *the fourth.*

Except there wasn't a fourth. Not really.

Richard had sat on the opposite side of the table from Ray and Bartov. Bartov took notes and nodded as the kid talked, and Ray's attention swung between the two.

Why couldn't Bartie see it?

Just over the boy's left shoulder, directly behind him, Ray saw, in jittering glimpses and out of focus, a shadow behind Richard Becker, flickering like some kind of anti-lightbulb on the fritz. At first, he thought the shadow was the boy's own, projected on the wall behind him, but it didn't align with the room's lighting. The shadow was disembodied from the boy, yet connected to him, and always over his left shoulder. Ray couldn't discern a shape. More of a *suggestion* of a shape. Possibly round. And definitely too close to the boy to be standing behind him. More like it was pressed against his back, or creeping over his shoulder and neck.

Ray counted five times it made itself visible. Popped in, then popped out.

He couldn't help but recall what he'd seen outside his SUV on the highway. The dead boy, Jeff, speaking without making a sound.

Ray did not believe in ghosts. Plain and simple. He didn't even believe in God, unlike so many in his line of work. Detective Ray "Al" Alverson believed in the power of deduction. He believed in what he could write in a report and corroborate with physical evidence.

But what he saw on the highway and in the conference room had been as real as the light emanating from his computer screen now, as real as the cursor hovering over the thumbnail of the video, the cursor that he slowly moved from the *play* button to the *x* in the corner.

He closed the file without playing it, shoved his earbuds back in his desk, and responded to the email saying they should transcribe the audio the best they could—and put a rush on it.

There were passageways that he did not intend to explore. Stairways he refused to descend, where figures stood in darkness with outstretched hands, tall and bony and beckoning, inviting him into madness. He had decided long ago never to explore such places.

He saved his work and shut off his computer and announced to the room that the time had come at last for him to get some fucking sleep, at which his coworkers mockingly cheered. He waved them away and headed down the long hallway to the elevator, conscious of passing by the conference room where he interviewed Richard Becker and a thousand witnesses and suspects before him and trying to ignore the hair that raised on the back of his neck.

6

Gertie and David crossed the Minnesota border at 10:27 Wednesday night, windows down and radio off, muggy air blasting through them. She made as few stops as possible, though David convinced her to take a nap at the halfway point. These were their typical roles. Gertie pushing too hard, David the cautionary voice in her head. They'd been at this nearly four years.

Four years since she had a home and a bed, with only David to talk to and nothing to listen to but the same CDs—preferable, still, to the stadium country and preachers on the radio.

Outside, the land was dark. In the day, the colors of the midwest had been tremendously green, with trees round and bunched together like giant heads of broccoli. She rarely remembered to take in the scenery, a shame since she'd seen most of the country through these windows. The red sand of the southwest. The forests of the east. The white-capped mountains of the northwest and the mosquito-thick marshes of the south. She passed through these places on her way to rooms marked off with crime scene tape, where blood stained the walls, floors, ceilings, carpets, pillows. Even when the clean-up crews had come and gone, leaving the places stinking of bleach, traces of blood remained like dirt caked under fingernails.

Four years.

It could end in Minnesota.

It could have ended in Kentucky, too.

Or Louisiana.

Or Nevada or Oregon or Maine or Florida or—

She was being morose.

She popped open the middle console and fished out a Five Hour Energy.

"How far?" she said around a mouthful of chalky syrup.

"Sixty miles," David said. "Give or take."

"Getting close."

"Yeah." He looked out the window. "Like a hundred times before."

"You don't need to say it."

"Sorry." After a pause, he said, "What I meant to say was, Gee whiz, I bet we'll run into him at the next gas station."

"There's the spirit that beat the Japanese."

"We do have to catch up sometime, don't we?"

She let the question hang.

All this silence was making them think too much.

She reached under her seat and slid out the leather CD case.

"Please no," David said.

She flipped through the sleeves one-handed, seeking an album to break the mood. She popped in Black Flag and shouted the first lines in David's ear: "Loose nut in my heeead! Loose nut rattling my skuuuull! Crying for a human touch! Or anything that'll reach my sooooul!"

David groaned.

• • •

She sensed the scene approaching. The air grew dense, and the night seemed to darken. She shut off the music.

"You feel it?"

David craned his neck. "I think so. Around the curve."

"Yeah."

They crossed an overpass and saw city lights nearby. Vast black plains on either side of the highway. In the grass on the southbound side, someone had staked two white crosses into the ground and hung wreaths from them.

"Here we go."

David sat on the edge of his seat.

She pulled to the shoulder and shut off the engine. Another car zipped by, too close. She checked her mirrors for approaching vehicles and threw open her door and stepped out.

The crosses were wooden. The wreaths plastic. Crude lettering between the arms of one read, "In Loving Memory of Jeffrey Patel. We Love and Miss You." On the other: "In Loving Memory of Henry Opal. Beloved Father and Friend."

Jeffrey and Henry. She was sure they flashed their photos on the TV, but she couldn't picture either. They were blanks. Breadcrumbs to join all the others.

She knelt beside the crosses. Soggy mud crept through the knees of her jeans. She touched the earth with her fingertips. Sensed the residue of darkness. It soaked into surfaces like radiation, a lingering stink as if something had burned there.

David practically bounced on his toes. "It is him, isn't it?"

She took her hand from the dirt and wiped it on her pants. "Let's go."

When she stood, her head swam, and she saw spots.

She leaned on the cross for balance.

"Whoa." She rested there, blinking.

"You all right?"

"Lightheaded."

"You're overtired. You need rest."

She wanted to snap at him. They were finally here. They couldn't stop now.

But she hadn't had a good night's sleep in days, and she needed energy to face what lay ahead. She was more talented than most, but the gift still drained her.

"You can't face him like this."

"No shit."

"So what do you wanna do?"

She pushed off the cross and started across the highway, paying no mind to the approaching headlights. A small pickup whipped by, missing her by feet, honking as it went.

Back in the van, David was just a blur of color beside her.

"Seriously, Gertie. You need to sleep."

"I get it." She turned the key. The engine roared. "Tomorrow," she said, "we're finding this fucker." She smacked the blinker and pulled onto the highway.

7

Thursday morning. A pale sun rose over the city of Fairfield, Minnesota, population 34,218. Fifty-two degrees outside and rising. Sometime in the night, a pale mist crept from the edges of the Great Blue River into the streets, diffusing first through the old downtown, sidling around brick buildings and into alleyways and covering monuments and parks and continuing outward into housing tracts with their identical structures and dead ends and into the farmer's fields surrounding the town. From above, as from a great eye in the sky or as on a map, such as the one taped across the glovebox of Gertrude Morgenstern's black 2013 Nissan NV Cargo Van, the city resembled an isosceles triangle that had been stretched and distorted, with the two longer sides coming to a point in the southwest, the shorter "base" facing east. The Great Blue River, not particularly blue nor particularly great, wiggled from one end of the city to the other, running the length of the triangle in rounded zigzags, its origins farther south and its finish farther north so that what the town contained was a mere segment of river, incomplete and unremarkable, which, for some, might have been an accurate description of the town itself. With the Twin Cities a two hour drive north, Sioux Falls three hours west, the flat expanse of Iowa to the south, no mall and one movie theater and a handful of bars downtown, two high schools, one private, one public, a community college and a smattering of small businesses, though the second largest city in this area of the state, it was practically interchangeable with any number like it across the Midwest, an unremarkable place with ambitions to be an economic center while clinging to a fierce sense of small-town pride and surface-level niceties, citizens waving at each other on the street and judging each other from their homes, *bless-her-heart* and *did-you-hear-about-her-husband*, with a simmering resentment toward outsiders, the sort of town teenagers hated until they realized they were just like their parents.

On this misty morning, the people went about their usual business. Here two homeless men dug through a dumpster searching for bottles and cans. Here a fast-food restaurant's lights had been on for an hour, and now cars lined its drive-thru. Here a group of young adults stumbled back to their apartment, drawing wide arcs from the sidewalk into the road and back. Here a patrol officer sat in his car drinking coffee while all around her vehicles slowed their approach and sped up when they passed, and soon the highway that had grown cold in the night would warm beneath the tires of a modest morning commute and those who still tuned into the news would hear their forecast of 92 degrees and humid with a possibility of thunderstorms in the evening and their lives would spin inevitably forward.

Detective Ray "Al" Alverson sat awake on the sofa in his living room wearing boxer briefs, alone but for his reflection in a black TV, killing time before work and still fighting his encroaching thoughts about the thing in the conference room and the silent boy on the highway.

Gertie slept in a towel with her laptop on her thighs and a bedside lamp still lit. On the laptop screen, browser tabs listed the names and addresses of those she intended to speak with once she woke. Meanwhile, David Arlo stood at the window with his face pushed through the fabric blinds. Their room was on the third story, but didn't have much of a view beyond the parking lot. He wondered if today would be the day he found peace and what that might mean for his future, if he had one. And what about Gertie? Were they destined to roam this world forever, like the spirit residing in this Holiday Inn? They'd sensed him when they first arrived—an older man who lost something and believed he could find it here. He was responsible for the banging on the walls some guests heard around 3 a.m. and which the staff blamed on old pipes.

Across town, Janelle Winters slept restlessly in her own room, kicking the covers off and pulling them up again, shaking her head and muttering through yet another nightmare.

And across town again, at the banks of the Great Blue River, on a paved path that hugged the water and used to be a popular bike trail, behind a gray wall of concrete and under the overpass already crowded with cars, Richard Becker squatted to defecate and watched the roiling black water of the river churn around a pillar of the bridge. What remained of his consciousness wondered at his actions. Why was he defecating here? Why had he spent the night in this spot? Why did he ride his bicycle to the hunting shop and buy the knife, the one he now held in his left hand, and why did he do what he did to Derby? He loved that cat. It was almost as old as he was. It wasn't as if he wanted to do it, but ever since the incident on the highway, he had been pushed to the sidelines of his mind, and it was not until he did what he did to Derby that he realized he was not in full control of his body. He made excuses until then, the way anyone excuses their baser impulses. Perhaps he'd bought the knife as a means of protection. Given what happened on the highway, he could use it. Never mind that the knife was identical to the one that killed his best friend. And when he thought about Janelle and the messages she'd sent since that night, he wanted to reply but knew there was something wrong inside him, that he needed to keep himself from her, and so he fought the urge to say they should meet in a private place where he could bring the knife and do things to her. Laughter had filled his head then—laughter not his own—so he ran his phone under the tap and threw it in the trash and retrieved his sleeping bag and what remained of the cat and rolled it all together and took his bike from the garage and intended to ride to the edge of town and keep going, to take whatever was wrong in his head into the wilderness where it might run its course and let him starve and die, but instead he went to the river, to the bridge, where he came upon a sleeping homeless man and stood there shaking while the laughter echoed in his head before the man woke, saw him, and ran off.

That was yesterday, and now he finished his business and wiped himself with his bare hand and moved to the edge of the water and scooted down the pavement and reached for the rushing current and dunked his hand in, felt the grit moving through the water, shook the filth from his palm. He thought: *Oh my God, what is happening?* and the thing in his head laughed and laughed.

His skin crawled. He returned to his camp and reached a jerky hand into the sleeping bag and felt around, felt the cold fur inside, the velvety tissue, and his hand came away coated in something like mucus and it wasn't him who put his hand in the sleeping bag any more than it was him who did that to Derby, and he thought again about the night on the highway, swinging the metal bar into a stranger's skull. As the man's brains oozed out, Richard felt something scrambling up his own body. Like a giant crab or snake, it wrapped itself around him. He looked down, but there was nothing. He felt it searching for a way in. Couldn't get it off. Invisible and secret and laughing, laughing, the thing that sat now behind his eyes.

He could almost feel it swimming around inside of him.

It swiveled Richard's head to the left, to the right. It stuck his hand down his pants and grabbed his balls and squeezed until his stomach ached.

Richard wanted to cry, but they were no longer his tear ducts.

He thought about Janelle, or the thing inside him did.

It knew she would come.

Maybe he could go find that homeless man again. Have some *fun*. It would be a nice appetizer, a preview of what was yet to come.

Shut up, Richard thought. They weren't his thoughts.

He stood. Or the thing stood, this Oppressor, using Richard's legs. It did a little shuffle-step and slashed the knife through the air.

8

It was still early, but Janelle gave up on sleep, propped herself against the headboard and found her phone on the bedside table. She had a text from Amy, received around two in the morning. So she wasn't the only one having trouble sleeping.

Her dreams left her clammy and unsettled. Dreams of meat, of whale carcasses rotting on sandy shores, things bulging inside their guts, making the blubbery flesh pulsate, dreams of roads covered in rain as slick as oil while she jerked the wheel of the jeep helplessly and careened toward the railing of the Golden Gate Bridge.

Amy's text read, *see u tomorrow/tonight?*

Relief bloomed through her. She'd been dreading Jeff's wake, terrified Amy would blame her for everything.

She replied: *yes will be there of course <3*

Minutes passed. She sent another message: *u up?*

Amy replied immediately: *yea. can't sleep.*

Janelle: *me either!!! :(can u talk??*

Amy: *yea*

A moment later, her phone buzzed.

Amy's face filled the screen, her headboard behind her. She looked awful. Her cheeks were puffy, her hair pulled back and greasy. Her voice was hoarse and low: "Hi."

"Hey."

They frowned at each other.

Janelle said, "Are, um—how are you doing?"

"I keep puking."

"Oh."

"Yeah."

Janelle felt tears coming, but forced them back.

"I keep thinking, like, what the fuck did Jeff do to deserve this? Did you hear what else that sick fuck did? Killed his own family. And his neighbor, and an old man at a gas station. They don't even know why."

Janelle didn't know what to say. She'd been avoiding the news and social media since that night. Her parents had told her the basics, but even then she had a hard time retaining it.

"Sorry," Amy said. "I feel like I'm on speed but I'm sober as shit." At least there was that. "Richard got him. Put an end to that fucker."

"Yeah." *Richard*. She had to ask. "Have you heard from him?"

"No. I saw him at the police station that night. Or, I guess it was morning. I texted him a couple times. Nothing. He needs time."

"I know. I just— I feel like we should talk. All of us. We're going through this together, right?"

"Yeah, I guess."

Janelle let Amy's words linger. What did she mean, *I guess*?

"Sorry," Amy said, picking up on Janelle's discomfort. "I feel so fucked up. Like, I keep thinking he's gonna call me." She meant Jeff. "It doesn't feel like he's gone." She bit her lip and a wave of anguish rippled across her face, flushing her pink. She pinched her eyes shut so hard her whole face clenched. Just as suddenly, she relaxed, went robot-blank. "Sorry."

"Don't be sorry. I don't know how to do this."

"Me either. I've been talking to Jeff's parents. I feel like an asshole. Like, here I am, crying my ass off, and they just lost their son. I'm a selfish cunt."

"That's not true."

"It's like…" She looked at the ceiling. "Like a bad joke. Like, is there a God, because if so, he's some kind of fucked up psycho. I don't know. Sorry. Are you okay, though?"

God, this girl, Janelle thought. *Asking how I'm doing right now. Saint Amy.*

"I don't know. My mom's making me see a therapist tomorrow."

"That's probably good."

"I guess."

Downstairs, someone rang the doorbell, and her mother's footsteps crossed the kitchen. She heard the door open, then muffled talking.

"I think someone's here," Janelle said.

"The cops again?"

"I don't know. Maybe a reporter. Mom sounds pissed."

"I'll let you go."

"No, it's fine."

"I mean, I should. I'm gonna try to be normal today. Charlee keeps telling me to take a shower and eat, and I'm like, I'm just gonna throw up and get nasty anyway. Might as well be consistent."

For the first time since the highway, Janelle almost laughed. "She's a good sister."

"So are you, boo. You da best."

This was one of their little sayings. Sort of an inside joke without a punchline. She didn't know where it came from, but it sounded forced and awkward now.

Whatever. Janelle followed up with her line: "Nah, boo. You da best."

Amy faked a smile. "I'll see you tonight."

"Okay. I love you."

"Love you too."

She hung up, feeling queasy. She wondered if she would ever again have a conversation with Amy that felt normal, or if every time they talked, this would hang over them. It was why people divorced after the death of a child, wasn't it?

Amy had always been there for her. It was no exaggeration to say that her arrival in town had changed the course of Janelle's life.

Amy moved to Fairfield halfway through Freshman year. She'd come from a small town in Iowa with her sister. Her first day at school, Miss Dyer paired Janelle and Amy together for a chemistry project. Janelle was reluctant to meet this pretty new face—certain that Amy would fall in with the other snobs—but Amy took a long look at Janelle and said, "Damn, girl, I wish I had that skin." It was a ridiculous, naïve, and sort of racist thing to say, and it made Janelle uncomfortable. This new girl had no idea how much Janelle had been bullied for her complexion. For having parents whose skin didn't match hers. Kids called her a dirty

Mexican, illegal, asked how she got over the border. What moron would want this baggage?

Amy was no stranger to hardship, though. Her parents were meth heads and everyone in her hometown knew it. Shady characters haunted their house. Men and women with grimy, grabby hands and fucked up teeth. Amy spent as little time at home as possible. Sometimes, during the summer, she and Charlee would sneak off with a couple of blankets to sleep in a nearby cornfield just to be away from the creeps. Amy suspected something happened to her sister, but she never knew for sure. Charlee was four years older than her, and when she turned 18, she filed for legal guardianship of Amy and moved across state lines. Amy was not bitter about any of it. She turned out to be one of the nicest, kindest, most genuine people Janelle knew. They hung out for the first time that weekend under the pretense of working on their project, but wound up making goofy videos in Janelle's room. Amy called her sister and asked to sleep over. They hardly spent a day apart since.

Somehow, Amy proved immune to the petty rivalries at Fairfield High. Maybe she was too nice to bully, or too pretty to hate. She got good grades but was never labeled a goodie-goodie and made friends easily. Boys liked her, but she wasn't snide about it. She maintained acquaintances in a variety of cliques without locking herself into any. This might have had something to do with her taking photos for the school website.

One afternoon, Amy dragged her to a junior varsity basketball game where Amy wanted to get some yearbook photos. Janelle moped the whole time, refusing to make eye contact with anyone in the crowd. She practically snarled at the cheerleaders who kept doing ridiculous head-cocked poses and shaking their pompoms for Amy's camera. When Amy asked her why she couldn't relax, Janelle told her, "I hate everyone at this school, and they hate me."

Amy laughed and clicked through the photos on her camera. "No they don't, boo. They're jealous of your shit and all the guys want you."

This was crazy. Clearly, Amy didn't understand Fairfield.

Janelle crossed her arms and sank into the bleachers and didn't say much for the rest of the night.

That marked a turning point of sorts. It didn't happen immediately, but Janelle noticed that people began to treat her differently. She thought it was because of Amy—that the shallow idiots at her school figured, hey, if the new girl saw something worth befriending in Janelle, then perhaps she wasn't so bad after all—but when she aired these suspicions to Amy, Amy said nothing had changed at all. Janelle had been expecting people to hate her, so that's what she saw. Janelle wasn't so sure, but some weeks after the basketball game, two girls who had bullied her all through middle school sat beside her at lunch and apologized for being mean in the past. If Amy put them up to this, she never said. Around the same time, she learned that several of the guys that used to tease her had crushes on her.

Whatever the true cause of these changes, Janelle would not have experienced them without Amy. She was the reason Janelle had a shot with Richard, too. He was Jeff's best friend, and Amy started dating Jeff sophomore year. Janelle didn't even know she could have a crush on a jock like Richard before that.

She owed Amy for these gifts. And now this… It wasn't fair.

There was a light knock on her door.

"Yeah?"

Mom's voice: "C'ai come in?"

"Sure."

Mom poked her head in. "You up?"

Janelle shrugged and pulled the covers to her chin.

"I was thinking we should get out of the house for a while. Maybe get you a dress for tonight."

Shopping was Mom's thing. It was how she bonded. She liked to talk through the dressing room door—*You sure you're doing okay, honey?*— and quickly switch the subject if it got too hard. *Oh, that shirt looks perfect with those pants. You look like J-Lo.* She was always saying Janelle looked like J-Lo.

"Sure," Janelle mumbled.

"When you're ready, I'll make breakfast, okay?"

"Okay."

Her mom paused in the doorway, gave one of those sad smiles.

"Mom?"

"Yeah."

"Who was at the door?"

"Another reporter."

"I could've talked to them."

"I don't think that's a good idea, hon. They just want a soundbite."

"I could say something about Jeff."

"I'm sure there'll be more."

Janelle said that would be okay.

"Don't stay in bed too long."

Her mom went out.

Janelle peeled off the covers.

Yeah, she thought, *okay. No more moping.*

Today, she was going to wear a nice dress and see Jeff one last time before they put him in the ground. She would be brave, and she would see Richard there, and she would tell him that, whatever he was going through, if he wanted his space and all that, that was fine, but she wanted him to be okay, and Amy to be okay, and then whatever happened, happened. She just wanted everyone to be okay.

9

Gertie had booked an expensive room in a Holiday Inn just off the highway, reluctantly handing over her credit card for incidentals. She'd taken the elevator to the third floor, found her room, and crashed face-first on the bed. She woke around 3 a.m. to take out her laptop and cyber stalk the people she sought. She fell asleep again with the laptop open.

In the morning, she savored a hot shower and wrinkled her nose at the stink of her clothes before slipping back into them. There was a laundromat downstairs, but no time to use it.

She took the stairs to the lobby and found the continental breakfast where she scarfed down a couple muffins and tucked a third and fourth into her sweatshirt pockets.

A tall, thin girl with very black hair worked the front desk. She smiled at Gertie's approach. "What can I do for you?"

"Checking out."

"Room number?"

Gertie hesitated, uncertain if she should part with the room's cost. She could push inside the girl's head—not far. Just deep enough to plant a little influence. Something that would tell her, no, this woman doesn't need to pay, or she has already paid, and she should have her information wiped from the computer like she was never here.

"We have enough," David said in her ear.

"I can look it up by name," the girl said.

"No. I remember."

She paid.

In the van, they leaned over a map of the town, purchased from a gas station on their way to the hotel last night.

"Where to first?"

"Janelle Winters is the closest. We'll work our way across the map." Luckily, the kids involved were at least 18, so the media released their names. All she needed was an internet connection to find them.

Janelle Winters lived in a two-story house on the far side of a cul-de-sac. Pristine white siding, new shingles on the roof, a basketball hoop in the driveway. It even had a white picket fence—sharp wooden slats that enclosed the backyard like a small fortress wall.

They parked on the street, clamored out of the van, and started up the driveway.

They planted themselves on the front stoop. Gertie rang the bell. Church chimes sounded inside. She breathed deep, focused.

"Use the Force," David whispered.

She'd have told him to shut up, but she was already concentrating.

The door opened to reveal Janelle's mother. Tall, thin, and blonde, with a severe jawline and an icy glare. "Help you?"

Like sinking into a cold bath, she let the other sense wash over her. A feeling of expansion, a sudden *blooming* as her mind clicked into a new mode, becoming a tongue that could prod beyond the prison of its skull and taste the world's hidden flavors. The woman before her radiated sadness and indignation. Her edges seemed to glow with outrage at this intrusion, which flew in the face of the sign on the door warning off reporters. Behind her, somber tones in the house so strong they trailed through the air like ribbons. Gertie located their source up the carpeted staircase.

She fought hard to keep her focus while working her vocal cords, lips, and tongue. "Mrs. Winters?"

"Yes?"

Gertie was in the upstairs hallway, and she was here on the stoop. Janelle's door was at the end of the hall. Mrs. Winters waited for a response. Gertie pushed into Janelle's room, saw her on her phone. "I don't know," the girl said, "maybe a reporter."

"My name's Francesca White," she told Mrs. Winters. "I'm an independent journalist doing a story—"

"Not interested." Mrs. Winters crossed her arms. "Didn't you see the sign?"

"If you could only hear me out, I think you'll see—"

"My daughter has been through something unthinkable, and I'm sick and tired of you people harassing us. The public has been informed. The rest is private."

"I understand. I was just—"

"No. I've said all I have to say." Mrs. Winters slammed the door.

Gertie and David lingered just a moment before heading back down the driveway.

"Anything?" David said.

"Just a teenager on her phone."

"No trace?"

"No."

His disappointment was palpable.

"It's just the first stop," she said.

"Yeah."

Next was Amy Pink's place. A couple articles named her as the teenage victim's girlfriend. That made her a likely target.

They found the mobile home despite its lack of a number and knocked on the door to be received by a six-foot-tall linebacker of a woman who identified herself as Amy's sister, Charlee.

After Gertie's preamble, Charlee sneered, "Haven't you people bothered her enough?" Before Gertie could respond, Charlee held up a long index finger, then retreated inside.

"She's getting Amy," Gertie whispered to David.

"It's not her, is it?"

Gertie shook her head. She felt nothing but more heartache here, so potent she had to shut herself off or it might overwhelm her.

Charlee reappeared with her sister at her side. Amy wore baggie pajama bottoms and a tank top with no bra, hair in a frizzy bun. She had lost her boyfriend at the start of what could have been their future. Big sad strings on the violin. Welcome to the tragicomedy, sister.

"Amy?" Gertie said.

"Yuh?"

"I'm Francesca White. I'm a freelance journalist. Sorry to bother you, but I was hoping you'd have some time to chat with me."

"I've pretty much said everything already."

"I understand. You've been through a lot. It must get annoying talking to reporter after reporter."

Behind Amy, Charlee muttered, "No shit."

Amy shot her sister a look, stepped out, and closed the door behind her. "Make it quick."

There wasn't much they needed from the girl, but they were here. Might as well gather some intel.

"You and Jeff were pretty close, right?"

"He was my boyfriend."

"How long were you dating?"

"Pass."

"Sorry?"

"Do your research, dude. I answered this like a hundred times."

"I'm sorry. I do have this information. It's just, I want to hear you tell it."

"Sure. What's your next question?"

"What about Richard?" David said.

Gertie said, "Richard Becker saved your life, didn't he?"

"He did."

"How's he holding up?"

"Why don't you ask him?"

"I intend to."

"Great."

"I was wondering about your interpretation. Has he been doing okay?"

"I don't know. I haven't talked to him."

"When's the last time you spoke with him?"

"That night. At the police station."

"And he seemed okay?"

"What do you think? Jeff was his best friend. And he just killed a guy, so, yeah, I don't think he was feeling great." Amy sighed and looked across the street. A neighbor, an old lady in a white cotton dress, came out of her trailer and stood in her lawn, glaring at Gertie.

"Listen," Amy said, "I need to take a shower. I'm done answering questions."

"Okay."

"Don't take this personally, but maybe you should stick with furniture or whatever," Amy said, glancing at the van.

"Probably."

On the road once more, Gertie tapped her fingers on the steering wheel and cursed every red light. David practically bounced in his seat. They had a lead. Richard Becker was acting weird. Richard Becker had isolated himself. Richard Becker had been the one to kill their attacker. They both felt it. Were certain.

Richard Becker was the new host.

. . .

Richard Becker was not home. This was not a shock, but still disappointing.

His father answered the door dressed in a blue sweat suit. A large man. Not fat, but round, with a belly that strained his clothes and shoulders that were once broad and intimidating but now slumped toward his chest. When Gertie asked where his son might be, he turned to face the living room like maybe Richard was there. "He'd been hanging around those girls a lot. I assume he's staying over one of their places." Somewhere in the house, a television personality prattled on about an amateur athlete's chances at the professional level.

"Which girls?" But she already knew.

"Amy and Janelle. They're good kids. I almost convinced Janelle to try out for basketball a few seasons ago, you know. She was only interested in softball."

Gertie took longer than must have seemed natural to respond. Her mind was elsewhere.

"I didn't know that."

"She was good, but a little timid."

"You're a coach?"

"And the Phys Ed teacher at Fairfield High. I'm taking some time off to be with my son. This is uncharted territory."

"Mr. Becker—"

"John."

"John, I just spoke with Amy and Janelle. Richard wasn't with them."

He pursed his lips and shook his head. "I guess I don't know then."

Beside her, David sighed.

"Any idea when he left?"

"I assume this morning, but could've been last night. I thought he was still up there sleeping until I went to wake him."

"You're not worried?"

"Of course I'm worried. It might seem strange to you, but I believe a teenage boy needs his space. When I was his age, I had my own car, and I'd take off for weekends at a time without telling anybody, and all he's got is a bicycle."

"He doesn't have a license?"

"He's moving to New York City."

"Mr. Becker, do you—"

"John."

"Do you think Richard's holding up okay? Has he been acting strange?"

"Strange? Meaning what?"

"Has he seemed different?"

Mr. Becker squinted into the distance. "Different is normal, given the circumstances, wouldn't you say?" He thought a moment. "When I was my son's age, I lost a buddy in the service. You know what that's like?"

She'd have to wait this speech out.

"It was like someone ripped out my heart and held it up for me to see and then set it on fire. So if Richie wants to vanish for a day or two, I think he's earned that right."

"Does he have a cell phone I could try?"

"He turned it off."

"What about his mother? Is she around?"

"She passed some years back. What did you say your newspaper was?"

"I'm a freelancer."

"Freelancer. That like a blogger?"

"Sort of."

"You want my advice?"

"Sure."

"Catch him at the wake tonight. I'm sure he'll be there."

"The wake?"

"Jeffrey's. They're putting him in the ground tomorrow. It seems soon to me, but I guess there's no point putting it off. He was younger than Richard, you know. Senseless."

"What time's the service?"

"Starts at four. I believe it's at Caldwell."

"Thank you. I'll stop by." She turned to go.

"You know they're calling Richard a hero." John Becker's voice wavered, but he cleared his throat and continued, "He saved those girls, but he killed a man doing it. You know what that feels like? Hurting somebody like that, even if it's to help someone else?"

"No," she lied.

"That's good. Pray you don't." There was no malice in what he said. "Good luck with your blog."

"Yeah. Thanks."

She regrouped with David in the street.

"Is it him?" David said.

"It's him." In the house, concentrated in the boy's room, she felt the same sour note as she had at the highway memorials. Not as strong, but still there.

"You think he skipped town?"

"I doubt it. He doesn't have a car. He could steal one, but why not steal his father's? It's right there in the driveway." She gestured at the yellow Fiat. "Plus, his father's still alive. So that's a good sign."

David plugged his hands into his pockets.

She pulled open the van door and hoisted herself inside.

"You holding up okay?"

"Just need a coffee."

David nodded. "What next?"

"His friend's service is at four. We'll cruise town. Maybe we'll get lucky and spot him."

"Sure. Lucky. That sounds just like us."

10

Ray spent most of Thursday morning at the county courthouse, testifying in what had until two days ago been Fairfield's most sensational homicide in recent history. A battered woman the whole department knew from her frequent calls to the station had finally had enough, and pressed her husband's revolver to his ear while he slept. She's tried to make it look like a suicide, but the body's position and the blood spatter told a different story. The defense attorney was new, his questions clumsy. The prosecutor ate him for breakfast. The woman would end up in prison for defending herself. Ray didn't like it, but sometimes that was the job.

He arrived at the station around noon. He greeted the desk sergeant and made his way to the bullpen. Bartov was the only other detective around. The others would be out beating pavement. Summer was the busy season, even in Fairfield.

Ray nodded to Bartov and sat at his desk. He checked his email to see that the interview transcripts were ready. He attached them to his report without reading them. There were no video clips this time, and Ray was grateful.

"How was court?" Bartov called from his cubicle, sounding bored.

"Thrilling as ever."

Bartie snorted. "I'll bet. Hey, question for you."

Ray leaned back from his monitor and studied the younger detective.

Freckle-faced and blonde, a purebred Midwesterner if ever there was one, Bartov was one of the newest investigators in the department, and one of the hardest working. He'd come up through the ranks, and was one of the few cops in this city who had fired his service weapon in the line of duty. It was more than six years ago now, back when he was on patrol. He'd been the first responder to an armed robbery at the BP gas station on Riverfront and rolled up on the suspect as he ran into an alley. Bartov went after him, on foot. When he turned the corner, the guy fired five rounds that winged by Bartie's head. Bartie dropped to a knee and took the guy out with a double-tap—*pop-pop*—that hit him squarely in the chest. The guy died instantly. Bartie's coolness during the subsequent investigation was one of the reasons Obermeyer accepted his application for detective. Ray liked him.

"Some of us are planning to stop by the Patel kid's service before drinks at Blue Bricks," Bartie said. "You interested?"

A lot of officers had kids at Fairfield High, some in the same grade as the dead kid.

"I've got a long night ahead," Ray said. "I won't make it till later."

Bartie nodded knowingly.

Ray was something of a recluse and everyone knew it. He participated in the summer softball league, but rarely joined other extracurriculars. People made him twitchy. They thought he didn't know how to relax, but he just had a different way of relaxing—lifting weights at the gym, more often than not. Putting his body through hell quieted his mind.

"Okay then," Bartie said. "Figured I'd ask." He turned back to his own computer and kept on typing.

Despite himself, Ray pulled up yesterday's email from the transcription agency. With the sound off, he maximized the attachment and only hesitated for a second before hitting play.

Richard Becker's mouth moved. Ray's right arm was in the shot, but Bartov was off screen to the left. Richard spoke for thirty seconds, and the video stopped.

He rewound it and watched again, studying the space behind the boy. Nothing. No shadow. No figure.

He closed the video and returned to his work, but thought he would go to the Patel kid's wake after all. He'd go alone. Richard Becker would show up, and when he did, Ray would get one last clear look and decide with finality if something strange was going on, or if he was merely losing his mind.

11

At a glance, Jeff's calling hours could have been mistaken for a high school formal. A line of students, recent graduates, and their parents stretched through the double doors of the front entrance and beyond the brick overhang to wrap around the side of the building and bunch together in the parking lot. Boys in black pants and white shirts with black ties, rich kids in suits, girls in black dresses and sensible flats except for Christina B who teetered on five-inch heels in a dress that pushed her boobs to her chin, everyone dabbing their eyes with the backs of their hands or wads of tissue. Janelle surveyed them through the window of her parents' SUV while they circled the parking lot.

She shouldn't have felt bitter, but she didn't want to see these people. She had imagined the wake as a private affair. Janelle, Amy, and Richard would stand around an empty room looking over a closed casket, and Richard would put an arm around Janelle and she'd put her arm around Amy and together they would say goodbye to their friend and make peace with all of this.

"He had a lot of friends," her mom said. "I'll have to park on a side street."

They drove out of the lot and down the residential street beside the funeral home in search of parking. If they had come earlier, the line wouldn't be so long, and maybe there wouldn't be so many people to gawk at her, but she couldn't get herself down the stairs and out the front door any sooner. She had sat in front of her vanity fully dressed for close to an hour, studying her own face and feeling nothing. She thought about Richard. What had been an eager desire to speak with him earlier in the day had transformed into fear of what it might lead to. She feared what he might say, what she might feel. Most of all, she feared the numbness that settled inside her.

They parked half a mile from the funeral home. Her parents pressed her between them as they walked up the street, Mom on her left, Dad on her right. Mom still held her elbow.

"If you can't do this," Mom said.

"Barbara," Dad warned.

Mom's hand squeezed.

They joined the procession in the parking lot. It was almost five o'clock. The sun still blasted down on these mourners in their somber clothes. A few kids nodded at her. Others elbowed each other and gestured in her direction. This was exactly what she didn't want. She had spent years as a bullied freak until Amy saved her. She was right back there, all progress erased. These people had power over her. They thought to themselves, *Poor girl*, and felt sorry. It made her want to puke.

She couldn't just leave. Had to see Amy. And Richard. And Jeff, one last time. Perhaps remembering him in his coffin would be better than remembering him bleeding on the highway.

She watched her feet. Her black stockings disappeared into her shoes.

Her father touched her shoulder. "Nelly."

She looked up, into the glowing face of Christina B. Her pouty lips had been painted bright red. She looked like movie star grief. "Janelle?"

"Hey."

"I was looking for you."

"Okay."

"You don't have to stand in line."

"What?"

"I was just inside. Amy said to grab you. She's with Jeff's parents. I think she's kind of freaking out. Come on. Your parents can come, too. Hi, Janelle's parents. I'm Christina B."

Mom blushed. "We know, sweetie."

"Right." Christina B's smile was perfectly charming. "So let's go." With a shampoo-commercial flip of hair, Christina B started toward the entrance. Janelle followed.

Dad said, "Hang on." He gripped Mom's elbow, holding her and Janelle in place.

"Honey," Mom said to Dad, "what is it?"

Dad said, "Nelly, why don't you go inside? We'll meet you in a little while."

Mom wore a pleading expression.

"Barbara." His eyebrows arched. Janelle wasn't quite sure what that look signified, but Mom's expression softened, as did her grip on Janelle's arm.

"Right," she said. "You go on, Nelly. We'll see you in a bit. If you need us—"

Dad placed his hand on Mom's lower back.

For a moment, the numbness in Janelle vanished, replaced with something broader than sadness. Even before the trip to California, her mother had hovered over her more than usual this summer. The morning she left for the trip, Mom sat with her in the front room at 5 a.m. until Jeff pulled up. She demanded to lug Janelle's suitcase down the front steps and into the driveway. She lectured them about being safe on the road and what to do if they broke down and not to talk to strange men and not to drink mixed drinks she didn't make herself. She'd always been slightly overprotective, but this was worse. She'd become fearful of everything. Terrified that something awful would happen to her daughter.

And it did. She had tried to warn Janelle, to protect her, but she couldn't. And it was not the world she blamed for this, not the killer, not the unrelenting madness of mankind, but herself.

She squeezed Mom's elbow. "I'll be fine."

Mom blinked back tears.

Janelle followed Christina B past the line and through the front doors, down the hallway with its intricately patterned carpet and into the room where Jeff's body lay in a wooden box with the lid propped. The room stank of lavender. Flowers and tissue boxes rested on end tables beside wicker baskets full of bottled water. As one line of people pressed into the room, another filed out. A constant motion of bodies not unlike a shopping mall, only here there was nothing to buy. Just a quick look before dashing off again, pretending death would remain in this building.

She had been to funerals before, but none so crowded. Great Uncle Chuck, Grandma Winters, Aunt Carolyn and Aunt Ruth. Jeff was Catholic, so the decorations were different, but the setup largely the same. Rows of chairs in the center of the room for mourners. Big wooden easels with corkboard collages. Some of the photos had been printed on cheap computer paper. Others were framed. A monitor on the table next to the guestbook played a continuous loop of photos and silent clips of cell phone footage. Many of the recent photos included Amy. She hung off Jeff like jewelry. Richard was in a lot, too. Janelle spotted herself once or twice and looked away.

Christina B said, "There's Amy."

Jeff's family stood to the left of the casket. First his mom, then dad, then little brother, sister, and, lastly, Amy. Her eyes were puffed up from crying and she was currently engaged in conversation with one of their classmates, a boy named Zach who played football with Richard. In the middle of her conversation, Amy peered over Zach's shoulder and opened her eyes wide in a *please help me* look that put Janelle at ease.

She wasn't the only one who wanted to crawl out of her skin.

"Excuse me," Christina B said to the kid in front of them, "would it be okay if we jump in here?"

Janelle was pretty sure the boy was a junior. He ogled Christina B's lips. He swallowed and nodded and said, "Yuh, yeah, sure."

Christina B remained at Janelle's side.

Soon it was her turn at the casket.

Christina B touched her shoulder. "Want me to go with?"

"I'll be okay."

"I'm gonna go back, then, all right?"

"Okay. Hey Christina?"

"Yeah."

"Thank you."

Christina B smiled and planted a peck on Janelle's cheek before dashing away. Janelle rubbed the spot with the heel of her hand, hoping that never happened again.

Jeff's casket was dark and shiny on the outside, reminding her of a bowling alley. He rested deep within, so at a distance she could just see his forehead. She put one foot in front of the other until she was looking down at him, his matte black hair curling onto his forehead, skin a little too ashy in places, too pink in others.

In her mind, he screamed as a man plunged a knife into his back.

His hands were crossed over his waist. A rosary drooped delicately toward his wrist.

She had to admit, he looked peaceful.

She remembered the kneeler and smoothed her dress over her legs, knelt on the padded surface. She did not pray. She did not cry. She closed her eyes.

I'm sorry, she thought.

She stood and smoothed her dress and before she could steady herself, Jeff's mom pulled her into a perfume-heavy embrace. She was a stout woman with kinky black hair. Janelle knew her as the stern figure standing in the doorways of Jeff's house, hands on hips, reminding him of some chore he had better not forget. Now she smothered Janelle into her dress and whispered in her ear, "It's okay. It's okay."

Janelle thought she should cry now, but it wouldn't come.

"I'm so sorry," she mumbled into Mrs. Patel's body. "I'm so, so sorry."

"It's okay, honey. It's okay."

Mrs. Patel released her, and she was hauled into a stiff hug by Jeff's father, a timid man she did not know at all. She shook hands with Jeff's brother and hugged his sister lightly and when she got to Amy, they hesitated a moment before Amy wrapped her arms around her and pressed her lips against Janelle's ear and whispered, "I don't think I can do this."

Now Janelle cried.

. . .

Amy excused herself from the Patel family and followed Janelle to the back of the room. She pulled a bottled water out of a basket, snapped it open and chugged it. "Fuck," she said, sweeping her arm to indicate the room.

Janelle said, "Yeah."

They found two empty chairs.

"Still doesn't feel real," Amy said.

"No."

They watched the newcomers. Hands clasped over their waists, their mouths thin lines.

Amy scoffed as a short blonde woman entered the room.

"What?" Janelle said.

"Fucking reporters. That chick came to my place earlier."

Janelle hadn't seen her before. A pale young woman in a simple black dress. She couldn't have been older than thirty, but age etched her features prematurely. Her eyes were rimmed with dark circles, and her cheekbones needed no makeup for emphasis.

She turned back to Amy. "Has Richard—"

"No. I've been looking for him."

Janelle fidgeted with the hem of her dress. At the mall earlier, her mom had convinced her to buy one with lace along the arms, neck, and hem. It made her look a little goth, and the lace tickled. "Maybe he couldn't handle it."

"Fuck that," Amy said, "If we can make it, so can he." She chewed her cheek. "Sorry. I'm just upset."

"What if he doesn't come?"

"I think he will."

"But what if he doesn't? You haven't seen him since that night, right?"

"Right."

"You think he's okay?"

"I don't know. Is anyone okay right now?"

"Yeah. But I mean, I'm worried."

"I know. So am I."

Amy wasn't getting it. They had to do something. Janelle didn't care anymore what happened with Richard romantically. He could tell her she was the most annoying person in the world and he never wanted to see her again as long as it meant he was okay.

"We have to find him," Janelle said. "If he doesn't come. Tonight."

"Yeah. Okay."

Janelle sat back, forced her hands to stop playing with her dress.

Amy chewed her cheek some more. Then she grinned. "Yo. Did Christina B kiss you?"

Janelle flushed.

"I knew she was into chicks."

Janelle mock-punched her in the thigh. "Shut up."

It was good to laugh, even if they were both forcing it.

12

Ray arrived an hour after Janelle. He stood in the line and exchanged forced pleasantries with familiar faces, saved from lengthier conversations by the somber nature of the venue. Father Childs told him he just missed a group from the department. So Bartov and his buddies had spared no time getting to the bar. He didn't blame them.

He signed the guestbook and scanned the photos, all that remained of the boy now. They would be added to the museum of Jeff Patel's life, like the contents of his bedroom, condensed into cardboard boxes and slid onto shelves in a basement. Eventually, this happens to us all.

Before he knew it, Ray was looking down on the boy in his casket.

This body was nothing like the one he'd viewed on the highway, or on the table at the morgue when Dr. Aire pointed her pen at the wounds and confirmed what Ray already knew: Jeffrey Patel had suffered terribly. Ray's heart skipped at the sight of the corpse, and his knees went to rubber.

He had his first panic attack around the time he decided to leave the Twin Cities. He was still waiting to hear about the job in Fairfield at the time, and his divorce was not yet finalized, though his wife had already left. He was alone and at home, making dinner, when it hit. It felt like his heart wanted to leap out of his throat, and he couldn't feel his hands. He curled up on the floor until it passed. He had several more episodes in the following months, but they occurred in private and passed quickly. He never told his shrink. When he fell through a sliding glass door and nearly cut his thumb off his left hand, he laughed it off and said he'd been drinking.

If he suspected for a moment that he would lose it at Jeff Patel's memorial service, he'd have gone straight home from the station. He'd been to plenty of services, had seen his share of victims, some much younger than this. Many in worse shape. Hell, he'd already seen Jeff's corpse in various states, first freshly dead and then drained on a metal table, yet when he looked into the silk-lined box, his knees buckled and he dropped to the kneeler with an audible *crack*. His spine went stiff, and he clutched at the side of the coffin.

Hard to breathe.

His body moved, despite his attempts to stop it. His face tilted forward, leaning closer to the boy's, as if the corpse had requested his confidence. His fingers spidered over the edge of the coffin, down the lining and along the boy's sleeve from elbow to wrist, seeking the waxy hand.

Stop this, Ray commanded his hands.

They did not listen. His breath would not come.

The index finger of his right hand tapped the tepid flesh on the back of Jeffrey Patel's hand and he looked out on a black highway as the storm that followed the jeep from Iowa wrung the last drops of water from the sky. He walked across the sodden median with his friends—Richard beside him, Janelle and Amy following—toward a man in the southbound lane who had propped up the back of his truck with a roadside jack. The man said, "Hell of a thing. That deer sure took to your headlights." Except it was not the man who said this. It was the thing that wrapped itself around the man, a thing the color of smoke and just as insubstantial, a thing that Ray mistook at first for a shadow or trick of light—a series of limbs like snakes that wriggled across the man's torso, pulsing with some perverse imitation of life. These worm-like appendages tapered as they climbed the man's body. Some disappeared up his nose and into the corners of his eyes. Just over his left shoulder, a bulbous round head peeked into view.

Ray gasped and leaped back as if jolted by an electric shock. Someone nearby released a mournful, wretched moan.

That person, he realized, was him.

He crash-landed into an empty chair.

Figures crowded him, asking if he was all right, what happened, should they call someone. Father Childs softly called his name and touched the back of his head.

"Holy cats," someone said.

"Give him air."

"Is he having a heart attack?"

"Should we call a doctor?"

He looked up into the soft, concerned face of Mrs. Patel.

"I saw him," he said. "I saw him."

. . . .

He sat in his Explorer with the AC blasting. Sweat soaked his shirt and dampened his hair. He felt like he'd run a marathon, swimming vision and shaky knees and all. He had parked behind the funeral home in the only spot available. He watched the brick side of the building with suspicion, like it might jump out and shout, *Gotcha!*

Only one of his previous attacks had been like this. Freaky how similar, in fact, complete with the loss of control—the sensation that he'd been drawn forward by some magnetic force—and the accompanying hallucination. At least he had convinced the onlookers not to call an ambulance. They'd been reluctant to let him leave. Said he shouldn't drive. Asked if he had someone to call, and when he said he did not, they offered to get him a ride or drive him home. He left on his own damn feet.

A momentary loss of control. He was fine. Everything was fine.

He waited until he was certain he could drive safely, then headed out.

He did not want to go home, but there was nowhere else to go. Most days, when he became restless or unsettled, he'd kill a few hours at the gym. He'd been working out regularly since high school. Played a little baseball back then and was a decent hitter and second baseman, though everyone said he was built for football. It wasn't until Shawna left that he began to stay at the gym for hours at a time, lifting with a fury that had nothing to do with self-improvement. His shrink called it a coping mechanism for his divorce. In truth, the divorce came as a relief.

He and Shawna were both workaholics. He was still on patrol when they met. She was a nurse. Came home smelling like the hospital, like chemicals and blood, and drank half a bottle of wine each night with dinner. Silence followed them in everything they did. They didn't fight it, let it fill their home until it pushed them out the doors.

Their passion was always mechanical. Bodily need brought them to the same bed. Convenience kept them in the house. One night, he came home from a late shift and found her in her usual spot at the table, except she had no wine and no glass. She sat with her palms on the wood and asked him if he would like to sit so they could talk. He knew immediately what she would say.

She'd been sleeping with her trainer at the rock climbing gym. It had been going on for almost a year. "He asked me if I want to go to Colorado. I said yes."

Ray nodded. "When do you go?"

"In about a month."

"That soon."

"Yeah."

"You're quitting the hospital?"

"There are hospitals in Colorado."

"I guess that's true. I'll have to move out."

"I can stay in a hotel if you want. I'm not asking for anything."

"Not like that. I mean I can't afford this place on my salary."

This was their big blowout. A civil conversation about the cost of their mortgage.

He saw her twice more before she left. She mailed him checks to help with the house until it sold.

He didn't miss her, exactly, but loneliness takes many forms.

He could have joined the others at Blue Bricks. Laughed off his shitty night behind a mask of alcohol until everything blurred. They would hear about his episode at the funeral home one way or the other. He'd blame it on exhaustion. Obermeyer would demand a psych eval. Might force him to take a paid leave. If it came to that, Ray would push back. He didn't need time off, but maybe he could do with a little more sleep. All this shit about shadows and visions and vanishing figures. This wasn't like him, giving into superstition and chasing ghosts. At the heart of it, he couldn't allow himself to believe in such things.

He believed in rational explanations—yes he goddamn did.

There had to be one here. He just needed to sleep on it.

13

"Hey." Amy elbowed Janelle in the ribs and gestured toward the front entryway.

Mr. Becker lingered in the hallway, hands in his pockets. She barely recognized him in his suit, so used to seeing him in basketball shorts and an Under Armour t-shirt.

The crowd had thinned. Most of their classmates had come and gone, and Janelle managed to convince her parents to leave without her. She'd get a ride home from Amy.

Mr. Becker hovered over the guestbook. He'd come alone.

She stood.

"Nelly?" Amy said.

She shuffled between the chairs and stormed up the aisle. Amy followed.

Mr. Becker didn't notice them until Janelle tapped him on the shoulder.

"Whoa, Janelle. You snuck up on me."

"Is Richard with you?"

Mr. Becker was a stoic. Even when he yelled at you to run after the ball, try harder, stop pretending you had period cramps and get your butt down the court, his expression rarely hardened, his inflection flat. Today, though, his cheeks were puffy, and he looked like he hadn't slept in a long time. "You mean he's not here? I thought I might catch him."

"I'm sorry, what?"

"I thought he might be with you."

"You don't know where he is?"

"He's been through a lot. Probably just needed to get away."

"When did you see him last?"

"I thought I heard him downstairs this morning."

"But you didn't see him?"

"Last I knew, he was in his room. But his bike's been gone since last night. I wouldn't worry. He's probably at a girl's house."

Janelle's skin went hot. All the girls Richard might have been with had come to the fucking wake.

She said, "When you see him, will you tell him to call me?"

"Okay."

"Actually, will *you* call me?"

"Yeah, sure. I'll do that."

Janelle didn't know what else to say. She thanked him and made for the back of the room, rubbing her temples.

"That was weird," Amy said.

"Yeah."

"How could he not come?"

"Something's wrong."

"I don't know. I mean, some people—" She broke off, seeing Janelle's determination. Whatever protest she almost offered, she swallowed it. "What do you wanna do?"

"Did you drive?"

"Yeah."

"I might know where he is."

"Okay. You wanna go?"

"There's like fifteen minutes left here."

"I'm ready to leave if you are, boo. I don't think I can stand it here much longer. Just let me say bye to Jeff's mom."

More hugs. More wiping of eyes. Amy stood for the last time over Jeff in his casket. She leaned across him. Janelle couldn't see it, but she was pretty sure she kissed him.

Amy rejoined her and wiped her cheeks with the heels of her hands. "Let's find our boy."

14

"So, where we going?"

They were in Amy's Honda Civic. On the radio, an advertisement squawked about used mattresses. Amy switched it off.

Janelle toyed with her dress. "The river."

Amy thought a moment. "By the park?"

"Yeah."

The Great Blue River ran diagonally through town, accessible only on the outskirts of the city. In the downtown area, it had been walled off years back. Janelle was too young to know much about it, but her parents had been furious at the time. For weeks, they muttered at the dinner table that you couldn't make a natural landmark off-limits: the paved walkways made for scenic biking or jogging, or you could sit on the banks and fish. Earlier that summer, when the water was high and fast, a group of teenagers made a game of swimming across. One of them got caught in the current and drown. It made statewide news. When another kid in a different group of friends drowned the same way a month later, the town had a full blown crisis on their hands.

First, they put up a fence. Within a year and a half, the people passed a referendum to erect a permanent wall. There weren't enough volunteers to monitor the wall, and the police had more important things to do, so instead of truly stopping anyone from reaching the river, the wall created something of a secluded hangout for vagrants and bored teenagers.

Amy drove to Rapprochement Park—which everyone mispronounced "reproachment"—near the stretch of river where the first kid died. The park itself had been built as a memorial to tragedy. 50

innocent Sioux men were hanged there in the late 1800s. The park was created in the 1980s, a small, circular area consisting mostly of a parking lot and a butterfly garden that butterflies never got the news about. A ten foot tall stone bison overlooked the lot. It appeared almost prehistoric, with legs thick as tree trunks and a hide bunched around its shoulders. Amy parked beside it.

The wall blocked the river on the park's north side, twelve feet high and garnished with razor wire. Janelle and Amy followed it west to where it cut behind an old railway station, a gray structure with plywood in the windows and graffiti on the bricks. The station hid one of the few access points to the river, a chain-link gate that broke up the otherwise seamless structure of the wall. A yellow sign declared that this was for city personnel only, but a portion of the gate had been peeled back like the tab of a pop can. Amy and Janelle squeezed through.

Richard brought them here last summer. They'd been hanging at Jeff's place, playing a videogame, when Richard put down his controller and said, "I want to show you something." He was still dating Christina B at the time, but Janelle thought maybe he directed this at her, though he faced the TV when he said it.

Jeff had just got his license. They took his dad's car. When Richard brought them to the abandoned railroad building, Amy whined: "Dude, we used to come here all the time." Richard rolled his eyes and waved them to the back of the building. They must have been smaller then, because Janelle remembered the gap being easier to slip through. He acted like he'd led them to some magical hideaway, a secret glen in a forest. It was more like an industrial wasteland.

The graffiti was impressive, though. Murals coated huge stretches of the wall. Across a twenty-foot area, somebody had created an elaborate African landscape. Tall green grass, a rhinoceros, giraffes, a zebra, some of those African trees you see on the covers of books and movie posters. Other pieces were not as inspired, but still impressive. Bart Simpson grinding a rail on his skateboard. SpongeBob and Patrick laughing hysterically, mouths wide and water spurting from their eyes. A giant joint over an even more giant pot leaf. Various initials drawn inside lopsided hearts, paint dripping like blood. There was your typical vulgarity, of course, like *FUCK TRUMP* repeated in vertical columns.

Amy said, "If I get mugged, I'm gonna be pissed."

Janelle said, "This is cool."

Richard waved them toward the bridge.

The river ran muddy brown. It was maybe fifty feet from one side to the other. The water rose to a few feet below the path and swirled around the pillars of the bridge, making trails of foam downriver. Richard walked backwards. "If you look at the water long enough, it kinda feels like you're on a boat." He sat with his back against the abutment.

Cars hummed overhead.

Amy and Jeff teased him, saying this was a creepy spot to chill, but he ignored them, sprawled in the bridge's shadow. Janelle sat beside him while Amy and Jeff ambled downstream.

Janelle and Richard sat in silence. She wondered if her feelings were obvious.

"It's good to be alone sometimes," he said. "Without your cell phone or whatever. My dad says our generation's gonna burn out our brains."

"I like the water," Janelle said. "I mean, it's kinda peaceful. Even though the scenery isn't pretty."

"I think it is. Pretty."

She looked at him, hopeful.

He watched the water.

Still, maybe he was trying to give her a sign. A glimpse of something possible. A spark.

Tonight, there was no such spark in the atmosphere. She emerged onto the concrete path sweaty all over, terrified that he wouldn't be here. What if he had truly run away, or worse?

No, she didn't believe that. He wanted her to find him. And she would.

15

The river was lower than the last time Janelle saw it. The water murky with a red tint from the approaching twilight. Someone had graffitied the graffiti. Crosshairs hovered over the animals on the African landscape. SpongeBob and Patrick were full of bullet holes. A crude dick sprouted out of Bart Simpson's shorts. It seemed somebody had gone at the wall with a hammer in spots. Pieces of cement blocks had been torn loose and scattered on the walkway so she had to watch her feet or risk tripping.

The walkway appeared otherwise empty. No sign of Richard.

"Shit," Amy said.

"Hang on." Janelle squinted toward the bridge. She saw something on the ground, in the bridge's shadow. It might have been a bag of garbage.

She flashed to the night on the highway. Seeing *something* on the ground behind the jeep.

She forced herself onward. The thing on the ground took shape.

A purple sleeping bag.

Amy gripped Janelle's arm. "That's Richard's. He used to bring it to Jeff's to sleep over."

Amy sped up, pulling Janelle forward.

They reached the bag. It appeared dirty, sodden. Amy crouched to touch a lump in the middle, perhaps to check that it was empty. She recoiled in disgust. "Ew! There's something in there. It's all soggy." The fabric over the lump had mottled, as if diseased.

Despite her trepidation, Janelle found herself crouching, reaching for the zipper that ran the length of the bag. The bag's discoloration reminded her of recent nightmares.

"Nelly!" Amy shot to her feet.

A haggard, lanky figure stepped out from behind the abutment. Richard's shoulders slumped and his head hung forward. He wore an oversized black t-shirt and skinny jeans streaked with filth, and held both hands behind his back. She almost didn't recognize him. When he raised his face, his eyes were sunken and tired and there was something foreign about them.

Amy didn't notice, or looked past these discrepancies. She ran toward him with outstretched arms. "Holy shit, Richard! What the hell are you doing out here!"

Janelle remained in place. The way Richard moved didn't seem right. Dread crept over her. She fought the urge to run back to the car.

This was all wrong.

Still, there was the bag and the thing in the bag. She needed to know.

She pinched the plastic zipper.

Amy flung her arms around Richard.

Janelle pulled the zipper and whipped the bag open.

She sprang backward and fell hard on her ass.

Tan, blood-crusted fur and purple-gray innards. Even with the mutilation, she recognized Richard's cat. It had been pulled apart, practically inside out.

Amy's arms hung around Richard's neck. He leered at Janelle.

Those were not Richard's eyes.

She tried to call for Amy, but her throat would not open.

Richard reached one hand behind Amy's head and tangled his fingers in her hair. He pressed her face into his chest. Amy said something, but his shirt muffled it. She placed her hands against his chest and pushed, but he gripped tighter. The other hand came out from behind his back.

It held a knife.

Janelle could not move. Could not scream. Could not breathe.

Richard grinned. He plunged the knife into the base of Amy's neck, where her spine connected to her skull. She went instantly limp. Richard's hand in her hair held her upright. He pulled the knife free and released her.

Amy crumpled. Her skull clapped against the concrete.

Janelle screamed.

Richard—who was not Richard—charged.

16

Janelle moved on instinct. She didn't think—only reacted. Somehow, her feet were under her and she was running toward the gate, leaping through the minefield of broken cinderblocks.

Richard pounded pavement behind her, snorting like a wild boar.

Her body tingled in anticipation of a blade piercing flesh.

Ten feet from the gate.

Another stride and another, feet slapping earth.

She was fast, but he was faster.

Even if she reached the gate before he caught her, she wouldn't make it through. He'd catch her there, grab her arm or hair or dress and slash her to ribbons.

But the next nearest exit was miles up the path. No choice.

She cut toward the gate, lost her footing on the rubble-strewn path and slammed knees-first onto the walkway. She cut her palms on bits of cement and rolled over broken blocks, ended up on her back, arms at her sides, something jagged under her right hand.

Then Richard was on her. He planted his feet on either side of her waist, alien eyes ablaze. He leaned over her and squeezed her throat with his free hand and pulled the knife back, preparing to strike.

She gripped the jagged thing under her hand and swung it against the side of his head.

The chunk of cement dropped beside her and Richard stumbled backward.

She rolled onto her stomach, got her legs under her, and dove for the gate.

A woman stood on the other side, small and blonde and holding a pistol.

. . .

Gertie should not have been shocked by what she saw. She should not have hesitated at the sight of the young woman clamoring at the fence, black dress dusty, knees and palms torn. She should have done what she trained herself to do—raised the tranquilizer gun and fired at her target, the young man who shuffled backward and pressed a palm to his blooded left ear. But it had been so long since she'd been near it. The darkness came off it in waves, and it hurt her eyes to look at directly. She caught glimpses of mottled appendages coated in thorn-like hooks, and a tumorous bulge where its head pressed into the crook of the boy's neck like an enormous white tick. The limbs circled the boy's neck and wormed into his eyes, ears, nose, and mouth.

He swayed like a drunk at the river's edge.

It saw her then, for just a moment. She felt its recognition.

The boy grinned.

She raised the pistol, but it was too late.

The boy careened off the walkway and disappeared with a splash.

The girl was trying to squeeze through the gate, blocking Gertie's path.

Gertie braced herself and shoved the girl with enough force to knock her backward, then ducked through the space where the girl had been and rushed to the water, tracking the fabric of the boy's black shirt as it rippled and swirled. If he drowned, it would all start again.

She sprinted alongside the river. The boy floated away, too fast. He was already at the bridge, leading her by 20 feet, now 30, now 50. She jumped the sleeping bag, ran under the bridge's shadow and past the dead girl, half registering the blood and the pungent stink marking the thing's handiwork.

"Gertie!" David screamed behind her.

Richard's shirt was a black bead in the water.

The river took him around a bend.

"He's too far, Gertie!"

She ran. There was no catching him, but she ran.

"Gertie, the girl!"

She came around the bend. Searched the water. Too many shadows. Never enough light.

He was gone.

17

Janelle's heels caught on the rubble and she crashed to the earth yet again.

This time, she did not try to stand or run. She expected Richard to return with his knife. She wouldn't fight him. She watched the sky without seeing it. Felt herself going numb.

It was peaceful, this letting go. She could die. It would be so easy. She could rejoin Amy and Jeff, who had gone ahead without her, like when they went hiking in the redwood park the second day of their trip. It was Jeff's idea. He thought they should do something more active than lounging and getting drunk. Janelle didn't see what was wrong with that, but agreed it would be nice to see the redwoods.

There were five or six cars parked at the start of the trailhead, but they saw no people, which made Janelle nervous. The forest was vast and denser than any she had seen, even more so than the boundary waters. They walked for hours. They'd each brought a single water bottle. She drank hers almost immediately. Her stomach growled and her feet ached. She wore flipflops. The scenery became unimpressive after a while, the same tangled bushes pressing in, and though Jeff promised that this was an out-and-back trail, she felt certain they walked in circles. Her friends didn't listen. They went ahead, chatting, pointing out things in the brush she didn't see.

She fell behind. They didn't slow. Not even Richard.

She had to rest, but couldn't get herself to call out. She sat on a fallen log beside the trail and removed her sandals, rubbing between her toes. She thought she might cry, but she was too dehydrated. She didn't have a watch, and left her phone in the car. She thought she might sit there alone until the sun went down, until the forest filled with night movement and menace.

Abandoned. Her friends had forgotten her.

In reality, no more than twenty minutes passed before they came back, asking what was wrong, apologizing and wondering why she left them. She didn't tell them they were the ones who left. She apologized and said they could continue, but when they saw her feet and understood the state she was in, they agreed to go back to the car.

She wished they would come back to her now. Lift her from the path head to the beach where they would lie in the sun and everything would be okay, they would all be perfectly fine.

•   •   •

Gertie stood above Amy Pink's corpse. Blood matted her hair and ran along the walkway. Flecks of dirt and dust and a single ant floated on the surface. Except for this, the girl could have been lying on her side watching the river.

This was a disaster. Not only had she failed to capture her target, but she let another person die. To top it off, she had a witness to deal with.

She returned to the gate where Janelle lay.

The girl had seen her face. Gertie had heard of gifted individuals who could wipe memories, but it was beyond her skill level. She could influence the mind of another—little more than a form of hypnosis. For minutes at a time, she could render herself invisible, and if she really concentrated, she could move tiny objects without touching them, like the pins inside a lock. Destroying a piece of someone's mind was on another level.

Janelle's teeth chattered, in a state of shock, oblivious to the world.

"We can't just leave her," David said.

Gertie kept her voice low, out of the girl's earshot. "We need to move. He's not done."

"I know. But look at her."

Gertie did. The shock would wear off soon. She would find her voice, and then she would talk to the police.

That was not an option. Gertie couldn't explain the tranquilizer gun, the van with the metal plating in the back, or why she was stalking a group of teenagers. Even if they didn't arrest her, they'd slow her down. More importantly, if the cops found Richard before she did, they'd lock him up. She'd never reach him after that. She couldn't risk it.

"We take her with us," she said.

"We *what*?"

"We don't have a choice."

"So now we're kidnappers?"

"Kidnappers request a ransom. This is technically abduction."

"Great. Thanks for the distinction."

"I'm open to suggestions, but we're wasting time."

It was a terrible idea, but they were in a corner.

"I don't know."

Gertie squatted beside the girl. She closed her eyes and breathed in deep.

Janelle's emotions erupted out of her in chaotic bursts that even Gertie could not make sense of. *Pain-rage-guilt-terror-hate-love-pain-pain-sorrow-terror-pain-terror-pain* all twisted into knots, each flash bombarding Gertie with images of Amy and Richard and Jeff, snapshots of the girl's memories, her friends smiling and laughing together in one image, dead on the street or holding a knife or stabbed in the base of the skull in the next.

To reach her, Gertie had to burrow deep. She pushed past these blasts of emotion and searched for the voice beneath it—Janelle's subconscious mind.

It was like striking oil. A torrent of sensations and language spewed forth:

RICHARD KILLED AMY KILLED HER DEAD RICHARD KILLED HIS CAT MY GOD RICHARD KILLED HER IT WASN'T RICHARD AMY DEAD DEATH CASKET JEFF I WAS DRIVING THE WOMAN WITH THE GUN WATCHING ME KILL ME PLEASE I WANT TO DIE RICHARD WHY HE KILLED HIS CAT I WANT TO DIE WHERE IS AMY KILLED AMY MY FAULT PLEASE HELP ME PLEASE NOT HAPPENING I CANNOT I CAN'TCAN'TICAN'T MY FAULT PLEASE NO AMY AMYAMYAMY RICHARDWHY JEFF PLEASE DON'T PLEASE DON'T DIE DON'T DIE PLEASE—

Gertie took the girl's hand in a gentle grip and spoke with her own mind: *It's okay.*

The stream shut off, and Janelle focused on the woman crouching beside her. *The woman in the black dress pushed me down pushed me out of the way pushed me ran and left me—*

Gertie thought, *Calm,* and Janelle's mind quieted again. *Just breathe.*

Breathe? I can't breathe. I'm dying. I deserve to die.

You can breathe. You did everything you could.

I can breathe. I did everything I could.

"That's right."

No. I deserve to die.

This was a stubborn one.

Your thoughts are going quiet.

My thoughts are going quiet.

In a moment, you're going to stand. You're going to follow me out of here, and we're going to get into my van.

Amy's car.

No. You're going to come with me. I'm going to take you somewhere safe.

Somewhere safe? Where?

You'll be with me. It's safe with me.

Safe with you.

That's right. Your cell phone is in your dress pocket. When I tell you, you're going to throw your phone into the river.

Okay.

Gertie searched the girl's mind for information about the river and the wall that followed it. She was looking for more gates. Anywhere Richard might be able to escape. Janelle didn't know for sure, but knew the wall ran all the way to the edge of town.

Richard took me here once. It was better then.

Don't think about that.

Okay.

She needed a little more information, and then she could back out of the girl's thoughts. They didn't have much time. *Janelle, who does Richard love more than anyone?*

He loves me, I think. I hope. I don't know. And Amy. He killed—

Don't think about that.

Okay.

Who else does he love? Where would he go if he's in trouble? Who would he see?

Mr. Becker. His dad. He wants to make his dad proud. He loves his dad.

Okay. You're calm now, right?

I'm calm now, right.

You're going to come with me.

Yes. It's safe with you.

That's right. Stand up, Janelle.

Blank-faced, entranced, Janelle stood. She blinked several times. "I feel weird."

"It'll wear off. Your phone. Toss it."

She fished around in her dress and took out the phone and looked into the screen a moment before lobbing it into the water.

Gertie took a moment to search the path, found the piece of concrete with Richard's blood on it, and cast it into the water, too.

"Come on," she said.

"I'm following you. It's safe with you."

They passed through the gate, leaving the river and Amy's body behind.

PART 2
CROSSROADS

1

Janelle's forehead pressed against smudged glass. Outside, familiar buildings passed. An engine chugged loudly, and a seatbelt chafed her neck. Her limbs seemed made of lead, anchoring her to the seat. The driver was a short woman with blonde hair and a long nose.

The memories leaked back in a slow trickle. The river. Amy. Richard. Like recalling a dream.

To the woman, she said, "Did you drug me?"

The woman didn't look at her. "No." A pause. "But I can see how it might feel that way."

The weight of Janelle's head strained her neck. She leaned on the headrest.

"It's sort of like hypnosis," the woman said. "I had to calm you down."

"Oh."

The woman drove them out of the downtown area, toward the suburbs. They passed a Wendy's where Janelle used to hang out with Jeff and Amy after Jeff got his license. They would sit in a booth for hours, just wasting time. Janelle never felt like a third wheel around them, but sometimes, when they got all gooey and kissy, she wished they would break up so she could have Amy to herself again. Shame always followed such thoughts.

Now Jeff and Amy were dead, and every negative thought she had about them distilled into a series of blips on the line of time. Her friends were like those cloudy jars in the back of their old biology classroom, the ones Mrs. Hale held up as examples of different species. A tapeworm here. A rat there. A pig's brain. How many jars would Amy and Jeff fit into? Twenty or thirty. They could share. Two hearts pressing against the glass and each other. Mrs. Hale would hold up the jar and rotate it slowly so everyone could see the purple vesicles and the weird stubs that once pumped life. "These are the hearts of two friends and lovers, Jeffrey Patel and Amy Pink. Janelle Winters watched them die. She stood helplessly by. Later, she cried."

A pitiful noise escaped her throat.

"You okay?" the driver said, startling her.

"Who are you?"

"My name's Francesca White. People call me Franny."

Janelle shifted and sat up straight. She had definitely been drugged.

"I feel strange. Like I'm not really here."

"Some of that's what I did. But I'm pretty sure you're in shock."

"What do you want with me?"

"Nothing. I'm trying to keep you safe."

"From Richard?" Her ears felt hot. "Richard killed Amy. Why would he do that?"

The woman, Franny, sighed. "It wasn't Richard."

"I feel like I'm going crazy."

"You're not. You're just catching up."

Janelle wondered how old this woman was. Twenty-five or thirty, maybe. Hard to tell. She wore no makeup and the shadows under her eyes seemed deeper and more pronounced than natural, like the sockets of a skull. A ghoul of a woman, pale skin and pale hair, like she'd been dipped in bleach.

"Were you following us?"

"Yes. I should've been faster." She turned to Janelle. "I'm sorry."

Janelle looked down at herself. Her hands lay flat on the cushion on either side of her legs, which hung out of her dress lifeless and still. Her feet wedged against a duffel bag stuffed under the glovebox. The cab of the vehicle smelled like a locker room.

"We need to call the police." Janelle patted down her dress. It had a pocket on the right.

"We can't do that."

Janelle found the pocket. Empty.

"Your phone's in the river, remember?"

"Why?" Janelle's voice rose an octave. "What are you talking about?"

"I need you to take a breath."

Janelle squeezed her hands into fists. Her heart thumped. "I don't even know who you are. You, like, what, hypnotized me? What the hell am I doing here? What's happening?"

"Janelle. Listen to me. I need you to calm down. Listen to my voice. Deep breath now. That's good. Another one. Good. Remember, I'm not the bad guy here. You're safe with me."

Weirdly, the panic subsided.

Janelle's attention drifted to the door. It had an old-school plunger lock. Unlocked. She slipped her fingers around the handle. She slid her other hand to the seatbelt's buckle.

They were in the suburbs now. Somewhere near Richard's neighborhood.

Next turn, when the vehicle slowed, Janelle would throw the door open and leap out.

"I can read your mind," Franny said.

Janelle went rigid. "What?"

"Sometimes it's hard to understand, but you get used to it. Not as exciting as you'd think. And it's exhausting, besides."

"You're crazy."

"If you want more people to die, by all means, jump out. Tuck and roll. But the only reason I brought you with me is because that thing's still out there, and you have no idea what it is or how to stop it. It was Richard, but it also wasn't. It was *him*."

"Who?"

"Mr. Ugly. That's what I call it. If you could see it, you'd understand."

Franny flipped on the right blinker. *Click-clock. Click-clock.* They slowed. Took a turn.

Janelle did not dive out the door. Not yet.

Franny continued, "You know what I'm talking about. It wasn't Richard. Mr. Ugly took him over. It's what he does. And if you call the cops and they arrest him, he'll just kill himself and switch bodies, and we'll have to start from scratch until we find the new host. That means waiting for him to kill again."

So the woman was insane. This was not surprising, given the circumstances. Janelle could play along. Keep her talking. Maybe get to some kernel of truth. "If he can switch bodies, why not just do it? If we know what he looks like, shouldn't he just find someone new?"

Franny shook her head. "First, he doesn't care that we know what he looks like. He thinks he's unstoppable. Secondly, he can't just leave a body once he's attached. It's sort of a rule of the spirit world. It's called tethering. Once you tether to someone, you're stuck. At least until that person dies. They can tether to objects, too, but Mr. Ugly has no interest in that." Now she glanced at Janelle, sensing her trepidation. "Most religions are dead wrong. They're run by men, anyway, and all men want to do is fuck and enslave the world. Sure, except you, David."

Janelle shivered. "David?"

"David's a perfect example. He's tethered to me."

Janelle's palm sweat on the handle. She didn't know what Franny was talking about, but she recognized this street. The back entrance to Richard's neighborhood.

"Where are we going?"

Franny gestured at the wall of the cab behind their heads. "I put a binding spell on the back of this van. Took me years to do it, but it should act like a container. If we can seal Mr. Ugly inside, he'll be trapped. And Richard cares deeply about his father, so we're going to his house to see if he shows up."

"Then what?"

Franny pointed under her seat. "Tranquilizer gun."

"Oh."

"I'm more concerned with the possibility that he doesn't show up. If he drowned in the river, we're fucked."

Janelle squinted through the windshield. Night had fallen all at once. This was a residential street. Similar houses with manicured lawns, some with their sprinklers on. Cars in the driveways. Dogs napping behind fences. Richard might have been crouched somewhere out there, watching them.

If what this woman said was true, he could be anywhere.

"Why would Richard— Why would Mr. Ugly hurt Amy? Why come after his dad?"

"Because he thinks it's fun." Franny thought a moment. "Did Richard have any reason to think you'd search for him at the river? Was that spot special to you?"

"Maybe," Janelle admitted. "Yeah."

"Mr. Ugly knew that. He wanted you to find him. You and Richard were dating?"

Janelle clenched her jaw and looked away. She didn't want to talk about this.

"I'm sorry," Franny said. "My point is, he wants to hurt people Richard cares about. So if he cares most about you and his father, then you and his father are prime targets."

They pulled onto Richard's street. Franny slowed the vehicle and parked some ten houses away from his.

"So what's it gonna be? You can keep telling yourself I'm full of shit, or you can ask yourself why Richard was using the same knife as the man who killed your friend on the highway, and I can tell you it's not a coincidence, that Mr. Ugly prefers to use a knife with a gut hook."

Janelle's grip tightened on the handle. She clicked the seatbelt free.

"Just know," Franny said, "if you go, and you tell the cops about me, and you tell them to look for Richard, they'll shoot him on sight. And while they're questioning me, Jeff and Amy's real killer will be out there looking for a new host. You can't see him, but he's seen you, and he holds one hell of a grudge."

The seatbelt wedged itself against Janelle's right arm as she maintained her grip on the door. The belt settled into the crook of her elbow. She locked eyes with Franny.

"I want to know everything."

Franny arched her eyebrows.

"Everything. If you're telling the truth, it should be easy. Tell me everything about this Mr. Ugly or whatever. And I want to know who you are. And I don't just mean your real name."

The woman leaned back. "What makes you think Franny isn't my real name?"

Janelle just looked at her.

"The real one's not much better."

"I don't care."

The woman nodded. "It's Gertie. Scout's honor. Gertie Morgenstern. I haven't logged onto Facebook in years, but you could find me on there if you looked. While we're at it, I was never a Scout. That's just something people say."

"Fine. You're Gertie. And you can read people's minds and talk to ghosts or whatever. Now tell me what the fuck is going *on*." She released the handle and slipped her arm out of the seatbelt.

Gertie nodded to herself. "Okay, yeah. But you'll need to keep an open mind."

Janelle glared.

"Knowing changes things. You have to understand that. No one will understand. If you try to explain it, they'll send you to a padded room. And they might be right to. If your mind won't bend, it'll snap." After a pause, she added, "I guess what I'm saying is I need you to trust me."

"I have no reason to trust you."

"Maybe not," Gertie said. "So you'll need to judge for yourself."

Janelle crossed her arms. "Talk."

2

Gertie was a lonely child. At daycare and at school, other kids had no problem talking to each other, playing with each other. What the parents called *socializing*. It wasn't that she didn't want to. But words got stuck in her mouth. Until she was six years old, she only spoke to her parents just above a whisper.

They lived in the suburbs of Rockwall, New York, the third largest city in the state after Buffalo. At the bottom of her backyard, the previous owners had erected a rusty swing set with frayed ropes and uncomfortable wooden seats. The sandbox was Gertie's favorite. One of those plastic turtle shaped things.

Summers were best. They meant Papa wasn't teaching, so she didn't have to go to daycare or school, and she was free to enjoy the backyard where she could invent her own games and not face that stomach-churning struggle to make her mouth work.

The summer after kindergarten, she started talking to a girl who wasn't there.

Her name was Francesca White. A fancy name that made Gertie think of rich people in old cartoons. She had curly hair, and she never said her exact age. She was older than Gertie. A big kid, but not *big*-big. For a long time, nobody else knew about her.

It was a sunny Sunday. Mama and Papa were both home, and she and Francesca had spent most of the day sifting sand into a plastic bucket through a piece of torn screen. Francesca said that was how you made gold. You sift enough sand, a gold nugget appears on the screen. By the time her mom called her inside for dinner, no gold had appeared, and they'd moved on to climbing up one leg of the swing set because the yard had turned to lava.

Dinner was pasta with meatballs. Sunday tradition, her parents called it. Gertie loved spaghetti. It reminded her of playdough squished through tiny holes. Tonight, as usual, Papa kept checking his phone under the table. Even when he wasn't teaching he always seemed to be doing work, or talking about work. *My courses*, he called them. *I have to figure out my courses.*

Mama kept giving Gertie strange looks. Happy looks, actually. Like she had a surprise. But Gertie knew better than to ask. Mama was scary when she got mad, and she always got mad if Gertie asked about secrets and surprises. Like sometimes Gertie heard her up in the attic, talking like she was having real conversations with someone. But if Gertie asked what she was doing, who she was talking to, Mama would snap, "It's rude to pry, and don't you even think about listening to my conversations with other people."

Like usual, Gertie helped Papa clean the table and put away the leftovers. After, Papa went into another room, his attention still glued to his phone, and Gertie was going to retreat to her room to see about some Legos, but Mama was suddenly beside her.

"*Hey,*" Mama whispered. She dragged a chair away from the table.

Gertie thought she was in trouble, but didn't know for what.

"Let's sit for a second," Mama said. "I want to ask you something."

Gertie did as she was told. The table had six chairs, even though there were only three people in the house. Mama and Papa usually sat at the ends, with Gertie on either side. But now, Mama sat in the middle and had Gertie sit at the end. It felt weird. She didn't like it.

Mama was still giving her that strange look, but now she placed her hands on the table in front of her and cocked her head and looked very proper, like she was preparing for an important announcement. She smiled pleasantly, but still had the same tired eyes that she always had.

"Sweetie."

Uh oh, Gertie thought.

"There's something I want to ask you. You don't have to be scared. That's the last thing I want."

Gertie tried to relax her face, but she didn't know how to not look scared if that's how she felt.

"When you were outside today, I saw you talking to someone."

Gertie swallowed. Mama had seen her playing with Francesca White.

"Can you tell me who that was?"

Gertie stared. She knew she should answer Mama's question, but she didn't want people to know about Francesca White.

"You don't have to worry. I won't tell anyone else, I promise. But there's something I need to check, and it's very important that you are totally honest with me. Okay?"

Hesitantly, Gertie nodded.

"So." Mama put fake happiness in her voice. "Who was it?"

Gertie swallowed hard.

"*Sweetie*," Mama said. There was a sudden harshness in her face. She was getting mad.

"Francesca," Gertie said in the bravest voice she could manage, which was just a squeak.

Mama smiled. "Good. Francesca. Does Francesca have a last name?"

"I dunno."

Mama frowned. "Sweetie."

"White. Her name is Francesca White."

"That's a pretty name. How old is Francesca?"

Gertie shrugged. "She doesn't say."

"Is she old, like me?"

Gertie shook her head.

"Is she young like you?"

Gertie shrugged. Then nodded.

"What are her parents' names?"

Gertie hadn't considered that Francesca had parents. That was a good point.

Mama moved on. "Does Francesca talk to you often?"

She shrugged.

"Do you know what she looks like?"

"She has big hair. And she likes dresses."

"What color hair does she have?"

Gertie thought about that. Brown? Blonde? Red? "Red," she decided.

"Do you see her all the time?"

She shook her head no.

"When's the first time you saw her?"

Shrug.

"Where did she grow up?" Mama leaned closer. "Did she say?"

Gertie was feeling scared again.

"Do you see her now? Is she here with us?"

Of course not, Gertie wanted to say. Why would she be here with us now?

"Has she asked something from you? Did she mention a tether?"

A tether? she wondered. *What's a tether?*

Mama fired off a series of questions, "When's her birthday. Where did she go to school? Did she say what happened to her? How did she find you? Where does she live? Does she have siblings? Is anyone looking for her? Gertie, when was the first time—"

"I don't know!" Gertie cried, and suddenly tears were pouring down her face, and she just wanted Mama to stop asking so much. "I don't know because she's not real!" Gertie wailed. She had known this, but didn't want to admit it. It meant she didn't have the friends she wanted—real ones who didn't tease her because her mouth didn't work. "I'm sorry! I won't do it anymore!"

Mama became very still, her glassy-eyed excitement fading. "That's okay, sweetie. Mama's not mad." She studied Gertie for what seemed a long time.

Upstairs, the floor creaked. Papa must have heard Gertie's outburst.

Suddenly, Mama reached under the table and grabbed Gertie's hand. It sort of hurt.

"I just thought—" Mama broke off suddenly, glancing at the corner of the room. She took a deep breath. She looked... nervous? "You know you can tell me anything, right?"

Gertie wanted to wipe her cheeks, but she was afraid to move.

"Some people really do see things that no one else can. I thought maybe you—" She stopped herself again. "I want you to know, if it happens to you, you don't go to a doctor. You don't tell your closest friend."

What is she talking about? Gertie thought.

"I'm talking about a gift," Mama said, her eyes narrowing.

Gertie's arms broke out in goosebumps.

Mama squeezed her hand tighter and her voice got hard. "If you ever see someone like Francesca White for real, someone you didn't make up, but nobody else can see or hear, you come talk to me. Do I make myself clear?"

Papa's footsteps thumped on the stairs.

"Do I make myself clear?"

"Yes." She forced out the word, but she didn't understand.

Mama released her and shoved back from the table.

Gertie wiped her cheeks.

Mama went to the trashcan in the corner and opened the lid.

Papa appeared in the doorway. "What's going on?"

Mama snapped the trash's lid closed. "Just a little accident," she sighed. "Gertie dropped a plate."

3

Over the years, Gertie forgot the conversation. It sank into the sea of childhood memories as her world expanded. Her social anxiety stayed with her, solidifying into resentment of her more socially adept peers, who in turn resented what they mistook as her stuck-up attitude. She was a moody pre-teen and an angry teenager, taking her frustrations out on her own body, self-harming with a collection of safety pins she kept in the back of her sock drawer. She drew red lines on her inner thighs, cursing what she thought of as her own weirdness and the world's unfairness.

Late in high school, she discovered alcohol, fell in with a group of punks from a different school, wore fishnet stockings and a leather jacket and fingerless gloves and stopped talking to her parents for weeks at a time. They had always been distant, her father preoccupied with his courses. He taught History, and Gertie spent significant portions of her adolescence rolling her eyes at some lecture he gave over dinner about how this or that social or political event today mirrored almost exactly this or that social or political event from a hundred years ago.

Her mother was distant in a different way. She harbored some unnamed reservation about her daughter—some cause for disappointment. Gertie often caught her staring, a sad expression on her face. For a long time, Gertie tried to please her in an attempt to stop those looks. She'd bring home report cards with straight A's. She doodled as a pastime, drawing intricate landscapes and portraits she thought her mother might like. And though her mother did not display outright disdain, every compliment came out forced, reserved.

Shortly after her eighteenth birthday, she enrolled in the studio art program at Nulleport College. It was not her top choice, but it was only an hour and a half northeast of Rockwall, and her mediocre grades meant she had to take what she could get. The school was large and private, placed directly on the southern shore of Lake Ontario.

She snoozed through the gen-eds of freshman year, but she loved her art classes. She'd developed something of a passion for painting at the tail end of high school, thanks in part to a young art teacher named Mrs. Jamie who Gertie thought was trying just a little too hard to be hip, but who pushed her to dig deep and share what she had always been afraid to. "No more bowls of fruit," she said one day. "I want you to show me the real shit. The deep down shit." Her work was often rough around the edges, full of jagged shapes and deep shadows.

At the start of her second year at Nulleport, her mother went to the hospital when the abdominal pain she'd been ignoring for months became so severe she couldn't stand upright. The doctors diagnosed her with stage two ovarian cancer. Gertie offered to put college on hold, but her parents wouldn't hear it. They said she needed to think about her future, not worry about her mom's. Besides, the doctors claimed they caught it in time.

Two surgeries and more than a year of chemo later, the doctors declared her mother cancer free.

Junior year, she was allowed to move off campus, so she rented a house with some acquaintances and converted her bedroom into a studio. She painted every day, disappeared into the act of creation. She cut back on drinking and smoking to maintain a clear head. She won a competition in the Art Department. The owner of a local bar bought two of her paintings and hung them near the little stage where musicians played on weekends.

Fall of senior year, her mother's cancer came back. It moved rapidly. By Christmas, the doctors were using the word "terminal" and spoke of making her mother "comfortable." They gave her three to six months.

Gertie left school before her final semester in order to move back home. Her mother never left her bed. A nurse checked in each day, but Dad and Gertie played caretaker. Her mother was often sedated beyond lucidity. She talked to people who weren't there, held one-sided conversations with no one that lasted for hours at a time.

Over the months, the disease reduced her to a stick figure. Her eyes, when open, were milky with pain. Dark clouds hung over the house. The stink of piss and shit lingered in the halls, settled into the furniture. Gertie had never cleaned an adult's ass before, let alone her mother's, but this became her daily life. Afternoons, she spoon-fed Mom a liquid diet of soup and Jell-O with a side of saltine crackers. She had been a steely woman, independent and brash. She'd worked at the same health food grocery chain for 25 years, climbing her way up from cashier to regional manager. A self-made woman who took very little shit and had no patience for ignorance. Nothing like this bald child-like thing that moaned and whimpered all day and night.

There were things Gertie wanted to ask her, but couldn't phrase if she tried. Why hadn't they gotten along better? Why had her mom always been so cold? What had she expected of Gertie, and why couldn't she look her in the face, even now, and say that she loved her unconditionally?

One afternoon in early May, after convincing her father to take a break and get some fresh air, Gertie headed upstairs to check in. As she crept down the hall to the room, she heard her mother's voice filter through the crack in the door. She'd been sedated for days, capable of little more than turning her head to push some dribble out between her lips.

Though muffled, the words seemed urgent.

Gertie hurried down the hall and pushed the door open.

Her mother sat upright in bed, flush with life and color.

A pang of hope. Were the doctors wrong? Could she somehow beat this?

She smiled like she hadn't in months. Maybe years. "*Sweetie.*"

"Mama?"

Mama's eyes glistened, sharp and discerning.

Gertie baby-stepped to her bedside.

Her mother's smile softened. "Why didn't you show me your paintings?"

"What?"

"Your paintings. I saw them."

"What do you mean? Dad showed you?"

"Give me your hand."

A memory flashed in Gertie's mind. Sitting at the kitchen table, her mother just as excited as she was now, acting just as strange. Asking odd questions.

"Mama?"

"Your hand."

Gertie put her hand out. Mama sandwiched it with her own, her touch so light Gertie hardly felt a thing.

"All this time," Mama said, "I didn't think you had it. But those paintings—" Gently, she pulled Gertie's hand toward her own forehead, placed her pointer finger between her eyebrows. "I forgot. It's not about having it or not. It's about letting it in. And letting it out." Her expression changed to one of sadness. Or pity. "Don't be afraid."

Gertie's tongue swelled. A sensation she had not felt in a long time.

"It's possible to hide things even from yourself." She tugged on Gertie's hand. "Closer."

Gertie knelt so that her face was even with her mother's.

Somehow, the age lines were gone from the woman's face. Her skin was perfectly smooth, youthful, and Gertie realized with a shock that her hair had grown back.

"Open your mouth."

A dream. It's just a dream.

"It's not a dream. Open your mouth."

Gertie's palms sweat. Her mother's hands were ice cold, but they had no texture.

"Mama?" The word barely escaped her lips.

"Don't be afraid. It's a gift."

She did as she was told, opening her mouth the slightest bit.

Her mother peered inside, inspecting her like a doctor. "Wider."

Holding her breath, Gertie stretched her jaw as wide as it would go.

Quick as a striking snake, her mother plunged a frigid hand down Gertie's throat.

She gagged, but could not pull away—her mother gripped something at the top of her esophagus, a burning, tearing sensation as something tore and her mother's hand came away, white as a lily, a small black object clutched between her fingertips. Gertie expected blood, but there was none.

The object was a stone the size of a large, oval marble. Perfectly smooth and glistening with saliva.

Her mother gazed at her in triumph.

The room seemed to grow brighter. A rushing sound filled her head. Strange lights danced in the air like golden motes.

It was—for a moment—beautiful.

"They're weak," her mother said. "They need a tether to remain. A place, or a person. Otherwise, they drift away. They'll come to you now. Help them. I tried but I— I couldn't."

Gertie looked up, past her mother, and saw the figure on the other side of the bed. The woman stood nearly six feet tall, with hair so dark it seemed tinged with blue. She wore a white camisole and Victorian-era bloomers. Her face was unnaturally white, and she grinned.

Gertie jerked backward so hard she lost her balance and banged her head on the hardwood floor. She scrambled away, bumped into the wall, and only then did she look back at the bed.

Her mother lay still, sunken deep into the mattress. Her eyes were closed, her flesh sallow, her scalp bald but for a few strands of unruly blonde. Her chest rose and fell in a shallow but steady rhythm. There was no woman on the other side of the bed.

No dust motes dancing.

Gertie's throat felt as though someone had held a hot poker to it.

She ran from the room.

● • ●

Her mother died the next day. It was May 12. She was 43 years old.

Afterward, Gertie excused herself, leaving the nurse and her father with the body. She sat on her own bed, in the room she grew up in, replaying the moment of death. The final rattle in her mother's throat, like something falling down a well. The way her cheeks, already sunken, sagged the slightest bit deeper. The feeling of sudden cold that made Gertie's hair stand on end—and the sound of a footstep behind her. She'd been too frightened to turn.

She wanted to believe the previous day's events had been a dream. Her mother had not reached down her throat and removed a black stone. There was no woman in early 1900s underwear across from her. None of that had happened. It couldn't have.

And yet.

Gertie's room had not changed since she left for college, except now canvases lined the perimeter, leaning against the walls beneath old band posters—Bad Brains, Minor Threat, The Ramones, Black Flag, Circle Jerks. She'd placed the canvases in rows, front to back. She had not even thought about touching them since she'd been home and now glanced disinterestedly at the works she could see. She liked working with charcoal and gouache, sometimes watercolors, and occasionally acrylics. So much work went into them. Piles of ruined clothes. Countless tubes of paint. Many paychecks' worth of brushes and canvas.

The finished work—and the unfinished—seemed somehow foreign.

The act of creation that spawned them was a mindless state. When she worked, she became an empty vessel, like entering a trance. Sometimes she worked for hours or days at a time just to step back and have no recollection of where the image had come from.

One particular row of canvases drew her attention now. Gingerly, she approached the stack and sifted through them, her fingers flicking over their tops as she pulled them apart. Before she knew what she was looking for, she found it.

She pulled the canvas out of the stack, held it in front of her with both hands, and set it on the bed. The figure stared straight up at the ceiling, grinning that unsettling grin.

I didn't think you had it. But those paintings—

The woman wore the same camisole and bloomers in the painting. The details were impressionistic, like a rendering of fog in the shape of a woman, but the face was unmistakable.

She had painted it ghost white.

4

Summer came, but even on the brightest days, the sun could not penetrate the gloom that overcame the house. Gertie's father rarely changed out of his bathrobe. With no work between semesters, he spent days in the same bed where his wife had breathed her last. He rarely met Gertie's gaze, and when she asked him once if he would consider talking to someone professionally, he stormed upstairs and slammed his bedroom door.

She walked the neighborhood often to escape, but soon this led to an even greater crisis.

It happened six weeks after her mother's death. She was on an ordinary walk. She had her earbuds in. Her path had become a mindless routine, so she watched her shoes, glancing up only to check for oncoming traffic. She spotted the first gawker on the street behind their house—an old Asian woman peering out from the Dubanowski's front window. The Dubanowskis were a young gay couple who had just adopted their first child. The old woman was most likely a relative, but something about the way she watched Gertie gave her the creeps.

She walked a little faster.

Three houses down, a man in work overalls crouched on the roof over an open garage. He, too, stared at Gertie as she passed.

Every third or fourth house, someone gaped at her with the same dull expression.

When she came to the intersection of her own street, she stopped in her tracks. A little girl in a plaid school uniform stood in the middle of the intersection, totally still, staring at Gertie. The girl's hair was brown, pin straight, and ended at her shoulders.

There were no cars. No parents on a nearby porch.

Gertie took one step forward, and the girl started shouting.

Gertie couldn't hear her over the music, so she popped hear earbuds free.

The girl's mouth still moved, and veins in her forehead bulged with the effort of her cries—but there was no sound. As if someone had switched off the volume of her voice.

The sudden roar of an engine drew Gertie's attention to the right. A rusty old minivan pulled out of someone's driveway, then headed down the street in the opposite direction.

When Gertie turned back, the girl was gone.

At home, she sat on her bed, shaking.

She stopped taking walks. When she did go out, she refused to look at the houses or at the intersection to the left. Even in the backyard, she sensed eyes in every direction.

She had to get away from the house, away from her father. Away from the neighborhood. The realization came with a wallop of guilt and shame, but it didn't matter. She couldn't stay.

She left for her final semester two months early.

. . .

Most of her friends had already graduated, but an acquaintance in the Art program agreed to let her sleep on her couch in her shared apartment. It was an old, drafty house, and the couch was sunken in the middle and smelled like dog, but she was grateful. She had just enough loan money saved that she could pay a small portion of rent and buy her own groceries. The arrangement was to be temporary, lasting perhaps a month until Gertie found a job and an apartment of her own. It lasted less than 72 hours.

The uncomfortable couch meant she didn't sleep well the first two nights. By the third, she gave up and decided to sleep on the floor. With a comforter for a mattress and a thin sheet her only covering, she tossed and turned until 2 a.m. She woke at exactly 3:05 a.m. to the sight of a naked middle-aged man peering down at her. A bear of a man, covered in curly hair. His flaccid penis bobbed above her, and she did not move for several seconds.

Realizing she was awake and staring up at him, the man cupped his genitals and shuffled backward. "She saw me!" he yelped.

Gertie bolted upright and dashed straight ahead, realizing too late that she was still wrapped in the sheet. She fell onto the couch.

The man backed into the kitchen like a frightened dog. "She sees me!"

She couldn't read his tone. He sounded afraid, but also elated.

Finally, she found her own voice. "Help!" she screamed.

The man patted the air with one hand, concealing himself with the other. "I'm sorry!"

"*Help me!*"

There were two bedrooms downstairs, both beyond the kitchen. One of the doors flung open, and Muhammad stormed into the hallway in just his boxers. "What's going on!"

It was still dark in the house, but Gertie did not dare move to reach for the lamp.

"Hey!" Muhammad called. "Gertie? What's going on!"

The naked man wedged himself against the kitchen cabinets where Muhammad couldn't see him.

"There!" Gertie pointed.

Footsteps thundered upstairs.

Muhammad did not hesitate. He rushed into the kitchen and smacked the light switch, lighting the yellowed linoleum and the grease-stained cabinets. He turned his head side to side, somehow failing to see the naked man directly to his right. "What is it?"

Gertie kept her trembling finger pointed at the lunatic.

The man tucked his face toward his chest, ashamed.

Muhammad spun in a circle.

Now the others were in the living room. Someone turned the lights on.

"What's going on?"

"Who was screaming?"

"Did someone have a nightmare?"

They were joking, Gertie thought. They were all about to burst out laughing, and Mr. Naked Lunatic would introduce himself as somebody's eccentric friend, always up for a prank.

Except nobody smiled. They stared at her, waiting for an explanation. She wept in silence as she gathered her things, some of her housemates trailing her and asking what happened. Muhammad crossed his arms and leaned against the fridge, pissed that he'd been awakened at 3 a.m. for *this*. The naked man kept his distance, but repeated the same two sentences over and over: "I can't get out. You have to help me."

To her relief, he did not follow her outside.

She slept in her car most nights. What money she would have spent on rent she used to buy gas, pizza, and liquor. By the time classes started, she'd found a steady rotation of young men who didn't mind sharing their beds. She couldn't stay long at any one place or with any one person. The hallucinations became a regular part of her life, with strange figures seeking her out wherever she went. Sometimes they just watched her. Other times, they turned hostile—started yelling. Once, in late September, while walking from campus to the house of a new lover, a snarling black dog streaked out of a construction site and chased her down the street, nipping at her heels. It wasn't until the dog leapt *through* her that she realized why nobody tried to help. While she watched, the dog lay down in front of her, remorseful, and faded into vapor.

But lunatics and dogs were just the beginning. There were auditory hallucinations and visual anomalies. Sometimes when the boys she bedded were sleeping, she could hear their voices deep in the recesses of their minds. If she saw anyone become particularly emotional, colors would drift out from the tops of their heads. She couldn't eat meat anymore. When she burst out crying after taking a bite of a burger over lunch one day, the only explanation she could offer at the time was, "I can taste their sadness."

Alcohol suppressed these visions—so she spent most of her waking life blackout drunk.

By midsemester, she was failing all of her classes. She hadn't painted since her mother's death. For the first time, she was afraid of what might appear on the canvas.

Her father called often, but she never answered. He left voicemails. He'd started going to church—something he used to mock. Now he tried to recruit Gertie, saying she was right when she asked him to talk with someone. That someone, he said, was God.

In her sober moments, she thought about her mother. Her fingers tearing something from the back of her throat. *It's possible to hide things even from yourself.*

She wanted to reach through the veil of time and grab her mother by the lapels and scream in her fucking face: *Whatever you did to me, undo it.*

By late October, she'd had enough.

Winter came early in Nulleport. The first big snowstorm hit six days before Halloween. After waking around 6 p.m., opening all the cupboards of her latest crash pad and finding nothing but soft drinks, she walked to the nearest Fastrac, bought three 40 oz bottles of Busch that she downed in the parking lot, then trudged determinedly down the snow-covered sidewalk toward the bridge.

The Nulle River split the town down the middle from north to south, dumping into the south side of Lake Ontario. The bridge spanned the river thirty feet above churning black water that rarely froze, even on the bitterest of days. Concealed by the blizzard, Gertie stumbled along the bridge and crossed the road to face the expansive lake.

The snow was too thick to see more than a few feet in any direction, but the water would be all whitecaps in this storm. The river would carry her to them, and they would batter her body until the spring thaw, when some hapless fisherman reeled her in, or—she thought with a giggle—an eager freshman dove into the shallows, opened his eyes, and bubbled out a scream at the sight of her corpse all jelly-eyed and fish-bit.

She climbed up the railing and swung one leg over at a time, fingers and toes numb from the alcohol and cold. She crouched low, stretching her arms, sticking her ass out over the water.

Fat snowflakes drifted into an infinite gray nothing below.

She turned her face up, let the snow land on it. It tasted like tears.

"Whatever's wrong, this won't fix it."

The voice was soft. It belonged to a pale young woman on the sidewalk. She seemed about Gertie's age. She wore shorts and a tank top, despite the cold. The snow blew through her.

Another phantom.

"Why won't you leave me alone?" Gertie moaned.

The girl rolled her eyes. "You chose *my* bridge."

"What do you want?"

"Who said I want anything?"

"Isn't that it? Isn't that why they keep coming?"

The girl screwed up her face. "I don't know what your problem is, but killing yourself won't solve it. Trust me."

Gertie studied the girl. Really saw her. Her hair lay flat against her skull, sopping wet, and her clothes were plastered to her bluish skin.

"You jumped."

The girl shrugged. "Kids used to come here at night. Said you could hear my heels clicking on the pavement before midnight. Bunch of hooey. I was barefoot at the time." She wiggled her painted toes for emphasis.

For a moment, the gray below the bridge cleared, and the water shown black as an opal.

All Gertie had to do was let go.

"Such a waste," the girl said. "Your type come around sometimes. I don't mean suicides. I mean your *type*. You can see, but you don't want to look. You hear me, but you're too scared to listen." The girl snorted, a mean spirited sound. "You have no idea."

Gertie mumbled, "About what?"

She went to Gertie's side, placed ethereal hands on the railing, and looked down. "Soon as I let go, I knew it was a mistake. It wasn't the impact. The bridge isn't tall enough. I had rocks in my pockets, like Ophelia. When it was over, I was back where I started. Right where I am now. Everything gray. I felt myself fading, like snow in the wind. I don't know what I did, but I rooted myself here somehow. Like I was—"

"Tethered," Gertie suggested.

"And this is where I'll be, I guess, until the bridge falls down, or—" She looked off into the haze of snow. "I made two bad choices that night. And I'm stuck with them. Forever."

Gertie flexed her toes in her boots. She imagined falling, weightless for a second or two before slamming against the water, then sinking into the freezing torrent as it invaded her mouth, her sinuses, her lungs, and sucked out whatever warmth remained.

Before she made a conscious decision, she climbed back over the railing, onto the sidewalk. Her entire body trembled, and tears formed crystalline shards on her eyelashes.

There on the bridge, accompanied by a ghost, she sobbed, and confessed that she didn't know what this was—any of it. What her mother had done to her, what she was meant to do. There were no answers, no signposts. And everywhere she looked, more specters. The ghost listened, smiling despite her visitor's pain. It was, the ghost thought, a beautiful pain—the pain of a soul searching for answers.

A plow rumbled by, spraying slush across Gertie's jacket and jeans.

The muck fell through the ghost.

They watched the vehicle roar away, spraying salt.

"Thank you," Gertie said at last.

The ghost shrugged.

"Is there something I can do for you? To help?"

"Me?" The girl had very blue eyes, like clear water. "No. They're out there." She indicated the storm. "Millions of them. Searching for anyone who can hear them."

The ghost broke away, moved several feet to Gertie's right, and sat on the curb with her arms crossed over her knees. She rested her chin on her forearms and stared ahead, unblinking.

5

Gertie tried not to give fear so much weight. If any phantoms sought her out, she would listen. But the streets that had seemed so full before went quiet. No eyes peered through shaded windows. No ghost dogs bit at her ankles. She drove to a graveyard and spoke to headstones. Nobody spoke back. She returned to the house where the naked man had woken her in the night. She stood on the porch at 2 a.m. and whispered at the door, asking if the man wanted help. He never said.

Her academic advisor recommended taking Incompletes in her classes. She moved back in with her father. He talked incessantly about church, telling her she ought to come. The day she returned home, she walked the house searching for the woman from her mother's bedside.

But the house, like the street, was empty.

She wondered if her gift had faded, or if the fear she once felt had drawn the spirits in.

She took a job in customer service at a cell phone company. Even through the phone, she learned to sense people's emotions. In time, she learned how to influence them directly. Without saying a word, she could lull an irate customer into a cooing babe.

Within a year, she bought a cheap fixer-upper in the rural town of Victoria, half an hour outside Rockwall. Got the place at a bargain—it seemed she had an uncanny talent for haggling. The house sat between a meth head and a trailer park, but she never had problems with either.

Like most of New York State, Victoria had been carved out of forest, so her backyard ended at a treeline. Her realtor assured her that the hunters who frequented these woods never neared the edge. She set up a studio in the backyard shed, but couldn't get herself to paint.

She liked to sit out back by the firepit, sipping a beer after work, letting her thoughts get lost in the greenery of the forest. It was quiet, peaceful living. At least for a while.

She was in the lone lawn chair, her feet propped on a piece of wood beside the fire, with two tofurky dogs skewered over the meager flames. She cracked open her first beer of the evening and pressed it to her lips, looked up, and saw something moving inside the treeline.

It could have been a hunter who'd lost his way. This was turkey season, after all, and despite her realtor's promises, men often traipsed through the woods with rifles. But as the figure drew near, she recognized naked flesh. A girl. She stood out like a pearl in the brush.

Gertie shot to her feet. Her beer hit the ground with a *thunk* and her tofurky dogs dropped into the fire to sizzle. She patted her pockets, seeking her phone, but she'd left it inside.

No matter. At the figure's approach, Gertie's scalp prickled in that telltale way.

The girl appeared to be in her late teens or early twenties. Slender and boney. Hair buzzed down to almost nothing. She stepped into the yard reaching for Gertie with limp hands.

For the first time, Gertie did not shun the wandering spirit. She moved forward, taking deep, slow breaths.

"Look what he did to me," the girl said.

"Who?"

"He won't stop. He'll never stop."

The girl shimmered like a hologram. Her eyes bulged. "I'm disappearing."

"What can I do?"

The girl offered a pale hand. "See."

Feeling less brave than she would have liked, Gertie extended her own.

The girl's fingers were textureless and weightless. The only sensation was cold.

Upon contact, strobing memories flooded Gertie's mind.

The girl's name was Devon O'Shanahan.

She grew up in a one-story house with a boarded-up window. Rusting Station Wagon always in the driveway. A man with a bottle or can in his hand, big gut and strong chin, smiling, red-nosed, with curly black hair. Not her father, but like a father. Mother a round thing with narrow eyes, yellow front teeth, quick to swing her fists.

Devon ran away. Flash of a shelter made of cardboard. Old men with filthy, grabby hands. Young women with the same. Now a kind woman behind a desk asking her about her parents and answering that she had none, she didn't know. Now another home, another family.

Flashes of masturbating in front of a laptop, chatting with shadow-faced men with headphones on. Snorting powder from a handheld mirror. Meeting clients in motels and fucking them without pleasure, hairy sagging bodies slapping against her.

Memories fragile and distant, a side note to what she meant to show.

It had been a bad day. Her cam session less than lucrative, one viewer telling her to put things inside of her that she had no intention of putting inside of her, and when she refused, insulting her. Ugly, fat, stupid. Cow, slut, cum-dumpster. Should freeze a log of shit and fuck that, I'd pay to see that. She banned him but it tainted the session, which she cut short.

Pissed off and depressed, she paid for a ride downtown to a club where she used to pick up clients the old-fashioned way. She was loaded by the time she met her murderer.

He was tall and dark and not exactly handsome, but not hideous. Broad shoulders and the start of a paunch. Chin sandpapery with stubble. He bought her drinks, and they danced, body pressed to body, and after some time and more drinks he suggested they go somewhere to talk. She tried to alert the bartender, which she always did in case things went south, but the man yanked her by the wrist in a way that hurt and she sort of didn't care.

They went to his van. Inside, she took out her pocket mirror and did a bump. She offered some to the man. He declined, but popped open his glovebox and produced a baggie of powder and said, "Try that."

She did. "Your turn."

He shook his head.

She woke in a garage or basement with metal rafters visible overhead, bright fluorescents hanging from them. She was naked. Sour fabric filled her mouth, sealed over by tape that wrapped around the back of her head. She tried to sit up. Found her arms stuck out at her sides in a cruciform pose, nylon rope lashed to something over the sides of the table she'd been strapped to. The same with her legs, which had been secured at the ankles and forced wide.

The man circled the table, grinning. He took a position at her feet and produced a hunting knife. Made a big show of holding it to the light. A small hook arced off the back.

She strained against her restraints. The table legs bounced, but the ties held.

The man rubbed her shins and knees with his free hand. He ran the knife along her right calf, teasing with the blade. He crawled onto the table and ran the blade up between her thighs.

He pushed the knife inside. Rush of bright pain.

Then she was gone.

When her vision returned, she still lay on her back, facing the ceiling, but she felt lighter than air, and somehow *bright*, though her surroundings had turned gray.

She sat up.

Her body lay before her. Mutilated. Ruined. It looked unreal, like a doll. She'd been disemboweled from between her legs. Her intestines hung out in loops over the table's edge, unidentifiable bits of pink tissue scattered about like discarded fabric.

She'd almost forgotten about the man. He stood beside the table, watching her body. There was something else. Something she couldn't see before. Something clinging to the man's back, wrapping around his chest with cord-like appendages. Its head was the size of a newborn's and rested on the man's left shoulder, lumpy and misshapen and, like the ropy limbs, crisscrossed with yellow-orange veins. Its face, if it had a face, must have been pressed into the man's flesh. Its color reminded her of the time her birth mom's boyfriend put his hand through the front window. He'd held it over the sink for a long time, wrapped in a spare t-shirt. When Devon approached him and asked what he was doing, he flashed a cockeyed grin and pulled the rag away. "Just hanging with my friend," he slurred. "Mr. Ugly." The wound like a mouth. Inside, knobby white protrusions of knuckle and bone.

Unlike even the sight of her own corpse, this creature's presence filled her with dread.

Somewhere far off, a voice called to her. Unlike any she'd heard. More like a musical note than a voice. Warm and welcoming. She felt herself lift from the table.

The man watched her. Not her corpse, but *her*.

In her mind, she saw a woman sitting in a chair in her backyard, feet propped in front of a fire. The woman would hear her, see her. Somehow, she knew this.

Devon fled from the man and the thing on his back. Straight through the nearest wall. She focused her thoughts on the woman, picturing her face, calling out with her mind, and felt her in the distance. Then she was in a forest at dusk, following the meagre glow of a fire into a backyard.

The memory sputtered out, and Gertie stood alone.

Black smoke curled up from the fire.

She found the can of beer that she'd dropped, picked it up, and drained it.

She didn't know the murderer's name, but she had enough information to find him.

In the vision, she saw what he drove. A black cargo van with a business decal on the side: *Arlo's Furniture Warehouse.*

6

Arlo's Furniture Warehouse was located in a rundown section of Rockwall. Decades back, it had been the industrial side of town. Now the factories were defunct, and the residences boarded up. The warehouse stood alone, the size of two houses side-by-side.

She parked in the empty lot and stared at the building for twenty minutes. She'd seen enough cop shows to know a psychic couldn't just show up and start babbling about ghosts and visions and expect results. She needed evidence. She'd find some, take a photo, run like hell, and call the police as soon as she was safely the fuck out of there.

She gathered what little courage remained, left her car, and approached the entrance, gripping a travel-sized can of mace.

The open sign was off. She tried the door.

Unlocked.

Easy enough—but her heart raced.

She opened the door.

Concrete floors. Bare metal beams for a ceiling. Fluorescent strip-lighting. Scent of sawdust and mildew and something foul. High windows shot slanting rays of light through the air. A glass counter straight ahead, a register on the left side. Behind the counter, an empty chair and a small room made of freestanding walls—a makeshift office space. Behind the office, a plywood wall extended from one side of the warehouse to the other, bisecting the building. It must have blocked off a storage area or workshop in the rear of the warehouse. Rows of old furniture crowded the sales floor, most of it antique and wooden. End tables and china cabinets and dining room sets and dressers and vanities. Plenty of things to hide behind, she thought.

Shaking terribly, she let the door click closed behind her.

She stood motionless, trying to feel the mood of the place.

She crept behind the counter and tested the office door. Also unlocked.

She readied her can of mace and whipped the door open.

Nothing inside but a microwave, minifridge, and a metal desk covered in knickknacks: collectible train parts and hand-knit toys. Inside the fridge, a bottle of ketchup and cans of Mountain Dew.

She left the office and crept to the right side of the building where she spotted a door in the bisecting wall. Each step closer to that door sent her heartrate skyrocketing.

The foul smell came from back there.

A piece of printer paper had been taped across the door:

NO CUSTOMERS BEYOND THIS POINT.

She swung the door open to reveal row after row of metal shelving occupied by cardboard boxes, each labeled in messy black handwriting: CAR PARTS, EBAY READY TO LIST, NEEDS RESEARCH, GLASSWARE, REPLACEMENT KNOBS, CASTER WHEELS.

She stood in the doorway a long time.

Finally, she started toward the back of the building, down a center aisle between rows of shelves. She held her mace in front of her. Each time she came to an aisle, she turned and swung the mace. The smell intensified with every step. The sweet-sour scent of decay.

She found the source in the workstation at the end of the cabinets. A tool bench had been set up against the back wall beside a loading bay door. Someone had abandoned several repair projects here: a chair with spindles missing from the back, an upside-down dining table, a dresser with one side sanded to the grain and a drawer with a clamp tightened around it. In the center of all this, a wooden table rested on a large gray tarp. Four nylon ropes lazed overs the table like sleeping snakes, each secured to the table legs. Black-red stains marred the surface.

Human remains had been arranged into neat piles at the corners of the tarp. Hands in one corner, feet in another. Torsos. Heads. Flies swarmed over them like a crawling black carpet.

A door slammed behind her. She spun, brandishing her mace.

A man stood at the far end of the shelves.

Fear froze her in place.

The man was smiling.

He strolled leisurely up the aisle.

Streaks of light from the side windows illuminated him in increments. Wriggly limbs crossed his chest. A bulbous off-white head peeked over his left shoulder.

"S-stay where you are! I h-have mace!"

The man paused, threw his hands up, his mouth a little "o." He shook his hands in a mock tremble, dropped them, and continued forward.

She realized she'd been walking, too. Backward.

Coagulated blood stuck to her shoes. She bumped into the edge of the table and released a pathetic yelp.

"Don't c-come any closer!"

She searched for anything she could use as a weapon. Tools lay about the bench and half-finished project: a sledgehammer by the bay door, a circular saw on the bench, a screwdriver on top of the dresser. Behind her, a hunting knife rested on the tabletop. Clutching the mace in her left hand, she picked up the knife with her right.

"I love a fighter," the man said. He stopped at the last set of shelves, his face a mask of shadows. The appendages over his chest shifted, tightened. "But allow me to introduce myself." He jumped and spun 180 degrees in the air, landing with his back to her, feet wide. He raised his fists above his shoulders, gestured at the center of his back with down-pointing thumbs. "Ain't I pretty?" The creature seemed an unlikely hybrid of human and reptile. Maybe three feet in length. A ridged spine ran from head to tail, a nubby protuberance that curled over the man's left ass cheek.

She could only stare.

The man turned to face her. His grin vanished as he dropped the semblance of playfulness.

She braced herself. It felt like she was on the bridge again, over the water.

The man charged. An all-out sprint, shoulders lowered, arms swinging, legs pounding.

She depressed the button on her mace. A spurt of liquid arced wide right.

She hadn't centered the can.

She thrust the knife forward as he slammed into her, his arms wrapping around her back. They came down on the table. It collapsed under their combined weight, and he pressed down on her, crushing her, squeezing the air from her lungs. In their collision, the knife handle slammed into her solar plexus and slid along her ribcage. Now it rested against her side, the blade secured in the man's belly. She gripped the handle tight, arched her back, and heaved, drawing the blade from the man's belly up to his chest where it lodged against his breastbone. Blood and organs slid from the wound.

His bear hug slackened.

She released the knife and slid out from under him, assisted by the slick blood. She crawled to the edge of the tarp and got her feet under her.

She tried to run, lost her balance, and tumbled headlong into the side wall.

She braced for another attack, but the man lay where she left him, on his side, clutching his gaping abdomen. His breathing came in labored gurgles.

Impossibly, he pulled the knife from his chest and pushed himself into a kneeling position, his guts rolling into his lap. "Yeah," a bubble of blood popped on his lips and he placed his hands on the wet mound of innards. "I love a fighter."

He got one leg under him, began to rise.

Gertie rushed to the bay door and yanked on the handle, but it didn't budge.

She spotted the latch on the track and pulled the pin free and tried again.

The door shuttered open, revealing the morning light.

They were on a raised loading dock. She leapt onto the blacktop and ran straight, putting ten feet between herself and the building before she looked back.

The man shuffled toward the opening, clutching his intestines. He smiled, then pitched over sideways, landing out of sight.

Gertie stumbled to the edge of the parking lot and into the grass where she curled against a crooked tree. She pressed her hands over her thumping heart. She sat like this for several minutes. The reek of bodies and the newly dead man wafted from the building.

From inside the warehouse, there came a sound like rats scrabbling inside a wall.

She looked up.

The sight of what clambered out of the doorway nailed every molecule of her being into place. She knew she should run. Scream. Fight. *Something*. She had murdered a man. Cut him open so his guts came out—and it had been for nothing. The creature scampered sideways on spindly legs. It seemed larger now that it was not clinging to someone's back. It raised what should have been a face—a shrunken, lumpy visage that hinted at cheekbones and a nose, with a single yellow eye that opened vertically in its forehead, and a ragged, misshapen hole of a mouth enveloped by folds of skin, much like the puckered edges of a wound.

It was on her in seconds.

It lashed a rubbery appendage around her ankle and plastered itself to her leg. She swung a fist, but it scrambled up her body so fast she only punched herself in the shin. She slapped and rolled and grabbed, but it was too quick as it eased around her back, tightening cephalopod arms around her chest, squeezing her breasts and ribs and centering its body over her spine. It pressed its mouth to her neck and something pinched and wiggled into her flesh. A silver cord unspooled within her. It was inside, and while she choked and foamed at the mouth, seized and contorted, her spirit spasmed and some new survival instinct kicked in.

She contracted all her energy, pulling her consciousness into the pit of her stomach, compacting all of her being down, down, until she was but the size of a pea—her very existence crumpled into this tiny speck within. There she coiled, pressurized.

The creature couldn't find her, though it searched.

She felt its anger, waves of black rage.

It meant to tether itself to her. It *needed* to.

All at once, she exploded from her coiled place, blasting a shockwave of energy in all directions. The grass on which she sat flattened, as if a giant stepped there, and the branches of the tree above her shook, loosing a cascade of leaves.

The thing had been thrown free. It landed on the pavement like a cat and scampered across the parking lot and around the side of the building, out of sight.

She wanted to scream, to curse, to laugh madly with glee and terror, but the world spun and her stomach spasmed and forced its contents out of her mouth and into the grass.

Her eyelids were so heavy, but she could not yet sleep, as a desperate moan drifted out of the warehouse and startled her awake—

"Somebody. Oh God!"

—and the man she murdered stepped to the edge of the loading dock.

He wavered like a mirage.

He spotted her in the grass. "Am I dead?" he said. "Did you kill me?"

What could she say?

"You killed me." It was not a question this time. "And that thing— Oh my God. It made me—" He looked at his hands.

She shook her head. "I'm sorry."

He studied her, suspicious. "You fought it. You resisted."

He flickered again. A candle low on fuel.

"Please." He jumped from the ledge and approached her with upturned hands, strobing now like a shorting bulb. "Please, help me." He chewed his lip.

Sad, puppy dog eyes.

She would come to know that look well.

"Oh, fuck." She extended a hand. "Do it."

"Do what?"

"Tether."

"What does that mean?"

"Tether yourself to me."

"How?"

"Just… try."

He indulged a final glance at the door before cupping his hands around Gertie's.

She felt an electric jolt or pinch at the base of her skull.

The man's strobing stopped. "What just happened?"

"Tethered..." she mumbled.

"I feel weird." He searched the sky. "Everything's gray."

She pushed into a squat, patted the urine stain on her jeans.

"Who are you?"

"Gertie."

He meandered to the open bay door. "That's my body. Holy shit."

She shoved herself upright, swayed on unsteady legs. "Welcome to the afterlife, Arlo."

"It's David."

David's body lay slumped on the tarp, looking unreal in the manner of corpses.

Her legs went to rubber, and she had to sit. When she looked up, she couldn't find the ghost. Fending off the creature had depleted her. She said to the air, assuming the ghost would hear, as he'd hear everything she said from now on: "I think, David, we have a lot to talk about."

7

Janelle checked the clock radio. Nearly two hours had passed since they parked on Richard's street. The night had sealed over black and the windows of the houses glowed eerily from within. She wondered how many ghosts peered out of those windows now.

She didn't believe all that, did she?

Gertie stared out her own window, pensive.

She was probably crazy.

"So what is it?" Janelle said. "The creature. What does it want?"

Gertie shook her head slowly side to side. "I asked David the same thing. We've been hunting it for years. Learning his methods. He doesn't just kill at random. He possesses a host and starts by killing everyone they love before moving to strangers. When he gets bored, or if the cops get close, he kills his host and finds another."

"Where did it come from?"

"I don't know. It's not a ghost. It's... something else."

"A demon?"

"Maybe. I don't know."

Janelle had broken out in chills. She didn't want to believe. "How do you stop him?"

"He might not be a ghost, but he follows the same rules. He needs to tether to survive, and he can't body hop. Once he tethers, he's stuck. But without a tether, *poof.* After what happened at the warehouse, I spent a lot of time researching witchcraft. Spells and that sort of thing. Most of it's bullshit, but some of it's not. I put a containment spell on the back of this van. If we get him back there without a body, he'll be stuck. Then... *poof.*"

"What about Richard? Isn't it tethered to him?"

Gertie hesitated. "I'll perform an exorcism."

"You can do that?"

"First, we have to find him. I fucked up at the river. I froze. I won't do that again."

Janelle studied the dark interior of the van. Her feet rested on a duffel bag. A map of Fairfield had been taped to the glovebox.

"What about David?" she said.

"What about him?"

"Is he... here now?"

"Yes. He's always near."

Janelle resisted the urge to wave her hands in front of her, trying to touch the ghost. "Why should I believe you?" she blurted.

"You saw your friend back there. Richard. Would he ever... do what he did, if it was really him?"

Janelle knew the answer.

"The night's not over, if you're still not convinced."

Janelle turned to the darkened neighborhood. The lawns and the houses, the people inside ignorant of what slipped through the night and saw them only as future victims. Playthings.

Richard would come. She sensed it.

All they had to do was wait.

8

In a series of fits and starts, Richard emerged into consciousness.

Water filled his mouth and nose. His lungs burned.

I'm going to die now.

There was no panic in this thought. It came as a relief after what he did to Amy. Though it wasn't really him. It was his body, his hands, but not his actions.

The Oppressor had done this.

They returned to the waking world together.

The Oppressor raised Richard's head from the river and gulped lungfuls of air. It vomited and coughed and studied their surroundings.

The banks of the river surged by. The concrete walkway and its walls were behind them now, replaced by scrub brush and trees.

The Oppressor paddled to the bank and clawed at the grass. They lurched up a hill through a stand of trees. Richard's clothes hung wet and heavy and the fabric of his jeans chafed his thighs and waist.

The Oppressor felt the side of his head and flinched at the sting of their wound. His left ear hung down, half torn away where Janelle hit him with a piece of cement. He pushed the ear back into place long enough for the clotting blood to hold it.

Nice one, Janelle, Richard thought.

They came out of the trees at the edge of a rock quarry. The earth here had been scraped down to raw crust between piles of sand and stone. Earthmovers and conveyer belts on tall platforms loomed in the darkness.

Richard felt the Oppressor working out its next move. It burrowed through his memories, seeking new modes of torment. He caught glimpses of its mind. Difficult to look. Like standing at the edge of a cliff. Things writhed in the pit below. A sea of shapes, hungry for suffering.

Back on the river path, after Janelle hit him with the cement block, the Oppressor had looked up, disoriented, and caught sight of a figure it recognized. Richard didn't know who the woman was, but he felt in the Oppressor a flutter of emotions—excitement and something else.

Hesitancy. Nervousness.

Fear?

Rage flared through him, through the Oppressor.

And for the first time, he heard its voice. A sound like cockroach wings flapping in unison. *Fear? I will show you fear.*

They came to a gravel road, followed it up a hill to a paved path in a residential neighborhood. Slate gray warehouses on one side of the path overlooked the quarry. Identical suburban houses on the other side. They stumbled through the neighborhood, across lawns, up driveways and through backyards. Dogs barked behind fences and whined and slunk away when the Oppressor glared. The land was mostly flat, so it was not difficult to spot the homeless woman moving between the driveways, plucking bottles and cans from recycling bins and adding them to her shopping cart.

They followed her a while, far enough that she didn't notice at first.

The Oppressor found half a cinderblock in the gutter and cradled it against Richard's hip. They had lost the knife in the river.

Don't, Richard said.

The Oppressor whistled an indistinct tune.

The homeless woman looked up from the bin she rummaged through. Eyes like raisins.

The Oppressor waved.

The woman dropped the bin's lid and pushed her cart up the street.

The Oppressor walked unevenly with the cinderblock, but they gained. She favored her left leg. The cart caught on something. She shoved it. Her mound of bags belched beer cans. She abandoned the cart and shuffled toward the grassy hill to her left. Beyond the hill lay the main road and beyond that the highway.

The Oppressor followed.

She'd been using the cart as a walker and limped badly without it, barely lifting her feet so that Richard heard the *shh-shh-shh* of her sneakers brushing grass. She tripped halfway up the hill. The Oppressor rushed upon her and lifted the cement block above Richard's head with both hands and heaved it onto the woman's lower back. Her spine snapped, and the block embedded there as if tossed into mud. The woman wheezed and pawed at the grass. The Oppressor crouched by her head. It ran Richard's fingers through her hair, her scalp dry and crusted with dandruff. The Oppressor stroked the back of her neck, slid Richard's fingers around her throat to rest across her jerking jugular. It caressed her face, the fuzzed eyebrows, porous nose, cracked lips—and slid Richard's fingers into her mouth.

Please! Richard begged.

The few teeth she had left scraped his knuckles. She tried to speak or scream but choked on his hand. He gripped her hair with his free hand and forced the other deeper into the warm velvet of her mouth. His fingernails gouged her tongue, the hand closing into a fist. Her jaw popped, and she blew snot across his wrist and hot vomit met his knuckles. She seized and jerked and clawed the earth.

Then she was still.

A bolt of energy surged through Richard, through the Oppressor. Richard didn't do drugs. Nothing more than weed and liquor, anyway, but he imagined this was better than any hit of coke or drag of meth. He could see the night with cat's eyes, could feel the bugs in the grass and circling his head. Someone had cranked up the intensity of the world— and it was beautiful. He saw colors he didn't even know existed.

The Oppressor released a post-coital sigh and slid Richard's hand free of the corpse.

What excitement Richard felt turned immediately to shame.

Satisfied, the Oppressor stood on Richard's legs, raised Richard's foot, and stomped on the back of the woman's head until it was nothing but hair and skin flattened into the grass.

Richard could not even weep. Something inside him went limp. He let the wind blow him over the cliff. He sank down, immaterial, into the depths of hopelessness, where he was nothing.

The Oppressor left the corpse, climbed the hill, and continued down the road.

9

For her sixth birthday, Gertie's mother bought her a Magic 8-Ball. She liked to whisper questions to it and shake it and flip it over to read the die floating in its blue water, convinced that it could predict the future and clarify the past. She eventually dropped it on the stairs and all that water drained out so the plastic die rattled around and made no more predictions. If she had it now, she would ask if she had done the right thing telling Janelle all she had.

David stood at the end of his tether down the road. She was glad for the distance. They hadn't known each other in life. Now they were inseparable, and not by choice. She doubted they would have been friends if they met when he was alive. He was too uptight, too twitchy. This van had been his, along with the furniture warehouse advertised on its side. Mr. Ugly put an end to all that, with Gertie's help. She failed back then. The same way she failed on the river.

And here she was, putting yet another person in harm's way. Janelle was just a teenager. Younger than Gertie when her mother passed. Gertie didn't know what would happen to her when all this was over, even if it went the way she hoped. And in the meantime, Janelle's parents might report her missing and call the police. That was the last thing she needed.

This was all beginning to feel like yet another mistake.

David, for his part, mulled over thoughts not unlike his partner's, but he feared success as much as he feared failure. Not that he wanted to fail. That would defeat the whole purpose of this grayed out, fucked up limbo of an afterlife. It was just that—well, if they failed, he could follow Gertie around a while longer.

In the years before his death, he focused all his time and energy on his furniture shop, which he never quite figured out how to make profitable. Sunup to sundown, he hauled tables and chairs and hutches and dressers and bedframes from here to there, back and forth in that van, from house calls to the warehouse, from the warehouse to homes for a middling delivery charge. By the time all that was done, the cost of his efforts was incalculable. He told himself that was okay because at least he got to choose how he spent his time rather than being forced to work for someone else.

That was bullshit.

He had a heart that beat and a nose that could smell and a tongue that could taste and hands that could feel and a functioning dick with two balls and he had one lifetime to use any of it, but he ground himself into dust. He hardly had the time to visit his grandfather in the hospital before that horrible thing got ahold of him and made him go there to—

He didn't want to think about that.

He hadn't wasted his life. Not really. It was easy to look back and feel regret, but he had made his choices consciously, and there had to be value in that. Then again, if someone told him that death would render the world cold and gray and a little rancid and soggy, like cardboard in a basement, he may have made some different choices.

Oh well. This existence was no paradise, but at least it was familiar. Predictable. What came next remained a blank, and that was the greatest terror he could face.

He wasn't raised religious, and never believed in God, but at the very least, he had assumed that if there was life after death, you would find answers there. But why should death be any different from life, any more certain, any fairer?

He'd been pacing in circles twenty feet ahead of the van, eyes cast downward.

Now he looked up—

And froze.

Straight up the road, a football field's length away, a tall figure walked toward him.

When it saw him looking, it waved.

10

"Gertie!" David ran toward the van. "He's here!"

Gertie stuck her head out the window.

Lit by the moon, Richard cast a faint shadow on the asphalt.

She slid the tranquilizer pistol out from under her seat and checked the breach for the hundredth time to confirm that it was loaded. The weapon was ten inches long with a black metal barrel and a wooden handle. She pumped the wooden grip beneath the barrel to pressurize it and checked her sweatshirt pocket for the spare darts. She'd filled five after the events on the river.

Janelle leaned forward. "That's Richard! Did he just *wave?*"

Gertie opened her door. "Get in the driver's seat and wait for my signal."

"What signal?"

"You'll know." She stepped out and quietly pressed the door closed and strode up the street.

Richard swaggered toward her. He spread his arms.

A hundred meters away and closing.

Gertie planted herself in front of Richard's house. Let the bastard come to her.

He strolled. Eighty paces away now.

Seventy-five.

He began to skip.

Sixty.

Forty.

She ran her finger along the pistol's safety latch to ensure it was off.

Twenty paces now.

Fifteen.

She inhaled.

Calming breath.

In.

Out.

He stopped directly in front of her. She saw him clearly, a network of wriggling yellow-white eels wrapped around the young man he possessed. "Hello again," he said, "old friend."

Gertie raised her weapon.

"What do you have in that little toy?"

The hubris. She'd been counting on it.

She fired.

He didn't even try to duck. The dart pinned his shirt to his abdomen like a thumbtack. He looked down at it, amused.

Then he charged.

Gertie tried to sidestep, but he was too fast. He clotheslined her, and she slammed onto her back. She tucked her chin to avoid hitting her skull on the road, and then he was all over her, clawing her face and gripping her throat. She pulled at his wrists—couldn't breathe. He straddled her, pressing on her windpipe.

She slapped at him with her right hand. With her left, she dug into her sweatshirt pocket and gripped one of the extra darts, popped the cap with her thumb, and drove it into the boy's neck.

Richard—or Mr. Ugly—yanked the dart free and flung it onto the roadway. The movement cost him his center of gravity. Gertie slammed the tranquilizer gun against his chest and he tipped over backwards.

Coughing through the burning, choking sensation in her throat, she rolled to her stomach, got her legs under her, and rushed over to check that the boy was still breathing.

He was awake, but barely.

She kicked him in the side of the head, and his eyelids fell.

11

Janelle sat breathless, helpless as Gertie struggled with Richard.

It's not Richard.

It didn't even move like Richard.

The tranquilizers must have done their work, because he went limp in the street. Gertie stood over him, kicked him in a way that made Janelle wince, and turned and waved both hands at Janelle.

Janelle felt around the steering column, found the key, and turned it. She eased the van forward, parked next to Gertie and Richard's body.

Richard's chest rose and fell, however shallowly.

Now that he was unconscious, he looked like Richard again.

"Is he okay?"

Gertie ignored the question. "Help me."

Janelle joined her in the road. Gertie pulled the rear doors open. They stuck straight out from the back to create something of a screen on either side, blocking everything above their knees. Inside, sheet metal had been bolted into all the surfaces, including the interior handles. Runic symbols had been scraped into the metal. Janelle saw some words in English: *protection; circle; barrier; containment; confinement.* A sleeping bag and pillow lay on the floor. Gertie grabbed these and tossed them to Janelle.

"Put them in the passenger seat."

"Shouldn't we leave them for him?"

"No."

Janelle threw the bedding into the cab and slammed the door.

"Quiet!" Gertie hissed.

"Sorry."

On her return to the back, she spotted a long, plastic syringe lying on the ground near the rear passenger wheel. The dart that Gertie had stabbed into Richard's neck. She'd nearly run it over. Janelle stooped to pick it up and carefully slid it into her dress pocket.

Gertie gripped Richard by the ankles and dragged him to the back of the van. His arms stretched over his head and his shirt rode up to his neck. He snorted once. Gertie released his ankles and took a position by his head. She slipped her elbows under his armpits and lifted his upper half. His ass and legs remained on the pavement and his head rolled into his chest. She swung him around so his upper body was positioned nearest the van.

"Take his legs," Gertie commanded.

Janelle grabbed at his ankles, but he was too heavy and awkward. He kept slipping out of her grip, even when she grabbed the fabric of his jeans.

"Hold him under the knees. I'll get him up on the edge. I just need you to push."

Janelle repositioned.

Before she could lift, she saw movement to the right. The doors of the van only came out so far, hiding Gertie and most of Richard's upper body, but Janelle stood past the doors, in full view of any onlookers.

Several of the lights in Richard's house had come on, including the porch light, which illuminated Richard's father. He stood on the front steps in a bathrobe with his mouth open, coffee mug half raised. When he saw Janelle, he dropped the mug. It clattered on the steps and splashed black liquid onto his feet.

Then he was running down the lawn shouting his son's name.

PART 3
PASSENGERS

1

Ray went home after the Patel kid's service, took a shower, and lay on the sofa with a crackling fireplace looped on the TV. His house with Shawna had a real fireplace, and he'd collapse in front of it after long shifts. Now he dozed uneasily before snapping awake with the same near-panic that roused him three nights prior.

Check the police scanner.

He fought the urge, but couldn't just lay there.

He paced the kitchen, glaring at the scanner and telling himself he didn't need to turn it on, didn't want to turn it on, and so he simply wouldn't.

If there's nothing to it, then it won't hurt to listen. You won't hear a thing.

Sixteen minutes later, he pulled up to the Becker residence. It was 11:48 p.m.

He parked in front of the house, behind two patrol cars and a detective's SUV. Carlson and Schmidt were already on scene. John Becker sat on his front steps with his head practically between his knees.

Detective Carlson met Ray halfway down the driveway.

"This a recreational trip for you, Al?"

"Heard on the radio. Thought you could use some help."

"I'm not one to turn away a pair of hands."

Carlson filled him in. Mr. Becker had been inside, watching Sports Center, when he heard a car door slam. He thought it might be his son getting dropped off by friends. When he went to check, he claimed to see two women loading a body into the back of a black cargo van. One of the women was his son's friend, Janelle Winters. He was adamant the body was his son, though he didn't get a clear view above the waist.

"He says he spoke with the driver of the van this morning. Blonde woman. Claiming to be a reporter."

"Name?"

"He can't recall."

"Then I guess he didn't catch the license plate."

"That'd be nice, but no. He says there was an advertisement on the van, a decal, but he doesn't remember for what."

"At least it's something."

"I haven't gotten to the best part. So, our guy sees these ladies loading up this body, okay, and he runs out to confront them, but before he's halfway down the lawn, he claims the van up and disappears."

"You mean it drove off?"

"That's what I said. I said, 'You mean it drove off?' And he says, 'No, sir. It *disappeared*.' Says it was like a soap bubble going *pop*. What do you make of that?"

"A soap bubble going *pop*," Ray repeated.

"The arriving officer gave him a breathalyzer. It came back clean. No sign of drugs in the house. The BOLO's out on the van and its occupants. Patrol's knocking on doors. So far, no one's seen a thing. We checked the road, too, Al. Not so much as a tire track. You know this fella's son is the one who survived that incident on the highway the other night?"

"So is the girl."

"That's right. I thought I knew that name. Winters."

"Have we sent someone to her residence?"

"There's a unit en route. Schmidt and me were gonna head there next."

"All right. If you don't mind, I'd like to speak to Mr. Becker."

"He's all yours. Doubt you'll get much out of him."

Mr. Becker might have tipped over if Ray poked him. A shell of a person. He held two pieces of a broken coffee mug and idly pressed them back together as he relayed the events.

"You said you thought Richard might be getting dropped off by friends. Which friends was he supposed to be with?"

"I don't know. I thought I would catch him at the service."

"Jeffrey Patel's service?"

"That's right."

"When's the last time you saw your son?"

"Like I said, it's been a couple days."

"Two days?"

"I guess so."

"Forty-eight hours?"

"I guess so."

"Weren't you worried about him, after what happened on the highway?"

"You know I damn well was. That's why I was up. I just thought he needed space to— He lost his best friend." He clanked the pieces of mug together. "Maybe Janelle had something to do with that, too, do you think? She was the driver that night, you know."

"We'll look into it."

"She snatched my son, Officer." His voice wavered. "They used to snatch black folks, you know. In the old days. I grew up outside Baltimore, and people used to talk about the doctors coming and snatching people. Giving them STDs. You ever hear of Tuskegee?"

"I'm familiar."

"They gave black folks syphilis. How do you justify something like that? My God, what are they doing to my son? You were gonna charge him with murder. For defending his own life."

"I just want to make sure you're confident in what you saw tonight."

"I can spot a foul ball from two hundred feet away if it's an inch over the line. You don't think I'd recognize my son laying in the street? I know what I saw. Those girls snatched him. I saw Janelle clear as day. She looked right at me, knew I caught her in the act, and I don't know why you're standing here talking to me instead of doing something about it."

Ray motioned for Carlson and Schmidt to meet him down the driveway.

"Someone should stay with him," Ray said. "Maybe the kid shows up and saves us all a lot of trouble."

"Wouldn't that be nice," Schmidt muttered.

Carlson said, "I'll see about posting a patrolman here."

"Okay. Listen, you boys have enough on your plate. Why don't I take this off your hands? I'll head to Janelle Winters' place and let you know what I find."

"You want it, you got it, Al."

• • •

Mrs. Winters answered the door. She wore gray sweats and sneakers like she was preparing for a jog. She'd been crying. Her expression began as elation, as if she expected good news. Seeing Ray, the expression soured. "H-Hi. Can I help you?"

"Mrs. Winters?"

"Yes?"

Behind her, her husband poked his head out of a corridor.

"I'm Detective Alverson with the Fairfield Police Department."

"I just spoke to another officer," Mrs. Winters said. "Is there news?"

The husband approached the door like a nervous puppy.

"I was hoping to talk to Janelle, if she's available."

"She isn't here. I told the other guy something was wrong. She was supposed to be home hours ago, and her phone's going straight to voicemail. It's not like her."

"How long has it been since you've heard from her?"

"Almost five hours."

"And where did you see her last?"

"At the wake. Jeff's wake. We left around six. Janelle said she'd get a ride with Amy."

"Amy Pink?"

"Yes."

"Have you been in contact with Amy at all tonight?"

"She's not answering her phone, either."

"They're both respectable girls," the husband added.

"Why are you looking for her?" Mrs. Winters said. "The other fella wouldn't say."

"Someone claims to have witnessed your daughter participating in suspicious activity this evening."

Mrs. Winters clutched at her husband as if she might faint.

"What kind of suspicious activity?"

"We're trying to determine that. Does your daughter know anyone who drives a cargo van? Black, with a decal on the side?"

Something flashed in Mrs. Winters face. Her husband touched the small of her back. She flinched at his touch and said, "There was a woman here earlier today. A reporter. She said her name was Francesca White. She drove a van like that. Is Janelle in danger?"

"I honestly don't know. Do you remember anything about the van? Rust, or markings?"

"An advertisement. On the side. It was for a furniture place. Arlo's Furniture Warehouse. I thought it was strange because it was based in New York."

"What about the woman? Can you describe her?"

"Blonde, with a pixie cut. Maybe five feet tall."

"You said you spoke with her? Can you recall any specifics of the conversation?"

"Well like I said, she claimed to be a reporter and asked to speak to Nelly. I said no. That was really the extent of it. Detective, is this woman dangerous?"

"Do you recall what she was wearing? Any discernible features? Tattoos?"

"I'm sorry, I don't remember what she wore. A hoodie, maybe."

"Could you tell me what your daughter was wearing when you saw her last?"

"A black dress. We bought it earlier today, at the mall. And black stockings."

"What about Amy Pink?"

"Black slacks and a matching blouse. I think it was long sleeved."

"Do you know what Amy drives?"

"A Honda Civic. It's red, but I don't know what year."

"That's okay. Mrs. Winters, what is Janelle's relationship with Richard Becker?"

"Richard? They're friends. They're all friends. Nelly, Amy, and Richard."

"Do you have any reason to believe Janelle would want to harm Richard?"

"Harm him? What are you talking about?"

"Detective," Mr. Winters cut in, "I think you owe us some explanations here. These questions— I don't know what you're getting at, but there's no way our daughter would intentionally hurt anyone, especially Richard."

"I didn't mean to startle you. Your daughter's probably with Amy. They've had a terrible trauma. If I were a betting man, I'd put money on Janelle coming home any time now. If she does, would you give me a call?"

He slipped Mrs. Winters his card. She took it gingerly, fingers trembling. "We'll do that."

. . .

A brief call to dispatch confirmed the make and model of Amy Pink's vehicle. 2015 Honda Civic, red. Her address put her down the hill and across the river, in the Westwood Manor Mobile Home Park. He took Glenwood to Warren St. down to Central Ave and headed toward the bridge past Rapprochement Park. As the park came up on his left, he spotted what appeared to be a Honda Civic parked near the stone bison. He couldn't tell the color in the dark until he pulled into the lot and shined his headlights on it. Red. The license plate matched Amy's.

There was nobody inside the car. He peered through the windows and shined his mag light on the front seat. Someone had left a cell phone in the cupholder. The notification light was blinking.

The park itself appeared abandoned. It was near midnight and the only people who came out here at this hour were not the sort teenage girls should hang around. He expanded his search from the parking lot to the butterfly garden. The benches sat empty, the flowers closed up.

He shined his light at every shadow. Maybe they parked here and walked to one of the bars in the area. They weren't of drinking age, but that didn't stop a lot of kids. Hell, they deserved a drink after all they'd been through. If he found them, he just might join them.

Or they had vanished into thin air.

That bothered him. John Becker saying the van disappeared before his eyes.

Sound familiar, Ray?

People didn't just vanish. Logic did not break down because someone saw something weird. You don't throw out the foundations of mathematics because one equation doesn't balance. So, when it came down to it, even if he believed Mr. Becker *thought* he saw a van disappear, he did not believe that it happened any more than he believed Amy Pink and Janelle Winters had gone *pop* in this car.

He was about to get in his vehicle and head to the nearest bar when a sound caught his attention. A sound in the background—it had been there all along, but just now registered, below the noise of traffic on the bridge. A rushing, almost roaring sound, not unlike wind or fire.

Water.

He'd gotten so used to the wall that he sometimes forgot about the river. You couldn't even see it over the sides of the bridge when driving. Now he shined his flashlight at the pale gray brick and the razor wire looped over the top. It stretched unbroken to the east for a great distance. To the west, it disappeared behind a squat old building. He had the strangest notion there was something waiting for him behind the building.

The gate was maybe a hundred feet from the park, concealed behind the railroad building. He tried to wedge himself through the gap without causing more damage to the gate, but he was too big by about a hundred and fifty pounds.

He grabbed hold of the bent frame and put his back to the wall for leverage and pushed until he was red in the face and his palms ached and the metal curled away, adding six inches to the gap.

He slid through.

He had never been on the opposite side of the wall, but from the graffiti and physical damage to its foundation, it was clear plenty of others had. He directed his light at the riverbank and saw nothing but black water and weeds climbing the path, though he couldn't shake the feeling that someone was watching him from below the surface of that blackness.

The same uncanny sensation that brought him here led him up the path toward the bridge.

The beam of his flashlight landed on two horrors in sequence.

The first lay on what appeared to be an open sleeping bag—a mutilated animal.

The second made his heart sink, so he had to crouch or risk losing his balance.

Directly below the bridge, a young woman in black slacks and a matching blouse lay in a pool of blood.

2

The back of the van was pitch black and humid. The humming of the tires on the road vibrated Gertie's bones. Sweat drenched her clothes, and she struggled to stay conscious. Her own thoughts seemed to buzz in the center of her forehead, existence itself nothing but a bad migraine. Richard lay over her, limp, all 180 pounds of him pinning her to the floor. She felt his abdomen rising and falling. Mr. Ugly was sandwiched between their bodies, a frigid glob of aethereal goo that made her sick to be near. She didn't know if the creature was conscious while Richard was, or if it was laughing at her even while Richard was out cold.

When Mr. Becker came out of the house and spotted them, Gertie had acted quickly, centering herself the best she could and throwing a veil over Mr. Becker's mind. He looked through them while she hugged Richard from behind and yanked him into the vehicle with the last of her strength. She hollered at Janelle to shut them in and drive the fucking van right fucking now.

She'd heard police cruisers coming, their sirens blasting, and saw each driver clearly in her mind as they approached. She pushed into their heads and wrapped them in the veil. The vehicles blasted by, and she felt Janelle pull over to avoid multiple collisions.

She never had to hide from so many people back to back before.

Light-headed and nauseous, she slid out from under Richard and flung herself at the panel that separated the rear from the cab and pounded with both fists. "Pull the fuck over!"

Janelle brought them to a gradual stop, the van tilting right and crunching on gravel.

A moment later, Janelle flung the doors open to reveal a narrow road in the middle of what appeared to be a field of tiny corn stalks. A soybean farm, Gertie guessed.

Gertie leapt past the girl, acid vomit rushing up her esophagus. She reached the grassy shoulder before it spilled from her mouth. She wiped her chin and turned and saw the van doors wide open. "Close the doors!"

Janelle flinched, then did as she was told.

Gertie's whole body gave out. She dropped into the grass.

Drained. She couldn't see or hear David. The ground slid beneath her like liquid.

This didn't feel like victory.

The fact that they'd been spotted changed things. The cops were looking for them. She couldn't keep them cloaked anymore. Not for a while, anyway. She needed sleep. Lots of it.

"Have to get off the road," she muttered.

"What?" Janelle stood behind her, chewing a thumbnail. "I didn't hear you. Hey, are you okay?"

"Need to get... somewhere. Don't know... what to do."

. . .

Janelle, too, felt the earth sliding beneath her. She had driven northwest on a whim because there wasn't much out here. She expected Gertie to take over.

"I thought you had this worked out."

Gertie groaned and spat. "You know anywhere... low profile... hide away... few days?"

"Uh. Like where?"

Gertie snorted, spat. "Dunno."

"I'm not, like, in the mafia."

Gertie sprawled backward onto the ground, arms above her head. "Everything... spinning."

Janelle racked her brain. She imagined camping out behind a Walmart, a big silver tarp draped over the van, Gertie whipping holy water at it and reading passages from the bible.

"Secluded place," Gertie rasped. "Abandoned... woods... crack house... something."

How long were they supposed to hide? Was she going to be in a criminal database now, her face on the wall of the DMV with the rest of America's Most Wanted?

No time to get anxious about that. Had to think. Where would a criminal hide a van, short of dumping it in a lake somewhere? She scanned the plains, the knee-high crops. If this were a cornfield, they could drive down one of the farmer's paths and listen for approaching vehicles while they decided what to do. Stay a day or two. Why not? Shuck corn right off the stalk and chew it like cartoon characters, crumbs flying out the corners of their mouths.

But this was not a cornfield. This was soy. A tent could come in handy. Or one of those old silver campers like the one she and her parents used to have at—

"Oh my God!"

"*What*?"

"My dad owns a farm!"

Gertie propped herself on an elbow. "Huh?"

"Well, sort of. I mean, it *was* a farm. We haven't been there in, like, ten years. It was my Great Uncle Chuck's. When he got sick, he was gonna give it to my cousin, but I guess my cousin was just gonna sell it, so Chuck gave it to my dad. He has no idea how to run a farm, but he didn't wanna sell it and, like, offend my dead uncle, so it's still ours."

"... kind of farm?"

"Hay, I think. There's a small lake in the back, and a camper. We stayed there sometimes when I was little."

"No one's there?"

"I don't think so."

"How far?"

"Two hours? I think I'd recognize the road. It's outside Darwin."

Gertie attempted to wobble to her feet. "Let's go." She lost her balance and went tumbling into the soy stalks.

Janelle helped her up. "Easy," she said. "What's wrong with you?"

"Wiped out."

She had to push Gertie up and into the passenger seat. Her head lolled.

"What about Richard?" Janelle said.

"Wuh 'bout 'im?"

"Is he okay?"

"Fine. Need rest… watch for… cops." Gertie shut her eyes. Saliva oozed out of her mouth and down her chin. Janelle pushed her legs out of the way and shut the door.

Little more than halfway to Darwin, they drove by a county sheriff's car in a speed trap on the decline of a hill. Janelle kept even pressure on the gas. The cruiser never moved. They must have caught him sleeping. Not long after that, Richard banged on the panel behind her head, screaming for help. Janelle set her jaw and tightened her grip on the wheel, thinking that somewhere on this road she must have crossed the border from sanity into madness.

3

Charlee Pink answered the door in pajamas. She took the news as well as anyone could.

She shook her head as if she'd been insulted. "Sorry, what?"

"Her body was discovered about an hour ago," Ray said. "Again, I'm very sorry."

The news dawned on her as it often does in these moments: gradually. She pressed a hand to her mouth and slumped against the doorway, lowering her body to the floor. She didn't howl or shout, but wept into her palms and asked questions he couldn't answer: "What? How? Who would do this? Why? What do you mean, foul play?" Each word forced out through sobs.

Bartov stooped to help the girl to her feet and escorted her inside. Ray followed.

In the kitchen, she fumbled with the electric stove and a tea kettle, a ritual that seemed to help her nerves. The detectives stood in silence and waited for the kettle to boil, and when it did, she offered them a cup. Bartov accepted, but never drank it. She led them into the main room.

It was a decent place. An AC hummed in the window. A large TV sat on an entertainment stand across from a half circle of mismatched sofas, scratched up coffee table in the center. In one corner, a plush armchair sat beside an end table occupied by textbooks and notebooks. Amy's schoolwork, probably.

Charlee sat on the largest sofa and draped a fleece blanket around her shoulders. She drew her legs beneath her and rested her tea on her thighs.

Ray said, "You're Amy's legal guardian?"

Amy shifted. "I don't think I can do this right now. I think I might throw up."

Bartov cleared his throat. "That's all right, we can come—"

"Your sister was murdered," Ray said.

Bartov's mouth snapped shut and Charlee went as rigid as if she'd been slapped.

"We need your help."

She laced her fingers around the front of her mug, then unlaced them. "I'll try."

"Do you know where Amy was tonight?"

"She went to Jeff's calling hours. She was there all afternoon."

Bartov scribbled notes.

"Had you spoken with her?"

"This morning, before I went to work. And on my way home, at the wake."

"Where do you work?"

"Walmart."

"How was Amy acting when you saw her last? Did you notice anything unusual?"

She shook her head and wiped her nose with her wrist.

Bartov chimed in: "Charlee, can you think of anyone who wanted to hurt your sister? An ex-boyfriend? A rival?"

"A rival? No. She was with Jeff for like three years. She never had another boyfriend. We didn't talk, like the way some sisters talk, but I would've known if there was something off. Everyone loved her." She pulled tissues from a box on the coffee table and blew her nose.

Ray said, "Did she know anyone who drives a cargo van?"

"Not that I know of."

"Someone I spoke with tonight mentioned a blonde woman who drove one. Francesca White. New York plates, with an advertisement on the side for a furniture store. Does that sound familiar?"

Amy's forehead wrinkled. "The reporter?"

"You know who I'm referring to?"

"I don't know her, but she was here this morning. She talked to Amy. Are you saying she had something to do with... with all this?"

"I'm just trying to get a clear picture. Do you know what she and Amy talked about?"

"I only caught some of it. She was asking the same things as other reporters. They talked for like five minutes."

"How did Amy seem afterward?"

"Fine. Annoyed, maybe."

Ray continued this line of questioning. Half an hour after "Francesca White's" visit, Charlee left for work and stopped at Jeff's wake around 4:30 p.m. She'd been home ever since, but Amy never returned. Yes, Charlee wondered why her sister didn't come home, but she wasn't worried—she figured she was still with Jeff's parents, or maybe Janelle. No, she hadn't seen Richard or Janelle since the highway incident. Other than the wake, Amy hadn't even left the house. The only people she saw were some of Jeff's relatives who came by for pictures and videos for the service.

She provided details about their relationship and family history. They used to live in Iowa, with their addict parents. It was a matter of time before something bad happened to Amy—she was fourteen when they left. A few of the creeps her parents kept around had started to notice her. Charlee got her out of there as soon as she could and they hadn't seen or heard from their parents since.

Charlee squeezed a tissue in her fist. "She was supposed to be better off up here. I know this place isn't much, but we were doing okay. I kept the lights on. She had good friends."

"How do you think her friends were holding up, after the events on the highway?"

"I don't know. I didn't see them."

"Janelle Winters was Amy's best friend, right? Besides Jeff."

"They were more like sisters than me and Amy sometimes."

"What about Janelle and Richard? Were they an item?"

"I didn't get involved with Amy's friends. Amy's embarrassed by the trailer." Tears swelled in her eyes.

"Did you ever hear of animosity between her friends? Someone getting jealous, getting angry? Anything like that?"

She sat up straight and placed her tea on the coffee table. "Amy had a good life. That's all I wanted for her. She was better than me, and I was glad. I never told her that. I never told her I was proud of her. I never even told her that I liked Jeff. They were gonna go to school together. She got scholarships. Did you know that? She was so determined." Charlee shut her eyes and failed to squeeze back a torrent of tears. At last she got her voice back enough to say, "This can't be real, right? Are you really here? Is this… is this happening?"

. . .

Ray and Bartov sat in their vehicle down the road, listening to chatter on the radio. Bartov read his notes and sucked his teeth. "You think this is connected with the abduction?"

Ray had brought him up to speed on Mr. Becker's story. The van linked the incidents, but if it had indeed gone *pop* like a soap bubble, it had yet to *pop* back. They'd expanded the BOLO to neighboring counties, but so far there were no sightings.

"Look at who's involved," Ray said. "Amy Pink and Janelle Winters are last seen at the wake of their mutual friend. A few hours later, Pink winds up with a fatal wound in the base of her skull and Winters is spotted loading an unconscious black male into the back of a van with the help of an unknown woman. Before you ask, I looked up this Francesca White."

"An alias?"

"Most likely."

"Still sounds like we have a suspect or two."

"It does, doesn't it."

Bartov stuck his notes in his pocket. "You seem skeptical."

Ray said nothing. The dots should have connected, but something was off.

"What are you thinking?"

"We need to find that van. And I want to talk to the Patels."

"The Patels?"

"Jeffrey Patel's folks. The dead boy. Maybe they saw something at the wake. We should keep some eyes on Janelle Winters' place, too. Becker's is covered."

Bartov had his pad out again. "Anything else?"

"A double cheeseburger, milkshake, and a large fry."

"Coming right up."

4

Janelle drove up and down the main road through Darwin looking for the turnoff. She was beginning to second-guess her memory. Richard screaming and flinging himself against the walls didn't help. She found what she thought was the right street, and thirty minutes later spotted the marker for the private drive.

At the bottom of the drive, the farmhouse stood on the left, half-hidden from the road by the massive walnut tree surrounded now by waist-high grass. The house's siding crawled with creeper vines. Aunt Carolyn would die all over again if she saw the state of the place.

Janelle parked in the driveway. Unseen animals rustled the grass.

Gertie still slept. Janelle prodded her in the ribs. "Hey."

Gertie cracked one eye.

"We're here."

Gertie sat up.

"Please!" Richard hollered. "Let me out! Janelle! Somebody!"

Gertie said, "That been going on long?"

"Yes."

"Lucky you." She nodded at the house. "Think it's unlocked?"

"I don't think we should stay in the house."

"I've slept in this van long enough. That's a perfectly good house."

"We're visible from the main road down here. We're at the bottom of a hill. See?"

Gertie craned her neck.

"There's a lake farther back. And there should be an old camper, unless they sold it."

Gertie wiped sleep-drool from her chin. "It's your world. I'm just living in it."

There should have been a tractor path beside the house, but it was so overgrown she couldn't find it. She had to get out of the van and kick through the grass until she uncovered the ruts. She climbed back into the van and eased through the overgrowth. Grass slapped at the undercarriage, pinging off the meal. Not far along the trail, the old barn loomed out of the dark like a ghost ship. The path went back another quarter mile. It took a long time to traverse. To stay on the path, Janelle had to feel for the tires riding up on the tractor ruts.

"What'd you say they grew?" Gertie said.

"Hay. All of this was hay."

She ran straight into the wooden sign. She remembered it as soon as she hit it, but the thump startled her more than it should have. She backed the van up and the headlights picked out the sign's bold white lettering: *St. Chuck's Lake.* It was an old joke she never understood, something between Uncle Chuck and her father.

The camp was just on the other side of the next hillock.

The lake was the only thing not covered in grass. Two hundred feet across, roughly circular, with a forest on the opposite bank. Uncle Chuck had owned a few acres of those woods.

The headlights glinted off the silver trailer to the right, roughly half the size of a school bus. Like the farmhouse, it too was being digested by nature.

"Park away from the trailer," Gertie said. "Over there." She pointed to the left bank.

"Why?"

Gertie gestured at the panel behind them.

"*Pleeeeaaaaase!*" Richard yowled.

"He's not gonna stop."

Janelle backed the van into the suggested area and shut it off. Night clapped over them the instant she flipped off the headlights. Gertie picked up the pillow and sleeping bag her feet rested on and tucked them under her arms. They both clamored out.

The night was a cacophony of crickets and frogs, the sky flat black.

"Please *heeelp!*"

Gertie kicked the side of the van. "You're wasting your breath, dumbshit!"

"Janelle! Don't leave me!"

Janelle clapped her hands over her ears. *It's not Richard.*

Gertie snapped on a flashlight. The ground was muddy from recent rain. They kicked through the grass, which was tall enough to scratch their chins. Crickets and grasshoppers and other flying things bounced around them, landed on their legs and arms and careened into the night. Fireflies winked along the lake's edge and bats chirruped and wheeled overhead.

The trailer was unlocked. The air inside stank of mildew and mothballs. There were bunks on either side. Janelle claimed the far bunk. There were no sheets. When she perched on the edge of the bunk, dust erupted from the mattress and spun in the flashlight's beam.

Gertie said, "Glad I don't have allergies."

"When do we do the exorcism?"

Gertie flopped onto her bunk. "We'll talk about it tomorrow."

"First thing."

"First thing, yeah."

"I'm serious."

"Me too."

Janelle studied her. Her pale, boney face skeletal in the light. "Okay."

Gertie was snoring within minutes, but Janelle lay there for what felt like hours. Every few minutes, Richard would release a wail: "Neeeellyyy! Pleeeaaaase!"

You aren't Richard. You killed Amy. You killed Jeff.

"Heeeelp meeeeeee!"

She couldn't listen to it. She crawled out of bed and opened the trailer door.

Outside, she whispered in case David was listening, "I'm going for a walk."

A portion of sky had cleared, revealing a bright moon mirrored in the lake. She pushed through the grass to the water's edge, crouched there a while. Every time a bug plopped onto the surface or a fish kissed the air, the moon's twin wavered.

"*Neeeellyyyy!*"

She made her way to the right bank, leapt a muddy rivulet and climbed a slight incline toward the trees. She stood at the edge of the forest searching for a deer trail she used to know. She couldn't find it, but continued anyway.

She didn't know how far she'd go. Far enough that she couldn't hear Richard.

Mosquitos buzzed in her ears and divebombed her neck. A familiar obstruction rose out of the darkness ahead. A misshapen lump two thirds the height of the trees.

Her parents called it The Fallen Star. A massive boulder at odds with the rest of the forest. One night, over the campfire and smores, her mom said it was a star that fell from the sky when God sneezed. Janelle was too old to believe it, but the nickname stuck. Now she ran her hands over its rough, lumpy surface. She found enough grip for her fingertips and bit her hands into the rock and hoisted herself up one handhold at a time.

It took more effort than she expected, but she made it to the top, where it was relatively flat. The mosquitos didn't bother her as much up here and she heard only the sounds of nature.

She curled up with her hands under her cheek and tried to sleep without dreaming.

5

Ray spent the night interviewing Jeff's family and most of the morning making phone calls. The majority of local gas stations never turned on their CCTV cameras, and those that did couldn't recall a black cargo van or anyone resembling the wanted individuals. For the last two hours, he'd been on the phone with folks in New York State.

Finding Arlo's Furniture Warehouse had been a piece of cake. The company website was still live. It listed the owner's contact information, but the phone was out of service. He followed the trail to New York's missing person database.

David Arlo had been missing for five years.

On a hunch, Ray called the police department in Arlo's hometown of Rockwall, New York. The desk sergeant connected him to the chief investigator, who retained an unusually good memory of the case. Arlo's disappearance was one of several unsolved missing persons cases from that time. Arlo's grandfather and his business partner had also vanished.

No evidence of foul play. No crime. No bodies. The investigator didn't know anything about a van, but gave him the number to a guy who handled estate sales. If Arlo owned a business in New York, he said, one bank or another had him by the balls.

The estate guy put him in touch with another, who connected him with a woman named Ashley Peterson, who had worked directly with David Arlo many times. He used to buy the furniture left over from her estate sales. She said Ray's hunch was correct; David Arlo was in debt when he disappeared. He had a habit of taking out high interest loans. Some who knew him suspected he skipped town to escape the credit card companies. Peterson didn't think so. He was a good, honest guy. When the bank came to collect Arlo's debts, Peterson ran the sale. Lucky for Ray, she kept detailed records of every transaction going back ten years.

The van was a 2013 Nissan NV Cargo van in black, with 165,000 miles on it at the time Arlo disappeared. Peterson sold it to a woman named Gertrude Morgenstern. She'd come to Peterson as if they'd known each other for years and offered to pay extra so it wouldn't go to auction. Strangely, Peterson had a difficult time remembering what she looked like—she had a great memory for faces.

Ray thanked Peterson profusely and hung up.

He had a name.

And for some reason, he recognized it.

Morgenstern. Why was that so familiar?

A hasty Google search jogged his memory.

He actually gasped.

Bartov glanced over the edge of his cubicle before ducking down again.

The Camp Daydream Antifreeze Massacre had made national news at the time, and the suspect's name was on the FBI's most wanted list. Shocking as this was, he put it aside to concentrate on the woman. Best not to jump to conclusions.

Gertrude Morgenstern had two outstanding speeding tickets. One from Virginia. The most recent from Oregon. They were issued less than three months apart.

What was she doing taking a cargo van from Virginia to Oregon?

And why the hell was she abducting teenagers in Minnesota?

The Camp Daydream Antifreeze Massacre.

Jesus.

Obermeyer wasn't in yet, so he called his personal cell.

He answered on the second ring. "Obermeyer here."

Ray told him what he'd found.

"Keep this quiet," Obermeyer said. "Not a word until we're sure."

"I know."

"It's probably nothing."

"I know."

"Call me if you find anything else."

His head swam. He tried to see a pattern in all this. Something logical.

When all else failed, follow the evidence. Use simple math.

What did they have? A dead girl, a dead cat, and a vanishing van—all linked to a serial killer from Kentucky and a woman with possible ties to a mass murderer in New York State. It felt like two mountains were about to converge, and Ray stood directly between them.

6

Janelle woke early. The air was humid. The trees wet with dew. She had dreamt all night of blood and rotting flesh. Mosquitos left welts down her arms and legs. She lay on her stomach and lowered her legs over the side of the boulder, clutching at the grooves in the rock. She was halfway down when she fell. It hurt her pride more than anything.

She walked to the trailer, stuck her head in.

Gertie snored and rolled over.

Janelle went out again.

She was thirsty. Gertie had a few water bottles in her duffel bag, but they would need more. Her parents always said the lake was full of bacteria and chemical runoff. The house might still have running water.

It was slow walking. She stuck to the ruts the van had left, but the grass was starting to spring back. She wished she had boots.

She detoured at the barn. The front doors were open. Old hay and a decade's worth of dead leaves matted the ground. It used to house bales of hay stacked so high she could touch the ceiling when she climbed them. A gray bucket sat on its side in one corner.

She continued to the house.

The front door was locked. She wondered if she could break a window, but wasn't that desperate. Gertie probably could have used her Jedi bullshit to open it in a jiffy.

She cupped her hands over her eyes and peered through the front window.

The front room was bare. No furniture. No area rugs. No bookshelves. No piano.

She circled to the back door. It opened right up. Inside, she drifted from room to room, finding nothing but daddy longlegs, dust, and memories. The faucets were all dry.

She locked the back door on her way out, feeling defeated.

She cut a line through the overgrown backyard toward the tractor ruts and nearly crashed into the old water pump. She'd forgotten that Uncle Chuck and Aunt Carolyn had a well.

She stomped around the grass near the spigot, matting it down to form a circle. She retrieved the old bucket from the barn and placed it under the spigot and pumped with both hands. It was so rusted the handle barely moved.

Finally, she got the handle to pump once, twice, three times.

A spurt of brown water burped into the bucket. She continued pumping until the water ran clear, and she dumped the rusty water and banged the bucket out in the grass and filled it again until it was nearly brimming. She cupped her hands and scooped the water from the bucket and drank.

. ▪ ▪ .

Gertie woke to the sound of birds chirping. She didn't know where she was. She lay in her sleeping bag with an unfamiliar, 70's-style floral fabric close overhead.

She sat up, and the interior of the trailer settled into the previous day's timeline.

She found David outside, leaning against the trailer and squinting into the distance. She didn't know what time it was, but the day was already humid and there was not a cloud in sight.

"Morning," David said.

She grunted. She could have slept another six hours. "Know where she went?"

"Toward the house. She slept in the woods."

"Think she's making a run for it?"

"If she's smart."

In the daytime, the lake was a beautiful blue oval. Dragonflies zipped across it like toy helicopters and a thousand tiny bugs divoted the surface.

"We did it, David."

"I know."

"We fucking got him. He's in the back of our fucking van."

"I'm still trying to wrap my head around it."

"You don't know how to relax. We should get a keg."

"I'd love a drink, but, uh, it goes right through me."

"Whoa, David. Could you be developing a sense of humor?

He ignored the comment.

"We got the motherfucker, man!" If she could have smacked David on the arm, she would have. She just wanted to see him smile for once. Not that she was Miss Chipper herself, but she sure as hell smiled now.

"There's still the other thing."

"What other thing?"

"Richard."

"Later. Right now," she pulled her dress over her head and unsnapped her bra and wiggled out of her underwear, "I'm going for a dip."

She kicked through the grass and picked her way over a patch of mud and stones and ran into the water halfway up her shins and dove headlong into the blue shallows, shocked awake by the sudden cold. The bottom of the lake blossomed with silt as she kicked back to the surface.

She came up in the middle of the lake and blew a spray of mist into the sky. David watched her from the shore. She wondered idly what would happen if he tried to swim. Would he skip across the surface, or sink to the bottom?

He had no interest in finding out, apparently.

She ducked back under, spinning, twirling, somersaulting until she was dizzy.

Giddy for the first time in years.

When she broke the surface again, Janelle was just cresting the hill. She carried what appeared to be a bucket of water. She hauled it to the lake's edge.

"David thought you ran away," Gertie said.

"I found water."

"I thought we had plenty right here."

"You'd have to boil it."

"We could do that."

"Do we have anything to boil it in?"

"Oh."

"There's no food in the house. I looked."

"We'll figure something out."

Janelle took her bucket to the trailer and went inside.

Gertie heard cupboards slamming. She swam ashore and found her dress where she left it and used it like a towel and slipped into her underwear and bra.

Inside the trailer, Janelle had all the drawers and cupboards open. She had placed a single can of baked beans on the counter.

"Good find," Gertie said.

"It won't last long."

"Are there fish in this pond?"

"There used to be."

Janelle reached deep into each drawer and cupboard.

Gertie sat on her bunk. "What are you looking for?"

"Why don't you read my mind and find out?"

"It's easier if you tell me."

Janelle knelt on the counter and felt around the top of the cupboards. She pulled down a dusty fishing pole in two pieces. It was small enough that Gertie thought it was a toy until she saw the fishing line wound around the poles and knotted in the reel.

Janelle pinched the rusty hook and held it to the light.

"Nice," Gertie said.

Janelle beamed. "This used to be mine."

Outside, Richard yowled like a rooster greeting the dawn: "*Heeeeelllp!*"

"Here we go," Gertie said.

Janelle placed the disassembled pole on the countertop. "When do we start?"

"Start what?"

"The exorcism."

"Told you," David called from outside.

Gertie stood and moved toward the door. "I gotta put on some clothes."

Janelle stepped into her path. "What aren't you telling me?"

Gertie leaned against her bunk. There was no easy way to say it, and the girl wasn't going anywhere. "I may have fudged certain details."

Janelle went stiff.

"Okay. Look. I lied about the exorcism."

"What do you mean? What about it?"

"I mean, we won't be doing it. It doesn't— They're not real. I mean, some are, but they're only for people with a ghost tethered to them. Plus, they're usually fatal."

"Fatal for who?"

"The host. But Mr. Ugly's not a ghost. He's got his hooks into Richard. There's no getting him off. Even if there was, I'd have to do it from inside the van, and that's not gonna happen."

"You never planned on saving him."

"I would love to. There's just no way."

"I don't understand. How does he get out of the van?"

Gertie let her work it out. No exorcisms. Richard and the creature in a sealed box. Mr. Ugly would dissipate without a host.

"You're gonna let him starve to death?"

"You have to understand. Richard was lost the moment Mr. Ugly got into him. I'm sorry. I really am."

Janelle's face flushed deep purple. Her friends had been killed. She and Richard were the only ones left. Now she was supposed to stand by and let Richard die, too?

Gertie understood how that felt. Better than Janelle knew.

"It'll take a few days, tops. He'll pass out from dehydration first. And when he's... Mr. Ugly won't last long."

"Fuck you."

"Janelle."

"You lied to me." Tears brimmed in her eyes. "You're a murderer."

"Yes," Gertie said.

Janelle flung open the door and stormed out.

Gertie watched her. She cut around the right bank of the lake and climbed the hill into the woods. She had every right to that anger. Gertie wasn't about to convince her this was a worthwhile sacrifice. It was just a death sentence, and Gertie would see it through. She had no choice, and despite what she may think, neither did Janelle.

7

Ray spent the rest of his morning in meetings. First with Obermeyer and the other investigators. Then with half the police force—a roomful of pissed off cops looking for the person or persons senselessly destroying lives in their community. They all had their tasks. The FPD, the state troopers, county boys, and everyone in between would be looking for Gertrude Morgenstern, Janelle Winters, and Richard Becker. After obtaining a warrant for her banking records, they confirmed that Morgenstern was in the area. She'd used her credit card Wednesday night at a Holiday Inn. Physical descriptions had gone out on social media and mainstream news.

In the afternoon, a call came in about a vagrant's body discovered near a suburban housing tract. Ray and Bartov interviewed the woman who discovered the corpse. The young woman had been walking her dog when she came across what she thought was a lump of clothes on the hill. That made five violent homicides in a week—more than the previous two years combined.

It was dark out by the time he returned to the office, feeling like an old gym sock.

Running on three hours of sleep in the past 48 hours, he sat at his desk and pulled up the video clip of Richard Becker the transcription agency had sent.

Why was he afraid to look? To listen?

He plugged his earbuds in and expanded the video and hit play.

Richard was explaining why Janelle had been driving the jeep for so long.

"We were all taking turns, and it was hers. That was all. She would have said something if—" The rest was cut off by some sort of static.

But there was something underlying the static. It was broken up. Staccato.

Hsssss-huc-huc-huc-ssssss.

It cleared.

"Did you wake up before or after she hit the man in the road?" Ray asked.

And the video ended.

Ray rewound, cranking the volume until Richard was practically screaming in his ears.

Then the static, and the other thing.

He flung the earbuds away. They smacked the screen and rebounded and dangled off the desk.

He closed the window and rubbed his face.

He was so exhausted he might have imagined it, like he imagined the dead boy on the highway and the shadow in the conference room and his vision at the funeral home.

So go ahead and take another listen. If it's not real, there's nothing to hear.

He did not take another listen. The noise still echoed in his ears.

He gripped the edge of his desk so hard his knuckles cracked.

It's your job to accept the evidence, Ray. Stop running from it.

That needling voice wasn't going to shut up. He knew this from experience. It would get louder and louder until his hands went numb, and he lost his breath and collapsed through another glass door or drove his SUV into a goddamn telephone pole.

He hadn't imagined what he heard any more than the transcriber who found it so troubling they emailed Ray to confirm that *they* weren't losing their shit.

Say it, Ray. What did you hear?

Laughter.

He heard laughter in the static.

<h1 style="text-align:center">8</h1>

Gertie retrieved her duffle bag from the van. Mr. Ugly screamed like he was on fire.

She slipped into gym shorts and a tank top and searched the camp for anything useful. Discovered a wooden picnic table beside the trailer, swallowed by grass. She set to tearing the grass out and tamping it down with her feet. When she had the space somewhat walkable, she took the child's fishing pole from the camper and placed it on the table and tried to fit it together. No one had ever taken her fishing. The pole clearly connected with the handle, but the line was a mess of knots.

David sat across from her. "You should talk to her."

"You ever go fishing? Help me out here."

"Gertie."

She set the pole down. "She wants to be alone."

"You should have told her."

"What difference does it make?"

David sulked.

"We shouldn't have brought her," Gertie said.

"Why did you, exactly?"

She said nothing.

David said, "You need to tell her about your father."

"That has nothing to do with this."

"Bullshit."

She fiddled with the fishing pole some more before flinging it into the grass. She cursed and followed Janelle's tracks to the woods. They took her to a narrow deer trail.

The girl was hiding nearby. Gertie sensed her.

She found the boulder, stood at the base and shouted up. "This is a good spot. I can't see you at all from down here."

Silence.

"Janelle, we need to talk. I'm coming up."

She was not as limber as she used to be. Years behind a steering wheel had softened her core. It took a long time and some short falls, but she made it to the top.

Janelle sat cross-legged in the center of the rock, her back to Gertie.

"I should have told you," Gertie said. "You're right. I'm an asshole."

More silence.

"Listen, there's more I should tell you."

Janelle said, "I don't care."

"I deserve that, but you should know the whole truth."

"Whatever."

MR. UGLY

9

After the events at the warehouse, David was not keen on being labeled a serial killer, and Gertie may not have been thinking all that clearly, so, in a panic, she used the tarp that the corpses lay on to transport them from the warehouse to David's van to the woods behind her house. She dug a mass grave and rolled the bodies in. She took the tools apart and flung them into various lakes around the region.

Weeks passed. She rarely left the house, stopped going to her job, avoided phone calls. Her supervisor came by one morning, calling out that if Gertie was inside she'd better open up or he'd call the cops to make sure she wasn't dead. She opened the door and said she was fine, but she would not be returning to work. Her manager smelled the alcohol on her breath. Said something about Gertie getting help if she needed it. Gertie shut the door.

She drank heavily. Between nightly binges, she interrogated David about the creature. He told her everything. He didn't know where it came from, but sensed a cold, vast emptiness. She filled notebooks with thoughts.

She took up smoking again. She hardly slept. One night, when her meth head neighbor threw one of his crowded parties with a bonfire as high as the trees, she joined in. She found new ways to escape reality, mainlined them into her veins and faded out, past the scolding visage of the ghost tethered to her body and into a drug-induced nothingness.

Her father called occasionally, and when she was sober enough to answer, she did. He still talked about Jesus too much, but she couldn't help sensing the sadness underlying his words.

One night, drunk and hazy from something her neighbor rolled into a joint, so fucked up she hadn't seen David in hours, she was startled out of something close to sleep by banging on her front door. She assumed it was her neighbor coming over to kill time. But when she got the door open, her father filled the frame. He wore a cockeyed grin.

"Dad? What're you doing here?"

"*Pew*," he said. "Have you been drinking?"

She squinted to keep him in focus. She swore he was supposed to be out of town that week. His church had a nature camp somewhere west of Rockwall, where parents took their kids to let others babysit them in the name of communing with God. Her father had volunteered there for the past several years, often for weeks at a time.

She must have had the date wrong.

Self-conscious, she stumbled through the kitchen in search of coffee and found some in the pot. She spilled half on its journey from pot to mug and sipped it cold. It tasted moldy, so she abandoned it on the kitchen counter and made her way to the living room to flop on the sofa.

Her father paced the house, eyeballing the mess. Dirty clothes on every surface. Empty bottles and cans. Carpet stains and dishes with bits of food caked on. At least the mice weren't out tonight.

"This is how you live?"

"I would have cleaned if I knew you were coming."

"I wouldn't worry about it."

She caught a flash of David standing behind her father, yelling, but she couldn't hear him. He hated when she got so fucked up she couldn't see him. Told her it was like dying all over again.

"Dad," she said, "aren't you supposed to be at camp?"

"I wanted to see you."

"Oh. Uh. Why?"

"I need a reason to see my daughter?"

"That's not what I— I just mean it's sort of late."

He trailed a finger through the white residue on the coffee table. "I've been worried about you."

"I'm fine."

"The state of your place says otherwise."

"Whatever. Are you, uh, planning to drive back tonight?"

"No."

"So then. You want to stay here?"

"The thought had occurred to me."

He was still blurry. There appeared to be two of him.

"I don't have, like, a guest room. But I've been sleeping on the couch. You can take my room if you want."

"That's generous." He was acting weird as hell. Or she was very stoned. Or both.

Her bladder spasmed. "I have to pee."

She sat on the toilet a long time, head in her hands.

When she came out, she had a bad case of the spins. She leaned on the wall for balance.

Her father was not in the living room. He stood in the center of the kitchen, facing her.

He held a steak knife.

"Um," she said. "You hungry?"

"In a sense."

Chills up her spine. The drugs kept the thought from surfacing.

"I thought you'd recognize me."

Another flash. David stood beside her now, screaming a single phrase into her ear. It was far away and full of static, but she heard it clear enough.

A wave of nausea rolled through her.

"I'm so glad you found me," her father said.

She shook her head. Tried to focus.

"You're wondering how I found you, but you forget. I was inside you, Gertrude."

"Get... Get away from my father." Helpless, pressed against the wall. The room tilted and spun.

Her father took small, deliberate steps toward her. "Or what? What will you do?"

"I'll kill you. Send you back where you came from."

He laughed. Not her father's laugh. "And tell me, where is that?" He positioned the knife in front of his body, the blade pointed inward, at his stomach. "I was born in the mind of a man, Gertrude. He called me here. Someone who, like me, revels in your suffering."

Her feet caught on a dirty t-shirt. She toppled backward, landed on her backside.

"Such delicious suffering." He touched the blade to her father's belly. "I took care of him a long time ago, much like this."

"Don't," she said. She wanted to rush forward and wrestle the knife away. But he would turn it on her, and she was too disoriented to fight. "Leave my father out of it. He doesn't— He has nothing to do with—"

"Oh, I don't think so." He sank the blade into his stomach. "*Aaah*," he sighed.

"Stop!"

"It's just a... gut wound. Oh, that hurts him. He can feel everything."

"St— Stop! Please!"

"Be seeing you, Gertrude." Grinning, Mr. Ugly pulled the knife toward his chest. Blood erupted from the unzipped flesh and organs bulged against the folds. Mr. Ugly released another moan of pleasure-pain. "Keep an eye... on the news."

"Dad..."

Blood dribbled down his chin. He dropped to his knees. "*Guh,*" he said.

"Dad..."

"*Uck.*" He fell sideways. "*Hnk.*" The air rattled in his throat. He did not inhale again.

Gertie collapsed. She expected Mr. Ugly to crawl across her, invade her like before. Drunk or not, she would fight him off. If it came to it, she'd take the knife from her father's belly and kill herself before he got control.

The attack never came.

Blood pooled on the kitchen floor.

Flies buzzed.

. . .

She did not move until morning.

She made her way to the backyard. Watched the woods a while.

"I'm sorry," David said.

She did not want to bury her father in these woods, beside the other victims in their unmarked grave. Another missing person for the creature's catalog.

What choice did she have?

She drove her father's car into Pennsylvania. Found a quiet road on the side of a mountain, wiped down the interior, removed the plates and registration stickers, put it in neutral, and rolled it off the embankment. It slammed through a stand of trees and disappeared into the brush.

She hitchhiked home.

It took another three days for the story about her father's camp to break. The Camp Daydream Antifreeze Massacre, they called it. There were 23 victims ranging from 4 to 46 years old. Most were children. Those that hadn't died from the poisoned punch had their throats cut while they slept.

Two FBI agents, accompanied by the Sheriff and one of his deputies, asked if they might look around her property. She let them. She had cleaned up the house, including all the drug paraphernalia. In her backyard, they stopped at the treeline. Had they gone just twenty feet ahead, they'd have stood on a mass grave. They thanked her on their way out, and she broke down crying, saying her father was a good man. She meant it.

There were more interviews. Phone calls and visits from reporters. A few more drop-ins from law enforcement. The case was never solved.

She quit the drugs and drinking. Suffered weeks of withdrawal. She bought atlases and maps, pinned a detailed poster of major US travel routes onto her wall. She kept a close eye on the news, violent crime databases, and most wanted lists. When David's debt collectors came to settle his bills, his belongings went up for auction, including his van. She found the woman handling the sale and bought the van privately. She read a hundred books on witchcraft, psychics, the paranormal. She experimented with containment fields. Her first success came after months of work on a coffee mug. She told David to stick his finger in the cup, but he couldn't. She bought sheet metal and a drill and fixed it to the interior of the van. She researched firearms, but killing Mr. Ugly's host was not an option. She considered stun guns, pepper spray, tasers, and cattle prods before finally settling on the tranquilizer gun.

When she successfully locked David in the back of the van, she knew she was as ready as she'd ever be. She jotted down the location of several of the most recent heinous murders, packed a bag, and took her map off the wall and burned it in the backyard with all of her notebooks that mentioned Mr. Ugly or David or her father.

She might have been reported missing, herself, if she had any friends left.

With David by her side, she climbed into the van, her home on the road for what might be the rest of her life.

10

An unusual quiet had fallen over the forest. Janelle's right leg had fallen asleep from sitting on the hard surface of The Fallen Star, and though it was just she and Gertie on the boulder, she felt a third presence behind her.

"I'm sorry about your dad, but there has to be another way."

Gertie said, "I know you want to save your friend, but he's already gone. And if we fail now, if we let him get away again, he'll remember you. He'll come after you, and everyone you love. He won't stop. Ever."

Janelle sobbed into her hands for a long time.

When she got her breath back, she said, "I need to talk to him."

"That's a bad idea."

"I need to."

"He's a slippery motherfucker."

"I know."

Gertie relented. "Just be careful."

They returned to camp. Gertie sat at the picnic table.

Janelle drank well water from the bucket and walked to the lake's edge and splashed water on her face. Then she approached the van.

She sat in the cab and closed the door. Richard banged against the front panel and yelled for her to please open up, let him out, it was so hot in there.

It *was* hot. Sweat soaked through her shirt and ran down her forehead.

"Hey, Richard."

"Nelly! Nelly, please, you gotta get me outta here." His voice was hoarse. "I'm so thirsty."

She didn't fight her tears. "I'm sorry. Gertie says we can't."

"Nelly, I know what you think, but you have to listen to me. That thing that made me hurt Amy is gone. It's gone! I think being back here did something to it." Through the panel, and with his wrecked voice, she couldn't tell if he sounded like Richard or someone else.

"What do you mean?"

"It was terrible." He was pushed up against the panel, his mouth inches from hers, separated by a thin sheet of metal. "That voice in my head. It told me I'd never get free. It told me I was gonna kill you. I believed it. After what I did... What *it* did to Amy. Oh God."

Janelle twisted sideways in the front seat so that she could press her ear to the panel. She heard whimpering.

"You don't believe me," Richard moaned. "I'm gonna die back here."

"Tell me what happened."

"I just woke up, and it was gone."

"So it's just been you back there this whole time?"

"Yes!"

It seemed possible.

"Nelly, don't let me die back here. It wasn't me. You know it wasn't me."

She pressed her hand to the panel, imagining Richard pressing his to the other side. How had things come this far? Just a few days back, she was plotting how they could date long distance. She recalled the feeling of his body on hers. The way he felt inside her. How they breathed into each other's mouths. It seemed like magic, that their paths would converge in that way, finally. She'd have gone to New York if he asked.

She forced her voice not to waver. "I don't believe you."

"What?"

"I don't believe you. You're not Richard. Gertie says we have to let you die."

He slammed his fists against the panel, making her jump. "That's crazy! Nelly, please!"

"The thing is—" Her voice cracked. She cleared her throat and tried again. She pretended she was in the school play, like in 5th grade. Just reading lines. "The thing is, even if you're telling the truth, and the demon is gone, we can't afford to risk it. Either way, you have to die, Richard. I'm sorry, but it's the only way to be sure."

A long stretch of silence. Then an enormous blow to the back panel. *"YOU PIG FUCK!"*

She pulled away so hard she hit her face on the steering wheel.

"Do you think you can defeat God! You think this tin can will contain me? I can still taste your rancid twat! When I get out of there, I am going to start there! I will slit you open from your cunt to your lopsided tits! I will make this boy eat your guts the way he ate your rotten pussy!" He slammed against the walls. The van rollicked like a boat in rough seas.

Janelle slapped at the door handle, shaking so badly she couldn't grip it.

Richard cackled, screamed, a rabid thing railing against its cage.

She got the door open and jumped out.

The sides of the van bulged every time Richard hit them.

She went to the water and sat at the edge for a long time.

When she joined Gertie at the picnic table, Gertie was still fiddling with the fishing pole, plucking at the rat's nest of line. She glanced up, went back to her task.

"You have to cut it," Janelle said, her voice flat. "It's too tangled."

"I've never fished before. I haven't eaten meat in years, but it's better than starving."

"I know. You said you can taste the animal's suffering."

"That's right. You know more about me than anyone in the world. Except David."

"Lucky me."

Gertie produced a pocketknife from her shorts and passed it over with the rod. Janelle cut the line and assembled the pole, threaded the line through the eyelets and retied the hook.

"We'll need worms," Janelle said. "I'll see if I can dig some up."

Gertie shut her eyes. "There's one beside the left leg of the table. On your side."

Janelle looked where she was told. The worm was just under the surface, nested in the dirt. Gertie winced as Janelle pushed the hook through the worm's skin. It twisted rigid around the metal. Janelle held the dying creature up, studied its writhing.

She took the pole to the water's edge. Gertie followed. She put her finger on the line and released the reel and cast the worm and hook into the lake. Ripples radiated outward.

"Nice," Gertie said.

"I don't want him to suffer."

"I know."

"It'll take days, even in this heat. That's too much."

"What do you suggest?"

Janelle tipped her chin at the lake.

Gertie said, "I don't understand."

"Drive the van into the water. It's deep enough."

"I don't know."

"Nobody comes here. They won't find it for years. Mr. Ugly will be gone by then, won't he?"

"We still need transportation."

"It's not far to town."

"What happens when they see our faces?"

"They don't have to see *your* face, do they?"

"What about you?"

"I was kidnapped by a man in a mask. I don't know. We can work out the details later."

Gertie thought a while. "That could work."

"Tomorrow," Janelle said. She didn't have the heart to do it tonight. Not yet.

"Okay."

The line jerked against her finger, a slight tug. "Hey."

"What?"

She yanked the pole back. "I caught dinner."

11

Amy Pink lay facedown and naked on the metal table. The back of her head had been shaved, revealing a puckered pink line at the base of her skull at a 30 degree angle.

Dr. Aire leaned over the body and gestured at the wound with her pen. "The incision punctured the brain stem. There's some irritation to the follicles at the crown of the skull, indicating that someone pulled her hair pretty hard. Beyond that, there's little sign of a struggle."

The room was chilly in the way of morgues, but Ray didn't mind. He preferred the cold to the heat, and the day had been brutal. "She never saw it coming," he said.

Aire stood upright and bobbed her head noncommittally. "In a sense. The angle of the puncture indicates that the attacker was standing in front of the victim."

Ray tried to picture it. The blow came from behind. Yet Amy and her attacker stood face to face. Aire mimed hugging someone in a tight embrace, then slamming a knife into the back of their head. "She fell to the ground, hitting her left temple." She snapped on a pair of gloves from the instrument tray and lifted Amy's head. There was a significant gash by the girl's left eyebrow, but it hadn't swelled as it would in life.

"You're sure it happened like that?"

"Pretty sure. I swabbed under the nails, but I doubt there's anything there."

"What about height? How tall was her attacker?"

"Taller than her. The angle was downward. She's five-four, so let's say our killer is five-ten, give or take."

"You really think they hugged?"

"You're the detective." She pulled off her gloves and tossed them in the trash. "On to the next." She walked to a neighboring table occupied by a rumpled sheet with a small lump in the center. She lifted the sheet to reveal the carcass. "Detective, meet Mr. Fuzzy."

"Mr. Fuzzy?"

"It's like John Doe, but for animals. You don't like it?"

"I just don't think *Fuzzy* applies anymore."

"Don't be cruel." She gestured with her pen. The cat had been opened up, its organs removed. He couldn't tell what Aire had done and what had been done by its killer. "I don't often perform animal autopsies. Mr. Fuzzy," she shot Ray a mischievous glare, "was not stabbed to death like his friend. He drowned." Reading the surprise on Ray's face, she clarified, "The mutilation was posthumous. Where was the corpse discovered?"

"On the side of the river."

"Interesting."

"What's interesting?"

"If you pressed me, I'd guess that's not where it drowned."

"How come?"

"Take a whiff."

"Excuse me?"

"Smell the fur."

Reluctantly, Ray put his nose close and sniffed. It smelled exactly like he expected—like guts. "What am I supposed to notice?"

"You'd know if it was there. That's the point."

"Sorry, what's the point?"

"The river stinks, Detective. This doesn't smell like river water to me."

"I doubt the scent of water is admissible in court."

"Catch the killer. Then worry about court."

"It doesn't really work that way. Tell me about the mutilation."

Aire grinned. Despite the circumstances, she seemed to glow. "You're gonna like this."

"Sometimes, Doctor, I don't think you know me at all."

"At least one penetrative wound matches that of the female victim."

"You mean it was the same weapon?"

"If a jury asked, I'd say it's very close to certain. And there's this." She jabbed her pen at a coil of purple intestine. "The intestine's been punctured by a small, hook-like object. The type of object a hunter uses to field dress prey."

"Like a knife with a gut hook."

"I checked these wounds against the knife recovered from the highway incident."

"They match?"

"They match."

Ray rubbed the back of his neck.

"What do you make of it?" Aire said.

"I have to think about it."

The highway killer, Ehblu Htoo, was dead. That was certain. And the type of knife he used was never made public, so it couldn't be a copycat. But he could think of a couple civilians who knew exactly what kind of weapon killed Jeffrey Patel.

"I'd be pleased if I were you. You have your murder weapon."

"We have a theoretical murder weapon."

"Theory's better than a thumb up the keister."

"Most things are."

"Now, Detective, that depends who you ask." She gestured at the wall of freezers. "I still have to examine our new arrival." She meant the vagrant, Jane Doe. "You're welcome to stick around."

"I'm afraid I have to pass. I'm running on fumes."

"Suit yourself."

. . .

Bartov was still at his desk. The others were out somewhere. It was almost 10 o'clock.

Bartie raised his coffee and Ray nodded and slouched into his chair, his brains slushing between his ears.

He took out a notepad and flipped to a fresh page. He wrote:

A.P. killing →Hunting knife. Gut hook. Same as highway homicides.
Survivors: Janelle Winters, Richard Becker.
A.P. hugged attacker?
Check stores for knife purchases last 3-5 days.
Killer taller than 5'4".

A search through the DMV database told him Janelle Winters was 5'2", Gertrude Morgenstern 5'4", and Richard Becker 5'11". He wrote this down.

Why use the same type of knife that killed his best friend? To send a message?

To whom?

Richard had been through hell. It could have broken him. And there were all sorts of relationships at play. Jeff and Amy. Janelle and Richard, at least according to Richard's father.

And what about the cat? Where had it come from?

Ray chewed the end of his pen.

Then there was Gertrude Morgenstern and Janelle Winters loading an unconscious Richard Becker into a van. Retribution, maybe? Had they caught Richard in the act? If so, why not go to the law? Why run?

What about the shadow?

He clamped his teeth on the back of his pen until his gums ached.

Fuck the shadow. Fuck the laughing in the video and the disappearing van and stress-induced hallucinations.

He did not believe in these things.

Did he?

Simple math.

He spit out the pen and tucked his notepad into his jacket.

He stood and watched Bartov typing what might have been the investigative action report from the Jane Doe crime scene. Bartov sensed him watching and looked up. "Al?"

"Can I ask you a favor, Bartie?"

"What do you need?"

"Wanna take a ride with me?"

"Where to?"

"I'd like to follow up with John Becker."

"What for?"

"We're gonna see about a cat."

. . .

Ray explained on the ride. Bartov listened and struggled to connect the dots in the same order. He nodded often and worked his tongue around as if sucking a lozenge. When Ray finished, Bartov said, "I see what you're getting at, I guess. So, okay. Sure. I'm with you."

"Jesus, Bartie. If that's how the county attorney reacts, we're in trouble."

Twelve hours ago, when John Becker heard about Amy Pink's death, he collapsed on his front steps. Bartov was there. He called for an ambulance, and Becker spent some hours in the hospital. The doctors sent him home with a sedative. When he answered the door this time, he swayed slightly and his mouth drooped. Before he could jump to conclusions about their arrival, Bartov explained they were just here to clarify Richard's actions in the past several days, and, by the way, did they have any pets? A dog or cat, by chance?

John Becker took his time digesting the question. "Derby was close to eighteen years old. Cats wander off when it's their time. It's instinct."

Ray said, "How did Richard feel about the cat?"

"Derby came along when Rich was barely a year old. He was a stray. Hissed and spit at me like the devil, but he loved Rich. What's this got to do with anything?"

"John, would you be willing to let us take another look around your property?"

"You didn't do that enough?"

"Can't be too thorough."

"Well, all right."

As they entered the house, Mr. Becker stiffened. "My son's not a suspect, is he?"

Ray said, "We're just trying to narrow things down."

"I already told you who's at fault. How come you're not out looking for her?"

"There's a lot of people doing that right now."

"Sure."

Ray took the kitchen sink first while Bartov went to the upstairs bathroom. They wore latex gloves and carried small forensic kits that resembled tackle boxes.

Mr. Becker followed Ray, asking what he was looking for.

Ray ran a finger along the sink drain. "When's the last time you used this?" His finger came back rimed with black residue. He flicked the switch on the wall and the garbage disposal roared. He shut it off.

"I don't know. After dinner. Why?"

"Where's the first floor bathroom?"

Becker led him to it.

Bartov came down the stairs shaking his head.

Bartov and Mr. Becker stood outside the bathroom while Ray leaned into the tub with a pen light. The tub had a perforated drain. There was a good amount of peach fuzz amid a wad of black hair covering the holes. He pinched the disc of hair and held it up for a better look.

"What color is your hair, Mr. Becker?"

Mr. Becker must have thought he was crazy. "My hair is black."

"What about your son?"

"What's this about? What's that you have there?"

"Looks like cat fur." Ray tucked the circle of hair into a paper evidence bag.

Mr. Becker stepped into the room. "What's this about?"

"I'd like to look around the boy's bedroom, if that's okay."

"You know, I think you've done enough here tonight."

Bartov started to argue, but Ray shut it down. "That's all right, John. I'm sorry we bothered you at this hour."

"I'm sure you are." He followed them out, breathing heavily.

When he shut the door behind them, Ray smacked Bartov's shoulder.

Bartov said, "So you got your cat hair, Al. Remind me why that matters."

They strolled down the driveway, Ray swinging his evidence bag like a prize.

"It matters, Bartie, because if Richard killed the cat, then he mutilated the cat, and if he mutilated the cat with the same weapon that killed Amy Pink…" They reached the SUV. Ray slipped inside and buckled and waited for Bartov to do the same. "You see where I'm going with this?"

"You think a jury would buy it? Or a judge?"

"I honestly don't know, but it tells me we've got our suspect. You in a rush to get home?"

"Not particularly. Why?"

"You owe me a beer."

Bartov cracked a grin. "Buckets. I guess I do."

12

Janelle caught a second fish and Gertie caught the third. Perch. They laid them on the grass and covered them with an overturned drawer. Janelle winced her way through gutting and cleaning them with Gertie's knife. She drew the blade along the spine and sliced the skin back and cut jagged fillets from either side. She tried to see what she was doing as something scientific, like a dissection in biology class, but she flashed to the knife entering the base of Amy's skull and had to sit down and wait for the shakes to pass.

Gertie searched for a rock large enough to cook the fish on. Near the picnic table, she stumbled over a ring of stones that made an old firepit. They stomped down the grass and collected dry twigs and branches. Gertie shaved kindling from the twigs and got a fire going with her lighter. They set the grilling rock at the edge of the pit and laid the fillets on. They ate with their fingers and spat out small bones.

Janelle looked to the van. Gertie knew what she was thinking. She'd been through it herself, and she wouldn't wish it upon anyone.

"It's not fair, is it?" Gertie said.

Janelle started. Her gaze sank into the fire. "What does it want?"

"Mr. Ugly?"

"Yeah."

Gertie had put a lot of thought into this. At first, she believed he merely wanted to hurt people, to make them suffer. But he was larger now than when she first saw him. Stronger. David had told her that when he killed, there was a jolt like electricity, energizing him.

"I think killing gives him strength. If he gets strong enough, one day, he might not need a tether."

"Why didn't he kill you? When he came to your house that time?"

"What he did was worse than death."

The fire crackled and something inside popped and spit sparks.

The bats were out again, and swarms of insects buzzed around David like a living aura. A symphony of crickets rose in volume, and soon the frogs joined in.

"One thing I don't understand," Janelle said. "If killing makes him stronger, why doesn't he just, like, blow up a building or hijack an airplane or something?"

"I don't think it's about killing the most people. It has to be intimate. Like a ritual."

The sun was fully down now. The fire reflected red in Janelle's eyes. She trailed her foot in the grass. "I'm not a killer."

"I know."

"Richard's still in there, isn't he?"

"I wish I could say he wasn't, but I think he is, yes."

David joined them at the fire. "Tell her it's better to be free and dead than to be trapped in your own body like that. I should know."

Gertie relayed the message.

"That doesn't make it easier."

"Without her friends," David continued, "we wouldn't have him now. She's fighting back. We're all soldiers in a war against this thing. We have to do everything we can."

Janelle just frowned in response.

Gertie said, "I'm scared for tomorrow, too, you know."

"You are?"

"I'm afraid it'll work."

Janelle and David gave her quizzical looks.

Gertie found a spare stick and poked the fire, releasing a fresh plume of embers. "How do I go back to a normal life after this? Am I supposed to go home and get a job? My house has probably been repo'ed. I guess nobody dug up the woods, at least. I'd have heard about that. Mr. Ugly's the only reason I get up in the morning. When he's gone, I might just disappear."

"Like a ghost?" David said.

Janelle leapt up and swatted at her legs.

"Spark?" Gertie said.

"Spider!"

Gertie laughed.

Janelle gestured at the trailer. "I'm exhausted. I didn't sleep at all last night."

"Yeah. I should go, too. I'm still beat from last night. Never had to hide from that many people before, or for so long. I'm sort of impressed with myself."

"Yeah. Thanks for that, by the way."

"Go to sleep."

Janelle took a breath. "Okay, then."

"Okay, then."

Janelle retreated into the trailer and David sat at the picnic table.

"How do you do that?" Gertie said, gesturing at the seat.

"Do what?"

"Sometimes you sit on things. Other times, you walk right through them."

David shrugged. "Ghost physics. Want to help me write the book?"

Something in the lake splashed.

"I thought she took it well."

David frowned.

"Gertie, listen. I know you feel guilty, even if—"

"David, stop."

"Just listen. I know you feel guilty, even if you won't admit it. I've been with you a long time, and I've been through every what-if scenario there is. What if I never owned a furniture shop? What if I hadn't stopped at that car crash? If I hadn't visited my grandpa in the hospital that night, I wouldn't have been on the highway in the first place."

That was how Mr. Ugly found David. He witnessed a wreck and stopped to help. Always the Good Samaritan. He stepped out of the car and felt something slithering up his legs. Turned out Mr. Ugly had driven his previous host into a bridge abutment at 80 miles an hour. It was regular old bad luck that David was the first to stop.

"My point is," David continued, "the past is fixed. All that matters is what you do in the present."

"It's a good speech, David. You should take it on the road."

"Oh, fuck off." He stood up, suddenly huffy.

"Hey. I'm kidding."

He turned from the fire, from Gertie. "It sucks being dead, all right? It fucking sucks. But it's better than being like that." He pointed to the van. "When you killed me, I was glad. I was glad." He walked to the water's edge.

Gertie remained at the fire until it reduced to coals and the coals turned gray. She wondered if David felt the tears running down her cheeks, too.

13

Ray and Bartov drooped in a booth at the back of the bar. This was Bartov's establishment of choice, as it was directly below his apartment. Ray had more than a hundred pounds on him, so he was still sober when Bartie was red in the cheeks.

The bar was sort of a hipster joint, but Bartie got free drinks because they knew he was a detective and he lived upstairs. A jazz trio was just finishing up a set when they arrived—bassist, keyboardist, and drummer, college-aged and terribly sincere.

Ray had begun to regret the outing.

It wasn't that he disliked people. It was just that—hell, he barely had a conversation with his wife that wasn't about groceries or bills. He never liked human contact.

When the jazz band finished their last song, Ray leaned back and ran his thumbs around the lip of his beer bottle and thought about how he could leave without being rude.

Bartov studied him with a smirk. "You ever play an instrument, Al?"

"Ray."

"Sorry?"

"I'm Ray tonight. Not Al or Alverson. Not Detective. Just a guy having a beer."

"All right then, Ray. That makes me Ethan."

"No, that's too weird. You're still Bartie."

"Fair enough. You didn't answer my question."

"How's that? Oh, an instrument. I tried to pick up bass while I was getting my Associates, but it didn't take."

"Bass? Who plays bass in college?"

"I like the blues. Blues is nothing without the rhythm section."

"The blues. Bass makes sense for you, actually."

"How's that?"

"You can tell a lot about a person by their instrument of choice, even hypothetical. See that girl at the bar? The one with the pink hair?"

Ray saw her. She wore a leather jacket with some loopy, illegible script on the back. She was in the midst of a loud conversation with two companions, both guys. She touched their arms and barked out laughter. "What about her?"

"She'd want to be a drummer."

"Why?"

"Drummers are bombastic. They want to be seen and heard, but they're not subtle enough to be singers or guitarists. The good ones are like mathematicians, though. She'd be a bad one."

"You've got a whole system worked out. Keep talking."

"Okay, so vocalists are assholes. Even the nice ones. Sure, they're pleasant enough when you're complimenting them, but just as soon as you turn your back, the resentment comes out."

"Seems a little unfair, but okay."

"Guitarists are difficult. A lot of them sing, so they're technically vocalists. The ones who only play guitar, though, they're good people, even if they're a little uptight."

The waitress brought Bartie another bottle. He thanked her.

"Now bassists. Okay, bassists are shy, but the good ones are brilliant. They're all the good things about drummers without the arrogance. They like to be behind the scenes, but they know they're essential, which is why they can be a pain in the ass when they've got an agenda."

"Are you hitting on me, Bartie?"

"Ah, fuck off."

"I'm not sure what you're getting at."

"I'm just saying you could play the bass, if you wanted to." He tipped his beer. "Cheers."

"Okay, Detective. You were obviously in a band. What did you play?"

"Guess."

Ray pictured Bartie in some dusky bar, beer on a stool beside him, a small crowd of heads bobbing along. What would he be holding? Not a bass. Definitely not drumsticks. Was there anything on his knee, cradled against his chest, or just a microphone in his hands?

"You were a singer."

Bartie grinned. "How'd you get that?"

"I'm right, aren't I?"

"Course you're right. Anyway, that was years back. I wasn't very good." He laughed to himself, remembering some stage, or carrying a PA system from a busted up van through a back door in the cold. "We called ourselves The Munchies. Buckets, that was a long time ago."

Maybe it was the alcohol or his exhaustion or the week's unrelenting weirdness, but Ray could openly admit to himself here tonight that he never intended to isolate himself. He only meant to protect certain things—from himself as much as anyone. There were doors in his mind that he did not want to open, and if he let someone in, they'd see those doors, too.

Bartie had shifted the subject to childrearing in the manner of new parents. His son was eighteen weeks old, which seemed a strange number to Ray. At what point did parents start counting in months instead of weeks?

"What I've come to realize," Bartie said, "is that all babies begin as drummers. Alex would be the worst of them, but it wouldn't stop him picking those sticks up and wailing away."

Ray envied the sheer normalcy of such a life.

Inside, a door rattled.

"I was married," he heard himself say, more to himself than Bartie.

Bartie's laughter cut off. "No kidding?"

"Too weird? Detective Alverson in the domicile?"

"I've just never heard you talk about a wife. Any kids?"

"No kids. Just the one marriage. We were together, then we weren't."

Bartie squinted. "That's the single greatest divorce story I've ever heard, Ray. That's why they call you the Hound." He sat up rigid and placed his hands flat on the table and made his voice deep: "Well, your honor, we were together, then we weren't." He howled with laughter, then gasped like he might suck it back in. "Oh, jeez, I think I'm drunk."

A handle was turning in Ray's brain. A crack formed to one side of a door, darkness blasting through. "I've seen ghosts," he blurted, and the door inched open.

Bartie flinched. "Ghosts?"

"Yeah. Spirits. Full-bodied apparitions."

"When?"

"The first time was about ten years ago, in Minneapolis."

"Are you pulling my leg?"

"The first ghost I saw is the reason I'm here, in Fairfield. It's why I left Minneapolis. It wasn't the divorce. It wasn't that I needed a change of scenery. I was running. But I think I traded that ghost for something worse."

Ray held his empty Corona in both hands and studied the label, couldn't look at Bartie for fear of the disbelief or ridicule or judgment he'd see there. He already said too much, but it was like running his head under a cold tap—after the initial shock, there was nothing but relief.

He forced himself to look up. Bartov had sobered significantly. He leaned forward and tapped the table with two fingers like a gambler taking a hit. "Tell me."

14

Ray always had a talent for finding things.

When he was seven, he came home from school one afternoon to find his father waiting on the stoop with somber news. The dog, Franco, had dug a hole under the backyard fence and snuck out. Before his father could suggest they print posters and walk the neighborhood, Ray said they needed to get in the car. It took some convincing, but his father humored him.

Ray pointed the way. East two blocks and north three.

"Here." He'd brought them to a house with green shutters. They idled in the street.

Who knows what his father thought? He played along, at least. "What's here?"

Ray was out of the car and racing toward the front door before his father could react.

He hit the doorbell, but it didn't go off, so he pounded the door with both fists until his father grabbed him from behind, cursing. Ray thrashed, kicking his father in the chest and groin.

"Now you cut that out!" His father didn't believe in hitting a child, but if anything could bring him to the edge, this was it.

They were halfway down the lawn when an old lady opened the door. "What's going on here?" She had big white hair.

Ray's father started to apologize.

Ray shouted over him, "You got Franco!"

"Franco?"

"I'm sorry," Ray's father said. "Our border collie got out. My son thought—"

"Hold on." The woman shut the door and opened it a moment later with Franco on a leash, in a collar that wasn't his, panting happily. "This him?"

His father set Ray on the grass. "How did…"

The lady said, "I was going to call the pound. Just to let them know I found him, not to take him there. He's a sweet dog."

Ray's father looked at him, hands on his hips, head pulled way back, like Ray was too big to hold in frame. Ray ran up and took the leash.

"Keep that collar," the lady said. "A dog should have a collar on him."

There were other things. He'd get feelings about places and people. Naturally, that led him to law enforcement.

After high school, he got his Associates Degree in Criminal Justice and joined the police academy, moving up the ranks quicker than most. He walked the beat. He drove patrol. He never stopped the wrong person. Never broke the arms of kids who talked shit. He knew how to talk people down. Not that he never used force. He'd grown large and had been going to the gym for a while, and some guys couldn't resist picking a fight with the biggest man in the room. He put some of those types in the hospital. Usually followed the ambulance there.

That was how he met Shawna.

She was a workaholic like him, and they coexisted with the help of something like love. A marriage, a mortgage, and almost eight years later, he made Investigator, where he wanted to be from the start. He was good. Uncanny, even. He convinced himself that his "gut feelings" were the same instincts everyone followed, though he was particularly lucky.

He was not special, he told himself. He just did his job well.

The murder of Abdullah Elmi was not extraordinary except for the brutality with which it had been executed. Abdullah was nineteen years old. A second-generation Somali immigrant three weeks away from his first semester of college. He would have been the first in his family to go. They said he was quick to smile, and had perfect white teeth. He had no connection to the gangs in the area, at least that anyone knew of, and no obvious enemies.

His body had been found on the stone steps leading to an abandoned bar below street-level two blocks from the Wells Fargo building. Someone had bludgeoned him in the back of the head with a heavy object, then jumped repeatedly on his chest. His torso had been flattened, forcing his innards out of his mouth and rectum.

There were no witnesses. No evidence. No suspects.

Two weeks after taking the case, Ray woke from a sound sleep at 3am, the estimated time of Elmi's death. Something—his gut—told him he needed to get out of bed, get dressed, and visit the crime scene. The feeling was so strong he wondered if he was still dreaming.

Shawna stirred when he woke. He told her he'd received a call.

At 0400, downtown Minneapolis was mostly deserted. A handful of latenighters milled on the sidewalks, and there was the occasional sound of a bottle breaking or trash being rummaged through. He used to walk the beat around here, and saw no reason to be afraid. Yet when he reached the stone staircase where Abdullah Elmi's body had been discovered, his heart became a block of ice.

The staircase was black as a catacomb, the gray sidewalk like gravestones laid end to end. It was summer, but the air wafting up from the stairwell felt like someone had opened a huge freezer down there, and the darkness was somehow wrong. The longer he looked, the more convinced he became that he was seeing past the bottom of the stairwell, into something beyond the darkness. A vast place of impossible geometry, so foreign his mind couldn't register it.

He was a cop. Had been for years. He didn't believe in threats he couldn't put handcuffs on. He wasn't religious. God was hard work. A perfect fingerprint. His feet on the pavement and his hand pressing pen to paper. Rationality and determination. That was how he succeeded, and that's what brought him here. But a dread unlike any he'd known before shot through him, and he wanted to turn and run and not stop until he collapsed. He commanded himself to do just that, but the darkness had him now, and something other than his conscious mind moved his feet down the steps. The dread thickened, but his legs took him halfway down and stopped, and something in the most concentrated darkness resolved into a denser black—a shadow among shadows. It lengthened, stretched upright, *unfolded.*

Abdullah Elmi looked up at him. Something red hung from his mouth. He slurped it in and threw both arms out, spidery hands grasping.

Ray had seen the medical technicians place this boy into a body bag. He stood over his corpse and spoke to the medical examiner about the size of the killer's boots and he spoke to the boy's grieving mother about this child that had been so hard working and genuine with nothing but possibilities ahead before his life was so brutally and senselessly ended and now here he was, grabbing at the space between them as if he was trying to pull Ray down to him.

The boy spoke, but Ray couldn't hear him. He knew what he'd learn if he went to him, though. If he could accept what he was seeing, embrace the darkness and the unreality of the moment. He knew this the same way he knew how to find his dog or to talk to this suspect instead of that or look in this drawer or visit this property and prioritize this warrant over another. He simply knew.

But he couldn't go.

He didn't want it. He never wanted it. Had convinced himself he didn't have it. He was normal, goddamn it, and there was nothing in this world but what you could see with your eyes and feel with your hands, nothing but the physical, the sane, the predictable, that which could be transcribed in plain language on a notepad.

Simple math.

He regained control of his legs, stumbled backward, tripped and bruised his ass on the steps, clawed upward on all fours until he was at street level.

Then he ran.

At home, in the morning light, he could almost believe he dreamed it, but at least once a week for the next twelve months he woke at 3 a.m. seeing in his mind the boy at the bottom of the staircase. When he was downtown, he felt the pit calling, beckoning him into the shadows.

His work suffered. He wasn't sleeping. He said the city no longer agreed with him, that he'd recently discovered his wife's adultery. After some long talks with his supervisors, he applied to an opening in a small town southeast of the city, a place called Fairfield that he passed through when visiting relatives in Iowa.

To this day, if he drove into Minneapolis, when he was in sight of the staggered levels of the Wells Fargo Center, he'd get the shakes, and he would flash to the image of the dead boy, reaching, lips moving, calling to the one person who might hear him, but refused to listen.

∙ ∙ ∙

Bartie polished off two more beers during the course of this story. Now he leaned into the corner of his booth and pulled at his right eyebrow, a nervous habit.

"I've never told that to anyone," Ray said.

"I didn't know you believed in all that."

"That's what's funny. I don't know that I do. But it happened. I lived it."

"I believe you, if that makes you feel any better."

"You do?"

"You bet. It's too nuts to make up. Must feel pretty good to get it off your chest."

"In a way." He realized he'd been peeling the labels from his bottles. The scraps lay in a pile on the table.

Bartie said, "There's a reason you're telling me this now."

"Yeah."

Bartie waited for Ray to continue. When he didn't, Bartie said, "You don't have to tell me," though he clearly wanted to know.

"All right." He wasn't ready to share. Not yet.

"Do you remember what you said when I made Investigator?"

"What's that?"

"You said it's our job to look where others don't want to. That's the oath we take. We take a vow to step into the ugliness and pick through it with a magnifying glass."

"I don't remember saying that."

"I'm probably paraphrasing."

Ray slapped the tabletop. "Well. It's late."

"You okay to drive?"

"Sober as can be."

"Too bad. I was about to tell you my own story."

"Oh yeah?"

"Mm-hmm."

"I'm listening."

Bartie leaned forward. "You can't laugh."

"You didn't laugh at me. I'll return the favor."

"When I was a kid, my mom had sort of a year-long freakout, and I had to stay with my stepdad in Iowa. I swear to God, Ray, an alien lived in his basement."

Just then, the waitress stopped to check on them. "You fellas about ready?"

Ray tapped a finger against one of his empties. "Let's have another."

15

Ray woke at 6am, groggy but not hungover, rolled out of bed and dropped to the floor for his morning pushups. He chugged water from the tap and drew a hot shower and let the water beat on his neck as he replayed the night's events. He trusted Bartov to keep the ghost story to himself, as Ray would with Bartov's tale of a minor alien invasion in Nowhere, Iowa.

He dressed and ate and called Bartie, who answered on the sixth ring. "Ullo?"

"I wake you?"

"Nuh— Nope. Lemon fresh."

"Meet me downstairs in an hour?"

"Sure."

He drove to the station and sealed up the cat hair from the Becker residence and filled out the requisite forms and left it with the rest of the evidence to be delivered to the lab, pending Obermeyer's approval. He stopped at Quik Trip on the way to Bartov's apartment.

Bartov waited on the curb looking wrung out. When he opened the door and saw the donuts on the passenger seat, he grinned. "A little on the nose, isn't it?"

"Would you refuse the offer?" Ray gestured at the coffee in the cupholder.

"Hell no." Bartov climbed in.

Ray pulled onto the road.

"So, ah, where we going?"

"I was thinking about what you said last night. About looking where others won't."

"I said that?"

"You were paraphrasing me."

"Oh. From when?"

"Never mind. You remember my story, at least?"

"Of course."

"Good. I'm going down the stairs."

Bartov chewed a glazed donut. "And you're taking me with you?"

"If you're willing."

"A little ghost hunting on the job? Sure."

"That's the spirit."

"Too hungover for puns, Al. Anyway, you haven't said where we're headed."

"The Winters place. John Becker thought he saw Janelle Winters loading his son into the back of Morgenstern's van. Everyone wants to discount the end of his story."

"You mean the part where a vehicle vanishes into thin air?"

"Yep."

"Are you suggesting it's possible?"

"I honestly don't know."

"Well, okay. So, why the Winters place?"

"I'm not sure."

"But you have a feeling."

"Yeah."

"Well okay then."

. . .

Mrs. Winters was worse than ever. Hair greasy, eyes puffy and shadowed, and Ray was pretty sure she wore the same clothes as the last time he saw her. Her husband fared no better. The skin of his face had gone sallow, sagging off his chin and cheeks. They were happy to let Ray and Bartie look around. "Anything that helps you find my baby," Mrs. Winters said.

Investigators had already gone through the place, but they'd come up empty. Janelle didn't keep a diary, and her messages and online accounts revealed nothing but the social life of a normal eighteen-year-old. Her bedroom was painted light blue with posters of musicians on the walls, some he recognized, others he didn't. Above her headboard, she'd tacked up a collage of photos printed on cheap computer paper. She was in some of them, but never without at least one of her friends—Amy, Jeff, or Richard. Nothing in them hinted at lurking malevolence.

He positioned himself in the center of the room and stood still.

How was this supposed to work? If he had some special power, how did he tap into it?

Mrs. Winters stood in the doorway. "You saw the backyard fence?" Her voice flat, emotionless. "It's new. We're going to get a puppy. When she goes to college."

Ray nodded, half-listening.

"I wanted a collie, but he said a German shepherd's more trainable. Those are police dogs. I guess you know that."

Ray thought he should offer some words of comfort, but she wasn't really talking to him.

"What is it you're looking for?" she said.

"We're just trying to be thorough."

Bartov came down the hallway behind her.

Ray felt foolish just standing here. He began riffling through the girl's belongings. He opened her dresser drawers, lifted her mattress, patted the pockets of her clothes.

"What are you *looking* for?" Mrs. Winters repeated.

Bartov, taking initiative, said, "Barbara, I'd like to ask you some more questions about the day of Janelle's disappearance. Can we go downstairs, maybe have a cup of coffee?"

"Sure, yes. I'll put a pot on."

They retreated down the stairs.

Alone again, Ray relaxed. He started over, returning to the center of the room. He shut his eyes and breathed in a long, slow breath. He rotated slowly, hoping something would jump out at him. That night he saw Abdullah Elmi, all he'd done was show up. For all he knew, this type of thing only worked at certain times, in the right light or when the clocks struck three.

After five minutes, he gave up and continued riffling. He searched along the edges and underside of the girl's vanity. Emptied her desk drawers and put it all back. Tapped on her closet walls with an ear pressed to the wood.

Nothing.

He left the room.

Mrs. Winters' voice murmured downstairs. She sniffled often.

There were two other rooms upstairs, plus a bathroom. He headed for the nearest room, which had been made into a workout space. A rowing machine, a stack of free weights, a yoga mat and a balance ball, elliptical machine, resistance bands and a jump rope hanging from a hook, a television mounted high on one wall.

Nothing stood out here, either.

The master bedroom was next. It was spotless. The bed made, and the dressers organized with their sets of cologne and perfume and jewelry boxes. There were pictures on the walls—a wedding photo and a couple amateur portraits sloppily painted.

This was shaping up to be a great waste of time.

His bladder ached. Too much gas station coffee.

The upstairs bathroom was just as neat as the master bedroom. A store-bought picture frame hung above the towel rack, one of those frames with places for multiple pictures. In the center, looping calligraphy declared, *Love Runs in the Family*.

He pissed, washed his hands, dried them, and he reached for the doorknob to leave.

Something stopped him.

Something about those photos.

Most were taken outdoors with all three members of the family, who were much younger then. Janelle must have been in grade school in the most recent. Here, they stood in front of a big white farmhouse. Here, they posed in exactly the same way in front of a barn with the doors open, bales of what appeared to be hay or straw stacked inside. Here, a toddler that must have been Janelle sat on the lap of a man who resembled a bald Santa, complete with the round spectacles. Here, Mrs. Winters held a baby beside a wooden sign that read, "St. Chuck's Lake."

Without thinking, Ray reached out to touch this photo.

A tearing sensation roared through his chest the instant his finger made contact.

He fell back gasping and collapsed onto the toilet seat, clutching his abdomen.

Heart attack?

No. The pain was already gone.

He lifted his shirt.

No marks. No sting. Nothing to explain the feeling.

He remained on the toilet a while, gathering his thoughts.

Downstairs, Mr. and Mrs. Winters sat at the kitchen table with Bartov.

"Saint Chuck's Lake," Ray said, entering the room. "Where is that?"

PART 4
COLLISION

1

Gertie couldn't sleep. She'd grown apprehensive about the new plan.

She didn't like the thought of losing the van. Driving it into the lake would anchor it here, to this place. Eventually, someone might find it, and open the doors. Wasn't that inevitable?

In all her time hunting Mr. Ugly, she never considered what to do with the van once she caught him. Now it seemed a good idea to bury it. But would the weight of dirt bend the frame around the doors? If a crack were to form at the seal, would Mr. Ugly squeeze through?

When the sun streamed through the gaps around the curtains, she crawled out of her sleeping bag and swiped the baked beans from the counter and headed outside.

Janelle snored lightly.

The grass sparkled with morning dew. Gertie gathered what dry kindling she could find and poked through the ashes of the firepit, uncovering the slightest of embers. She set the kindling there and stoked modest flames. She opened the beans with her pocketknife and set the can at the edge of the fire and grabbed the water bucket from inside the trailer. It was nearly empty. She lifted it like a giant cup and drank the dregs.

She sat at the picnic table and watched the sun ascend.

It was already hot. Worse than yesterday.

She left the beans by the flames and walked to the van and put her ear against the side.

Silence.

David had followed her. He cocked his head. "Do you think he's—"

Richard slammed against the side so hard the van rocked.

Gertie pulled away. "Would've been too easy."

Richard growled, "Let me out."

"Are you enjoying your last hours in a body? I'm sure it's nice and toasty in there."

"Your mother wanted to abort you, Gertrude. I learned that from your father. He convinced her not to, but she resented him for it. Every day she saw your little face, always wanting food, wanting love, she wished she'd done it."

"He's lying," David said.

"No, he's not." She sat on the rear bumper. "It must get boring spreading nothing but misery."

Richard—Mr. Ugly—barked out a laugh. "How's that?"

"You think you're special because you destroy lives. Because you leave a trail of destruction. But there are plenty of people like you. You're not unique. If you had any real talent, if you were truly special, or god-like, you'd *make* something. That shit is difficult. It's difficult because it's rare, because it's unusual in nature. It's the scariest thing in the world to make something, to do something more than sow disorder."

Shuffling inside the van. When Mr. Ugly spoke, he seemed to be just on the other side of the doors. Then a sound like drumming on the floor.

Mr. Ugly tittered. "You hear that, Gertrude? That's me taking a piss."

Gertie left the van wondering why she went there in the first place. Seeking an excuse not to drive it into the water, maybe. Some sign Richard could be saved.

The can of beans steamed. The label had charred and peeled from the metal. She plucked it up by the lid and brought it to the table, stirred it with her knife. She tilted it to her lips and sucked out beans and sauce. Warm, but not hot.

David wandered to the path that led to the house, far enough to strain his tether. A cloud of insects followed. He hadn't said much, but she knew he didn't feel good about this, either. They both expected the new host to be sacrificed, but they hadn't planned to take such an active role in their death. The last time David did that, he hadn't been at the helm of his own body.

Last night, she allowed herself to indulge thoughts of what she'd do when this was over. If she wanted to lie drunk in a gutter until she decomposed, she could. But what about David, who had traded his ticket to heaven for a chain to the woman who killed him? As far as she knew, he'd be with her until her own time came. And then what? Would he get the chance to join the rest of the dead on the other side, or was that train long gone?

She was glad for his presence. She never admitted that before. He could be a pain in the ass, sure. His seriousness, his nagging. But his sacrifice was real. And she might not have made it this far without him.

The trailer door opened and Janelle stepped out, mid-yawn. She nearly tripped over the water bucket. "Ow. Oh, it's empty."

"Yeah, sorry."

"S'okay." She squinted at the van.

"He's alive." Gertie held out the beans. "Want some?"

Janelle started to refuse, but her stomach changed her mind. When she finished, she wiped sauce from her chin and tapped the empty water bucket with her toes. "I'll get more. Could use a walk."

"Bad dreams?"

"Yeah."

Gertie chewed.

"When I get back…"

"Yeah."

"Okay." She grabbed the bucket and started up the trail. She walked right through David.

He watched her go down the path. "You think she'll be okay?"

Gertie twirled a finger in the beans. "No. But we can't really help that."

"I guess not."

She tried to eat more, but she'd lost her appetite.

2

Janelle struggled with the handpump as nothing but gurgles sounded in the pipes.

Her walk to the house did not clear her head as she hoped. She kept replaying last night's dream in her mind. She'd been drowning in a literal sea of gore. Tissue and blood roiled and churned and bubbled around her and things flailed below the surface. It was so thick she could hardly move, and when she did, the sea sucked her down. She sank up to her chin, then her lips, mouth filling with rot. Drowning in death. Things below rubbed her ankles, rough as sandpaper. Before she woke, something like seaweed or vines slid up her calves, tightened, and dragged her down into that red hell.

She pumped furiously at the well as if it could force these images out of her head.

She paused when she heard a rumble that had nothing to do with the gurgling pipe.

She crept around the side of the house and peeked around the corner—

And ducked back out of sight, suddenly panting and lightheaded.

An SUV was coming down the drive.

. . .

Ray and Bartov arrived at the Winters's farm at 0937. The house was smaller than it appeared in the photos, and neglect had taken a toll. The tire tracks in the grass indicated it was not entirely abandoned.

Bartov voiced the observation. "Somebody's been here."

"Winters said a cousin tends the property."

"Doesn't look like they've kept up, does it?"

"Let's check the house."

They walked the perimeter. Bartov kept a hand inside his suitcoat, near his shoulder holster. Ray felt the weight of his own weapon, but hadn't thought of using it. He'd never discharged his weapon in the line of duty. Been in a few scrapes, though, including a wrestling match with an amped up tweaker who nearly wrested his pistol out of the holster. Ray cold-cocked the guy before it went that way. After that, he invested in a safety holster. Extra latches needed to be unclipped in the right order and from the right angle. It was no good for a quickdraw, but he didn't see himself getting into many duels these days.

There were clear fingerprints on the front doorknob. Ray made a mental note and tried the knob, careful to preserve the prints.

Around back, they found a cast-iron well pump in a circle of matted grass. The spigot dripped into a bucket below. There was an inch of water in the bucket. Mud had squelched up between the blades of grass, stamped there by narrow shoes. Women's shoes.

You could see she'd run from the pump through the grass, away from the house.

"Someone left in a hurry," Ray said.

.   .   .

Janelle had been one of the fastest players on her softball team, but she'd never run like this. This was not about beating a neon ball to first base. This was everything.

Her lungs burned, thighs and shins and calves, arms and chest, fueled by adrenaline. Weeds whipped so hard against her legs they drew blood. She carried her shoes, one in each hand. The grass tore her feet raw but she forced the pain to the back of her mind.

How far to camp?

How long was the trail?

How much farther?

How much time before the SUV rushed her from behind?

She cursed herself for locking the backdoor. They'd probably check the house first, and if they got inside, they'd waste precious minutes checking empty rooms.

Please.

Somehow, she crested the final hill, with no sign of the vehicle behind her.

Gertie was at the picnic table. When she saw Janelle, she nearly toppled backward. She shot up and ran to Janelle and caught her by the shoulders. "What is it?"

Janelle couldn't catch her breath, but Gertie understood.

"Oh, fuck."

• • •

Ray eased the SUV over the premade ruts through the farmland. There was only one set of tracks, and unless the path let out somewhere, the vehicle that made them was still back there. He could tell from the depth of the impressions it was a heavy vehicle. Possibly a van.

They bounced over the hills, eyes peeled for movement. They passed the sign for St. Chuck's Lake, climbed a hill, and came to a small body of water.

More like a pond than a lake. The surface was perfectly smooth— serene, displaying an inversion of the sky with its popcorn clouds. He recognized the silver trailer from one of the pictures in the Winters' bathroom. A fire burned nearby, its smoke curlicuing upward.

The tire tracks cut to the left side of the lake, then stopped.

"Where's the vehicle?" Bartie said.

"I don't know. Let's check the trailer."

He eased the SUV to the right, already working through the next steps: get a mold of the tire tracks, lift the prints from the house and trailer and test them against Janelle and Richard's.

As soon as he shut off the engine, Bartov was out the door and halfway to the trailer.

Ray eased out and stood still, listening.

Bartov mouthed at him, *Coming?*

Ray held up a hand.

Something didn't feel right. He sensed it in his chest, his gut, his balls.

They were being watched. Not from the trailer. Maybe from the woods, but he didn't think so. He felt as though he were standing beside a trap door. Any second, it would spring open and whoever hid below would come flying out like a stage magician.

"Ray?" Bartov whisper-yelled. "You good?"

Ray wanted a closer look at the place where the tire tracks ended. Because that didn't make sense, did it? Tracks didn't just end like that without another set leading somewhere else, and these ones simply stopped dead, like footprints in the snow that just…

"What is it, Ray?"

"I'm gonna check something."

He cocked his head, listening hard. He pointed at his ear, mouthed back, *Hear that?*

Bartov gave a confused shrug.

Ray wasn't sure what he heard. Days ago, he'd have dismissed it as nerves. Not today. It was real. A bassy rumble or growl emanating from the place where the tracks stopped.

He stepped in that direction.

Something shimmered ahead.

It lasted only a second or less. A waver, like heat lines on blacktop, obscuring the treeline, about as tall as a cargo van.

A soap bubble going pop.

He was at the bottom of the staircase now, searching in the dark beyond dark.

What he heard was the idling of an engine.

He unholstered his weapon.

• • •

"Gertie." Janelle gasped for air in the driver's seat.

"Yeah."

"He's coming… right… toward us."

"I know."

They were both soaked with sweat. Janelle from her run and Gertie from the effort of hiding the van from the men. The cop could not have seen them. Yet here he was, gun in hand, creeping through the grass like he could *smell* them. Either Gertie was weaker than she realized, or the guy had some talent of his own.

If they didn't do something, he would bump right into them.

She considered having Janelle drive them into the lake. Turn the wheel and hit the gas. But the point wasn't simply to kill Richard. It was to keep Mr. Ugly contained and disembodied long enough to fade away, like stars at sunrise.

A bead of sweat rolled between her eyebrows, along the bridge of her nose, and dropped off the tip.

The cop was ten strides away and closing.

"Hit the gas," Gertie said.

"*What*?"

"Before it's too late."

"I'll hit him."

"He'll move."

"He can't even see us."

"Yes, he can."

Five strides away.

David said, "She's right, Gertie. You could kill him."

"Then kill him," Gertie shot back. "Now, Nelly."

Janelle leaned over the wheel, stomped the gas.

∙ ∙ ∙

Ray saw it clearly. Just a blink, a flash.

Or he saw nothing at all.

He saw empty air, yes. Space. But the van was in that space, too.

Two tons of black metal and glass. He *felt* it, and he felt the occupants—two females in the front, a boy crouching in the back, two other figures inside that he couldn't make heads or tails of, one like the dotted lines of an invisible man in a comic book, the other even stranger, impossible to get a bead on, a slippery form, bleach white and yet dark like a stain, sitting with the boy, or on top of the boy, or inside the boy.

He dove right just as a column of displaced air blew his jacket back.

Exhaust fumes hit him in the face.

New treads appeared in the grass as the ghost van tore up the hill.

"What in the hell!" Bartov howled. "What is that!"

Ray aimed his pistol at the space between the tracks. Dirt flung into the air, kicked up by tires he couldn't see. He slid his finger from trigger guard to trigger.

He thought of the boy in the back. A prisoner.

Richard Becker.

He holstered his weapon and pounced up and ran to the SUV.

"Bartie, get in!"

Bartov was too stunned to move.

The wake of dust crested the hill and continued out of sight.

"Bartie!" Ray hung out of the driver's side door. He started the SUV, gripped the doorframe with one hand and steered with the other. He reversed, drew up beside Bartov. "Let's go!"

Bartov found his way into the passenger seat.

Ray punched it.

They lurched up the hill.

Bartov pointed at the settling dust. "Was that…"

"That was your alien in the basement, Bartie."

3

Janelle white-knuckled the wheel.

The van bounced crazily, fishtailing and cutting scars in the grass.

Gertie kept one part of her mind searching for the men behind them. If they neared, she'd continue to cloak the van, though she didn't know what good it would do if the big cop had the gift. They needed distance. They needed speed.

Simple enough, but the van topped out at 70 mph.

"What do we do?" Janelle said.

"I don't know."

"We're not gonna make it."

Hearing it out loud, Gertie almost wept. "We have to."

Any moment, the policemen would appear in the mirrors.

Janelle said, "I have an idea."

"What?"

"Take the wheel."

"What are you—"

"I'll jump out."

"*What?*"

"I'll be a distraction. Slow them down."

Gertie started to protest, but caught herself.

They had to try.

Grass thrashed the grill and undercarriage. The speedometer read barely twelve mile an hour.

"Okay," Gertie said.

"Yeah?"

"It's worth a shot."

David whined, "I don't like this."

"Okay, then," Janelle said. She eased her foot from the gas.

Gertie took the wheel with her left hand.

Janelle slowed to five miles an hour and cracked her door. "Here goes."

"Good luck."

Janelle kicked the door wide and leapt out. She vanished in the grass.

Gertie clamored over the center console and for a horrible moment lost control of the vehicle, which stuttered out of the tractor tracks and straight into the grass. She got herself seated and corrected the wheel. The tires slipped in mud, then jerked forward as they regained traction.

"She fell," David said, craning his neck through the window.

Gertie steered them onto the path. "She'll be fine."

She slid her seatbelt on and pressed the accelerator.

. . .

Dust and bits of grass glided across Ray's windshield like flotsam at the bottom of the sea. He felt a little like that, like he was underwater, in a submersible, traversing some godforsaken trench unknown to man. The world he knew was far away. He could drown here, and if he didn't, if he surfaced to breathe ordinary air again, he would not be the same.

Bartov was facing a similar realization. He made strange noises in his throat, gulping and gasping, and at some point he had removed his weapon to cradle it in his lap.

They were less than halfway to the house when a figure appeared in the middle of the path, running toward them.

Janelle Winters.

Bartov yelped, "*Ay!*"

Ray swerved left, out of the ruts and into the grass around the girl. He did not slow or stop. Janelle slapped the passenger window and shouted something he couldn't make out.

Bartov twisted in his seat to watch her fade behind them. "That's the missing girl!"

They thumped back into the path. "It's a trick."

"What are you talking about!"

"She's trying to slow us down." Like so much else, he couldn't explain how he knew this. Anyway, he'd already called the locals on the radio. They'd secure the girl before long. "Morgenstern is in that van with Richard Becker."

Bartov pressed a hand to the top of his head as if to keep it from bursting. "What van?"

• • •

The van's tires squealed as it shot out of the grass onto pavement, the bumpy ride smooth again. Gertie whipped the vehicle onto the private drive and gunned it toward the main road.

Something slammed into them.

She checked her mirrors, saw nothing.

It came again, followed by Richard's howling laughter.

He was throwing himself against the walls, trying to distract her, or maybe tip the van over.

The SUV spurted out of the field behind them.

She hoped to lose them on the main road.

At the intersection atop the hill, she swung a hard left. The tires screamed and smoked. She heard and felt Richard thump onto his ass.

This road stretched out on a flat plain, so she could watch the intersection in her sideview mirror as she picked up speed, leaving the farm behind. If her plan had any hope of succeeding, the big cop would either pause at the intersection, uncertain where to go, or he would turn right.

He turned left.

The cop switched on his emergency lights. Red and blue blinked at the top of his windshield and between the slats of his grill.

Gaining on her.

She bared down. Her vision wavered and her sweat went cold and feverish. She was pushing her abilities to the limits again. Only now she was not hiding in the back of the van where she could concentrate. She had split her consciousness in half. One half guided her hands on the wheel and watched the road. The other held the feeble cloaks over the minds of the men following her. She could not maintain this split for long.

. . .

"There." Ray tipped his chin at the blur in the road, maybe a quarter mile ahead. He guessed its speed between 60 and 70 mph. He was creeping up behind it.

Bartov placed a shaking hand on the dashboard. "I don't see a thing."

"It's there."

Bartov shook his head and released a long, labored breath. He rolled down his window and hung his head out, either to get air or search for what Ray saw.

It had been a mistake to bring him. Ray thought he would need the support, that having company would keep him from losing it if things got weird. But as strange as all this was, none of it shook Ray like he expected. All his life, while he willed himself to believe in nothing but sound reasoning and the powers of deduction, intuition pointed him toward something less sane. When you look deep enough, to the core of things, you see the emptiness at the center. All things drifting without anchor.

It was time to be honest about this. To be honest with himself.

He had to catch the van. It wasn't just about recovering Richard Becker and bringing justice to Amy Pink. He would chase Gertrude Morgenstern to the end of the earth, until she ran her transmission into a smoking, seized hunk of metal. He would ask her what it's like not to just walk down the stairway to meet the dead, but to live there and learn their secrets.

He pulled behind the blurry object, catching flashes of the rear doors through a haze. He honked his horn to let her know he wasn't going anywhere.

She showed no sign of slowing.

He drew back a car length, checked the opposite lane and found it empty.

He crossed the yellow line and accelerated, drawing up beside her.

. . .

She squinted into her mirror as the SUV eased along the driver side. The cop in the passenger seat leaned out the window and looked straight ahead, his mouth hanging open. The driver grinned in her direction. He couldn't get a lock on her, but whatever he saw, he drank it in.

She was all but tapped out, could barely keep her eyes open. If this went on much longer, she would pass out.

"Y—kay?" David's voice was a bad radio signal.

"No."

"Don't—any—ng stupid."

She tried to wipe the sweat from her eyes with the back of her wrist, but her wrist was sweaty, too. Her eyes burned. "Any ideas?"

"—on't know."

Her vision slurred. She meant to pull her hand from the wheel and wipe her brow again, only to find that her hand was no longer on the wheel, but on the seat beside her.

Her other hand was in her lap.

In the passenger seat, David flickered in and out.

"—ertie? Are y—oka—"

Everything plunged into blackness.

When she came to, the van had drifted over the white line. There wasn't much of a shoulder. The passenger side tires growled over dirt and the van vibrated.

She yanked the wheel left, overcorrecting and swerving into the cop's lane.

Both cops watched her with eyes popping out of their sockets.

She was fully visible.

They *saw* her.

• • •

It was just like John Becker said, only Ray experienced it in reverse. The van was not there, and then it was. *Pop!* Where there had been a blurry distortion speeding along at 70 miles an hour, there was suddenly an ordinary cargo van, black, with a faded decal on the side advertising Arlo's Furniture Warehouse: Quality Secondhand Furniture at Great Prices.

Ray laughed. He was enthralled.

This sensation did not last long.

The van drifted dangerously onto the shoulder, and he could see that the driver—Gertrude Morgenstern, short girl with blonde hair plastered to her face and neck—slumped in her seat.

"Whoa, whoa," he said.

Gertrude jolted, suddenly awake, grabbed the wheel, and pulled it hard left.

Too hard. She veered toward him.

He edged toward the shoulder on his side. At the same time, he became aware of a tortured groan coming from the passenger seat, the sound of a mind cracking in half, followed immediately by the *pop!* of Bartov discharging his weapon into the van's driver side window. A double-tap. Ray only heard the first round, the second muffled by the ringing in his ears. He screamed, "Don't!" and hit the brakes, but it was too late.

The van swerved right, over the shoulder and off the road. It tipped sideways and slammed onto its passenger side in a plume of dirt and dust.

. . .

The first round came through the window inches from her head, shattering the glass. The bullet bit the air in front of her nose. She flung herself over the center console, flattening her body. She could not tell where the second round went.

The van shook as the passenger tires drifted onto the shoulder. There must have been a culvert, because suddenly the van fell to the right, forcing her first against the door and then the center console, the seatbelt yanking on her ribs and knocking the air from her lungs so hard she barely noticed the roaring noise or the grass and dirt spitting through the shattered passenger window.

4

The van lay on its passenger side in the field. The wheels spun idly. It had cut a path through the sod like a meteorite.

Bartov still pointed his weapon.

In a calm, even voice, Ray said, "Stay here, Bartie. Don't move."

Bartov made no sign that he heard.

Ray left the SUV and sprinted to the wreck. He thought he saw someone coming around its other side. A man with dark features. Shorter than him, with the start of a belly and stubble on his cheeks, eyes wild with shock. Ray called, "Sir, did you—"

But the man was gone. *Pop!*

No time to figure that one out.

He climbed up onto the driver side paneling and lay on his stomach.

Gertrude Morgenstern gazed up at him, suspended in her seat by the seatbelt.

"Are you okay?" Ray said.

She coughed.

"I'll get you out, but I need you to shut the vehicle off and put it in park."

"You don't understand." Her words were slightly slushy.

"Now."

She did as she was told, and before she could react, he reached inside, gripped her wrist, and pulled the keys from her hand. She pawed at him. "Wait!"

Back on the road, a door slammed.

Bartov approached at a jog, his weapon holstered. "I didn't— I just thought— Is everyone okay?"

Ray tossed him the keys. "Check the back."

Gertrude went bug-eyed. "Don't," she croaked. "Please."

"You're okay. We'll get you outta here."

Like a rabid animal, Gertrude clawed at her restraints.

Bartov called, "Ray! It's not looking good back here!"

Gertrude grabbed his shirt. "You'll let him out!"

.   .   .

David had never been in an accident before. Already being dead was probably the best way to experience it. When it was over, he drifted out through the ceiling and surveyed the damage. The van looked okay. Might still drive if they got it upright.

He circled to the front as the big cop ran over. Curiously, the cop paused and looked directly into David's face and started to say something, then shook his head and continued on. The other cop—the one who shot at Gertie—lagged behind.

The big cop told the other to check the rear.

David thought, *Oh shit.*

He reached the back doors first. They were still closed.

But the smaller cop came around with a set of jangling keys. He rushed forward in what he must have thought an act of heroism and plugged the keys in place and yanked at the first door, which dropped open like the bottom jaw of a massive animal. Richard lay just inside the compartment, face bloody, neck twisted at an unusual angle.

"Ray!" the copy yelled, "It's not looking good back here!"

No, David thought. *Not after all this.*

.   .   .

The woman was in shock. No doubt about it. She struggled against the seatbelt, pulling at it like she could tear it in half.

Ray had a million questions, but he would get to them later. He told her to calm down.

Her daze wore off. "I'm not the fucking threat here!"

He reached his left arm into the cab and grabbed her around her right armpit, lifting her enough that she could click the seatbelt free. She struggled to balance herself against the center console, stood up through the window frame, and slid herself out as Ray gripped her under the arms to assist. She cursed at him the entire time.

"I need you calm."

She slithered on her belly and swung her legs over the side and dropped to the grass. At the last second, Ray caught her wrist. She tried to squirm free, but he had her tight.

"Let me go!"

"Calm down."

He maneuvered off the side of the van and onto the grass beside her, twisting her arm behind her back as he did. She was small but wiry.

"Let's go," he grunted, and steered her toward the back end of the vehicle. If Bartov secured Richard, they could get them both into Ray's SUV and have a nice chat.

Gertie snarled, "You have no fucking idea— Let me go!"

"You'll have plenty of time to explain—"

A series of grunts and snorts behind the van cut him off.

"It's too late," Gertrude said, voice soft with resignation. "He's free."

5

Mr. Ugly unfolded from the compartment. The creature was not the three-foot-long thing it had once been. It still had the same basic shape—a central column with many limbs radiating outward. But what had been like octopus arms a foot in length had grown into appendages as long as David was tall. They were a variety of shapes, some cylindrical and tapered at the tips, some like four-inch wide flatworms, others spaghetti-thin and prickling with cilia. At least four were stiffer, fuller, and jointed, with an underlying structure that might have been bone. These ended in deformed, paddle-like hands with stubby digits. Atop the central trunk of the body sat the head—defined cheekbones and only the impression of a nose, the mouth a round orifice ringed with something like stringy meat, and a single eye in the center of what constituted its forehead. It supported itself on its lower limbs like a centipede straining to walk upright. The upper limbs slid along the van like elongated slugs.

The cop never saw it. Not when those limbs were mere inches from his face. Not when they crowded around him, teasingly, closing in. Not when Mr. Ugly plastered himself to the cop's body and twisted tight as shrink-wrap and forced the limbs into his mouth, nose, eyes, and ears, squeezing into him like jelly oozing down a drain. Even when the cop backed away and shook in seizure, gurgling and hacking, he had no idea what was happening to him.

. . .

Gertie dug her heels into the dirt. "Do you have handcuffs?"

"What?"

"Zip-ties. Anything."

She'd never get the tranquilizer gun from the van now. If Mr. Ugly went after the other cop, maybe they could restrain him in time. And maybe, if the big guy had the gift, she could convince him what they were up against.

"What are you—"

"Do you have them or not!"

"In my vehicle."

"You need to get them. You have to hurry."

He shoved her forward, ignoring her.

She limped. Her left knee ached something terrible, and her head wobbled strangely on her neck. But she was alive. For now.

The smaller cop—the one who shot at her—waited behind the van with a blank expression. He pointed his pistol at Gertie's chest. This close, he wouldn't miss.

The big guy released her and patted the air in a peacemaking gesture. "Put it away, Bartie. It's under control."

She was too fatigued to see Mr. Ugly clearly, but she knew he was wrapped around the guy. The cop stood off-balance, and he twitched spasmodically except for his hands, which held his weapon steady. Two minds vied for control of his flesh, so when he spoke, it came out slurred: "Nische to shee you, again, ol' friend."

• • •

Ray didn't understand. There was something wrong with Bartov. It wasn't merely the physical signs—the darting eyes that were not his and the way his skin seemed to ripple. It went beyond that. A *wrongness* that wafted off of him like poison fumes.

Bartie chuckled. *Huc-huc-huc.*

Ray had heard that laugh before.

On some basic level, below conscious understanding, he must have known all along what he was chasing. The shadow in the video. The vision of Ehblu Htoo on the highway with *something* wrapped around him. The same *something* he'd sensed in the back of the van. The laughter in the static. All symptoms of the same disease.

"Hey, Bartie. Take it easy now." His words were worthless, and he recognized, somehow, that this man was no longer Bartie. If he bought a few seconds, he could reach into his holster and unsnap the safety catches. Maybe the Bartie-thing would listen with a weapon pointed at it.

Bartie's face spasmed. One eye winked while the other widened, one corner of his mouth drooped while the other curled upward. "Oh hiya, Ray. Nysh to shee yo, too. Owe you a detch of grashichude. It wush shtuffy in the back of that van."

Keep him talking. "I wish I could say it's good to see you, too, but I don't even know what you are."

Bartov whipped his head back and inhaled. He raised his trembling left hand. With a violent snort, he snapped his fingers, and the seizing and twitching stopped.

Whatever had been fighting for control just won the battle. The pistol never wavered.

"It's lovely down here at the bottom of the stairs, isn't it, Ray? Your new friend there can tell you all about the fun we have down here, can't you, Gertrude?"

"Okay, pal," Ray said. "Why don't you put the gun down and we can talk all about the stairs."

Bartov rolled his eyes.

If Ray concentrated, really strained, he could see *something* coating Bartov's body, shielded by the same wavy heat-lines that hid the van. He wasn't sure he wanted a clear view of whatever it was, but he'd aim there. Once he got his weapon out.

Out of the corner of her mouth, Gertrude whispered, "You have to run."

"What's that you're whispering about, Gertrude? You think he should run? Well, that's prudent, but you see, the detective here thinks he can kill me before I kill you. Isn't that funny? He thinks I want to *kill* you. He thinks I want to kill *you!*" With a flick of his wrist, Bartov turned his weapon on Ray and fired.

Pop-pop.

Hot white pain slammed through Ray's chest.

Bartov arched his eyebrows as if he'd just made a compelling argument.

Shot me, Ray thought. *Bartie shot me.*
Not Bartie. The shadow.
It was always the shadow.
He fell.

6

Gertie ducked and spun and dashed to the road. She expected to hear gunshots ricocheting in the dirt behind her, but Mr. Ugly called: "Where are you going, Gertrude!" Her movements were sluggish, and something in her chest ached terribly. If she hadn't broken a rib, she had at least bruised them. It was all she could do to stay on her feet.

She ducked around the driver's side of the cop's SUV, putting the vehicle between her and Mr. Ugly. She made her way to the driver's side door and pulled the handle. The door opened. Staying low, she reached in and felt around the steering column for the ignition slot. Smooth and empty. No key.

She leaned across the seat, searching the interior. No sign of the cuffs the cop mentioned.

She spotted a duffel bag in the back.

In the distance, sirens sounded.

If she stalled Mr. Ugly, maybe the cop's backup would subdue him without killing him.

She poked her head up, peeked through the window.

Mr. Ugly was at the passenger window, smiling.

She ducked, circled to the back of the SUV. She would keep the vehicle between them.

"It was always right in front of you," he called. "You just didn't want to see."

She crouched behind the back bumper and clicked open the rear hatch. The hydraulic cylinder raised it up. She grabbed the duffel bag and ducked out again.

"Do you know what a binary star is, Gertrude? I learned about them from a professor I knew. The name is deceiving. It's not a single star, but a pairing of two. Two stars, locked in a dance, circling around each other, spinning faster and faster until the stronger rips the weaker apart. Eats it right up." He made an obscene slurping sound. "You see?"

His voice had been coming around the driver side.

Now he went quiet.

She opened the bag and dug through the equipment: camera case, crime scene tape, chalk, tape measure, plastic crime scene markers, and here, a bundle of something like heavy-duty zipties. If she could get behind him, take him by surprise, she'd slip one of the zipties around his wrists.

She took out the bundle and poked her head around the driver side.

Mr. Ugly wasn't there.

She dropped to her belly and peered under the SUV, searching for the cop's feet.

Nothing. He must have been standing behind one of the tires. Or he—

A hand gripped the back of her shirt, yanked her back and flung her through the air.

She flailed, kicking at empty space. Lost the zipties.

She landed hard on her ass.

The cop towered over her. He held the gun out, displaying it like a sacred artifact. "This is a Glock 22. It holds fifteen rounds. There are eleven left." He raised it.

She threw her hands out and winced, ready, at last, to die.

He pointed the weapon straight up and fired 1-2-3-4-5-6-7-8-9-10 rounds into the sky, pressed it under the cop's chin, and blew his brains through his skull.

7

The cop collapsed. Blood pumped from the hole in his chin and the top of his head and pooled bright on the pavement.

The sound of sirens grew louder, minutes away.

Movement in her peripheral vision. David, jumping up and down. Just a flash. Pointing at the cop's fresh corpse.

She knew what David saw. She figured it out the instant Mr. Ugly blew the cop's head off. Like he said, it was always right in front of her. Right now, he was unwinding from his host, rising and chuckling through that asshole of a mouth.

A cruel joke. The whole thing. He hadn't been strong enough to possess her before. And he wouldn't try it again until he was sure he'd win. All along, he knew she was following him. All those crime scenes were custom made for her. She'd been speeding toward this trap for years.

She shoved herself upright, grunting at the new pain in her joints and tailbone and the steady ache in her chest. She rushed to the dead cop and tore the pistol from his hand. She put the gun to her temple and squeezed the trigger.

Nothing happened. The trigger didn't even click. The top of the gun looked funny. Like it needed to be cocked.

Empty.

A cold tendril wrapped around her waist. She looked down, but couldn't see it.

She stood.

Another invisible limb lashed over her left arm.

There was no gun in the SUV that she had seen. There was some broken glass by the van, but it was all safety glass, little diamonds. The bigger cop would have a weapon, wouldn't he?

She lurched toward the shoulder of the road, more steely appendages latching onto her. A nearby voice giggled. She forced her feet, one after the other, to carry her out of the road and into the grass, to the big guy who lay on his back with his eyes open, staring at the blue void.

Mr. Ugly's limbs circled her neck, her thighs. One drilled into her right ear and thrummed like a mosquito.

She dropped onto the cop, straddling his waist.

He blinked. Not dead, but close.

She slipped her hands inside his jacket, felt for his holster.

He swatted at her. "Don't," he wheezed.

One of Mr. Ugly's tentacles found its way into her left nostril and slid down her airway.

She yanked at the handle of the cop's gun.

Hacking at the fibers wiggling in her throat, she coughed, "Please."

The cop pushed at her.

There was something wrong with his holster. It was made of hard plastic, and there seemed to be multiple straps holding the gun in place. Some kind of safety mechanism.

"You have to kill me," she said.

A bristly tendril wormed up her belly and over her chest and up her neck and chin.

This was it. Her last moment of freedom.

She leaned close to the big cop's ear and forced out the words: "It has what it wants."

A prickly tentacle darted into her mouth and something pinched inside of her and Mr. Ugly's laughter echoed all around.

8

After the cops left her on the farm, Janelle stood for several long minutes, chest heaving, arms dangling, useless. Soon the sound of the blowing grass replaced the noise of the motors.

Far off, tires squealed.

A grasshopper whirred heavy wings and landed on her dress above her belly button. It studied her before flying off again.

If she closed her eyes, she could imagine she was a little girl on a camping trip at Uncle Chuck's farm. She used to make this walk to the house to use the bathroom. Usually, she peed in the lake or squatted by the creek, but she enjoyed these walks. It was the only time her mom let her run off by herself. She had two minds about that time alone. On the one hand, she could dally and stop and look at whatever she wanted without anyone telling her to hurry or asking what she was so curious about. On the other hand, it was scary to know she was on her own. She'd get a strange feeling, like she could vanish, as if the sky might open and suck her away. And with that feeling came a creeping sensation along her flesh, hyper-alertness of her own vulnerability. If something scary—or hungry—came along the path, there was no one to lift her out of its reach. No one would even hear her cry.

If these walks began as leisurely strolls, dark thoughts nudged her into a speedwalk and sometimes into a jog. When she reached the house, she'd feel silly for her fear. Aunt Carolyn would be tapping out some waltz on the piano, and Uncle Chuck, if he was around, would let her grab two cookies from the jar and pat her on the head and tell her she'd better get back before Mom and Dad worried. Safe in the presence of grownups.

Authority figures. Those who knew the world and its dark corners and could tell her there was nothing lurking there.

How their ability to comfort faded over the years. The growing suspicion, as she got older, that these adults were just as afraid of the shadows as she had been, only they knew to lie about it. She had been developing that same skill until recently. Legally, she was all grown up, but felt very much like a child, and had been eager to be like them—so certain of the world.

She knew better now.

There was nowhere to go. No warm house smelling of cookies with a chipper tune in the air. Aunt Carolyn and Uncle Chuck died years ago. All of her friends were dead. Gertie was gone, and the police, though she knew none personally, had seemed like the enemy since the day she first registered skin tones. Who was there to rely on now?

The sirens were close.

She walked to camp, crossed the stream, and entered the woods.

She climbed the Fallen Star and sat there, arms around her legs. She listened to the emergency vehicles roll into camp, their doors slamming, voices barking. Too distant to make out the words.

Time marched forward. People thrashed through the woods. She flattened herself to the top of the rock. They called her name. Voices she did not recognize. They retreated for a while, and when they returned, they were joined by the sound of heavy breathing, snorting, chuffing.

Dogs.

The animals and their handlers shot through the woods like rockets. Twigs snapped and popped and leaves crunched on the forest floor. They came to the boulder, sniffing.

Then barking.

She lay there another minute, knowing that she had been discovered.

"Okay," she said to herself, quietly. Then louder: "Okay!" She stood up. "Okay!"

She leaned over the edge of the boulder. A man stared up at her. He wore a brown uniform. His dog was a German shepherd. It barked wildly. The man blew a whistle.

PART 5
ROAD'S END

1

Ray woke alone in a hospital room.

Machines beeped. A plastic tube ran under his nose, feeding him oxygen. This was called a nasal cannula, he remembered. He'd learned that from Shawna. An IV in his forearm connected to a bag of saline on a metal rack above him. There was not much else in the room. A sink, a jar of cotton balls on the counter. A garbage pail with a bloody pad hanging out from under the lid.

He saw it all through a drug-addled fog. It hurt to turn his neck, and he was aware of a steady pain in his body that he couldn't pinpoint. A bandage had been taped over the left side of his chest, under his pectoral.

A deputy he didn't recognize poked his head into the room and ducked out again. Voices in the hallway. The deputy returned with a middle-aged woman in pink scrubs who greeted him with a big smile and asked questions he only sort of understood, though she seemed satisfied by his answers. She informed him that he was in Abbot Northwestern Hospital in Minneapolis. "Do you know why you're here, Ray?"

"Shot." His voice cracked.

"That's right." She explained that he had undergone emergency surgery, but he was stable, and would be moved upstairs for recovery shortly. "You're on the news, you know."

"The news?"

"You should rest. I just wanted to say thank you." She must have read the confusion on his face. "My cousin's a police officer. It's dangerous work. But I don't need to tell you that."

He felt his lips moving.

"What's that?" the woman said. "Who's Shawna?"

The world blurred, and he found himself in a different room with less oppressive lighting. A TV hung on the wall past the foot of his bed and there was an empty bed to his right. The same unfamiliar deputy sat in a chair by the door, twiddling away on his phone.

Ray felt a sudden release of pressure below his waist and realized that he'd been given a catheter and was using it now. The deputy glanced up. Ray shut his eyes, pretending to sleep.

Hazy hours passed in this realm of semi-wakefulness. At one point, a nurse entered with a computer on a rolling stand. He checked Ray's blood pressure and heartrate and walked him through more questions. What year was it, who was the president, rate your pain on a scale of one to ten, what's your date of birth. His pain localized in his abdomen. Felt like someone stood on his chest, digging toenails into his ribs.

The nurse did something to his IV, and the pain eased off.

The doctor who came to speak with him was a tired looking Indian man with hairy knuckles. He spoke with the emotional detachment Ray expected of doctors.

"Upon entrance, the projectile fractured your left ninth and tenth ribs and grazed your left lung. We're giving you oxygen as a precautionary measure, but there was only a slight hemorrhage that we were able to stitch up quite nicely. The projectile came to a stop in the posterior mediastinum and was removed during surgery. We don't usually do this, but I have it if you want it. As a souvenir, perhaps?"

"No thanks." He'd seen enough bullets.

The doctor smiled. "You're going to be okay, Ray. We'll keep you for several days, assessing along the way. How does that sound?"

Ray gave a feeble thumbs up.

The doctor lowered his clipboard. "For this type of injury, things couldn't have gone any better. I hope that's some relief. You've been very lucky."

Luck had nothing to do with it. That only one of Bartie's shots hit its target was not lost on him. It wasn't the result of chance. It was Bartie. When his finger squeezed the trigger, he was still fighting the shadow. He must have been. Otherwise, Ray would be in a different room, naked on a metal table with Dr. Aire pointing her pen at two holes over his heart.

Obermeyer arrived sometime later, accompanied by two men. Ray recognized one as the sheriff of Marsh County, a middle-aged man named Cruise—black goatee and a flattop, badge pinned to the right side of his chest, a small American flag pin on the left. Ray didn't recognize the other man, but he wore plain clothes and a badge on his hip. An investigator. Upon their arrival, the deputy stood and saluted. The sheriff said, "You don't have to do that, Benson." Benson nodded with embarrassment and went into the hall.

The men dragged chairs to Ray's bedside. Obermeyer lifted a plastic Walmart bag. "They told me you'd need a change of clothes. I got a cheap sweatshirt and pants. They said loose fitting, so I got extra-large. Hope that works." He set the bag on a shelf above Ray's head.

Ray thanked him. His chest felt like a blast furnace.

Obermeyer gestured at the other men. "This here is Sheriff Cruise and Detective Sergeant Wheeler, from Marsh County. I hate to do this now, Ray, but we're trying to piece together what happened this morning."

"Hell of a mess," Cruise agreed.

The Detective Sergeant balanced a notepad on his knee.

"Where's Bartie?" Ray said.

Obermeyer cleared his throat and rubbed at the fabric over his knees. "Let's start at the beginning, if we can."

Ray's heart skipped a beat, though the monitor didn't notice. He remembered hearing gunshots—one after the other, like firecrackers— but he'd been on his back, lost in the red fog of pain. Everything else blurred.

"Ed? He's okay, isn't he?"

Obermeyer said, "What made you go to the farm, Ray?"

He told them about the picture in the Winters' bathroom. He skipped the part about touching the photo and feeling—

Pain in his chest.

It hadn't been an invitation, he realized. It was a warning.

"So you drove up there. What did you find?"

He said how they found the well and the footprints and drove on to St. Chuck's Lake.

Here he paused, unsure how he could explain what happened next.

"We found the van, and we pursued."

Sheriff Cruise cut in, "Did you approach on foot before or after calling it in?"

They must have had guys analyzing the tire tracks and boot prints at the lake. What they'd see was Ray's SUV parked off to one side, his footprints approaching the van to the left, and Bartov's tracks leading to the right, toward the trailer. These were minor details, but they didn't add up with the van sitting there in plain sight, which is how it would appear. No detail was too minor when talking about the wounding of an officer.

"I wish I could remember," Ray lied. "It's all foggy."

Obermeyer said, "What happened next?"

They'd never understand that although Bartie shot him, it wasn't Bartie.

"I'm sorry. I don't remember much, other than the pursuit."

The Detective Sergeant muttered to the sheriff, "He's on a lot of painkillers."

"That's all right, Al," Obermeyer said. "We should let you rest. We'll come by tomorrow."

Before they could stand, Ray said, "What happened to Bartie, Chief?"

All of the men shifted uncomfortably.

"Al," Obermeyer sighed and dropped his voice. "Bartov appears to have taken his own life."

"That can't be right," Ray said.

"You're sure you don't remember anything else?"

Detective Sergeant Wheeler said, "Who shot you, Detective?"

"I don't know," Ray lied. "I'm sorry. Maybe it's shock."

"What about the driver?" the sheriff said. "Did you get an ID? Did you see anyone else?"

He felt like shit for holding his tongue. This wasn't why he'd become a police officer—to obstruct an investigation. But through their questioning, something he'd forgotten had returned to him. Something Gertrude Morgenstern said before he blacked out.

It has what it wants.

"I'm sorry," he said. "Christ, I wish I could be more help."

"Okay, Al," Obermeyer said. "All right."

The sheriff sucked his teeth. "What about—"

"That's enough for now. Ray, you need to rest. If you remember anything, we're gonna keep the deputy posted at the door a while. You just holler when you're good and ready."

All three men stood and pushed their chairs back.

"Chief?" Ray said.

"Yeah."

"Did you find the kids? Becker and Winters?"

Obermeyer stuck his hands in his pockets. "The Becker kid was in the back of the van when it went off the road. He perished in the crash. We found Janelle Winters on the farm this afternoon. She's at the Sheriff's Office. We'll take her back to Fairfield in the morning. Looks like she may have been involved in the Becker kid's abduction, after all."

"How's that?"

"We found some kind of tranquilizers in the cargo van. Likely a sedative. She had one in her pocket. We'll get toxicology from the Becker kid soon, but I'd put money on the sedative being in his blood."

And just like that, Ray understood. Morgenstern, the shadow, Janelle Winters, Richard Becker, the incident on the highway. What happened to Bartov had happened to the Becker kid. Morgenstern and Winters must have sedated the boy and loaded him up just like his father said. But it wasn't Richard Becker they meant to abduct. They were trying to stop the shadow.

"Any sign of the driver?" Ray said.

"Looks like they stole your SUV. The sheriff's guys found it at a Shell station up the road. Right in town, but nobody saw anything. Half the state's out there knocking on doors. If it was Morgenstern, we'll find her."

"Just wish I could help."

"You will." Obermeyer tapped his own temple. "Rest up and rack your brains. And when the doctor says eat your Jell-O, you say, 'How much?'"

"Yes sir."

With a curt nod and sympathetic smile, Obermeyer led the others out.

Ray lay there a while longer, resting and preparing for what came next.

It was going to hurt.

The machines beeped. The clock ticked. Deputy Benson played a game on his phone.

It was most likely a courtesy to post the deputy here. Ray didn't have a family, and it sent a message that, regardless of your county or station, the boys in blue took care of each other.

Either that, or the sheriff considered Ray a flight risk. In which case, he was right.

"Benson," he croaked.

The boy didn't hear.

"Hey, Benson."

The deputy tucked his phone away. "Sir?"

The boy was stiff. Nervous. Ray could use that.

"What's your first name, Benson?"

"Eric."

"What time is it, Eric?"

Benson checked his watch. "Ten o'clock."

"That late?"

"Yes, sir."

"You see this IV in my arm, Benson?"

"Sure."

"It's not doing much to quench my thirst. I thought I saw a vending machine in the hall."

"Oh, I don't know if—"

"You ever been shot, Benson?"

"Well, no."

"It makes you thirsty. Like you've been wandering a desert for forty days and forty nights. I swear when they wheeled me in here I saw a vending machine just out there. All I want in this world is a blue Gatorade, Benson. It's all I can think about."

"I just don't know if you should drink anything but water. The nurse—"

"Oh, hell," Ray huffed. "Never mind." He made a point of smacking his lips.

The deputy went back to his phone. After a minute, he grunted, "Oh, cats." He stood. "Blue Gatorade, was it?"

"The dark blue," Ray said. "Not the light kind."

"Right."

"You're a saint, Deputy."

"Yeah, sure." The deputy left, easing the door closed behind him.

Ray waited thirty seconds. When he was sure the deputy had gone, he sat up, gritting his teeth against the pain in his chest. He tore away the nasal cannula and yanked out his IV. The machine at his bedside released a frenzy of beeps. He pressed the power button, and it went silent. He was more careful removing the catheter.

He leaned on the bed and tugged on the gray sweat suit Obermeyer brought him. His shoes had been placed at the end of the bed. Squeezing into the sweatshirt, he thought he might pass out from the tearing sensation in his left side, but he managed to keep awake and upright. He found a Ziplock bag containing his belongings on the shelf above his bed—wallet, keys, cell phone, badge. His service weapon wasn't there. It would be locked in a secure location.

He eased open the door and peeked down either side of the hallway.

The nightshift. Quiet.

He shuffled toward the elevators.

On the first floor, he followed the exit signs to a security desk. The guard glanced up.

Ray flashed his badge. "Hell of a night," he said, trying not to favor his right side.

"I bet."

On the sign-out sheet, he wrote *Eric Benson.*

He continued down the hallway, following signs for the parking garage. When the security desk was out of sight behind him, he leaned against the wall and fought a wave of dizziness. Nausea churned his stomach and white-hot pain burned through his upper body.

He forced himself forward.

The parking garage was less than half full. He stalked around the level he came out on, looking for vehicles most likely to have what he needed. They'd see him on the hospital cameras, but it didn't matter. He'd be gone before they reviewed the tapes.

He found a black Land Rover that seemed a likely candidate. It wasn't just intuition that pointed him to this vehicle. He could admit that now.

He crouched at the rear of the vehicle and felt around the undercarriage. The lockbox was unmistakable. He wrapped his fingers around it, pulled it free, and set it on the pavement beside him. The entire box was about the size of his palm, a combination lock with three numbers. Breathing heavily and scanning the garage for onlookers, he took the box in both hands and ran his thumbs over the dials, feeling the numbers.

Just know, he told himself. *Just know the combination.*

Nothing came to mind.

He resisted the urge to throw the lockbox across the garage.

He tried to relax, though the entire left side of his chest had clenched up.

How the hell was he supposed to do this?

He thought back to all the times the gift had helped him. Was there some trick to activating it? Some magic phrase he could utter like in a children's book?

No, it was never like that. It wasn't something you could switch on and off, consciously. In fact, he'd never *consciously* used it at all—even when it brought him answers. It wasn't like he *knew* the picture in the Winters' bathroom would zap him when he touched it. This thing he had—this gift—guided him, but it never truly revealed itself. He didn't command it. In a sense, it commanded him.

So he shut his eyes, and he willed the gift to take over.

He let his fingers scroll through the lockbox's dials.

It popped open with ease. He pulled out the key.

He never even read the combination.

Inside the vehicle, he let the cold air of the AC soothe him. He resisted the fatigue that weighed on his eyelids, fought against the voice that told him it was okay to sleep, that his body needed to heal, he'd been shot and opened up on an operating table and if he wasn't careful he'd tear his stitches—inside and out.

He couldn't stop now. There were only two people in the world who could provide the answers he needed. One had gone missing. He knew exactly where the other was.

He adjusted the seat and the mirrors the best he could with his limited mobility, shifted the vehicle into gear, and guided it toward the exit.

2

Some years ago, Gertie had been driving through a state park in Florida—
a thickly forested place of trees and swamps. Around a curve, a spot of
bright red caught her eye in one of the trees. She pulled over, shut the
engine off, and left the van. The midday sun beat down. The air was
humid, the forest like a jungle with its endless green. She crept between
the trees. David, who had been asking the whole time, "What is it? What
did you see?" looked up and fell silent.

About halfway up a tree, an antique bicycle had been absorbed into
the bark except for the front wheel and handlebars. It must have been
leaned there decades prior, and the tree grew up around it. It was both
beautiful and disturbing. This bicycle had once belonged to someone. It
had been left alone—forgotten—so long the tree swallowed it, claimed it,
and raised it up. Now it belonged to no one, conjoined with slow-moving,
unstoppable nature.

Gertie recalled this scene from deep within the recesses of her mind.
She was the bicycle now, the object absorbed and not her own. Mr. Ugly
was the tree.

His winding roots wrapped her, stole into her, crushed her into
stillness. She felt his membranes—unreal yet substantial—great and
small, tunneling into her mouth, nose eyes, ears, between her legs, a
network of psychic veins rippling without and within.

She could do nothing but watch as he used her body for a toy.

She'd meant to kill herself, but couldn't get the wounded cop's gun
from its holster.

When Mr. Ugly took control, he forced her hand into the cop's pocket
and fished out his keys. They took his SUV, ripping down the road and

into the town of Darwin, a modest suburb on the prairie. They parked behind a gas station across from a grain silo. Mr. Ugly left the vehicle there, using her legs to walk into the residential neighborhood.

He made her jog when sirens blared down parallel streets, blue and red lights flaring between the houses. He cut through the front yard of a colonial style house and climbed the wooden privacy fence behind it, clutching the planks and dragging her over the top. They clattered into a heap on the other side.

Human flesh is so pathetic. This thought was not hers.

He righted her and stumbled to the house's back door.

Locked.

He elbowed one of the back windows. It bruised her arm, but the glass cracked. Another blow sent shards tinkling to the ground. He knocked the hanging pieces free and pulled her through. She rolled over the back of a floral patterned couch. Cheap paneling covered the walls. Thrift store sofas and empty pizza boxes the only furnishings.

No one was home.

Mr. Ugly went straight to the kitchen. He rummaged through the drawers until he found a steak knife. He took it with him down the hall and entered the master bedroom where he flung her onto the unmade bed.

They would rest now. Then they would eat.

Relegated to a prison inside herself, she did not truly sleep. Neither did he. They vibrated against each other, his foulness tainting her, an unnamable sickness, black oil coating her insides.

She saw him like never before, like no ungifted individual could, and attempting to make sense of him threatened the soundness of her mind. His was no mind at all. There was no will, no conscience, no fears or hopes or sensations—those colorful ribbons that drifted from people's skulls. There was only a chasm, at once empty and full of shadows, radiating vileness.

This thing she had been chasing, what she called Mr. Ugly, was but the surface of a vast and terrible construct concealed beneath a mirage. In the depths, she glimpsed a disjointed jumble of what might have been memories. First, an endless darkness in the midst of an expansive nowhere, beyond time. Sensations of emptiness, drifting aimless, formless, a near eternity in the seamless darkness. This was *before*. This was its womb.

Until, at last, a moment collapsed *nowhere* into *somewhere*, rending the fabric of its existence in two: the change came like an explosion of sound. Like a pinprick of light. A breach, dilating the dark. The sensation of suffering called to it from somewhere *out there*, somewhere *above*, or *under*. Like a shark scenting blood, it followed the siren call of pain, and there it found its path into the real, a world of glorious physicality and violence.

It tunneled through the breach into the mind of a man—a murderer.

Gertie saw what it had seen. Looking through human eyes, the eyes of a killer, upon a fresh scene of brutality. Blood on the floor and walls, victim sprawled with innards out. Some anonymous woman. It mattered who she was, but it didn't matter at all. She was dead. No longer a person. She was meat. Her murderer looked on—a man as anonymous as his victim—unaware of the stowaway in his mind. This was Mr. Ugly's birthright. Somehow, this act of evil had torn the fabric of reality and summoned it forth. Here it took its first greedy sip of suffering.

It sought more.

It learned to control its host, the first of so many.

It killed.

It fed, gained power.

When the host body was lost to a police officer's gunshot, it found another.

And another.

And another.

In time, it found Gertie, or she found it. It studied her in the warehouse as she moved between the furniture, radiating like a star. Its twin, its binary. It had not been strong enough to take her then. It raged at that failure, and resolved to rectify it.

It had her now, all it wanted.

She was one in a million.

Her pain, a delicacy.

⋅ ⋅ ⋅

The clock on the nightstand read 10:17 p.m. when keys jangled in the front door.

Mr. Ugly sat up, shook her head and felt around the bed for the steak knife. She had no adrenaline left. Every joint felt hyperextended and her ribs ached with each breath. Mr. Ugly may have controlled her body, but she felt her pain as sharply as ever.

Mr. Ugly slipped off the bed and pressed her back to the wall beside the bedroom door.

The owner of the house stomped down the hallway in heavy boots. He entered the room. He was in his early 20's, blonde and tan. He wore a filthy white t-shirt with holes in the back and faded blue jeans. Dirt or sand coated him and he smelled of sweat, dust, and alcohol.

He had just peeled off his shirt when Mr. Ugly brought the knife down on his head. His eyes crossed, and he stood there moaning, t-shirt clutched in a fist. Mr. Ugly yanked the blade out with a burst of blood and drew it across the man's throat. The man fell onto the bed.

In the instant of death, Mr. Ugly shuddered, pulsing with renewed strength.

So did Gertie. Her ribs no longer ached. Her joints loosened. Everything felt brand new.

Mr. Ugly sucked in a breath and released it with perverse pleasure.

He took the time to carve out the dead man's eyes and place them in his mouth.

Why? Why mutilate the bodies?

He sawed off the fingers, one at a time. Next, he removed the genitals and flayed the legs below the knees. He placed strips of flesh on the bedspread, creating a halo around the man's head.

He did not choose for humankind to be his hosts. He could enter animals, too, but it would be no use. He'd done it once, and was trapped there without a hold until the thing went under a moving tire. Such creatures were too innocent, incompatible with his form. But humanity received him, welcomed him, even. They were made for each other.

Deep down, we all tend the soil where he plants his roots.

"Don't listen to it," David said. He stood in the corner of the room, glaring. "I can feel it too." He touched his forehead. "He's trying to wear you down."

Even so, there was some truth in these thoughts. Just this morning, she confessed that he was not unique in the world. People didn't need him as an excuse to kill and mutilate. They were clever apes, but they could never save themselves from their darker nature. Just look at her now, her hand carving flesh from bone. It was satisfying, how it tore, how she could pull a man to pieces and spread him before her. She hated her species nearly as much as Mr. Ugly did.

No! she screamed within, and felt her cage rattle.

The prison trembled with laughter.

Drenched in blood, she tracked red footprints though the house.

Mr. Ugly took the man's keys from the kitchen table and went outside and climbed into the rusting Ford pickup and drove through town. Gertie's gift, like her body, was his now, and he burrowed into the mind of a deputy at the first roadblock they came to and saw that Janelle Winters was being held at the Marsh County Department of Corrections.

3

Janelle had never seen the inside of a jail. She expected metal bars and dimly lit corridors, inmates shouting and reaching through the bars while a mean looking guard slammed a baton and hollered threats. The reality was more mundane, though she only saw the holding area. There were no bars on any cells, just plain rooms with gray doors and off-white walls. More clinical than she expected, like a kennel for people.

She was searched and fingerprinted and taken to a conference room with bad lighting where a series of investigators questioned her for hours. They told her in calm, reasonable voices that she had to explain everything that happened up until her capture or she would be going to prison for a long, long time. She didn't doubt this. By now, the life she once expected had shriveled up and blown away.

They told her about the crash. How a detective had been killed, another seriously injured. How the driver fled. If she just talked, they promised, she'd get a lighter sentence.

She hardly heard a word. She asked, "You saw Richard's body?"

They seemed very interested in this question. "Yes."

So she knew that somebody had opened the van doors. Mr. Ugly was free. He could be anyone now. One of the people questioning her. A stranger on the street. Her mom or dad.

"Why did you abduct Richard, Janelle?"

They took her to a holding cell, a rectangular room, maybe fifteen feet long and ten wide. Metal benches lined the walls, one of the few features that matched her preconceived notions, in addition to the toilet-sink combo at the far end. The toilet was concealed by a waist-high barrier that offered no real privacy. She resisted as long as she could, but finally used it out of necessity.

The only other woman in the cell had long, greasy gray hair and wore tattered clothes that smelled like pee. Two more women were brought in sometime later, guided by a deputy. They stumbled to the bench across from Janelle, plopped down, and proceeded to drunkenly slur out a song that had no apparent melody and words Janelle couldn't understand. They looked to be in their mid-20s. Janelle didn't know what time it was when they entered, but it couldn't have been more than an hour before they both slumped on the bench, snoring.

The old woman muttered to herself and avoided eye contact.

Janelle cried on and off. She hid it the best she could. She hated feeling this weak, this scared, this helpless. She wished she could be the hardened criminal the police thought she was.

Before they put her in the cell, they promised that she'd be taken to Fairfield first thing in the morning and charged with a slew of crimes: conspiracy, assault in the second degree, use of drugs to injure or facilitate a crime, false imprisonment.

None of it mattered. They had failed. *She* had failed. Her life was over.

She only hoped that Gertie was still out there, fighting.

4

At 11:11 p.m., Mr. Ugly parked his stolen pickup truck outside the main entrance of the Marsh County correctional facility. The doors had been locked two hours ago, but he stood before them in Gertie's body and slid the mechanism free without ever touching it.

He pushed the doors open and stepped into the dim lobby.

Empty chairs in rows. During business hours, visitors would wait here before passing through security. Straight ahead, at the far end of the room, a bright rectangular window looked into a small office occupied by a female deputy with a headset on. She sat behind the glass and stared at a series of computer screens that displayed the lobby and holding cells.

Mr. Ugly approached the glass.

The woman looked up.

Her name was Darcy Childs. She was twenty-two years old, born in Minnetonka to a family of law enforcement officers, had been a deputy for two years, and worked in this building for just over eight months. She was engaged to a State Trooper by the name of Linden McNamara. They had a big ceremony planned for next spring at a cabin venue they reserved a year and a half back. They wanted a baby, and agreed that working patrol was too dangerous for a future mother. But the job was boring. She wished she could be out responding to calls instead of stuck at a desk. It was mind numbing, and hardly felt like law enforcement except for the occasional disturbance in the holding cells.

When she saw the woman in the lobby, she was almost glad for the disruption.

Then she saw the dried blood on the woman's hands and face.

Deputy Childs stood and practically shouted, "Miss, are you all—"

She never finished the question. A sudden warmth spread from the crown of her head down through the center of her chest, into her groin, her toes. A soothing voice cooed that everything was all right, all she had to do was hit the buzzer for the security door and let the woman through.

Childs met the woman in the hallway, at the security scanner. The woman grinned, cracking the flecks of blood on her cheeks, and for a moment Childs wondered who she was and why Childs had let her through. But her skepticism passed, the calm returned, and the voice told her to kneel.

The concrete was hard on Deputy Childs' knees, but she didn't mind.

She would do anything for the voice.

She felt no alarm at the sight of the knife.

. . .

Janelle's ass kept falling asleep. She tried crossing her legs, uncrossing them, slouching, sitting straight up. Nothing helped. Finally, she lay on the bench and stretched out. The old woman watched her disinterestedly. Janelle almost asked how she could sit there for so long without moving, like some Buddhist monk, but decided against it.

Her primary feeling, beyond the waves of fatigue and despair, was hunger. All she'd eaten in the last 48 hours was the fish she and Gertie caught, a mouthful of beans, and a soggy Salisbury steak an investigator brought her during the interrogation. When she shut her eyes, she pictured burgers, fries, and a strawberry milkshake. She could practically see the sweat dripping down the cup. Her parents used to take her out for that exact meal after softball games.

Would she ever eat such food again?

She'd seen enough crime shows to know she could've asked for a lawyer. Truth was, she didn't care. There was nowhere to go, nothing to do. With Mr. Ugly free, she was safer in a cell than on the street. But her next thought made her sit up straight: *What about her parents?*

Mr. Ugly held a grudge. That's what Gertie said. He'd gone after Gertie's father to punish her. What stopped him from going after Janelle's family?

She wasn't hungry anymore. Her palms sweat, and she tapped her feet, fighting the urge to pace. Her only comfort was that Gertie hadn't been caught, unless they picked her up sometime after—

Click click click.

A noise at the cell door.

At first, she didn't recognize the face peering through the little window. She'd never seen her grinning like that.

Gertie tapped the knife against the glass again—*click click click*—and opened the door.

5

The old woman had heard the tapping, too, and watched the door swing open. Gertie slid into the room, eyes glassy, knife in her fist. The old woman did not react.

"Gertie?" Janelle whimpered. She stood and backed toward the corner of the cell, bumping into one of the sleeping drunks, who snorted and sat up.

"Yo, why's the door open?"

The other drunk cracked an eye. "What's going on?"

They couldn't see her, Janelle realized.

Gertie had used that trick before. Except, this time, it wasn't Gertie doing it. She was *his* puppet now. Janelle couldn't see him, but the mad glee in Gertie's eyes told her so. He forced Gertie to step slowly, deliberately across the room, knife out like a torch.

He paused in front of the old woman.

The woman leaned forward to look through the door.

Gertie grabbed her by the hair.

The woman yelped.

Gertie plunged the knife into her throat.

The drunk girls screamed.

Janelle wanted to tell them to run, but Gertie blocked the exit, invisible to them.

The woman slumped to the floor. Blood arched from her wound in diminishing pulses.

"They shot her?" one of the girls screamed.

"What the fuck!"

"Help! Help us!"

"What's happening!"

One of them started for the door.

"Wait!" Janelle yelped

Mr. Ugly thrust the knife into the girl's gut, pulled it out, and plunged it again and again, before sinking it into the back of her head. The remaining girl yowled and pulled herself into a ball. She shook her head and cried into the space between her knees. Mr. Ugly cut her throat.

The only sound now was the dripping of blood—a leaky faucet.

Mr. Ugly turned to Janelle.

She had to run. It was her only chance.

"Try it," Gertie said. "How far will I let you go?" Mr. Ugly touched the knife to Gertie's forehead. Bits of ragged flesh clung to the serrated blade. "I see you."

Janelle was in the driver's seat of a jeep, speeding along the highway while torrents of rain sluiced across the windshield. She could hardly see the lines of the road.

"I'm pulling over," she said to her sleeping companions. "It's too dangerous."

She flipped on her hazard lights and pulled to the shoulder.

Richard stirred beside her. "What's going on?" He placed a warm hand on her thigh. "Are we home?"

"Not yet."

Amy and Jeff woke, too.

"Chicken," Jeff said. "Afraid of a little storm?"

Janelle stuck out her tongue.

"Probably for the best," Jeff admitted. "It's my mom's jeep."

Amy agreed. "It's nasty out."

They arrived at Richard's house three hours later. His father waited up. He opened the front door and placed his hands on his hips and waved as his son pulled a suitcase from the jeep.

Richard came around the driver's side and wrapped his knuckles on the window. Janelle cracked the door. He leaned in, pecked her on the lips.

"Ooooh." Jeff made kissy faces in the back.

Richard flicked him off.

Amy laughed.

Richard trudged his suitcase up the front steps. In the light of the porch, she saw the blood running out of his ears and nose. The left side of his head had collapsed

"Okay, chaperone," Amy said. "Drive us home."

In the rearview, Janelle saw Amy curled on the seat with her head in Jeff's lap, her back to Janelle. Blood poured from the hole in the base of her skull.

"Aw man," Jeff said. "You'll stain the upholstery."

He coughed, splashing blood across the dashboard.

"They died because of you."

A hand gripped Janelle's throat and pressed her to the wall.

No air. Spots of light swimming. Gertie's face a funhouse distortion.

"It's your turn," Mr. Ugly said, "but it's not the end. I'll be seeing your parents, just like you thought. Don't worry, you'll be there with them. Your head, anyway. Think I'll do your father first, make your mother watch. Then I'll stop by Richard's place. Say hi to his dad. And Amy's sister, Charlee? I'm looking forward to that. I'll take my time with Jeff's family. Tie them up, do them one at a time. Let them listen from the living room. Yeah."

He raised the knife.

Barely conscious, Janelle imagined someone standing in the doorway behind Gertie. Imagined a voice calling out, demanding the Gertie put down the knife and step away from the girl. "Do it now," she imagined the figure saying. "I know what you are."

6

The pistol shook in Ray's grip. He'd requisitioned it from the deputy's body at the security gate. He'd passed two other bodies in the hall. When he first looked into the room, he saw the three women on the floor and Janelle leaning against the far wall, hands up.

Then he registered the shape that pinned her there.

Morgenstern was a smear of color, a sort of shimmer.

It has what it wants.

"I'll put a hole through that head you're hiding in," he said, matter-of-factly.

"Is that right?"

"Try me."

A ripple of energy passed over the shimmer.

"You've got two seconds," he said. "One."

Morgenstern released Janelle. The girl slid wheezing to the bench.

Morgenstern ended whatever spell kept her hidden. Ray saw her clearly now.

And he saw *it.* A white, misshapen twist of jelly-like flesh, the central trunk extending from a lumpy head in the crook of Gertrude's neck. He couldn't tell where the trunk ended—lost among the mess of limbs, like giant worms winding round.

"My God."

"That's right, Detective. Behold."

He tightened his grip on the pistol. "S— Step away from the girl."

"I can see inside you, Ray." She still had her back to him.

"Drop the weapon and place your hands on the wall!"

"You don't know a thing."

"I said now!"

She didn't react. "You've been running from shadows so long. Do yourself a favor."

Keep running, the voice spoke inside his mind—a filthy, repugnant sensation. A series of flashing images. Every corpse he'd seen—on streets, on highways, in apartments, on beds, on sidewalks, in bathrooms, on metal tables in cold morgues naked and pale with their pink wounds circled in blue and black marker and all at once they sat up and glared with accusation in their fishdead eyes and he knew that he had failed them all, that their killers had never been found or had gotten off light or were enjoying three square meals a day and trading cigarettes for porn and sleeping like babies and meanwhile a million more murderers were out there plotting, lifting weapons, squeezing triggers, slashing blades, swinging fists as their victims raised meek hands and fell backward on the streets and highways and apartments and beds and sidewalks and bathrooms and metal tables and Ray gaped, helpless, hopeless, sinking into an abyss of despair.

"*RESIST!*" a male voice screamed.

Pressure in his head like he'd never felt.

"*RESIST!*"

Back in the holding cell.

Bodies on the floor.

Gertrude Morgenstern approaching, knife in hand.

Behind her, a man, red in the face, screaming, spittle flying. He was translucent, almost gray. The same man Ray saw briefly after the van went off the road.

David Arlo.

"*Fight it!*" the ghost screamed. "*It's in your head!*"

Ray had lowered the pistol. Gertrude within arm's reach. No time to raise the pistol. She had him. Even with his pounding head and the remnants of his vision like the afterimage of a flashbang, he knew he was about to die.

Gertrude's arm cocked, the steak knife too gory to glint.

Behind her, Janelle lifted her head and dove forward.

She hit Morgenstern at waist-level. They veered to Ray's left. Gertrude's knees clipped as they collided with the bench on the wall and she brought the knife down toward the back of Janelle's head.

The strangest thing happened then.

The ghost of David Arlo lunged—

And grabbed Gertrude's arm.

Rather, he grabbed the steely appendage of the creature wrapping her arm.

Time stood still. David and Gertie's eyes locked. Even Ray gaped, unsure what he was seeing. A ghost gripping a thing that had no body.

David marveled at his own hand, then tightened his grip and, with his free hand, raked at the creature's head. They rolled off the bench, onto the floor. Ghost and demon locked in a wrestling match. Gertie grunting and contorting and David rending at the creature as if he could squeeze out whatever imitation of life animated it. Appendages loosened from Gertie's torso and whipped at the ghost, knocking him back.

David lost his grip.

Gertrude righted herself, stunned and horrified.

Ray had plenty of time to aim. He lined up the shot.

"Don't!" Janelle, who had fallen at his feet, slapped the weapon. "You'll set it free!"

Gertrude dashed to the exit.

Ray reached for her, but she slashed. The blade narrowly missed his fingers.

He allowed her to pass, thinking, *What am I doing?*

She ran from the cell, pursued by David's ghost, then Janelle, who paused in the door and barked at Ray, "Come on!"

7

Janelle burst from the cell as Gertie ducked around the corner. Shocked faces stared through portholes of other holding cells. A deputy lay on the floor, a stream of blood curling along the linoleum.

The big cop followed Janelle, favoring his right side.

Janelle calling over her shoulder, "Hurry!"

In the main hallway, she leapt another body, a middle-aged man on his back, his neck opened up, blood spatter on the walls and ceiling. At the security gate, she avoided looking directly at the young woman dead in front of the lobby doors.

She entered the lobby just as Gertie pushed through the exit.

Halfway across the room, Janelle paused. What would she do if she caught up?

An engine roared outside.

She shook off her doubt, crossed to the exit and entered the night.

Gertie was clear behind the truck's windshield. She peeled out as she swung out of the parking lot and onto the main road. Then, in a flash, the vehicle vanished.

The cop crashed through the lobby doors at a loping jog, his face pale yellow. He made his way to the only other vehicle in the lot—a Range Rover parked near the main entrance.

Janelle beat him to the driver's side. "Keys!"

He didn't argue. He tossed the key over and limped to the passenger door.

She had the engine running by the time he grunted his way inside, and they ripped out of the parking before he could close his door.

"You can see her, right?" she said.

The cop leaned against the headrest and squeezed his eyes shut.

She snapped her fingers in front of him. "Hey! I need your help!"

She didn't know where they were. The buildings were old and quaint. The downtown area of a modest, rural city. Few cars out tonight. A small mercy.

"Do you see her?"

"No," the cop hissed.

They sped toward a red light.

She slowed. "Which way?"

The cop shook his head.

"You're like Gertie aren't you? Which way did she go!"

He spasmed, arching his back and groaning. She recalled what her interrogators said about the detectives who pursued Gertie from the farm. One had been killed. The other shot.

This guy had at least one bullet hole in him.

She turned right at the intersection, an arbitrary choice.

The cop settled back in his seat. Through gritted teeth, he said, "I'm not like Gertie."

"You saw her at the farm."

"Where are we going?"

"I was hoping you could tell me."

He snorted a cynical laugh. "I went to the station to find you. Thought you could tell me what's going on." He rolled his eyes and turned away, jaw clenched.

"Are you okay?"

"Meds are wearing off."

She blew through a red light. The buildings thinned out near the edge of town.

She said, "You did something to her in the cell, didn't you? She let me go."

He shook his head. "Not me. The ghost."

"The ghost? David?"

"Yeah."

She eased off the gas.

"What are you doing?"

She turned down a residential street and pulled to the side of the road. "We lost them."

The engine purred, and the AC blasted. The houses were mostly dark.

She needed to think. She had assumed the cop knew some secret, or had a secret weapon. But he was just as clueless as she was. And with Gertie's gift, Mr. Ugly was practically unstoppable. He'd gone on a killing spree at a sheriff's office. He could vanish if he wanted, hide out far from the only two people who knew to look for him.

But that wasn't his style.

"I know where he's going," she said.

"Where?"

"It doesn't matter. If you shoot her, he'll just find a new host."

"What then?"

"Gertie's van. Is it totaled?"

He attempted to shrug. "Don't know."

"Where is it?"

"Local impound, maybe."

"Where's that?"

Gingerly, he tapped the screen in the center of the dashboard. A GPS logo popped up.

"That should work," Janelle said.

"I'm Ray, by the way."

"Janelle."

"I know."

"Right. You're a cop."

"Detective."

"Whatever." She typed into the GPS.

They didn't have much time.

8

Mr. Ugly drove erratically out of town, crossing the painted lines, blasting through red lights, hopping curbs, sideswiping parked cars. Gertie expected sirens. It was only a matter of time before someone discovered the bodies at the sheriff's office.

But it wasn't the police that worried Mr. Ugly. It was the ghost riding shotgun.

David sat with his hands upturned in his lap. No one had considered the possibility that he could touch the creature. They'd become so used to his status as a mere observer.

The creature brooded. He was rattled. Afraid, even.

"Afraid?" Mr. Ugly seethed. "I'll show you fear."

They were beyond the edge of town, headlights carving southeast on Route 12, toward Darwin. In another ten miles, the town appeared as a dome of dull light in the distance.

David glared. "What are you planning?"

"Wait and see." Gertie despised the feeling of the creature moving her lips, speaking in her voice. Like hearing a recording of herself, or an evil doppelganger. And yet—

And yet, in a way, it was a relief. She had no control, so she had nothing to fight against, no choices to make. She could gaze from the windows of her eyes while he steered her body. Her will didn't matter, and likely never had. It was always Mr. Ugly she was meant for. They had traveled the same road so long, headed for collision. Only one would survive, and she knew it would be—

These aren't my thoughts.

She wanted to cry, but even her tear ducts were his.

David said, "Don't give up."

A couple sheriff's cruisers had set up a checkpoint at the edge of Darwin. Road flares painted the air toxic red. A deputy leaned against his vehicle and smoked a cigarette.

Mr. Ugly slowed.

David stiffened. "Leave them alone."

"Or what?"

Mr. Ugly reached into the officers' minds and cloaked the truck from their sight. They passed unnoticed. Half a mile later, they pulled into the parking lot of a Speedway.

"Low on gas," Mr. Ugly said.

David checked the gauge. "The fuck we are."

The lights were on in the station, two cars parked at the edge of the lot.

Mr. Ugly parked alongside the building, blocking the windows.

"Don't," David said.

Mr. Ugly shut off the engine and exited the truck.

David followed. "I said stop."

Coming around the front of the truck, Gertie counted three people through the windows of the shop. Two young men chatted with a blonde girl working the register. One of the boys wore a blue baseball cap and leaned on the counter with a sly smile. The girl got a kick out of whatever he said. The other boy had dark hair and Greek features. He pretended to be interested in a tub of snacks behind his friend, but stole bashful glances at the flirting couple.

Mr. Ugly pushed through the front doors. The bell jingled, and Baseball Cap jerked upright like he'd been caught cheating on a test. The Greek boy smiled at Gertie.

Her clothes were black, and the blood on her cheeks had faded.

Mr. Ugly didn't prod their minds, didn't cloak himself. Just walked up the aisle and took the knife from behind his back and went for the Greek boy.

"I said stop!" From behind, David grabbed Mr. Ugly's head.

Mr. Ugly was prepared. He wrapped three tendrils around David's wrists and neck. David yelped and tried to pull away, but the multitude of arms wrenched him to the ground.

The Greek boy's eyes lit up as the blade sank into his gut, then in and out in rapid succession—five times. Fifteen. Twenty.

Baseball Cap grabbed at Gertie.

Mr. Ugly swung the knife, catching the boy's right wrist. The boy staggered backward, pink bone visible in the gash on his arm.

The Greek boy coughed and pawed at Gertie.

Mr. Ugly pressed the tip of the blade to the boy's jugular.

Somehow, David got his feet under him. Still tied in the creature's restraints, he heaved himself toward the back of the store. Mr. Ugly hadn't expected that. He stumbled, lost his grip on the kid, who slumped to the floor clutching his gory abdomen.

A flash of color appeared behind the counter: the cashier leveling a shotgun.

Mr. Ugly ducked just as the weapon roared.

Buckshot blasted gum and chips from the shelves above Gertie's head.

Mr. Ugly released David and spun on Gertie's heel.

The cashier ejected the spent shell.

Mr. Ugly dashed behind a shelf as another round boomed.

Something tore into Gertie's right shoulder and bicep.

Mr. Ugly sprinted for the exit. Debris like confetti in the air.

Another shot. Pellets punched through the glass six inches above Gertie's head.

They pushed into the night and dashed around the front of the truck. Mr. Ugly reached for the driver side door handle with Gertie's right hand, but incredible pain jolted through her arm.

"I see fear!" David screamed from the doorway of the gas station.

Mr. Ugly used her left hand to open the door and found the keys on the seat.

He fumbled with the key in the ignition.

David was in the passenger seat, rage etching his features. "I see fear, you motherfucker!" Through him, Gertie saw the blonde girl rushing to the gas station door, raising the shotgun as she came. If Gertie still controlled her mouth, she would have smiled.

Mr. Ugly turned the key, shifted into drive, and stomped the gas. The truck lurched forward as a fourth shot shattered the passenger window and tore through the ceiling.

The truck bounced over the curb and onto the road.

Blood bubbled from Gertie's arm. The wounds throbbed.

Up ahead, another roadblock.

Gertie's heart raced. It was Mr. Ugly's heart, too. And David's.

They would pass this roadblock like they passed the others. They would drive south, toward Fairfield. The night was not over, and Mr. Ugly was more furious than ever.

9

It soon became clear that finding the van was more complicated than driving to the nearest impound. For starters, they didn't know which agency had taken it. If the Fairfield PD had it, it could have been processed and brought to a local tow yard for storage. If awaiting processing, it would be at the station in Fairfield, where Ray and Janelle would never gain access. If the Marsh County Sheriff had it, it could be at any of the towing companies in and around the city of Graywood. Ray didn't know if the county had a processing facility.

"We don't have time to drive all over," Janelle said, fighting to keep her voice steady.

"No."

"So where do we go?"

Ray shook his head, wincing. The pain had become severe since the station. He hadn't checked his bandages, but had likely split his stitches. "I don't know."

Janelle wanted to scream. She shut her eyes and took a breath. "You said it might be at a local impound. Three came up on the map. Is one more likely than the others?"

Ray focused on the screen. Instead of a map, he saw video of a sailboat cutting through blue water. That seemed odd, but he was in too much pain to dwell on it.

"All right," Janelle said. "I'll try the closest. That's Townline Towing Company."

Ray whistled through his teeth. "Sure."

He leaned against the headrest, shut his eyes, and felt Janelle turn them around.

In another moment, he checked the GPS to see how far they had to travel.

Now the screen displayed an ordinary map. No video. No sailboat.

"What are the other names?"

"What?"

"Of the towing companies."

"Big Jim's Tow and Repair, and, um, Anchor Towing."

"Anchor," Ray said. "It's at Anchor."

Janelle studied him, processing. "Okay."

Careful to keep her eyes on the road, she typed into the GPS.

Anchor Towing was just south of Graywood on an otherwise empty stretch of land. The property extended for half a football field, unpaved fields occupied by rows of rusted old junkers. Almost immediately, they spotted the van at the end of one of the rows. The damage wasn't clear until Janelle pointed the brights at it. The passenger side was in bad shape—dented and scratched to reveal the metal beneath the paint, one headlight busted, bumper hanging at an odd angle, grill streaked with clots of dirt, passenger window shattered. As far as they could tell, the wheels were intact and the tires full. Around the back, the doors were closed and apparently functional.

"It looks okay," Janelle said.

The main building was a nondescript, blocky gray structure. Two garages stretched out from either side, each with six bay doors. The keys to the van would be inside the main building.

Lucky for them, the front door was made of glass.

Ray was in bad shape, so Janelle agreed to go alone. Approaching the door, she spotted a rock twice the size of her fist just beside the entrance—a makeshift doorstopper, she guessed.

She lifted the rock, wound up, and whipped it at the door as if she were in the outfield throwing home. The rock punched through the glass like a bullet, leaving a nearly perfect outline of itself. She reached through the hole and found the lock.

Inside, she hit the light switch and winced at the sudden brightness.

Towers of tires lined one side of the room, but the space was otherwise cleaner than she expected. The rock sat in the middle of the room between a couple racks of pine tree air fresheners, windshield wipers, and other auto accessories. She hurried behind the counter.

A small black cabinet hung on the wall. Rows of keys inside, about thirty in total. Each had a plastic band attached, names scrawled in black marker. She flipped through the keys, dropping those that didn't suit her needs. At last, she came upon a key with the words *Sheriff* and *Nissan* scrawled on the plastic identifier. She ripped the key off the hook and turned to leave.

The phone on the counter caught her eye.

Maybe she could buy everyone just a little more time.

She practically pounced on the phone and lifted the receiver. She typed in the first three numbers to her parents' home phone, then stopped. She had to be smart about this.

She replaced the receiver and ran outside.

Ray was already getting out of the Land Rover. "Find it?" he called.

She held the key up for him to see. "I need you to make some calls first."

"Calls?"

"They'll listen to you. You're a cop."

"Detective."

"Whatever."

10

By the time Mr. Ugly arrived at the Winters place, a thunderstorm had rolled out of the southwest and unleashed a fury of wind and rain. Lightning drew black mountains in the sky and thunder rolled like the shouts of giants.

He pulled into the driveway. The house was dark. If Janelle's parents were inside, they would be sleeping. Gertie was too drained for Mr. Ugly to search the house with her mind. He would have to search it the old fashioned way.

All through the drive, blood had run down her ruined right arm and pooled in her seat. As Mr. Ugly forced her out of the vehicle and into the rain, it trickled down her legs and soaked her shoes. He stood a long time with the rain beating down, fighting Gertie's wooziness.

He had been thwarted twice. He knew his anger made him reckless, tired of this game, but not ready to give up Gertie's body or gift. She was, in truth, one in a million. The perfect vessel—the perfect toy. If he killed the parents here, he could gather the energy he'd lost at the gas station. In all likelihood, it would heal her arm.

He started up the sidewalk to the front porch.

Gertie pleaded, *Leave the girl alone. She hasn't done anything.*

Mr. Ugly ignored her, amused at her begging.

It was me. I brought her into this. Punish me.

Mr. Ugly assured her, "I am."

David stayed several feet behind. Mr. Ugly poised his limbs in the air behind Gertie's back, daring David to try something. The ghost had merely distracted him at the gas station. The Greek boy had suffered nicely. That was something. If not for that fucking cashier, things would have gone much better.

The front door contained a small window. Mr. Ugly smashed it, reached in, and turned the handle. The front room was still and empty. He stepped inside and left the door open. He considered the carpeted stairs to the right, then continued ahead, to the kitchen.

He had lost his weapon at the gas station. He approached the knife block on the counter like a connoisseur. He gripped each handle and slid his options free one at a time, clattering all that did not please him to the floor. None were to his liking, so he opened drawers and selected another steak knife with a serrated blade. He preferred weapons with teeth.

The downstairs was empty. He returned to the front entrance and started up the staircase slowly, mindful of Gertie's lightheadedness. He paused at the top of the stairs. To his left, at the end of the hallway, cracks of light outlined a bedroom door. He smiled. All the other doors were opened, their insides dark.

Please, Gertie begged.

The doorway neared. The seams of light seemed to vibrate around the black rectangle. In the distance, at the base of the stairs, Gertie heard rain drumming the hardwood floor. Thunder boomed and wind howled and something outside thudded along the road, battered by the night.

"Please," David said. Like begging fire not to burn.

Mr. Ugly clamped the knife between Gertie's teeth, gripped the handle with her good hand, and flung the door inward.

The room was just as empty as the others. A bedside lamp had been left on. The drawers of both dressers—his and hers—were still open. Anonymous articles of clothing lay on the floor, and a glance at the closet showed empty hangers.

Janelle's parents had left in a hurry. It didn't make them safe, and there were three other families Mr. Ugly intended to visit. But for now, these people were free of him.

Mr. Ugly sat on the bed. Gertie's shoulders slumped.

This was disappointing, but he knew he'd been impatient. Foolish, even. Maybe the psychic bitch and the impotent ghost were right. Maybe he *had* been scared.

Certainly, he'd been rash.

He blamed the proximity of human thoughts. He'd been in their company too long, absorbing their neuroses. They obsessed over the inevitability of their own deaths, always attempting to outrun it or distract themselves from it. When faced with it head on, they lost their minds. Like he had tonight, charging into a gas station to prove a point that could have been made if he'd come directly here, before Janelle's parents packed their panties. He was a god, not some foolish mortal. He had all the time in the world.

More, in fact.

The blood in Gertie's wounds had mostly clotted. She was not going to die from them as long as he kept them clean. He would rest some moments longer, then go to a neighbor's house.

And why stop there? He'd been thinking so *small*, used to bodies with fewer talents. He could remain in this house for weeks if he wanted. This street—this neighborhood and all neighborhoods like it—was open for feasting.

He would feast.

He would grow. In time, he wouldn't need these pathetic hosts. Then he would show them all the extent of his power.

These people were but a blip in this timeline. He'd have them all, eventually.

• • •

David paced half circles through the bedroom while the creature sat. Its vertical slit of an eye studied him with reptilian indifference. When it took hold of him at the gas station, he felt the power in its limbs, their intent, and he understood its true nature.

It was just a stomach. Its limbs were the esophagus that swallowed prey. Once trapped, it digested the mind and soul, dissolving sanity and hope. It could do that to David still. It had taken his body. Years ago, it tried to take his soul—and failed. Now they were tethered again, through Gertie. If it trapped him in its arms, the digestion would begin anew.

How much time before Gertie dissolved?

He had one last thing to try, but he would have to get close. That would be challenging enough. Even now the limbs protruding from

Gertie's back tracked him, waving like antennae as he paced. Masked by the thunder and rain, he didn't hear the van pull into the driveway, but a creaking on the stairs shortly afterward announced the distraction he needed. He was not a religious man in life—or death for that matter—but he prayed that Gertie had the strength to do what he needed her to do. If she didn't, there would soon be more ghosts in this house.

11

In Minneapolis, Ray had spent two years on the Emergency Response team and participated in a handful of no-knock warrants. Even accompanied by a dozen other officers, adrenaline would course through him so he had to hide his shaking hands by gripping his service weapon so tight it hurt. People became addicted to that kind of rush, like soldiers to war. Not Ray. He dreaded those assignments, standing before the locked door awaiting the breach, never knowing if the people inside would be zonked out on heroin or amped on meth and eager to die in a hailstorm of bullets. If it weren't for the endless training drills that taught him to ignore the doubt and fear, he'd have stood frozen and stupid while his brothers and sisters in blue rushed into harm's way.

Tonight, as then, it was duty that sent him into Janelle's darkened house.

To serve. To protect.

To step into the ugliness.

He limped inside with the requisitioned pistol tight against the right side of his chest, left hand over his right to steady his aim. His body ached, but adrenaline kept the pain at equilibrium.

Janelle followed him inside. He'd told her to stay in the van, but she refused.

He gestured at the door and mouthed, *Close it.*

She eased it shut, careful not to make a sound.

The sudden quiet risked alerting anyone within, but he had to hear the sounds of the house. All he heard now were the muffled storm and the patter of rainwater dropping from their bodies onto the floor. He sensed the first floor's emptiness, and turned to the stairs.

Willing the floorboards not to creak, he shuffled to the bottom step.

A dim yellow light illuminated the upper hallway.

He gestured to Janelle to remain where she was. She frowned.

He started up.

Creeeaak. He winced at the sound his foot made on the second step.

Thunder boomed.

He continued, leaning on the railing for support.

Janelle followed.

He waved at her to go back.

She shook her head.

He tucked the pistol in tight as he neared the top of the stairs.

Two steps remained.

The light came from the left side of the hallway: the parents' bedroom.

He paused on the final step. He sensed a presence in the hallway, pressed against the wall directly beside the stairs, just out of view. Waiting for him.

His palm sweat against the pistol's grip. If he shot, he couldn't kill. Had to be strategic.

Now or never, Ray.

He stepped forward, into the light of the hallway.

She was there, where he expected. Gertie, a small, thin woman, soaking wet and grinning, had flattened herself against the wall. Now she lunged, and in her quickness she was less than human, something white and wicked. The blade of the knife she held flashed like scales in water.

Ray deflected with his left hand. With his injuries, the movement was sluggish, and the blade arced across the meat of his palm. He closed his fingers around her fist and slammed it into the wall. At the same time, he swung at her head with the pistol.

She ducked.

The pistol thumped a hole into the wall.

She lowered her shoulders and bucked forward, head-butting his chest.

The pain was enormous. His vision went white, and he stumbled backward.

She came at him. He saw the creature clearly. Like some long, thin jungle snake, its body encircled hers, that head on her shoulder, watching him with one vertical yellow eye. Some of the limbs sprouted like feelers. All pointed at him.

David saw his chance. He'd been waiting in the bedroom, hoping Mr. Ugly would forget him. As the big cop stumbled and Gertie charged, David rushed from behind.

But he'd miscalculated. He was too far. Gertie swung the knife at the cop's neck while David was still several paces away.

Something darted from the staircase, a howling thing that collided with Gertie and pinned her against the opposite wall.

Janelle.

The girl shrieked and flailed and battered Gertie with imprecise blows, thumping her chest and shoulders and ruined right arm.

Mr. Ugly's limbs flashed upon Janelle, wrapping her wrists, waist, throat. Impossibly, they wrenched her arms above her head and lifted her into the air.

David went for Mr. Ugly's head. It whipped tentacles at him. He dodged them and wrapped his arms around its head and yanked backward with all his might.

Ray grabbed the wrist of Gertie's knife-wielding hand. Slick tendrils wriggled under his grip, sliding up his forearm. Others found their way around his neck and squeezed until he saw spots.

"GERTIE!" David screamed. "FIGHT! PUSH HIM OUT!"

A passive observer in the center of this struggle, Gertie could only watch. What did David expect from her? Even if she could fight back, what would be the point? Mr. Ugly had been invited into this world by human acts of evil. Was it so bad that He returned the favor? She couldn't fight, anyway. Not with Him inside of her. David could tug at Him all he wanted, but he was just a mortal's spirit. His pathetic, ethereal hands were no match for the many arms of God. Arms that, with Gertie's gift, could reach out and touch the living like never before, choke the life out of them, tear them apart like the chattel they were.

"FIGHT!" David shrieked. "*GERTIE, YOU STUBBORN BITCH!*"

Something in Gertie flinched, as if slapped. David never talked to her like that.

"Did you come all this way just to watch? This is your fight! It's always been your fight! You're stronger than him! Fight, you shithead! You morose, nihilist ass! *FIGHT*!"

Like climbing out of a nightmare, she saw clearly the scene at hand and the inevitable outcome. Ray with his hands restraining hers, Mr. Ugly choking the life from the big man whose eyes were beginning to roll, Janelle held aloft, bones straining in their sockets, and inside herself, the creature's wicked tongue at work, spewing its poison thoughts.

It had called itself God, but David pried at its perch on her shoulder, and she felt something loosen—that tongue rocking free like a stake shaking in mud.

"*GERTIE, PLEASE!*"

She felt her own body in this struggle. Felt it keenly.

Not Mr. Ugly's body. *Hers.*

She concentrated on the index finger of her left hand, straining to take it back—just make it flex, make it twitch. Just one fucking finger, goddamn it.

Nothing.

Mr. Ugly laughed within. Wild, mocking laughter.

But David's fingers found the corner of the creature's eye.

He hollered, "*NOW!*"

David dug into the socket.

Mr. Ugly had never felt pain. It shocked him, and in that instant, his tongue slipped.

Janelle fell half-conscious to the floor, and before she could get her footing, she tumbled backward down the stairs.

Ray still gripped Gertie tight. The tendrils around his throat released, and he sucked in a breath, locked eyes with Gertie, and saw her consciousness shoot to the surface.

She opened her left hand, dropping the knife.

David struggled to maintain his hold. Mr. Ugly focused his attacks on him, wrapped him in a cocoon of limbs and unleashing a series of vicious blows.

Gertie took a step.

Mr. Ugly pulled David loose, lifted him, and flung him down the hall. He soared through the open doorway and into the bedroom he had only just left.

Mr. Ugly returned his attention to Gertie.

His tongue found purchase.

Her eyes shut, but she didn't tell them to.

Her hands clasped, but she didn't tell them to.

No, she pleaded. *I was free.*

Ray saw her body go stiff, as if electrified. He felt her despair as her captor enclosed her again.

Ray did the only thing he could think of. He dove for the weird bulbous head on her left shoulder, just as the ghost of David Arlo had. Ungifted hands would have passed through the creature, but he focused his energy there, and found the eye. The creature spasmed, giving Gertie a second and final chance.

The tongue did not come fully free this time, but loosened. She fought with all her might to move, just *move, damn you.*

Her right arm—the wounded arm—responded.

Except, it didn't. It dangled useless at her side, even while she raised the hand to her mouth. She had grown a third arm, she thought. It protruded from her shoulder above the useless one, but it had no wounds, no blood streaking down the bicep. It felt powerful and pure.

It was her spirit arm, she realized. Somehow, she had popped it loose from her body.

There was no time to marvel at the accomplishment.

With this empyreal hand, she gripped the bundle of tendrils Mr. Ugly had forced inside her mouth and down her throat. She pulled with all her strength.

Fireworks of pain shot through her core, as if she were ripping out her intestines.

Ray kept one thumb inside the creature's gelatinous eye and reached back with the other hand to help Gertie pull. Coils of slick white snakes slid from her lips. She gagged and coughed as they came. The last ended in a curving white barb that glowed white as an ember. She gripped it with her left hand, her body her own at last. The barbed tongue strained to re-enter her, reared back, and snapped forward like a scorpion tail. She lost her grip and went sprawling down the hall.

Her spirit arm back in its housing, she lay on her back, dazed. David stood in the doorway above her, watching helpless as Ray tangled with the beast in the middle of the hallway.

With one hand, the detective held Mr. Ugly's head at bay above him. With the other, he struggled to fend off a hundred thrashing limbs—and failed.

The glowing barb was already between his teeth, scratching at his tongue.

Ray knew the score. This was a losing battle. It always had been. Gertie was far more powerful than he'd ever be. The creature would get its hooks in him now. Once it did, he'd never pry it loose. But Janelle had explained about the van.

The creature was weightless now. It clung to him desperately, a cold, ethereal eel.

Ray planted his feet, felt his shoes gripping the hardwood. He braced himself, ignoring the terrible pain in his body. He pivoted away from the parents' room where Gertrude lay and David Arlo stood. The shock on their faces said they understood what he needed to do, but doubted he had the strength.

He burst into a sprint, tearing down the hallway toward Janelle's open bedroom door.

He felt a vague sadness as he ran, knowing so much would remain unfinished. He'd never rectify his mistakes, tell Shawna he was sorry, and he hoped she found happiness. He would never find the ghost of Abdullah Elmi and hear what he had to say. Would never tell the wife and child of Ethan Bartov that his death had been honorable, and he had not taken his own life, that he was a good man who did his best until the end.

Death knows nothing of convenience.

He dashed through the doorway, into Janelle's room.

He tried to bite the barb in his mouth, but more tendrils forced his jaw wide.

The window, feet away, looked out on the storm. Rivers swirled down the glass.

The barb cut across his tongue, darted down his throat.

He leapt. His toes were the last to leave the ground.

In his final moment of control, he stretched horizontally in the air, threw his fists out in front of himself. Something pinched at the base of his neck, and a hideous voice in his head cried out.

They crashed through the window together and fell with the rain in darkness.

12

Gertie struggled to her feet. Her limbs responded in jerky, spasmodic motions as her brain relearned control. Past the doorway at the end of the hall, Janelle's bedroom window was a broken lattice of glass and wood. Rain fell sideways through the opening, intermittently illuminated by flashes of lightning. Gertie stumbled to the opening and looked down.

David appeared beside her. "Holy shit."

"We have to hurry," she said.

She tottered down the stairs on uncertain legs, every step a hazard.

At the bottom, Janelle lay in a tangle of limbs that stopped Gertie's heart. Gertie reached out to touch her cheek, but before she made contact, the girl gasped and flailed, nearly kicking Gertie in the chest. Gertie fell back onto the steps. Janelle flashed to her feet, blinked several times, looked down at her body as if disbelieving her lack of injuries—and saw Gertie.

Rage and terror ignited, and she leaned over Gertie, pressed one hand to her neck, and pulled the other into a fist.

Gertie braced herself. "It's me! It's me!"

"How would I know?" Janelle snarled.

"He's outside! There's no time!"

Skeptical, Janelle grabbed Gertie's good arm and helped her to her feet.

They rushed out the front door together and leaned into the storm, hobbled down the steps and around the corner of the house. The sight of what lay on the grass below Janelle's window made the girl stop in her tracks.

Gertie rushed forward.

Ray had landed directly on the corner of the picket fence, six feet from the house. The corner post with its pyramidal point had impaled him through the stomach. His weight and momentum had snapped the base, so that only a jagged shock of wood protruded from the earth like a broken tree. He lay in a fetal position, his hands limp on the pink-stained paint. The rain made red ribbons of his blood as it ran from his wound down the length of the post.

Janelle fiddled with the hem of her dress. "Is he—"

"Alive," Gertie said. "For now."

Mr. Ugly held fast to the dying man. As Ray's life faded, so did their chance to end this.

Janelle snapped to attention, turned, and sprinted across the lawn.

Gertie was about to call and ask where she was going when she saw the van parked at the bottom of the driveway. Her own pulse quickened.

"Gertie!" David's voice.

She turned, but couldn't see him.

Then—a flash. He appeared beside her, staring at his hands. They flickered.

"David?"

"I can barely hear you." He held up his hands. He flashed again like a sputtering candle. "What's happening?"

"The tether," she said softly.

"Oh," David said, half cry, half moan.

When pulling Mr. Ugly free, she must have dislodged David, too.

As she had nearly five years ago, she offered her hand. "Hurry."

She shut her eyes, waiting for that subtle pinch.

It never came.

"David?"

"It's okay," he said, his voice a distant radio signal.

"What?"

"You got him."

David flickered in rapid succession. The fear was gone from his eyes. He gestured to the driveway, where the van roared and Janelle turned the wheel so the back doors faced them. The vehicle sank into the sod as she backed it over the lawn.

"It's over," David said. The rain fell through him, as it always did.

Selfishly, she didn't want him to leave. "Where will you go?"

He reached up to touch her cheek, where her tears mingled with the rain. "I'll see you there, eventually."

Her flesh tingled at his touch. ·

She laughed.

"What's funny?"

"You called me a bitch."

He grinned. "Well…"

"Morose, nihilist ass?" She raised her left arm for an embrace, and he opened his, and leaned into her. As their limbs closed, he winked out for the last time.

"See ya, dickhead," she said, fighting back a sob.

Janelle parked the van as close to Ray as possible, nearly colliding with Gertie. She jumped out of the vehicle and ran to the back and popped open the rear doors. She hurried to Ray's body and slipped her hands under his armpits. When she looked up, Gertie was at the van doors, pulling at something above the bumper.

"Help me!" Janelle practically shrieked.

"I am." Like a magic trick, Gertie slid a silver loading ramp out of the back of the van and thumped it onto the ground just inches from Ray. "This time, we'll do it the easy way."

Even with the ramp in place, it wasn't easy. Ray weighed nearly three hundred pounds. Inch by inch, they dragged him. His wounds were terrible. He groaned while they worked him along, and though another life had been lost to the creature they called Mr. Ugly, there was some pleasure in knowing these sounds of pain did not belong to Ray alone.

At last, they slid him inside and closed the doors.

PART 6
WRECKAGE

1

Fairfield Free Press
September 14
"Few answers after week of unprecedented tragedy" by Octavia Winn

Fairfield, MN — After a string of violence in and around the city of Fairfield, Chief of Police Edmund Obermeyer held a press conference Tuesday morning to assure residents that authorities were using all available resources to bring justice to the community.

In the past week, eight residents of Fairfield have been killed or declared missing. On Saturday, two members of the Fairfield Police Department became involved in a high speed chase that ended in tragedy when the pursued vehicle lost control. Authorities have not released details about the incident, but named Detectives Ethan Bartov and Ray Alverson as the officers involved. Local teenager Richard Becker perished in the crash. Gertrude Morgenstern, 26, of Victoria, New York, is the suspected driver of the vehicle.

Morgenstern is the prime suspect in a spree of violence late Saturday evening, including a deadly attack on the Marsh County Department of Corrections which left six deputies and three prisoners dead. A separate attack at a Speedway gas station in the township of Darwin left one teenage victim in critical condition and another with non-life-threatening injuries. The Sheriff's Office released a statement early Monday naming Janelle

Winters and Detective Ray Alverson in connection with these incidents. Their whereabouts are unknown.

The violence began last Tuesday, when serial murderer Ehblu Htoo attacked and killed Eagle Lake resident Gerald Whitney before stealing Whitney's truck and slaying local residents Jeffrey Patel and Henry Opal on I-690 North. Richard Becker, Janelle Winters, and Amy Pink survived the incident. The body of Amy Pink was discovered two days later, the result of a homicide.

In addition, an unidentified woman's remains were discovered near Tanager Commons on the northeast side of town Friday afternoon.

Despite the questions surrounding these incidents, Obermeyer urged the community to remain calm and to allow the Fairfield Police Department to complete their investigations.

"The families affected by these tragedies deserve to understand why their loved ones have been taken," Obermeyer said. "We are partnering with law enforcement around the state to find those responsible and bring them to justice. As painful as this time may be, we must trust in each other and the strength of our community. We must come together to bring peace back to our city."

. . .

Two weeks.

Up front, it seemed like nothing. Janelle was no stranger to boredom. She considered herself an introvert. Two weeks in a motel room by herself after a week in hell? Call it a vacation. Anyway, it would give her time to recite the tale she and Gertie had agreed upon.

She slept through most of the first three days, awake long enough to pick bread out of the minifridge or one of the apples Gertie left. She was to eat no more than six slices of bread and one apple a day. You couldn't fake malnutrition.

By the fourth day, sleep became as much of a burden as her stomach pains. Terrible visions flooded her dreams. Amy and Jeff's deaths replayed on endless loops. Richard wept in a pitch black space no larger than a cupboard, encased in amber. Plastic zipties cut her wrists and a cold bench put her ass to sleep while a demented Gertie crept through the holding cell. The dreams were awash in blood, and she woke up dirty and sweating.

She couldn't take a shower. Had to let the grime build up, allow herself and her funeral dress with Ray's blood on it to absorb every drop of sweat, every odor her body emitted. At least the motel had a little window AC, though it buzzed like an old fridge.

On the fifth day, she thought obsessively about her parents. How were they holding up not knowing if she was alive or dead? What if they lost their jobs because of her? What if they divorced? What if, when she finally reappeared, they saw through her story, knew she was a liar, and cast her out? She paced the room and eyeballed the phone, pointing at it and scolding herself aloud that she couldn't use it. She thought about unplugging it, but there was always a chance that Gertie called early.

The room had basic cable. Gertie had forbidden her from watching the news, in case she learned something and let it slip later. The first three days, she kept the TV off and listened to the sounds around her: car doors slamming in the parking lot outside, the occasional gurgle of a pipe after someone flushed a toilet, the deep vibrations of a male voice in the room beside hers. She never opened the curtains, allowing only gauzy light to filter in. When she wasn't sleeping, she paced, pressed her ear to the walls and door, hungry for sounds of life. She finally turned the television on, avoiding channels that might even chance the occasional news bulletin between commercial breaks. She stuck to reality TV with its forced drama and manufactured crises. When shows that Amy liked came on, she sobbed and changed the channel, then switched it back and sobbed some more.

She cried for long periods, stuffing her face into pillows and blankets or running the bath and sink to mask the sound. She cried until the tears dried up and her limbs went limp from exhaustion. She burst a blood vessel in her left eye. She would chug water from the tap and wonder if she had simply exhausted the well of pain, then stare at the flashing colors on the TV before some memory or thought triggered another round of sobs.

The only time she opened the door was to retrieve the package. She'd been expecting it, but still the knock startled her, and she stared through the peephole into the empty night for a long time before cracking the door and snatching the unmarked box. She placed the contents in the top drawer of the dresser where she would not be tempted by it.

Aside from this, the days were all the same. Reality blended with dreams as starvation set in. She worried that she'd forget the story she had to tell the authorities, so she wrote it on the motel's legal pad, then tore it up and flushed it down the toilet. She took to repeating the story every fifteen minutes—four times an hour—until it became second nature. She spoke it in her dreams, woke up reciting it. She pictured every moment and forced herself to feel it, shutting her eyes and willing it to have happened. It worked to the point that she occasionally forgot why she was in the motel. She should run to the police immediately, tell them she'd been abducted and forced to do terrible things. Things she could never forgive herself for.

Yet she managed to keep one foot in reality. She had to.

Gertie had not shared the finer details of her own plan, but while Janelle suffered through alternating emotional torment and boredom and starvation, Gertie was out there working to shape the narrative. When Janelle asked if she intended to tamper with police evidence, Gertie shrugged and said, "What evidence?" Janelle imagined her walking into police stations past bored desk attendants, whistling while she opened locked doors in search of an evidence room, strolling back out with overflowing cardboard boxes.

Maybe that was too rudimentary. There were so many bodies, a good number of them law enforcement. There'd be video. Documents saved on hard drives, drifting in cyberspace. Gertie couldn't destroy it all, could she?

The call came as promised. Janelle lay naked on the floor, disgusted by her own clothes. She did not have a scale, but guessed she had lost twenty pounds, and she did not have much to spare. Her ribs shone through her skin, a thin shroud over rotting bones. When the ringing began, it broke through a hallucination of the sea. She was a diver at the ocean bottom, exploring the ivory cathedral of an enormous skeleton she soon recognized as her own. A submarine whirred overhead and shined a light, and its sonar bleated: *Brrrriiiiing! Brrrriiiiing!*

She rolled over and pawed at the bed for balance. The room spun.

She scanned for the phone and saw it on the nightstand, vibrating like in a cartoon.

She lifted the receiver and pressed it to her ear. "'lo?"

"Janelle?" said a female voice.

Janelle cleared her throat.

"Janelle, if that's you, tell me what you're supposed to do."

Janelle leaned over the nightstand. She was so heavy. She forced her spine upright.

"Medicine," she said. "The pill."

"What about it?"

She slapped her face, trying to force lucidity. "I know what to do."

"Tell me."

Janelle did.

Satisfied, Gertie said, "You're going to be okay," and hung up.

Janelle checked the clock. 11:13. Day or night?

She pulled back the curtains. Dark.

She found her clothes and dressed, wincing at the rancid fabric.

She searched the room for evidence. All she had brought were her clothes and the food, and the food was long gone. She opened the dresser drawer and removed the Aspirin bottle.

A single pill rattled within like a dead insect. She fumbled with the cap, struggling to line up the markings. They kept wiggling around. Finally, she pushed it loose with her thumbs.

Pop!

She dumped the unmarked pill into her palm.

She hesitated only a moment—there was a slight chance this pill would kill her—then popped it into her mouth and swallowed.

Had to hurry now.

She checked through the peephole, saw an empty parking lot, and opened the door.

The night was impossibly vast. The parking lot stretched for miles. She took a step. Had to sit and let a wave of vertigo pass. Headlights skimmed the parking lot at a distance. Not supposed to let anyone see her.

She stood. Her feet carried her over grass, over curbs and pavement. When lights moved on the road, she ducked aside. She had no particular destination, but one thing still to do. She walked what could have been miles or less than a hundred feet until she found herself in the middle of the road in front of a gas station. Its lights were a blur on the otherwise flat landscape. Anticipating this next part, she became hyper aware of her body. Felt her heartbeat in her chest. Felt her stomach pains, her greasy, tangled hair on her scalp and how it itched. The humid air lazing on her skin and in her nostrils, her lungs. The soles of her feet, sore in her simple flats.

It was not easy to run. Not at first.

She was so weak, and the drugs had her even more off-balance. She fought for the first several steps. Each footfall sent shockwaves through her skull. She found her stride. Fast as she could, she ran, feet slapping, the sound reverberating off the gas station and echoing through the night. She felt power within her, and she knew that, despite all she'd been through, she was not done. This was not the end for her.

At the peak of her sprint, she let her body drop, flinging herself to the pavement so hard she felt the impact in her eye sockets. She threw her hands out, felt the skin sheer from her palms, her knees, her elbows. She rolled along the street, flailing her limbs and banging her head. She pinioned through the universe, stars and earth rolling around and around.

She was supposed to walk to the gas station and ask for help. That was the plan.

In the early morning, an off-duty firefighter found her on the side of the road and called the police.

. .

Fairfield Free Press
September 8
"UPDATE: Charges dropped against local suspect in killings" by
Octavia Winn

Fairfield, MN — Janelle Winters, 18, a former suspect in the deaths of Amy Pink and Richard Becker and the disappearance of Detective Ray Alverson, has been released from police custody. According to a statement from the Fairfield Police Department, all charges have been dropped.

Winters was found last Saturday morning in Joliet, Illinois, suffering from malnourishment and displaying signs of physical trauma. She was treated at a local hospital before being taken into police custody.

In a statement to the press, Winters' lawyer, Kent Herington, said that the teenager had been held captive by Gertrude Morgenstern, the prime suspect in a spate of recent violence in and around the city of Fairfield. A blood test confirmed that Winters had been dosed with Fentanyl, a powerful opiate found in a toxicology report performed on Richard Becker. Becker died when a vehicle believed to be driven by Morgenstern went off the road during a high speed police pursuit. Becker is believed to have been abducted by Morgenstern prior to his death.

In a harrowing tale, Winters told authorities that Morgenstern held her against her will in the back of a vehicle for two weeks. Winters leapt from the moving vehicle when the lock malfunctioned. Authorities could not say why Winters was targeted. Winters is the only remaining survivor of last month's attack by serial murderer Ehblu Htoo on I-690 North.

"My client is grateful for the work of the fine officers of the Fairfield Police Department," Herington said. "She is a victim. She has cooperated with this investigation from the beginning, and hopes that justice will finally be served for the families of those affected by these heinous crimes." Herington asked members of the community and press to respect the privacy of Winters and her family at this time.

Gertrude Morgenstern is described as 5'2", 130 pounds, blonde, and is believed to drive a black 2013 Nissan NV Cargo Van. Authorities are offering a cash reward for anyone with information about her whereabouts.

. . .

Every once in a while, an unmarked car parked outside of Janelle's house. No one ever mentioned it, but they knew it was the police. Her parents believed it was for their protection. They told the cops about Ray's phone call warning them to leave the house the night of Janelle's disappearance. For several weeks, her bedroom window had been replaced with a crude piece of plywood, but it had since been repaired, along with the fence. No one could explain what happened after the attack at the sheriff's office. Janelle claimed to have no memory of it, and Ray was still missing. Janelle assumed they had video evidence, but Gertie saw to that. Anyway, Janelle knew the police were watching her. She wasn't upset about it. She was culpable, after all. Amy's sister would never know the truth. Neither would Mr. Becker, Jeff's family, or the family of the other cop who was killed—Bartov. Even Ray must have had family.

Gertie had told her it was best this way, but Janelle wasn't so sure. Yes, ordinary people might crack knowing what she knew, but that wasn't the point. Concealing the truth didn't protect anyone but herself and Gertie. At the same time, she conceded that sharing the truth wouldn't do much good, either. How would Mr. Becker react if she told him his son had been possessed by a demon, that it forced him to murder Amy and a handful of others? How likely was that to comfort him, to ease his suffering, to resolve his son's death?

She would take the truth to her grave, and there it would rot.

She saw Gertie only once after the motel.

Three weeks had passed. Janelle was still spending most of her time in pajamas, matting a path of footprints in the carpeting between her bedroom, the bathroom, and the kitchen. Burger King told her she could take as much time as she needed before returning to work, but she hadn't decided if she would. Neither of her parents had vacation time left, but they called multiple times a day to check on her. They were working on fattening her up, leaving elaborate dishes in the fridge with heating instructions.

She left her bed to answer the demands of her stomach and found last night's tuna casserole. She placed the dish on the table and scooped a heaping spoonful onto her plate and reached for the microwave.

A figure stood in the hallway, silhouetted by the light in the front room.

Janelle nearly dropped the plate.

"Sorry," Gertie said. "Didn't mean to scare you."

"You could try knocking."

"Would you have answered?"

"I guess not."

Gertie gestured at the casserole. "Mind if I have some?"

Janelle prepared her a dish, and Gertie sat at the table, staring at the window blinds.

They ate without talking.

Janelle had a million questions, but didn't see much use in asking them. Gertie had come here to say something. When she cleared her plate, she leaned back, patted her belly, and released a thunderous burp. "Whew," she said, and waved at the air.

Janelle couldn't help laughing.

Gertie smiled. Apparently, she was waiting for Janelle's cue.

"What brings you here?" Janelle said at last.

"Just checking in."

"BS."

"I wanted to let you know you're in the clear, as far as I can tell."

"In the clear," Janelle repeated.

"I thought you'd like to know."

"How?"

Gertie raised her hands, splayed the fingers, and wiggled them. "Magic," she said flatly.

"What about you? You're, like, America's most wanted thanks to me."

It hadn't come out in the papers, but Janelle offered the authorities information on some missing persons cases from Upstate New York. Gertie had told her about the killings, she said, because she planned to bury Janelle right where she had the others—in the backyard of her old house. Janelle's lawyer used that information to work out a fine deal. Just as Gertie planned.

Gertie watched the window. Daylight struggled around the blinds. "You're gonna be all right," she said.

Janelle's right eye twitched. It had been doing that lately.

She sighed and picked up their plates and brought them to the sink. She flicked on the garbage disposal and rinsed them before placing them in the dishwasher.

She half expected Gertie's chair to be empty when she looked again, but she was still there, looking blank and exhausted. "I'm gonna go now," she said.

"Okay. Will I— Will you—"

Gertie stood abruptly and embraced her. She squeezed Janelle so tight it hurt. Janelle squeezed back. They held each other for a long while. When they let go, both had tears in their eyes. Gertie took a step backward and nodded curtly. Janelle returned the gesture. She followed Gertie to the front door.

Gertie pushed through the screen door. It slapped shut behind her and shaded her face on the other side. "Okay, then," she said.

"Okay, then."

Gertie nodded again, then started down the yard toward a small red Volvo, a rental.

Janelle closed the door.

2

Janelle stuck with her job flipping burgers, despite her parents' reservations. They still wanted her to try community college, and although she hadn't taken it off the table, she didn't know what she would major in, and she'd heard too much about college debt to jump at the concept. If she later decided it would be of use, she'd enroll. In the meantime, she drifted from day to day, not quite aimless, but close enough. She saved enough money to buy a used car—a 2010 Chrysler Sebring with the bottom rusted out so badly she'd be lucky to get two years out of the thing—and was promoted to shift manager at work. She took overtime whenever it was available, working fifty-five hour weeks on a regular basis. Her parents said she was overdoing it, but she didn't think so. She needed to stay busy, keep moving even if she went nowhere.

Nearly a year passed this way.

In mid-July, she started researching cities near San Francisco. The notion of leaving had been in the back of her mind for a while, but it didn't gel until she had a list of prospective apartments and jobs. Even then, it seemed more like a fantasy than something she'd go through with. She supposed that was how most things felt until you did them.

The bay area was too expensive, but she found an affordable studio apartment in the nearby city of Merced. She'd never been there, of course, but a little online research showed it was a decent place to live, if a bit boring. Lots of chain restaurants and white people, according to someone on Quora. That made it sound like Minnesota, with more sun. She figured if she hated it, she'd move somewhere else. If she ran out of money, she'd come home.

It was something to do, anyway. A way to move forward.

Even as the fantasy resolved itself into a series of mundane tasks, she put off telling her parents. The studio apartment fell through, but she found another in the same city, spoke with the property manager over the phone, signed a two-month lease and faxed it back, and mailed out her security deposit for September. She applied to all the jobs she was qualified for and got one callback from a Red Lobster. They wouldn't hire her more than two weeks out, but she took this as a good sign.

With three weeks left, she decided to inform her parents over dinner. Dad grilled pork chops and Mom made hot dish. Janelle picked at her plate, her stomach in knots. Mom was about to get up and start cleaning dishes when Janelle forced out the words. She straightened her back and looked at them sheepishly and said, "There's something I need to tell you guys."

Dad dabbed at his mouth with his napkin. Mom leaned her elbows on either side of her plate.

"Before I say what it is, I want you to know I've thought long and hard about it, and everything's already in motion." A long beat. She inhaled. "I'm moving to California."

Dad nodded.

Mom said, "When?"

This was not the reaction she expected. "September."

"That soon," Dad said.

"Will you be staying with someone?"

"No. I don't know anyone. Well, there's Richard's cousin, but we don't really know each other."

"Did you tell work?" Mom asked.

"Not yet. I'm gonna put in my two weeks soon."

"Job prospects?" Dad said.

She told them about the Red Lobster call.

"You'll find something better," Dad said.

Growing suspicious, Janelle said, "You're not, like, mad?"

Mom frowned, and Dad blurted out a laugh that he immediately stifled.

"Honey," Mom said, "we're not blind. We'll be sad not to have you in the house, but you're not happy here. You haven't been the same since..." There was no need to finish the statement. "It's why we kept pushing you toward college. We'll miss you like crazy, but if this is what you want, we'll support you. I just want you to know we're here for you, as your support network, to quote the doctor." They'd attended a handful of Janelle's therapy sessions as a family, where Janelle had to repeat the lies that she and Gertie came up with.

She felt herself tearing up, and all the tension she'd been carrying, all the guilt about her secret decision, melted away. "I'll visit as much as I can."

"So will we."

The remaining weeks blinked by. She worked right up until the day of the move, and every time she came home there was a new shopping bag of household items waiting in her bedroom. They bought her dishes, silverware, towels, dishrags, a shower rack, plus a number of items to prepare her for a life of sun: sunblock, sunglasses, tank tops, shorts, a couple new bathing suits and strapless bras, sandals, and lots of aloe. Because she wasn't bringing her bed and didn't know yet how long she'd stay with her current lease, they got her an air mattress and a new sleeping bag, but returned the sleeping bag when she broke down crying at the sight of it, seeing in her mind Richard's bag with his cat inside reduced to matted fur and blue-gray innards.

It took some convincing before they agreed to let her drive down alone. This was important to her. It was how she pictured it from the start—open road, wind in her hair, sun ahead. She wasn't foolish enough to drive in one straight shot. She had developed a mild phobia of night driving, and if she ran into a bad storm, she would pull over until it passed. As an additional precaution, she kept a baseball bat in her trunk and carried a four-inch folding knife in her purse. She had been keeping the knife in an ankle holster, but her therapist was concerned and wore her down over the months until she agreed that her purse was more socially acceptable.

The morning of her move, she woke up to a light knocking on her bedroom door. It came and went, and when she sat up, the door was closed. Usually, Mom cracked it even if Janelle didn't invite her in. She could have imagined the knock, like the time she woke up because she thought someone had kissed her forehead, but she doubted it. She'd been in the middle of a vivid dream, a pleasant one for a change, and could have stayed in it a while longer.

She checked her phone. It was 4:31 a.m. She'd set her alarm for 4:45 so she could hit the road as soon as possible. She considered sleeping those additional fifteen minutes, but the dream was gone, and she might as well see if someone had really knocked.

She rolled out from under her sheets and took two shuffling steps toward the door before she spotted the piece of computer paper someone had slipped underneath. It had been placed face-down. On the other side, something had been written in blocky black letters. Some of the ink had run through, like blood through fabric.

Her heart thumped and her palms sweat.

She had been waiting for something like this to happen. Something *unusual.* Something that would confirm that Gertie was wrong— everything was *not* okay. Every day since the motel had been like their last day on the farm, when they foolishly believed they had everything under control.

She fished her knife out of her purse, then rushed to the paper and flipped it over.

A crude smiley face had been scrawled next to a single word: *OUTSIDE.*

A chill raced across her arms and scalp, raising the finer hairs.

In her night shorts and a t-shirt, she opened her door and stood in the upstairs hallway, which seemed especially dark in the morning gloom. At the far end of the hall, her parents' bedroom door was closed. She shook her head at the memory of invisible restraints on her wrists and ankles and made her way down the carpeted staircase, avoiding the creaky steps.

Downstairs, everything was where it should be. She resisted the urge to explore the house, throwing out precaution for the sake of getting this over with, gripped the front door's knob, steeled herself, and yanked it open.

She gaped at what waited for her, her fear slowly ebbing, replaced by numb shock.

She clipped the knife into her waistband and hid it beneath her shirt.

She went out.

Mom sidestepped up the driveway with her arms straightened beside her and her hands splayed, like a gameshow host revealing The Grand Prize. Dad wasn't so theatrical. He stood beaming, hands in his pockets. When he removed his right hand, he held a set of car keys, which he dangled in the air, wiggling his eyebrows.

"It's a Honda!" Mom announced. "Very good safety rating."

Dad added, "We couldn't let you take that old junker."

Janelle had to sit on the steps.

Suddenly, she was balling.

Her parents shared a look, then rushed to her side.

Her mom rubbed her back. "Hey, what's wrong, Nelly?"

She pressed her face into her knees. She was shaking, and struggled to get air through the sobs.

"What is it?"

She couldn't explain it to them. How their perfect little surprise had threatened to erase a year's worth of progress. How she mentally and emotionally prepared herself to find their bodies strewn about like gory party favors. How part of her would always believe that the worst was still ahead.

When she got herself under control, she lied. She pretended these were tears of joy, that she was so happy about the gift it made her sad to leave, and she would miss them terribly.

Her parents weren't convinced. She read fresh concern in their faces, but they did her the favor of pretending to believe. They cradled her like she was a child again, like they could protect her from harm.

She cleaned herself up and ate a big breakfast Mom had concealed in the oven. They asked if she wanted to test drive the new car, but she said it would be fine, and when she got on the road, right on schedule, she saw that it was—fine.

Her phone called out directions through the vehicle's speakers, so she was able to crack the windows and still hear. She left the radio off, preferring the sound of the road and the wind. It was not exactly how she imagined it. Her face was puffy and fatigued, she was not filled purely with hope—but a mix of emotions, especially nervousness—and the sun was not ahead, but to the left. Still, she was going through with this, taking a step into the unknown, away from a place she knew she could never truly live, and heading near the place where, only a year ago, she and her friends had shared their last truly happy moments together. She intended to revisit those sites once settled in. She'd walk the Golden Gate Bridge and think of Jeff's morbid facts about suicides. She would go to the trail she made them abandon, and she would walk it in its entirety, with hiking boots and a backpack full of water and power bars. She hoped she could make peace or something like it with everything that happened.

She believed such a thing to be possible. She'd felt it in last night's dream.

She couldn't remember how it began, but she knew it was more than a dream even before she woke. It was too vivid, too consistent, and had too much texture. She sat in a wooden dinghy without oars, adrift on a great blue ocean. There was no wind and no waves, though every now and then the boat rose on a gentle swell as massive things shifted the water below. A great orange sun hung in the sky, and despite being utterly alone with no land in sight and incapable of directing her craft, she felt perfectly calm. She was not even thirsty, and she believed if she had been, she could have cupped a hand and reached over the side and drank from the sea.

There was nothing to fear in this place.

She sat in the boat a long time, content.

She was not alarmed when things began to bump against the underside of the craft. She knew who it was. She half expected them to arrive, after all, and now that they had, she realized they were the reason she felt so content to be alone—because she wasn't alone. Not really. They were there with her, had been waiting for her, and always would be. They pressed their hands to the underside of the dinghy's boards, and she pressed hers over them, feeling them through the wood. She dared not lean over the side to look. They wouldn't want her to see them like that. All the same, it was good to know her friends were down there, gliding through the water like a pod of dolphins, keeping a place for her, so that when her time came, they would greet her open-armed, laughing in watery silence, together again in the boundless sea.

3

Snakehead, Arizona had once been a booming mining town of more than 10,000 people. Now the population hovered around 450 residents. Situated ten miles from the entrance to the Grand Canyon, half the buildings had been declared National Historic Landmarks in the latter half of the 20th century. Unfamiliar faces were common, and it was not unheard of for the occasional some-time tourists to return as a full-time resident, if not in the town proper then one of the larger towns just two miles down the road. So no one thought much at all about the young, indistinct woman who appeared in late June.

Nobody, that is, except Carlito Moreno.

Carlito was the town's only mechanic, and before the shop was his, it was his father's, and before that, his grandfather had trekked from Venezuela to Mexico to Arizona with nothing but the sandals on his feet and a clawing hunger for a better life. That hunger led to Carlito's birth in this country, and though his father and grandfather had not been wealthy at the time of their deaths, they had settled for a particular type of happiness in this little tourist spot where the heat was only unbearable one month out of the year, the cost of living cheap, and the residents loyal enough to their local mechanic.

As a young man, Carlito hadn't understood why his father did not aspire to something greater. Yet as he matured, married, and had children of his own, the fantasy of a business empire sounded more like a stress heart attack than a jacuzzi, and his ambitions for wealth transformed into goals for his children—that they should have a stable home and the opportunity to choose their own paths.

At 22, his oldest son, who had spent two years in Phoenix studying business, returned home to announce that his only desire was to take over Moreno Auto when Carlito retired. The boy persisted despite Carlito's objections, and at 63, Carlito knew he could not run the shop forever. He turned his attention to teaching the boy everything he knew. In another two years, the townspeople Carlito had worked with for twenty years expressed surprise when he answered the phone, and—after a brief conversation—asked for Ronniel. It was impressive, if a touch emasculating, but Carlito had seen his own father die stubbornly on his feet clutching his chest in one hand and a socket wrench in the other and hoped to spare his family that particular sight.

Nowadays, he took his time heading to the shop in the morning, knowing Ronniel ran a tighter ship than he ever did, and the boy preferred it when his father was not underfoot.

This morning, as he pulled into the same lot he'd pulled into for more than 40 years, he thought his eyes were playing tricks on him. A young lady stood in the garage wearing a pair of the shop's coveralls. Perhaps a hair over five feet tall, she stood beside Ronniel as he leaned under the open hood of Jen Hardanger's Ford Bronco.

Carlito parked and approached the open garage.

Todd popped out of the door to the front office and gave Carlito a half-hearted wave.

"Rony?" Carlito said.

Ronniel poked his head around the side of the Bronco and grinned. "Morning, Pop."

Carlito gestured at the woman. "Are we selling overalls now?" Carlito said.

The woman looked on with uncurious eyes.

Ronniel stepped out from behind the vehicle and placed his hands on his hips. "Que?"

"Quién es este?"

"Oh, right. This is our newest employee. Her name is, uh—"

"Frannie," the woman added.

Ronniel nodded, satisfied. "Right."

"New employee? Desde cuando?"

"This morning."

"Who decided?"

"I did."

Carlito studied the woman, or tried to. He'd never seen a plainer face in his life. Her hair was a shade of colors he could not identify. Was it blonde? Red? Brunette? It would not resolve itself—and the same of her face. It had all the features of a face, and yet she could have been a mannequin that walked out of a store display.

"What are her qualifications?" Carlito said. He realized he was shouting and didn't care.

Todd pretended to study the undercarriage of the Honda CRV he had on the lift.

"Qualifications?"

"Does she have experience working on automobiles?"

Ronniel started to answer, then turned to the woman. They spoke quietly.

"No," Ronniel answered.

This was very unlike Ronniel. He did not hire people off the street.

"References?"

Again, Ronniel spoke to the woman.

She shook her head.

This was too much.

"Ronniel, ven aquí."

"Que?"

"Ahora!"

They talked in private behind the garage. Carlito scolded the boy and asked him what he was thinking hiring this woman who stood there like she owned the place in a pair of coveralls so big she had to fold the ankle and wrist cuffs five times. Ronniel could not explain it. She had simply showed up, chatted for a few moments, and the next thing he knew he was handing her the overalls and telling her he could make a copy of the shop key that afternoon.

Ronniel finally agreed that, although they needed a new pair of hands since Carlito had begun his steady creep into retirement, this particular stranger was not who they needed.

When they walked back to the open bay doors, the woman was elbow deep in the Bronco's engine with Todd standing at her side. Todd peered up at the father and son and, responding to something the woman said, handed her a wrench and a fresh serpentine belt. A moment later, she stood upright and said, "Belt's done, but you didn't need to replace those spark plugs. Run the diagnostic again. You'll see that same misfire. Let Mrs. Hardanger know it's a head gasket. She won't be happy, but it'll save her trouble in the long run." She wiped her hands on her coveralls and walked straight past the baffled men on her way out the bay door.

Ten minutes later, Carlito and Ronniel found her leaning against the garage and picking at her nails.

"What did you say your name was?" Carlito said.

"Frannie White."

"What makes you think it's a head gasket, Frannie?"

Frannie smiled and tapped her pinky against the corner of one eye. "X-ray vision."

Carlito recalled this episode over an evening cup of coffee to Jacinta, who had raised her eyebrows hopefully at the mention of Ronniel meeting a woman. She pressed her husband for details, but Carlito could recall virtually nothing of the woman, though he'd spent nearly eight hours in her company. He pegged her for a drifter, unlikely to stay beyond that first day.

Yet she was there again the next day. And the day after, and the next, and so on, until she became as much a fixture of the shop as Carlito himself, and more reliable than Todd and Chico combined. It did not take long before she and Ronniel became romantically involved. Ronniel never came out and said it, but a father knows. He didn't understand, seeing no charm in the woman.

She was not a talker, but Carlito dragged out bits of information over the next several weeks. She had moved into Crazy Roger Sherman's house, of all places. As far as Carlito knew, the place had been condemned. Ronniel agreed to help her fix it up. Carlito offered to assist, and thereby get a glimpse of the woman's dwelling place, but she refused. She was a very private woman, Ronniel said. She wouldn't even let him go into the shed in the backyard.

That caught Carlito's attention.

Crazy Roger Sherman had always been crazy. Some said he climbed out a second story window the day he learned to crawl. Or he was kicked by a mule in his teens. Or he fell into the gas tank at his father's old station and that's why Roger Sr. closed shop. Or he'd simply come out of his mama half cooked. Regardless, he *was* crazy. At the end of his life, he'd grown destitute, and tried his hand at a series of schemes to derive income from the seasonal tourists. One such scheme involved what he called "Roger Sherman's Diary [sic] Cow's Milk Strait [sic] from the Unfowled [sic] Tit."

The idea was to sell unpasteurized milk at a roadside stand.

He bought six dairy cows, God-knows-how or from where. To house them, he'd built a ramshackle stable behind his house. Mostly built it himself, which explained the southward lean of the roof. It was more an oversized shed than a stable or barn, and after three months of squeezing the cow's teets raw with nothing to show but sore forearms, he sold the animals to Biggie Cordero, the local butcher. That was a year before he got himself killed by a sheriff's deputy in Mohave County for robbing a liquor store with what turned out to be a broken broom handle.

Carlito parked his F-150 in front of Crazy Roger's place, shaking his head at the state of the house. The porch slumped in the middle and the siding had been peeled off and replaced with fresh Tyvek wrap. Two black windows with fresh frames studied him. The old scrub brush around the perimeter had been removed, lending an impression of nakedness. A pile of debris lay on the northern side of the house, beside a neat stack of new siding.

How much of this had Ronniel paid for? The boy had a soft heart, which made him a lousy haggler at the shop. Some customers were enthusiastic about sapping their profit margins, and Ronniel couldn't resist a sob story. Still, the place looked better than it had in decades, dilapidated porch or no.

The old dairy shack, on the other hand, had not been touched.

It could have been constructed entirely of splinters. Cheap plywood bleached sickly gray had been haphazardly nailed to an underlying frame, the construction of which Carlito could only guess at. At each corner, rusted nails ran vertically from the top of the wall to the bottom, separated by an inch or less. Other nails had been punched seemingly at random through the sides, along with a smattering of screws, as if Crazy Roger had shut his eyes and hoped for the best. Strangest of all were the nails that protruded from within, their sharp points forming thousands of tiny spikes. It was a wonder the man hadn't died of tetanus. The plywood had been applied in patches, like a wooden quilt. Gaps formed where the pieces came together, two inches wide in some areas.

Carlito left his truck, approached the dilapidated shack and, without thought, pressed his eye to one of the many cracks. Darkness on the other side. A sheet of it. Slightly shiny.

A black tarp.

All the cracks were blocked up that way. Apparently, Frannie didn't want anyone peeping at what she had inside.

He made his way to the doors of the structure, at its rear and hidden from the road. These, too, had a significant gap where they came together and where they sat in their frame. Also blocked from the inside. A rusted latch secured with a brand new combination lock held the doors together. If he were so inclined, he could get the prybar from his truck and pull the lock right off the brittle wood.

The doors had no handles. Almost lazily, he set his fingers in the gap between them.

The moment he set them there, he snatched them back, hissing through his teeth.

What the hell was that?

He stepped away, nearly tripping over himself.

The sensation was indescribable. A feeling of *wrongness* that cut straight to his center.

He swallowed repeatedly, fighting the urge to vomit.

A noise behind him—a scrape of shoe on dirt.

His heart froze.

"Can I help you, Carlito?"

He turned slowly, stiff as a corpse.

He saw her clearly, the veneer gone. She was blonde and thin, with brown eyes and a slightly upturned nose. It was the first time he saw her dressed in something other than the shop's coveralls. Her pale legs stuck out of cutoff jean shorts, the bottoms frayed. Her top was a spaghetti strap thing that revealed two long scars on her right arm, one a ragged circle on her bicep and the other a discolored strip that ran around the ball of her shoulder.

He stammered for an explanation. "I— I— Uh— Just wanted to come see the work— On the house. Rony told me about it. Said he was helping you."

She watched him. She seemed very tired.

"It looks good," he added, sounding to himself like a child caught in a lie.

Frannie gestured at the shed. "The real project's in there."

A fresh wave of fear prickled his scalp. "Yeah?"

"I think you'll appreciate it."

Was it his imagination, or had her expression changed just then? A flicker of a smile?

"Oh, that's okay."

"No, really. You should take a look."

She stepped toward him.

Ridiculously, he flinched.

She pretended not to notice and went straight for the lock. She entered the combination and creaked the flimsy doors open and pulled back the tarpaulin. He cast his eyes aside, not so sure he wanted to see. He couldn't think straight, floating loose inside his body.

Frannie said, "Needs a lot of work, but I couldn't just dump it."

In his peripheral, he saw the shadowy interior of the building broken by columns of light cutting through the roof. And in the center, barely fitting within the chaotic network of beams: a vehicle. The angle of the bumper caught his attention, and he could no longer resist the temptation. He looked, and his jaw fell open.

It was the car. *The car*. The body was in rough shape, and he could only guess if it still ran, but it shocked him to see it here, in this woman's shed, surrounded by hanging tarps and decaying wood. He'd restored one just like it decades before. A 1977 Pontiac Trans Am Y82. The *Smokey and the Bandit* car. It was that restoration project that convinced his own father that he was worthy of taking over the shop. Took him nearly a decade to finish, but in that time he came to know every part, every curve, and every sound that machine could make. It hurt him deeply to sell it, but that was his father's final challenge—not just loving the beast that had put him through his paces, but learning to part with it. He put the money straight back into the shop, buying both lifts and a couple grand in new tools. He had said goodbye to it once before, and could not make sense of his emotions seeing it again.

"Only thing I ask," Frannie said, "is that you don't touch it."

He understood.

"It came from up north, so the salt and cold did a number on it, but the frame's still solid. Belonged to a friend of mine. I couldn't get rid of it, or leave it behind. Figure I'll keep plugging away until it runs right."

Carlito ran his eyes over the machine. It had been black once, but the paint was just about gone, scraped from the paneling by decades of wind and ice. The bonnet was a jagged hole exposing the shaker scoop.

His vision blurred with tears. He had a hundred questions—yet as much as he wanted to lift the hood and run his hands over her parts, his very gaze seemed an invasion of privacy.

He cleared his throat and wiped at his eyes. "I should probably get back."

She shrugged. "Will you do me one favor?"

"What's that?"

"Don't tell Ronniel about this. You know how he is. He'll want to take over."

"Of course." He understood better than she could possibly know.

He returned to his truck. Frannie had parked behind it—she'd bought a used Camry from the shop her second week on the job. He sat in his truck and watched her come around the side of the shed and wipe her hands on her shorts. She smiled at him. The veneer was back. He could no longer see the scars on her arm, and again her hair seemed to shimmer different tints in the sun.

That was odd, but he felt he had misjudged her. Nobody who treasured that car could be all that bad. Hadn't his father disapproved of Jacinta when they started dating, too?

He'd do his son a favor and set aside his suspicions. If not forever, then for a while.

.   .   .

Gertie watched Carlito drive off, a cloud of dust following.

When he was out of range, she sighed and dropped her guard, and a fresh wave of fatigue rolled over her.

It was a risk to settle anywhere, but she couldn't remain on the road forever.

She hadn't intended to get so involved with these people. Originally, all she wanted was to learn about car repair. The van wouldn't run indefinitely, and it would be easier to fix it herself when it broke down. But now that she had a house to sleep in and a warm body to keep her company, she liked it—and that scared her.

She was not pretending to like Ronniel.

Or his suspicious father, for that matter.

Rony, as he liked to be called, was tall and warm and good with his hands. Confident and quiet, yet rich with secret passions even he didn't know about. He often said he had no imagination, yet she caught glimpses of his thoughts and drifted into their current, like floating down a stream under a perfect, clear sky. That was Rony, a peaceful river. She felt a touch guilty for stealing into his mind at their first meeting, but she needed a job. At least she didn't rob him like she might have in the old days. David would have been glad for that.

She did not know what the future held, or if she'd stay here very long. Eventually, Carlito would try sneaking another peek at what she had in the shed. She'd conjured the car out of his memory, knowing the effect it would have. It bought her time, but how much?

Rony, too, would eventually grow wary of her secrets. A single Google search could do her in. She could picture him standing in a doorway somewhere, a pained look on his face, his fingers twitching like they did when he fell deep into thought. *I saw your picture online,* he'd say. *All those people.*

The dust on the road settled, and Carlito's truck had faded out of sight. She returned to the open shed, replaced the tarp across the entrance, shut the doors, and slid the lock through the hasp. She paused, the lock still open.

The temptation was there again. As always. To check.

To *know*.

Every night, this temptation stirred her awake. She would slip from the covers and, if Ronniel had stayed over, tiptoe barefoot across the warped floorboards and out of the room. At the front door, she would tip each boot upside down to check for scorpions, slip them over her sockless feet and step out to greet the night on the funhouse of a porch. If the moon was out, the desert would fold open blue-gray, the shed standing fifty feet away like a giant tombstone. On clouded nights, she scuffed her way across the barren lawn until her fingertips grazed the splintered wood or the jagged nails of the building. She did not need to see the lock or its combination to align the tumbler and pop it open.

Her pulse would rise, as it did now.

And then, as now, she'd slide the lock free, pull the doors open, brush aside the veil of tarp, and stand at the brink of deeper dark.

The van's rear doors faced the opening. The smell had faded, but she covered her nose out of habit. As always, she hesitated before approaching, thinking, *What if this is the day?*

She drifted closer, set her fingertips gingerly on the surface, lay her ear to the paneling—and listened.

ACKNOWLEDGEMENTS

I love adventure documentaries. The kind of documentaries that follow eager sportsmen and sportswomen who have fixated on climbing The Impossible Climb or spelunking The Very Treacherous Cave. I'm particularly drawn to mountaineering—probably because it scares me the most. These stories are all approximately the same: the adventurers spend years preparing, researching, training their bodies and minds, buying better gear, etc., until, at last, they embark.

At some point, things become more difficult than they anticipated. Occasionally, someone gets injured, so the real adventure becomes trekking down the mountain in search of medical help. Most often, though, because we all love a happy ending, our adventurers reach the summit, too exhausted and oxygen-deprived to cry tears of joy. Then they turn back.

Oftentimes, it's more difficult getting down the mountain than getting up.

I would never compare myself in a literal way to such adventurers. Sure, I've hiked a medium-difficulty trail or two in the Adirondacks, but that's a bit like comparing shooting hoops on the basketball court behind my apartment to playing in the NBA. Figuratively, however, writing a novel and climbing a mountain have their similarities. They both entail years of research and painstaking work. Both require a particular brand of mental fortitude that from the outside may present as a mild form of insanity.

But I'm not writing this to boost my own ego. This is the acknowledgements section, after all. The other vital similarity between novelists and adventurers (again, figuratively) is that nobody goes adventuring alone. Well, some do, but they usually end up dead, lost, or short a limb. To make it safely up and down a mountain, you need a team, and I am lucky enough to have one.

When I get lost in my writing journey, the person I turn to more than anyone is my best friend and wife, Carey Feagan-Allocco. She is my first editor, my sounding board, and my Sherpa. Without her, I would certainly lose a limb or two along the way. Thank you for your love, support, and guidance.

I also owe an incredible debt of gratitude to the following friends and beta readers: Sam Hastings, Tyler Ianuzi, Ryan "Squid" Greenfield, Ben Wheeler-Floyd, and Ashley McNamara. If I found myself delirious and lost, they steered me back to the path. Thank you all for your honest feedback, encouragement, and enthusiasm.

I must extend a heartfelt thank you to Investigator Brandon Gotham of the Rochester, New York Police Department for generously answering my endless questions about law enforcement and investigative police work. Any discrepancies between the realities of that difficult, important work and the story I have written are the result of my own creative liberties or ignorance. This book simply would not have worked without Investigator Gotham's input. I'm considering starting a new detective story just so I'll have an excuse to continue our email chain.

And if I can sufficiently drive this metaphor into the ground, I want to thank the team that helped me back down the mountain. If finishing a novel is the journey to the summit, then publishing it is the return trip ending at a medical tent. The team at Black Rose Writing has been a joy to work with, and I am thrilled to be joining their catalog. Thank you for your belief in this story and for unleashing Mr. Ugly on the world. May his reign be long and brutal.

Lastly, my sincerest thanks to *you*. If you're reading this, you've not only taken the time to read a story I wrote for you, but you've gone on to see what I had to say about the people who helped make it a reality. That's a magical thing to me. I think you're magical. Please keep reading and supporting authors and presses. Thank you, thank you, thank you.

ABOUT THE AUTHOR

Benjamin Allocco is an author, podcaster, and occasional musician. He lives in the Syracuse, New York area with his wife and their two rambunctious cats. He received his MFA from Minnesota State University, Mankato. He prefers his fiction dark and his monsters ravenous. To keep up with his writing and other projects, visit www.benjaminallocco.com.

NOTE FROM THE AUTHOR

Word-of-mouth is crucial for any author to succeed. If you enjoyed *Mr. Ugly*, please leave a review online—anywhere you are able. Even if it's just a sentence or two. It would make all the difference and would be very much appreciated.

Thanks!
Benjamin Allocco

We hope you enjoyed reading this title from:

www.blackrosewriting.com

Subscribe to our mailing list – *The Rosevine* – and receive **FREE** books, daily deals, and stay current with news about upcoming releases and our hottest authors.
Scan the QR code below to sign up.

Already a subscriber? Please accept a sincere thank you for being a fan of Black Rose Writing authors.

View other Black Rose Writing titles at www.blackrosewriting.com/books and use promo code **PRINT** to receive a **20% discount** when purchasing.

www.ingramcontent.com/pod-product-compliance
Lightning Source LLC
Chambersburg PA
CBHW010727100726
47899CB00009B/2962